ELLERY QUEEN'S
BLIGHTED DWELLINGS

ELLERY QUEEN'S
BLIGHTED
DWELLINGS

Stories collected from issues
of *Ellery Queen's Mystery Magazine*
edited by Ellery Queen

Edited by Eleanor Sullivan

LONGMEADOW PRESS

Published exclusively for Longmeadow Press by

Davis Publications, Inc.
380 Lexington Avenue
New York, New York 10017

SECOND PRINTING

Copyright © 1986 by Davis Publications, Inc.
All rights reserved.
Library of Congress Catalog Card Number: 59-13341
Printed in the U.S.A.

CONTENTS

Introduction   8

The Haunting of Shawley Rectory   *Ruth Rendell*   9
The Living End   *Dana Lyon*   24
I Wish He Hadn't Said That   *George Baxt*   35
The Yellow Wallpaper   *Charlotte Perkins Gilman*   43
The Inner Voices   *Jean Potts*   58
Over There—Darkness   *William O'Farrell*   76
In the House Next Door   *William Bankier*   89
The Third-Floor Closet   *Jack Ritchie*   95
The Crime in Nobody's Room   *John Dickson Carr* 105
Locked Doors   *Lilly Carlson* 121
Le Château de L'Arsenic   *Georges Simenon* 130
My Neighbor, Ay   *Joyce Harrington* 144
The Dwelling Place of the Proud   *Charles B. Child* 164

The Thief   *Helen Hudson* 177
The Name on the Window   *Edmund Crispin* 186
The Hump in the Basement   *Suzanne Blanc* 196
The Ghost of Greenwich Village *Donald McNutt Douglass* 203
The Dark Place   *Richard A. Selzer* 214
The Problem of the Whispering House *Edward D. Hoch* 224
A Hearse Is Not a Home   *Jean L. Backus* 243
No Place To Live   *Ellery Queen* 252
A Nice Place To Stay   *Nedra Tyre* 261
The Mysterious Mansion   *Honoré de Balzac* 271

INTRODUCTION

One of the first signs of our maturity is the awareness that wherever we live, wherever we go, we have to take ourselves with us—that we ourselves are dwelling places. Which is not to say we aren't affected by the dwellings in which we live or those with whom we choose—or are forced—to live.

While putting together this new collection of stories from *Ellery Queen's Mystery Magazine,* our television set was tuned to a favorite program, Elsa Klensch's *Style* on CNN, and one of that week's showings was the elegant 1985 fall collection by Karl Lagerfeld with its splendidly rendered and harmonious theme, "Home Sweet Home." *Our* collection is also splendidly rendered by the contributing authors, but the word "harmonious" is not quite so apt.

In *The Garrison of Cape Ann,* John Greenleaf Whittier wrote: "Soon or late to all our dwellings come the spectres of the mind." This is proven out in each of the 23 stories in this anthology, from Honoré de Balzac's great classic "The Mysterious Mansion," written in the early 1800s, to Lilly Carlson's "Locked Doors," which won the Robert L. Fish Award for best first mystery short story written in 1983.

"Where dwellest *thou?*" asks the servant in *Coriolanus.* Wherever it is, if it is the source of serious discontent, we hope you're planning to do something to sweeten your situation. Non-criminal, please. Crime is for fiction.

—Eleanor Sullivan

Ruth Rendell

The Haunting of Shawley Rectory

I don't believe in the supernatural, but just the same I wouldn't live in Shawley Rectory.

That was what I had been thinking and what Gordon Scott said to me when we heard we were to have a new Rector at St. Mary's. Our wives gave us quizzical looks.

"Not very logical," said Eleanor, my wife.

"What I mean is," said Gordon, "that however certain you might be that ghosts don't exist, if you lived in a place that was reputedly haunted you wouldn't be able to help wondering every time you heard a stair creak. All the normal sounds of an old house would take on a different significance."

I agreed with him. It wouldn't be very pleasant feeling uneasy every time one was alone in one's own home at night.

"Personally," said Patsy Scott, "I've always believed there are no ghosts in the Rectory that a good central-heating system wouldn't get rid of."

We laughed at that, but Eleanor said, "You can't just dismiss it like that. The Cobworths heard and felt things even if they didn't actually see anything. And so did the Bucklands before them. And you won't find anyone more level-headed than Kate Cobworth."

Patsy shrugged. "The Loys didn't even hear or feel anything. They'd heard the stories, they *expected* to hear the footsteps and the carriage wheels. Diana Loy told me. And Diana was quite a nervy, highly strung sort of person. But absolutely nothing happened while they were there."

"Well, maybe the Church of England or whoever's responsible will install central heating for the new parson," I said, "and we'll see if your theory's right, Patsy."

Eleanor and I went home after that. We went on foot because our house is only about a quarter of a mile up Shawley Lane. On the way we stopped in front of the Rectory, which is about a hundred yards along. We stood and looked over the gate.

I may as well describe the Rectory to you before I get on with this story. The date of it is around 1760 and it's built of pale dun-colored

9

brick with plain classical windows and a front door in the middle with a pediment over it. It's a big house with three reception rooms, six bedrooms, two kitchens, and two staircases—and one poky little bathroom made by having converted a linen closet. The house is a bit stark to look at, a bit forbidding; it seems to stare straight back at you, but the trees round it are pretty enough and so are the stables on the left-hand side with a clock in their gable and a weathervane on top. Tom Cobworth, the last Rector, kept his old Morris in there. The garden is huge, a wilderness that no one could keep tidy these days—eight acres of it, including the glebe.

It was years since I had been inside the Rectory. I remember wondering if the interior was as shabby and in need of paint as the outside. The windows had that black, blank, hazy look of windows at which no curtains hang and which no one has cleaned for months or even years.

"Who exactly does it *belong* to?" said Eleanor.

"Lazarus College, Oxford," I said. "Tom was a Fellow of Lazarus."

"And what about this new man?"

"I don't know," I said. "I think all that system of livings has changed but I'm pretty vague about it."

I'm not a churchgoer, not religious at all really. Perhaps that was why I hadn't got to know the Cobworths all that well. I used to feel a bit uneasy in Tom's company, I used to have the feeling he might suddenly round on me and demand to know why he never saw me in church. Eleanor had no such inhibitions with Kate. They were friends, close friends, and Eleanor had missed her after Tom died suddenly of a heart attack and she had had to leave the Rectory. She had gone back to her people up north, taking her fifteen-year-old daughter Louise with her.

Kate is a practical down-to-earth Yorkshirewoman. She had been a nurse—a ward sister, I believe—before her marriage. When Tom got the living of Shawley she several times met Mrs. Buckland, the wife of the retiring incumbent, and from her learned to expect what Mrs. Buckland called "manifestations."

"I couldn't believe she was actually saying it," Kate had said to Eleanor. "I thought I was dreaming and then I thought she was mad. I mean really psychotic, mentally ill. Ghosts! I ask you—people believing things like that in this day and age. And then we moved in and I heard them, too."

The crunch of carriage wheels on the gravel drive when there was no carriage or any kind of vehicle to be seen. Doors closing softly when no doors had been left open. Footsteps crossing the landing and going downstairs, crossing the hall, then the front door opening softly and closing softly.

"But how could you bear it?" Eleanor said. "Weren't you afraid? Weren't you terrified?"

"We got used to it. We had to, you see. It wasn't as if we could sell the house and buy another. Besides, I love Shawley—I loved it from the first moment I set foot in the village. After the harshness of the north, Dorset is so gentle and mild and pretty. The doors closing and the footsteps and the wheels on the drive—they didn't do us any harm. And we had each other, we weren't alone. You can get used to anything—to ghosts as much as to damp and woodworm and dry rot. There's all that in the Rectory, too, and I found it much more trying!"

The Bucklands, apparently, had got used to it, too. Thirty years he had been Rector of the parish, thirty years they had lived there with the wheels and the footsteps, and had brought up their son and daughter there. No harm had come to them; they slept soundly, and their grownup children used to joke about their haunted house.

"Nobody ever seems to *see* anything," I said to Eleanor as we walked home. "And no one ever comes up with a story, a sort of background to all this walking about and banging and crunching. Is there supposed to have been a murder there or some other sort of violent death?"

She said she didn't know, Kate had never said. The sound of the wheels, the closing of the doors, always took place at about nine in the evening, followed by the footsteps and the opening and closing of the front door. After that there was silence, and it hadn't happened every evening by any means. The only other thing was that Kate had never cared to use the big drawing room in the evenings. She and Tom and Louise had always stayed in the dining room or the morning room.

They did use the drawing room in the daytime—it was just that in the evenings the room felt strange to her, chilly even in summer, and indefinably hostile. Once she had had to go in there at ten-thirty. She needed her reading glasses, which she had left in the drawing room during the afternoon. She ran into the room and ran out again. She hadn't looked about her, just rushed in, keeping her eyes fixed on the eyeglass case on the mantelpiece. The icy hostility in that room had really frightened her, and that had been the only time she had felt dislike and fear of Shawley Rectory.

Of course one doesn't have to find explanations for an icy hostility. It's much more easily understood as being the product of tension and fear than aural phenomena are. I didn't have much faith in Kate's feelings about the drawing room. I thought, with a kind of admiration of Jack and Diana Loy, that elderly couple who had rented the Rectory for a year after Kate's departure, had been primed with stories of hauntings by Kate, yet had neither heard nor felt a thing. As far as I know, they had used that drawing room constantly. Often, when I had passed the gate in their time, I had seen lights in the drawing-room windows, at nine, at ten-thirty, and even at midnight.

The Loys had been gone three months. When Lazarus had first offered the Rectory for rent, the idea had been that Shawley should do without a clergyman of its own. I think this must have been the Church economizing—nothing to do certainly with ghosts. The services at St. Mary's were to be undertaken by the Vicar of the next parish, Mr. Hartley. Whether he found this too much for him in conjunction with the duties of his own parish or whether the powers-that-be in affairs Anglican had second thoughts, I can't say, but on the departure of the Loys it was decided there should be an incumbent to replace Tom.

The first hint of this we had from local gossip; next the facts appeared in our monthly news sheet, the *Shawley Post*. Couched in its customary parish magazine journalese it said: "Shawley residents all extend a hearty welcome to their new Rector, the Reverend Stephen Galton, whose coming to the parish with his charming wife will fill a long-felt need."

"He's very young," said Eleanor a few days after our discussion of haunting with the Scotts. "Under thirty."

"That won't bother me," I said. "I don't intend to be preached at by him. Anyway, why not? Out of the mouths of babes and sucklings," I said, "hast Thou ordained strength."

"Hark at the devil quoting scripture," said Eleanor. "They say his wife's only twenty-three."

I thought she must have met them, she knew so much. But no.

"It's just what's being said. Patsy got it from Judy Lawrence. Judy said they're moving in next month and her mother's coming with them."

"Who, Judy's?" I said.

"Don't be silly," said my wife. "Mrs. Galton's mother, the Rector's mother-in-law. She's coming to live with them."

Move in they did. And out again two days later.

The first we knew that something had gone very wrong for the Galtons was when I was out for my usual evening walk with our Irish setter Liam. We were coming back past the cottage that belongs to Charlie Lawrence (who is by way of being Shawley's squire) and which he keeps for the occupation of his gardener when he is lucky enough to have a gardener. At that time, last June, he hadn't had a gardener for at least six months and the cottage should have been empty. As I approached, however, I saw a woman's face, young, fair, very pretty, at one of the upstairs windows.

I rounded the hedge and Liam began an insane barking, for just inside the cottage gate, on the drive, peering in under the hood of an aged Wolseley, was a tall young man wearing a tweed sports jacket over one of those black-top things the clergy wear, and a clerical collar.

"Good evening," I said. "Shut up, Liam, will you?"

"Good evening," he said in a quiet, abstracted sort of way.

I told Eleanor. She couldn't account for the Galtons occupying Charlie Lawrence's gardener's cottage instead of Shawley Rectory, their proper abode. But Patsy Scott could. She came round on the following morning with a punnet of strawberries for us. The Scotts grow the best strawberries for miles around.

"They've been driven out by the ghosts," she said. "Can you credit it? A clergyman of the Church of England! An educated man! They were in that place not forty-eight hours before they were screaming to Charlie Lawrence to find them somewhere else to go."

I asked if she was sure it wasn't just the damp and the dry rot.

"Look, you know me. *I* don't believe the Rectory's haunted or anywhere *can* be haunted, come to that. I'm telling you what Mrs. Galton told me. She came in to us on Thursday morning and said did I think there was anyone in Shawley had a house or a cottage to rent because they couldn't stick the Rectory another night. I asked her what was wrong. And she said she knew it sounded crazy—it did, too, she was right there—she knew it sounded mad, but they'd been terrified out of their lives by what they'd heard and seen since they moved in."

"Seen?" I said. "She actually claims to have seen something?"

"She said her mother did. She said her mother saw something in the drawing room the first evening they were there. They'd already heard the carriage wheels and the doors closing and the footsteps and all that. The second evening no one dared go in the drawing room. They heard all the sounds again and Mrs. Grainger—that's the mother—heard voices in the drawing room, and it was then that they decided they couldn't stand it, they'd have to get out."

"I don't believe it!" I said. "I don't believe any of it. The woman's a psychopath, she's playing some sort of ghastly joke."

"Just as Kate was and the Bucklands," said Eleanor quietly.

Patsy ignored her and turned to me. "I feel just like you. It's awful, but what can you do? These stories grow and they sort of infect people and the more suggestible the people are, the worse the infection. Charlie and Judy are furious, they don't want it getting in the papers that Shawley Rectory is haunted. Think of all the people we shall get coming in cars on Sundays and gawping over the gates. But they had to let them have the cottage in common humanity. Mrs. Grainger was hysterical and poor little Mrs. Galton wasn't much better. Who told them to expect all those horrors? That's what I'd like to know."

"What does Gordon say?" I said.

"He's keeping an open mind, but he says he'd like to spend an evening there."

In spite of the Lawrences' fury, the haunting of Shawley Rectory did get quite a lot of publicity. There was a sensational story about it in one of the popular Sundays and then Stephen Galton's mother-in-law went on television. Western TV interviewed her on a local news program. I hadn't ever seen Mrs. Grainger in the flesh and her youthful appearance rather surprised me. She looked no more than thirty-five, though she must be into her forties.

The interviewer asked her if she had ever heard any stories of ghosts at Shawley Rectory before she went there and she said she hadn't. Did she believe in ghosts? Now she did. What had happened, asked the interviewer, after they had moved in?

It had started at nine o'clock, she said, at nine on their first evening. She and her daughter were sitting in the bigger of the two kitchens, having a cup of coffee. They had been moving in all day, unpacking, putting things away. They heard two doors close upstairs, then footsteps coming down the main staircase. She had thought it was her son-in-law, except that it couldn't have been because as the footsteps died away he came in through the door from the back kitchen. They couldn't understand what it had been, but they weren't frightened. Not then.

"We were all planning on going to bed early," said Mrs. Grainger. She was very articulate, very much at her ease in front of the cameras.

"Just about half-past ten I had to go into the big room they call the drawing room. The removal men had put some of our boxes in there and my radio was in one of them. I wanted to listen to my radio in bed. I opened the drawing-room door and put my hand to the light switch. I didn't put the light on. The moon was quite bright that night and it was shining into the room.

"There were two people, two figures, I don't know what to call them, between the windows. One of them, the girl, was lying huddled on the floor. The other figure, an older woman, was bending over her. She stood up when I opened the door and looked at me. I knew I wasn't seeing real people. I don't know how but I knew that. I remember I couldn't move my hand to switch the light on. I was frozen, just staring at that pale tragic face while it stared back at me. I did manage at last to back out and close the door, and I got back to my daughter and my son-in-law in the kitchen and I—well, I collapsed. It was the most terrifying experience of my life."

Yet you stayed a night and a day and another night in the Rectory? said the interviewer. Yes, well, her daughter and her son-in-law had persuaded her it had been some sort of hallucination, the consequence of being overtired. Not that she had ever really believed that. The night had been quiet and so had the next day, until nine in the evening when they were all this time in the morning room and they had heard a car drive up to the front door. They had all heard it, wheels crunching on the gravel, the sound of the engine, the brakes going on. Then had followed the closing of the doors upstairs and the footsteps, the opening and closing of the front door.

Yes, they had been very frightened, or she and her daughter had. Her son-in-law had made a thorough search of the whole house but found nothing, seen or heard no one. At ten-thirty they had all gone into the hall and listened outside the drawing-room door and she and her daughter had heard voices from inside the room, women's voices. Stephen had wanted to go in, but they had stopped him, they had been so frightened.

Now the interesting thing was that there had been something in the *Sunday Express* account about the Rectory being haunted by the ghosts of two women. The story quoted someone it described as a "local antiquarian," a man named Joseph Lamb, whom I had heard of but never met. Lamb had told the *Express* there was an old tradition that the ghosts were of a mother and her daughter and that the mother had killed the daughter in the drawing room.

"I never heard any of that before," I said to Gordon Scott, "and I'm sure Kate Cobworth hadn't. Who is this Joseph Lamb?"

"He's a nice chap," said Gordon. "And he's supposed to know more of local history than anyone else around. I'll ask him over and you can come and meet him if you like."

Joseph Lamb lives in a rather fine Jacobean house in a hamlet—you could hardly call it a village—about a mile to the north of Shawley. I had often admired it without knowing who lived there. The Scotts asked him and his wife to dinner shortly after Mrs. Grainger's appearance on television, and after dinner we got him onto the subject of the hauntings. Lamb wasn't at all unwilling to enlighten us. He's a man of about sixty and he said he first heard the story of the two women from his nurse when he was a little boy. Not a very suitable subject with which to regale a seven-year-old, he said.

"These two are supposed to have lived in the Rectory at one time," he said. "The story is that the mother had a lover or a man friend or whatever, and the daughter took him away from her. When the daughter confessed it, the mother killed her in a jealous rage."

It was Eleanor who objected to this. "But surely if they lived in the Rectory they must have been the wife and daughter of a Rector. I don't really see how in those circumstances the mother could have had a lover or the daughter could steal him away."

"No, it doesn't sound much like what we've come to think of as the domestic life of the English country parson, does it?" said Lamb. "And the strange thing is, although my nanny used to swear by the story and I heard it later from someone who worked at the Rectory, I haven't been able to find any trace of these women in the Rectory's history. It's not hard to research, you see, because only the Rectors of Shawley had ever lived there until the Loys rented it, and the Rectors' names are all up on that plaque in the church from 1380 onwards. There was another house on the site before this present one, of course, and parts of the older building are incorporated in the newer.

"My nanny used to say that the elder lady hadn't got a husband, he had presumably died. She was supposed to be forty years old and the girl nineteen. Well, I tracked back through the families of the various Rectors and I found a good many cases where the Rectors had predeceased their wives. But none of them fitted my nanny's story. They were either too old—one was much too young—or their daughters were too old or they had no daughters."

"It's a pity Mrs. Grainger didn't tell us what kind of clothes her ghosts were wearing," said Patsy with sarcasm. "You could have pinpointed the date then, couldn't you?"

"You mean that if the lady had had a steeple hat on she'd be medieval or around 1850 if she was wearing a crinoline?"

"Something like that," said Patsy.

At this point Gordon repeated his wish to spend an evening in the Rectory. "I think I'll write to the Master of Lazarus and ask permission," he said.

Very soon after, we heard that the Rectory was to be sold. Notice boards appeared by the front gate and at the corner where the glebe abutted Shawley Lane, announcing that the house would go up for auction on October 30th. Patsy, who always seems to know everything, told us that a reserve price of 60,000 pounds had been put on it.

"Not as much as I'd have expected," she said. "It must be the ghosts keeping the price down."

"Whoever buys it will have to spend another ten thousand on it," said Eleanor.

"And central heating will be a priority."

Whatever was keeping the price down—ghosts, cold, or dry rot—there were plenty of people anxious to view the house and land with, I supposed, an idea of buying it. I could hardly be at work in my garden or out with Liam without a car stopping and the driver asking me the way to the Rectory. Gordon and Patsy got quite irritable about what they described as "crowds milling about" in the lane and trippers everywhere, waving orders to view.

The estate agents handling the sale were a firm called Curlew, Pond and Co. Gordon didn't bother with the Master of Lazarus but managed to get the key from Graham Curlew, whom he knew quite well, and permission to spend an evening in the Rectory. Curlew didn't like the idea of anyone staying the night, but Gordon didn't want to do that anyway; no one had ever heard or seen anything after ten-thirty. He asked me if I'd go with him. Patsy wouldn't—she thought it was all too adolescent and stupid.

"Of course I will," I said. "As long as you'll agree to our taking some sort of heating arrangement with us and brandy in case of need."

By then it was the beginning of October and the evenings were turning cool. The day on which we decided to have our vigil happened also to be the one on which Stephen Galton and his wife moved out of Charlie Lawrence's cottage and left Shawley for good. According to the *Shawley Post*, he had got a living in Manchester. Mrs. Grainger had gone back to her own home in London from where she had written an article about the Rectory for *Psychic News*.

Patsy shrieked with laughter to see the two of us setting forth with our oil stove, a dozen candles, two torches, and half a bottle of Courvoisier. She did well to laugh, her amusement wasn't misplaced. We crossed the lane and opened the Rectory gate and went up the gravel drive on which those spirit wheels had so often been heard to crunch. It was seven o'clock in the evening and still light. The day had been fine and the sky was red with the aftermath of a spectacular sunset. I unlocked the front door and in we went.

The first thing I did was put a match to one of the candles because it wasn't at all light inside. We walked down the passage to the kitchens, I carrying the candle and Gordon shining one of the torches across the walls. The place was a mess. I suppose it hadn't had anything done to it, not even a cleaning, since the Loys moved out. It smelled damp and there was even fungus growing in patches on the kitchen walls. And it was extremely cold. There was a kind of deathly chill in the air, far more of a chill than one would have expected on a warm day in October. That kitchen had the feel you get when you open the door of a refrigerator that hasn't been kept too clean and is in need of defrosting.

We put our stuff down on a kitchen table someone had left behind and made our way up the back stairs. All the bedroom doors were open and we closed them. The upstairs had a neglected, dreary feel but it was less cold. We went down the main staircase, a rather fine curving affair with elegant banisters and carved newel posts, and entered the drawing room. It was empty, palely lit by the evening light from two windows. On the mantelpiece was a glass jar with greenish water in it, a half-burnt candle in a saucer, and a screwed-up paper table napkin. We had decided not to remain in this room but to open the door and look in at ten-thirty; so accordingly we returned to the kitchen, fetched out candles and torches and brandy, and settled down in the morning room, which was at the front of the house, on the other side of the front door.

Curlew had told Gordon there were a couple of deckchairs in this room. We found them resting against the wall and we put them up.

We lit our oil stove and a second candle, and we set one candle on the window sill and one on the floor between us. It was still and silent and cold. The dark closed in fairly rapidly, the red fading from the sky which became a deep hard blue, then indigo.

We sat and talked. It was about the haunting that we talked, collating the various pieces of evidence, assessing the times this or that was supposed to happen and making sure we both knew the sequence in which things happened. We were both wearing watches and I remember that we constantly checked the time. At half-past eight we again opened the drawing-room door and looked inside. The moon had come up and was shining through the windows as it had shone for Mrs. Grainger.

Gordon went upstairs with a torch and checked that all the doors remained closed and then we both looked into the other large downstairs room—the dining room, I suppose. Here a fanlight in one of the windows was open. That accounted for some of the feeling of cold and damp, Gordon said. The window must have been opened by some prospective buyer, viewing the place. We closed it and went back into the morning room to wait.

The silence was absolute. We didn't talk any more. We waited, watching the candles and the glow of the stove, which had taken some of the chill from the air. Outside it was pitch-dark. The hands of our watches slowly approached nine.

At three minutes to nine we heard the noise.

Not wheels or doors closing or a tread on the stairs but a faint, dainty, pattering sound. It was very faint, it was distant, it was on the ground floor. It was as if made by something less than human, lighter than that, tiptoeing. I had never thought about this moment beyond telling myself that if anything did happen, if there was a manifestation, it would be enormously interesting. It had never occurred to me even once that I should be so dreadfully, so hideously, afraid.

I didn't look at Gordon, I couldn't. I couldn't move, either. The pattering feet were less faint now, were coming closer. I felt myself go white, the blood all drawn in from the surface of my skin, as I was gripped by that awful primitive terror that has nothing to do with reason or with knowing what you believe in and what you don't.

Gordon got to his feet and stood there looking at the door. And then I couldn't stand it any more. I jumped up and threw open the door, holding the candle aloft—and looked into a pair of brilliant, golden-green eyes, staring steadily back at me about a foot from the ground.

"My God," said Gordon. "My God, it's Lawrences' cat. It must have got in through the window."

He bent down and picked up the cat, a soft, stout, marmalade-colored creature. I felt sick at the anticlimax. The time was exactly nine o'clock. With the cat draped over his arm, Gordon went back into the morning room and I followed him. We didn't sit down. We stood waiting for the wheels and the closing of the doors.

Nothing happened.

I have no business to keep you in suspense any longer, for the fact is that after that business with the cat nothing happened at all. At nine-fifteen we sat down in our deckchairs. The cat lay on the floor beside the oil stove and went to sleep. Twice we heard a car pass along Shawley Lane, a remotely distant sound, but we heard nothing else.

"Feel like a spot of brandy?" said Gordon.

"Why not?" I said.

So we each had a nip of brandy and at ten we had another look in the drawing room. By then we were both feeling bored and quite sure that since nothing had happened at nine nothing would happen at ten-thirty, either. Of course we stayed till ten-thirty and for half an hour after that, and then we decamped. We put the cat over the wall into Lawrences' grounds and went back to Gordon's house, where Patsy awaited us, smiling cynically.

I had had quite enough of the Rectory but that wasn't true of Gordon. He said it was well known that the phenomena didn't take place every night; we had simply struck an off-night, and he was going back on his own. He did, too, half a dozen times between then and the 30th, even going so far as to have (rather unethically) a key cut from the one Curlew had lent him. Patsy would never go with him, though he tried hard to persuade her.

But in all those visits he never saw or heard anything. And the effect on him was to make him as great a skeptic as Patsy.

"I've a good mind to make an offer for the Rectory myself," he said. "It's a fine house and I've got quite attached to it."

"You're not serious," I said.

"I'm perfectly serious. I'll go to the auction with a view to buying it if I can get Patsy to agree."

But Patsy preferred her own house and, very reluctantly, Gordon had to give up the idea. The Rectory was sold for 62,000 pounds to an American woman, a friend of Judy Lawrence. About a month after the sale, the builders moved in. Eleanor used to get progress reports from Patsy, how they had rewired and treated the whole place for woodworm and painted and relaid floors. The central-heating engineers came, too, much to Patsy's satisfaction.

We met Carol Marcus, the Rectory's new owner, when we were asked round to the Hall for drinks one Sunday morning. She was staying there with the Lawrences until such time as the improvements and decorations to the Rectory were complete. We were introduced by Judy to a very pretty, well dressed woman in young middle age. I asked her when she expected to move in. April, she hoped, as soon as the builders had finished the two extra bathrooms. She had heard rumors that the Rectory was supposed to be haunted and these had amused her very much. A haunted house in the English countryside! It was too good to be true.

"It's all nonsense, you know," said Gordon, who had joined us. "It's all purely imaginary." And he went on to tell her of his own experiences in the house during October—or his non-experiences, I should say.

"Well, for goodness' sake, I didn't *believe* it!" she said, and she laughed and went on to say how much she loved the house and wanted to make it a real home for her children to come to. She had three, she said, all in their teens, two boys away at school and a girl a bit older.

That was the only time I ever talked to her and I remember thinking she would be a welcome addition to the neighborhood. A nice woman. Serene is the word that best described her. There was a man friend of hers there, too. I didn't catch his surname but she called him Guy. He was staying at one of the local hotels, to be near her presumably.

"I should think those two would get married, wouldn't you?" said Eleanor on the way home. "Judy told me she's waiting to get her divorce."

Later that day I took Liam for a walk along Shawley Lane and when I came to the Rectory I found the gate open. So I walked up the gravel drive and looked through the drawing-room windows at the new woodblock floor and ivory-painted walls and radiators. The place was swiftly being transformed. It was no longer sinister or grim.

I walked round the back and peered in at the splendidly fitted kitchens, one a laundry now, and wondered what on earth had made sensible women like Mrs. Buckland and Kate spread such vulgar tales and the Galtons panic. What had come over them? I could only imagine that they felt a need to attract attention to themselves, which they perhaps could do in no other way.

I whistled for Liam and strolled down to the gate and looked back at the Rectory. It stared back at me. Is it hindsight that makes me say this or did I really feel it then? I think I did feel it, that the house stared at me with a kind of steady insolence.

Carol Marcus moved in three weeks ago, on a sunny day in the middle of April. Two nights later, just before eleven, there came a sustained ringing at Gordon's front door as if someone were leaning on the bell. Gordon went to the door. Carol Marcus stood outside, absolutely calm but deathly white.

She said to him, "May I use your phone, please? Mine isn't in yet and I have to call the police. I just shot my daughter."

She took a step forward and crumpled in a heap on the threshold.

Gordon picked her up and carried her into the house and Patsy gave her brandy, and then he went across the road to the Rectory. There were lights on all over the house; the front door was open and light was streaming out onto the drive and the little Citroen Diane that was parked there.

He went into the house. The drawing-room door was open and he walked in there and saw a young girl lying on the carpet between the windows. She was dead. There was blood from a bullet wound on the front of her dress, and on a low round table lay the small automatic that Carol Marcus had used.

In the meantime Patsy had been the unwilling listener to a confession. Carol Marcus told her that the girl, who was nineteen, had unexpectedly driven down from London, arriving at the Rectory at nine o'clock. She had had a drink and something to eat and then said she had something to tell her mother, that was why she had come down. While in London she had been seeing a lot of the man called Guy and now they found that they were in love with each other. She knew it would hurt her mother, but she wanted to tell her at once, she wanted to be honest about it.

Carol Marcus told Patsy she felt nothing, no shock, no hatred or resentment, no jealousy. It was as if she were impelled by some external force to do what she did—take the gun she always kept with her from a drawer in the writing desk and kill her daughter.

At this point, Gordon came back and they phoned the police.

Within a quarter of an hour, the police were at the house. They arrested Carol Marcus and took her away and now she is on remand, awaiting trial on a charge of murder.

So what is the explanation of all this? Or does there, in fact, have to be an explanation? Eleanor and I were so shocked by what had happened—and awed, too—that for a while we were somehow wary of talking about it even to each other. Then Eleanor said, "It's as if all this time the coming event cast its shadow before it."

I nodded, yet it didn't seem quite that to me. It was more that the Rectory was waiting for the right people to come along, the people who would *fit* its still un-played scenario, the woman of forty, the daughter of nineteen, the lover. And only to those who approximated these characters could it show shadows and whispers of the drama—the closer the approximation, the clearer the sounds and signs.

The Loys were old and childless, so they saw nothing. Nor did Gordon and I—we were of the wrong sex. But the Bucklands who had a daughter heard and felt things, and so did Kate, though she was too old for the tragic leading role and her adolescent girl too young for victim. The Galtons had been nearly right—had Mrs. Grainger once hoped the young Rector would marry her before he showed his preference for her daughter?—but the women had been a few years too senior for the parts. Even so, they had come closer to participation than those before them.

All this is very fanciful and I haven't mentioned a word of it to Gordon and Patsy. They wouldn't listen if I did. They persist in seeing the events of three weeks ago as no more than a sordid murder, a crime of jealousy committed by someone whose mind was disturbed.

But I haven't been able to keep from asking myself what would have happened if Gordon had bought the Rectory when he talked of doing so. Patsy will be forty this year. I don't think I've mentioned that she has a daughter by her first marriage who is away at the university and going on nineteen now, a girl that they say is extravagantly fond of Gordon.

He is talking once more of buying, since Carol Marcus, whatever may become of her, will hardly keep the place now. The play is played out, but need that mean there will never be a repeat performance?

Dana Lyon

The Living End

The living arrangements that Nell had made with her friend Emma had not been in effect a month before she realized that it had been a devastating mistake. Why, she asked herself, sitting trembling at her desk while she was going over her bills, hadn't she left well enough alone, without worrying about money all the time? She had her little house, her so-so job with Civil Service and a pension not far in the offing, her solitude at night, her peace and quiet, even if inflation *was* taking a large piece out of her accumulated savings while the little apartment above was standing idle; so why hadn't she left it that way?

Money, she thought. Worrying about the future. Seeing the savings growing smaller instead of larger, feeling the need for an increased income which she'd never get from her job now that she was this close to retirement. So that apartment upstairs that she had built and used herself years ago while her parents were still living in the downstairs quarters was the answer to her need for increased income, just sitting there waiting for another tenant.

She had tried: the nice young couple, both of whom worked and were therefore out of the house all day—until she discovered that the girl had been three months' pregnant at the time of signing the lease, and then there was the baby, waking Nell at night with its incessant crying, until she had finally had to give them their notice. What was eighty-five dollars a month weighed against her quiet and peace of mind?

And then the nice-looking middle-aged woman who worked downtown and brought home man after man and was such a wretched housekeeper that some of her roaches had finally invaded Nell's living quarters. Notice served.

And there were others, even less desirable, particularly the ones who managed to evade rent day, and those who wanted to be sociable, wanting to use her telephone or her washer, wanting her to accept C.O.D. packages and forgetting to repay her, and always and forever the excuses for not being able to pay the rent. ("Just a week or two, Nell dear—I'm expecting a check in the mail any day.")

She had hated being a landlady, but now she was hating, even

24

more, seeing her small savings depleted in order to take up the slack caused by inflation. Nevertheless, no more bothersome tenants—until suddenly she had thought of Emma.

Emma had been her closest friend, her chum, when they were in high school together, her confidante, nearer to her than anyone else had ever been. Arms entwined, heads together, whispering about boys, daringly discussing the origins of life—a commitment they knew would last for life. It didn't, of course.

Nell had gone her way to college and other friends, to love affairs and marriage, to divorce and finally a job wih the state, and somewhere along the way Emma had been almost forgotten. Except for one definite and unfailing commitment that had lasted all these years: they exchanged long letters on each other's birthday and thus at least kept in touch once a year. But as time went on there was little to tell each other about their lives, which had remained almost static in their later years.

They were both in their early sixties now, but this one contact remained; they dared not neglect this birthday acknowledgment for fear that whoever didn't write would be considered dead by the other. So they had continued writing.

Emma, Nell thought now. I know she doesn't have much money. I wonder if she'd like to take the apartment overhead. I could bring the rent down to seventy-five dollars, and I'd be company for her, and she'd be company for me—but not too much, not as if, heaven forbid, we had to live in the same rooms. Nell enjoyed her privacy too much, her own way of doing things—letting the dishes go if she felt like it, or flying at the cleaning chores some weekend if that was what possessed her at the time, or playing the radio late at night, or the TV, or painting in her little studio room. Snacks at any hour of the day when she was home, instead of regular meals. Quiet reading. Walks alone along the country road where she lived. Just to be alone when she wanted to be—

However, the apartment upstairs was entirely separate, and even had an outside staircase of its own, and someone like Emma, who had always been so thoughtful of others, would not make much noise. The seventy-five dollars would help; it would just about take over the depletion that present-day prices had made in her savings. Well—a few more years and she'd be able to retire on her pension and what she had managed to save during the years of her enslavement. But there'd be no savings left unless she rented the apartment.

Emma was delighted. She wrote, "I have been so depressed, dearest Nell, because I thought the rest of my life would have to be spent alone, no family, even my friends here are dying off; and you make the little apartment sound so fascinating. I'll give notice on this dinky room I live in." Room, thought Nell; is that all she has?—and began to feel qualms along with the Good Samaritan warmth within her. "I'll just pack up my things and get a bus ticket and be with you in a week."

More qualms. Why was Emma in such a hurry? What was she doing that she could pack up and leave her way of life and her job and what friends she had without another thought—too eager, perhaps, to join Nell's life? Well, no matter, they could still lead their individual lives. Emma would be getting a cheap apartment and Nell would be getting an increased income.

Nell spent the following weekend giving the little apartment—sitting room, kitchen, bedroom, and bath—a thorough cleaning. She laundered the curtains, put everything in place, even added a little bouquet of flowers from the garden just before she went off to the bus station to greet her friend.

"I can't believe it!" Nell exclaimed over and over as they drove back to the house. "You seem just the same, dear. I just can't believe it, how long has it been, you've hardly changed at all—"

"Nor you," said Emma, beaming, both of them fully aware they were lying. "How could we ever have been separated for so long?"

"Well, like everyone else, we got busy with our own lives. Here we are," and Nell pulled into the carport at the side of the house. "Do come into my little nest for a bite before I take you upstairs."

"What a darling place!" Emma exclaimed, looking around Nell's cozy living room. "Don't bother with anything, dear, I won't want to put you to any trouble."

Nell beamed. "Well, if you're not hungry, how about a little glass of sherry?"

"No, thanks, but you go ahead."

They sat there, in Nell's charming little living room, and for a moment said nothing. What was left to say? They had chattered all the way from the bus station, but now there was nothing left that hadn't already been said in their long exchange of letters. They had changed, indeed: Nell, the tall, graceful dark-haired high-school girl, was now lean rather than slender, her dark hair mostly white, her once lovely eyes shadowed by glasses, her lipstick not quite even; and Emma, the plump, plain little high-school girl was now plumper and plainer. Her faded blonde-white hair was cut in a Buster Brown fashion, making her look like a prematurely aging kindergartener, her dress was flowery, her shawl askew, and her face, as always, bland.

Out of the silence, Emma finally said, "What a lovely home you have here, dear. Shall we go upstairs and look at mine?"

She exclaimed joyfully over the neat little apartment. "Just right for me!" she said. "And with you downstairs for company I'll never get lonely—"

Apprehension washed over Nell like a sudden splash of cold water. "Well, I keep pretty busy all the time," she explained hastily. "Working all day, then doing my chores at night, and I've kind of taken up painting—oh, not commercially, of course, just for my own amusement—though it might develop into something someday. Now about the rent, dear. As I told you, seventy-five a month for *you*, though I usually get a lot more, but I decided I just didn't want strangers up there any longer."

"Oh, yes," said Emma. And then, "But I don't guess you want a deposit of a month's rent or a lease or anything like that, do you? Being friends and all."

"No," said Nell patiently. "I don't think a lease is necessary between us. Just the month's rent."

Emma paid her. In cash. "And I promise," she added, smiling, "that I'll be very careful with the utilities so they won't add too much extra onto your expenses."

Nell thought: Who said anything about my paying the utilities? But she kept silent, more apprehensive now than ever.

The first month was quiet and calm and Nell could now figure on replenishing her savings account toward her retirement. Except, of course, that it wasn't a full $75.00 since the gas and electricity and water took up well over $10.00.

And it soon became apparent that Emma was far from solvent herself, so she started looking for a job. She found nothing, until finally she put an ad in the paper as baby sitter, and was repaid by a rash of answers on the telephone—Nell's telephone, of course, since Emma claimed she couldn't afford one of her own. Therefore Nell gave her a key to her own apartment and Emma ran down her outside stairs whenever the phone rang.

And at night, when Nell answered, she had to go out and call Emma, who never answered until Nell had climbed the stairs and knocked on the door. If she can hear the telephone when I'm not at home, Nell asked herself, why doesn't she hear me when I call? She finally resorted to banging her broom handle on the ceiling and Emma learned that if she didn't respond Nell would simply hang up the phone.

No matter. Emma was delighted with the two dollars an hour she was paid for her services, although occasionally she was called on to supply her own transportation, which, of course, meant Nell's, and soon this became intolerable as Nell was expected to pick her up any time after midnight, as well as to take her earlier, and what with the telephone ringing almost constantly, Nell was soon at her wits' end. Until finally she informed Emma that she must take jobs only where transportation was provided.

"Oh," said Emma, looking downcast. "That means I'll have to lose a lot of my jobs because most of them expect me to drive myself. Maybe I could learn to drive your car?" she asked hopefully.

"No," said Nell, and that was that. Until the first of the following month when the rent was due. Emma did not offer it and finally, five days late, Nell brought up the subject.

"Oh," said Emma. "Well, dear, would it be all right if I just paid half of the rent this time and made it up later? You see, with business falling off and everything, I'm a little short of cash. Just for this month, of course," she added hastily.

Nell said, "Will next month be any better? Emma, I think you should have made your financial circumstances clearer before you pulled up stakes and came here. You told me you had an income from your brother's estate and also your Social Security that you took at sixty-two instead of waiting till sixty-five when you'd have gotten more, and that you felt you would have no trouble getting a job here. After all, dear, seventy-five dollars a month, utilities included, is very low rent for these days."

"Yes, I know," Emma said hurriedly, "but it's a lot more than I paid back home where I stayed with friends. Only I thought you needed me, that you were lonely and that's why you wanted me to come and keep you company, and then I thought how you might be pleased for me to help with the work in your dear little house, cleaning and cooking and laundering, and that would take care of the rent, and so everything would turn out fine."

Too late Nell remembered Emma's proclivities of the past that had earned her the name of Pollyanna Emma, who always knew that tomorrow would be sunny and happy and that everything would turn out right for little Emma. But it never had, because little

Emma, being so sure of God's grace, had done little to prepare for the inevitable rainy day. "Oh, I'm sure everything will turn out for the best," Emma was always saying, and it frequently did but only because of the services of people around her.

So now she said, "I'm sure everything will turn out fine for both of us," and Nell could have slapped her. But she couldn't bear to come down too hard on her. After all, she'd given up what home she'd had (whatever *that* was) to do something she thought would help her friend. Emma couldn't pay, that was certain, and so Nell said resignedly, "All right, Emma, you can help with my place," and went back to it in despair.

So now, she thought, I have a dependent for the first time since I got my divorce.

Emma was always underfoot and always in need—she had to use the telephone, she had to go to the library, the dentist, the supermarket, everything for which she had no transportation and for which Nell did. Nell would come home tired out from her job of coping with people, her boss, her co-workers, the public; and even though she tried to be as quiet as possible, hoping for a few moments of peace, there would be Emma on her doorstep saying, "Oh, Nell dear, do you suppose you could run me down to the store—or would you have an extra can of tunafish?" or, "Drat it, I have to go to the dentist's tomorrow, only appointment I could get was three o'clock. Do you suppose you could take a weensy bit of time off and run me to his office?"

"Emma," said Nell, pushed to the wall, "I'm afraid this arrangement isn't going to work out very well, after all—"

And then the little round face under the white bangs would grow old and pinched and frightened and Nell would sigh and say, "Well, we'll see—" and the little face would brighten with relief and things would go on as before . . .

Emma was idle and lonely. She still had a few baby-sitting jobs when the transportation was included, but the rest of her time was spent without purpose. She didn't really care much for reading, she hated any sort of handiwork, gardens did not interest her; she had no TV set nor the wherewithal to buy one since she did not even have the wherewithal to pay the rent. This last was an unmentioned, rather sordid matter that Emma refused to acknowledge, and which Nell, exhausted, would no longer bring up after the three times she had mentioned it and as a result suffered excruciatingly from guilt qualms when she'd seen the bleak, frightened look on her little friend's face.

Little friend, hell, Nell said to herself. She's a *leech!* But she doesn't know it. She keeps saying that she'd do the same for me if our positions were reversed, take me in and give me a home and look out for me—she knows damn well our positions could never be reversed, but in the meantime she gets credit for being noble enough to offer her beneficence to me!

Nell was getting frantic. Emma said, at various times: The roof leaks. The heater doesn't work properly. Now that summer's here the heat is terrible—perhaps if I could have an air conditioner?

Winter again. Emma growing plumper, Nell growing leaner. And more tired. Pitter-patter up and down the outside staircase, knocking on the door the minute Nell got home, sitting there chatting but unable to keep the disapproval out of her eyes while Nell sipped her sherry and yearned to read the paper at the same time. Why am I such a fool? Nell asked herself countless times. So, okay, I made a mistake but God knows I've paid for it over and over. Do I have to pay forever?

One wintry day Emma tapped lightly on the door and when Nell appeared she said, "Dear, could I just show you something for a minute?"

"What?" said Nell. "I'm busy with supper."

"O-oh, it smells wonderful. Swiss steak, is it? Haven't had any for years, it seems. Just scrambled eggs. Or tuna. Gets kind of tiresome."

The wind blew a blast of cold air into Nell's cozy living room.

"What is it, Emma?" she asked impatiently. I'm damned if I'm going to ask her *again* to have supper with me. She'll end up a permanent unpaid boarder.

"Well, it's just the staircase outside. It shakes a little when I use it. That nice Mr. Brown who brought me home the other night noticed it—you know, the one with the two children I sit for, they're really darling but they do keep me busy, they get into such mischief—where was I?"

"The staircase," said Nell with foreboding. "What about it?"

"Well, Mr. Brown noticed how it shook when he took me to my door—so polite, the other fathers never do—and he said I should tell my landlady about it."

Nell went out and inspected the staircase. It did shake. The main post holding it up was beginning to rot at the bottom. Without Emma up there, she thought, I could just let the thing go and close up the apartment. Wait till I get ahead a little with my finances, and then I'll have it repaired. But not with Emma there.

She said briefly, "I'll see about it," and went into her apartment again, ignoring the mewling plea behind her, "Oh, but Nell darling—"

Shut up, said Nell to herself. Shut up!

She sat erect in her chair and cried.

And thus Nell's life became a shambles. There was now no further talk of paying the rent—Emma was always low on funds. And there were constant complaints (delicately put) of things that should be done to the apartment to make it more habitable, other things that were needed—like transportation, telephone, air conditioning, television—that would make Emma more comfortable and happy. With always the offer to take care of Nell's house, cook her meals, do her cleaning, refusing to believe Nell when she said, in a moment of exasperation, that all she wanted when she got home at night was peace and quiet and solitude, a look at the paper, and her drink in private.

"You're just saying that," said Emma, beaming her bland smile. "But I know that you just don't want an old friend like me doing menial work for you. But honestly, dear, I don't mind. I'm very independent, you know, but I like to do my share—"

Another time, a day when Nell was more exhausted than usual, Emma was waiting for her at the door. "I could hardly wait," she said excitedly. "I've had the most wonderful idea that would do wonders for both of us! Look, dear, it's just that— Oh, let's go in first and I'll tell you while you have your little drink—it's really a solution to everything."

There's only one solution, Nell thought drearily, and that's for you to pack up and leave. They went in.

"It's so simple," said Emma, her voice rising. "Look, I know you could use a little more money and of course I hardly have any at all, so—why don't I move into that little studio room of yours, where you paint, and rent the upstairs apartment, then we'd both be better off. We could split the rent money because I'd be giving up my own apartment, of course—"

Nell looked at her incredulously. She did not go into explanations. She simply said no, and did not speak again.

Emma left, her head bowed like a child who has been unjustly disciplined, and Nell poured herself a drink and sat trembling in her chair, her thoughts black and deep.

She spoke aloud. "This," she said, "is the living end. The absolute living *end*."

A storm rose slowly, unobserved, from the north, and then came rushing like a wild insane creature of the elements, swooping down in blackness and noise and torrents and terrible sounds until the small house shook. Nell roused and lifted her face and said, "Storm, why don't you blow off the roof of my house?" The thought felt good.

She got up finally and went outside and saw that the steps leading up to the apartment were trembling in the wind. She went to the unsteady post and examined it, the wind and rain lashing at her. Nell did not notice. She smiled and kept her hand on the fragile support, then gave it a violent shove. It moved dangerously, almost loose from its moorings, ready to go with the least pressure put upon the steps. She smiled, and went into her warm little nest, humming happily to herself.

When would Emma come? She was frightened of storms. There had been other times of wildness in the elements when she would come shivering with fear to Nell's door and plead to spend the night there. How soon? She must come now—now when the storm was raging.

Still humming, Nell went into the kitchen, got the broom, and banged its handle on the ceiling. That should fetch her.

The storm, the wild screaming wind, pounded on the small house and shook it like an angry giant and the torrents fell and the air was filled with noise and confusion and terrifying threats; and suddenly there was another sound, the wrenching crash of the steps outside as they were torn from their moorings; and then a single human scream . . . At last, as if finally satisfied, the wind held itself in abeyance for an instant, and suddenly there was no sound at all. Just silence.

And Nell sat on, drink in hand, still smiling, still humming. She was alone at last.

Emma did not die.

She lay in traction from head to foot in the hospital to which she had been taken. Her back had been so shattered that she was given little hope of ever being able to walk again. A wheelchair possibly, after months spent in bed.

Nell did not go to see her. Not, that is, until Emma fully regained consciousness. She went then only because the hospital called her and said that Emma was asking for her and that since she was Emma's only living relative— "I am not a relative," said Nell sharply. "I am her landlady only."

But she went. Emma smiled wanly from the bed. "Hello, dear," she said. "It's so good to see you. I'll bet you were here every day while I was unconscious."

Nell said nothing.

After a brief silence Emma said bluntly, "The bills are enormous. I don't know what I'm going to do."

"Well, I'm sure the county will take care of you. They always do in cases like yours."

"County! What do you mean, county? I have never accepted charity from anyone."

Oh, no? Nell thought. No free rent, no free transportation, no free food half of the time? "And," the pathetic little voice continued, "I don't intend to start now."

"Then what *do* you propose to do?" said Nell, monumentally uninterested. "You certainly can't pay these bills yourself."

"I don't have to!" said Emma triumphantly. "You know that nice Mr. Brown who used to bring me home after I sat with his kids? Well, he's a lawyer, and he was the one who pointed out how rickety those stairs were, so he was in to see me this morning and he told me—"

There was an uneasy silence. Then Nell said, not really wanting to know, "Well? What did he say?"

"He said," Emma explained carefully, "that you should have had those stairs fixed after I complained about them, and that undoubtedly your insurance company would come through with plenty of money to take care of me—"

There was a brief silence. Then Nell spoke. "Emma," she said carefully, "there *is* no insurance company."

"Then of course you should have had the stairs fixed. Mr. Brown inspected the hole where the post had been and he said it looked as if the post had been even more damaged than when he first saw it."

"The storm—"

"No," said Emma. "The storm knocked away the post but the hole was cement and it was broken all around the top—he said the post must have been hanging by a thread when the storm came. No insurance, hm? Well, dear, then I guess I'll just have to sue you personally."

"Sue *me?* What do you mean? You know I haven't done anything to be sued for—it would just be a waste of money on your part. You can't get blood out of a turnip. It wasn't *my* fault the storm blew down the steps, so there's no use threatening me with a lawsuit—"

Nell's voice rose hysterically, and the impulse to murder was there in her hands. She could almost feel them moving of their own volition, twisting in her lap, struggling to be free in order to silence this hateful creature forever.

"I have nothing, do you hear?" she cried, her voice rising out of control. "Nothing!"

"Well, then, what am I to do?" said Emma helplessly. "And of course you have something, dear. Your little house—you told me once it was free and clear—and your car and your little, or big, savings account that you plan for when you retire— Oh dear me, yes, you have a lot and of course it is only fair for you to take care of me for the rest of my life since you ought to have had the stairs fixed, you ought to have had the stairs fixed, you ought to . . ." She smiled contentedly, and dozed off.

George Baxt

I Wish He Hadn't Said That

"Now that I've rung in the new year, I'd like to wring my neighbor's neck." Malcolm Brodsky was seated at his desk, glaring at the blank sheet of paper in his typewriter and balancing the telephone receiver between his shoulder and his fleshy chin. The rest of the instrument was on the floor at his feet, anchor for twenty-five feet of telephone line which usually made it possible for Malcolm to pace the length and width of his attractive living room, with the occasional airy indulgence of a heavy-footed entrechat or timestep. Even seated, at least one foot was active. It was tapping angrily, causing Malcolm's new best friend, Andy Agouta, who was on the other end of the wire, to inquire anxiously, "What's that banging on your end?"

"My foot," snapped Malcolm. "Now she's murdering 'Getting To Know You.'"

The "she" murdering "Getting To Know You" lived across the court, two stories up. She was learning how to play the piano. She practiced from two to three hours every night when she got home from work, usually around five o'clock. Saturdays and Sundays was open season for her. There were no set hours for practising. On weekends she attacked the ivories when the spirit moved her, which was frequently. Obviously a beginner and working from sheet music, her repertoire was limited. The limitations were exclusively show tunes.

The Saturday she had moved into the apartment, 11-H, a very warm June day, she had flung open her windows and then zeroed in on the upright. "Send In the Clowns," which a gifted musician could demolish in under four minutes, took her more than fifteen with no time off for good behavior. Malcolm had been spared this tortuous initiation because he was away for the weekend visiting his sister out in Montauk on the tip of Long Island. Andy Agouta, an aspiring architect, had come to brunch on Sunday and, fascinated by Malcolm's outrageous wit and apparently cavalier attitude toward everything and everyone, himself included, promptly offered to drive Malcolm back to New York and Malcolm had accepted with alacrity. It saved on the train fare.

Halfway to New York, when he found a chance to speak (Malcolm was blowing his nose), Andy asked, "Why are you so mean to your nephew?"

"He's noisy."

"I didn't notice he was particularly noisy."

"I hate noise."

"If you hate noise you shouldn't be living in New York."

"I don't live in New York, I *survive* in New York." Andy, who was a very good driver and kept his hands on the wheel and his eyes on the road in front of him, nevertheless stole frequent looks at Malcolm's agitated face, because the steady succession of one-liners were funnier when you caught the accompanying expressions on Malcolm's face.

"Thank God I finally have a quiet apartment. I mean I've lived all over the city and been driven to near self-destruction by neighborly stereos, radios, hi-fi's, overhead heels clicking on uncarpeted floors. Across the courtyard from me, two floors up, there used to be a clarinetist—of all the ugly instruments. Complain? Did I complain? I almost got terminal from complaints. Fortunately, early Thanksgiving morning he jumped out of the window. Bless his heart, he took the clarinet with him. The apartment has been blissfully empty ever since. The building is trying to go co-op, so they haven't been that anxious to rent it again. How about you, Andy? Is it quiet where you live?"

"I never notice."

Malcolm stared stonily at Andy's well made profile. "You never notice? What kind of a neurotic are you?"

The following day a little after five P.M. Malcolm's complacence was shattered. He was seated at the desk revising a chapter of his work in progress, an essay on the dangerous mental pollution being spread by television soap operas for an obscure, esoteric magazine that published four times a year, when he heard the piano.

His right hand froze in midair. His left had gripped the edge of the desk until the knuckles turned white. His eyes narrowed, his nose twitched, and his inner radar, always in superb working condition, signaled in the direction of apartment 11-H. His eyes lifted slowly. The windows of 11-H were flung wide and he saw the back of an upright piano, placed smack against the windows. He couldn't see the villain at the keyboard.

He looked frantically at the windows of other apartments. There was no one in sight. Was no one else annoyed enough to look and try to detect the origin of this cacophonic obscenity? He hurried to the telephone table and snatched up his personal directory, searching for the building superintendent's phone number, when the telephone rang. "Hello!" he shrieked, grabbing the receiver.

"Dear heaven," shouted Andy at the other end, "don't destroy my eardrum! It's Andy!"

"It's hell! There's someone in eleven-H!"

Andy wondered if his new friend took drugs. "What's eleven-H?"

"What do you mean what's eleven-H! The suicidal clarinet player, remember? *Now* there's someone up there murdering 'Send In the Clowns' on the piano! The composer ought to thank his lucky stars he doesn't live in the neighborhood. Listen to it! Just listen!" He carried the phone across the room to his desk, then leaned across the desk and held the telephone out the window.

"Sure sounds awful," commiserated Andy.

"*Awful?* Are you always given to such understatement?"

"Are we on for dinner tonight?"

"I can't think about food while my stomach's turning. I'll call you back. Stay home and stay off the phone!" Malcolm slammed down the receiver, found the building superintendent's number, dialed it, and waited. There was no reply. Slamming the phone down, he grabbed his keys from the table near the door and hurried down to the lobby. Hassim, the Iranian student who served as part-time doorman, told him the superintendent was in the laundry room. Malcolm hurried down to the basement. In the laundry room he found the superintendent working with a monkey wrench on a pipe above the sink.

"Walter!"

Walter Midzik froze on the stepladder. He recognized the hysteria. Nine-B. Brodsky comma Malcolm. Malcolm was tugging at one of Walter's pantlegs. Walter resented the familiarity and pulled his foot away, almost upsetting the ladder.

"Walter!" Malcolm's voice was up several octaves.

"Calm yourself, Mr. Brodsky, calm yourself. The exterminator comes on Friday."

"I don't need the exterminator." His hands were on his hips, which signaled he meant business. "What's that atrocity in eleven-H?"

Hell, thought Walter, here we go again. His mouth formed into one of its best building-superintendent smiles. "A very nice young lady moved in on Saturday."

"With a piano! That piano has got to stop!"

Walter remembered the piano all right. It didn't fit into the elevator and had to be hauled up eleven flights of stairs, with the young lady accompanying it every step of the way to make sure it wasn't bruised or damaged. Walter continued to dwell on thoughts of the young lady—her inviting lips, her boudoir eyes, those long exciting legs that seemed to begin at her waist, the way she looked at him when he arrived at the apartment to have a look at the air-conditioner she said wasn't working. Which it wasn't, thereby proving she was honorable.

"Why are you smirking at me?" Malcolm demanded.

Walter was aroused from his reverie. "Her air-conditioner is on the blink. The engineers can't get here until sometime next week."

"What's one thing got to do with the other? I can't work! You tell her to shut those windows when she's torturing that piano, you hear me?"

Walter didn't like the menace in Malcolm's voice. Slowly, he descended the stepladder with the practiced sexuality of yesteryear's showgirl. Standing eyeball to eyeball with Malcolm, he said, "Mr. Brodsky, nobody talks to me like that." Walter was young and muscular and he was very angry. The anger made him tremble and the building keys that hung from his belt tinkled.

"I'm sorry," said Malcolm, backing away. "But you know I'm a very nervous person. I can't stand noise. *Everybody* complained about Fenuski." That was the clarinet player. "Hasn't anybody else complained about this this this *thing?*"

Walter shook his head. "Maybe you're painting it worse than it is."

Malcolm drew himself up to his full five foot seven. "Very well, Walter," he said, "I'll take care of it myself."

Back in the apartment, he paced back and forth, building up a stronger head of steam. Eleven-H, whose name was Tansy Glunt (tansy? wasn't that a weed?), had entered her second hour of malpractice. Now she was attempting "Climb Every Mountain," and the ascent was as difficult and arduous as Hillary's attempt to conquer Everest. Malcolm was beating at his temple with his fists when the phone rang. It was Andy again.

"I thought you said you'd call right back." Andy was calm, collected, unruffled, and hungry. "If we're not meeting for dinner, I'd like to go out and do some food shopping."

Malcolm responded with a maniacal laugh that chilled Andy's spine. "Of course we're having dinner. I have to get *out* of this place. I'm going crazy!"

They made a date to rendezvous at Malcolm's favorite Italian restaurant on West Forty-eighth Street in thirty minutes, then Malcolm crossed to his desk, composed himself, and then composed a note.

"Hi there, Good Neighbor 11-H—welcome to the building! Good luck in your valiant attempt to master the keyboard! But could you kindly close your windows when doing your exercises? Many many thanks!

—9-B"

An hour after the note had been slipped under her door, Tansy noticed it. Walter had rung her doorbell and before admitting him she picked up the note and read it. When Walter entered, she handed it to him. He read it, shrugged, set it on the foyer table, took her in his arms, and kissed her passionately.

Shortly after midnight, Malcolm came home. He rescued the note he had sent 11-H from the floor as he entered the apartment. Under the note he had sent her, she had penciled, in an adolescent scrawl: "Sorry. My air-conditioner is on the fritz."

Malcolm let out a howl of rage as he crossed to his desk and under Tansy's note he scribbled in large block letters: "SO ARE YOU!"

He took the elevator to the eleventh floor and was about to slip the note back under Tansy's door when he heard muffled voices from within the apartment. One of the voices, which Malcolm recognized as Walter Midzik's, dripped with ardor. So he's added another scalp to his belt, thought Malcolm. He stared at the note in his hand and slowly crumpled it. He returned to his apartment and sat at the desk and looked up at her windows. In time the light went out. Malcolm leaned back, lost in thought.

For another two weeks, he continued to endure the torture. The exchange of notes continued, but even after Tansy Glunt's air-conditioner was repaired, her windows remained open. There was during this period a three-day heat wave and yet when she massacred the keyboard the windows were open. Malcolm tried canvassing some of the other tenants who might be affected by her fanatical fingers and succeeded in getting only three signatures on the petition he was circulating (he suspected they were three of Walter's abandoned conquests). He phoned the main office of the building management and was told that Tansy Glunt, by law, could be censured only if she was heard playing after eleven P.M. or before nine in the morning.

That night, at dinner in a Spanish restaurant in Greenwich Village, Andy was shocked at Malcolm's appearance. He hadn't seen him in a week. Where once there had been a buoyant, cherubic expression there were now dark circles under the eyes, a nervous twitch to the lips, and deep frown lines around the mouth.

"Now she's doing it on purpose," he muttered. Andy knew he meant Tansy Glunt. Tansy Glunt was now as much a part of Andy's life as was the President of the United States and the Mayor of the city, both of whom Malcolm also disapproved of. "Now she plays every night at five for three hours and all day Saturday and Sunday, with no hope of going on tour."

Andy smiled. At least Malcolm was still in control of his sense of humor.

"I thought of packing a bag, making it known I was going away, and then slipping back in through the basement, figuring if she thought I was out of town she'd give it a rest for a while. But then I'd be trapped in the apartment."

"I could slip you groceries."

"No, thanks. I've got a full freezer."

"Why don't you move?"

"Who can afford it?"

"Your sister will help you."

"She's helped me too much." He picked moodily at his *paella*. "And why should *I* move? I was there first!"

"She still entertaining the superintendent?"

"So the handyman tells me."

"Well, summer's almost over. She won't keep her windows open when it starts getting chilly."

"What are you talking about? July doesn't begin for three days!"

"Would you like the spare bedroom in my place for a while?"

"No! I mean no thanks." Malcolm drew himself up and a superior look took possession of his face. "I shall overcome."

One Saturday a week later, Walter Midzik was astonished to receive a call from Malcolm inviting him up for a drink, specifying

Walter's favorite brand of bourbon. Walter couldn't resist. He entered Malcolm's apartment jauntily, the keys on his belt jingling merrily. It was six months until Christmas, but he was almost tintinnabulating with a holiday spirit. Malcolm shut the door and gestured Walter to the sofa. On the coffee table was a glass of bourbon on the rocks. Walter took a deep swig and said, "Ah!"

"Good?" asked Malcolm, sitting across from him, holding what looked like a tumbler of vodka and ice.

"*Very* good," said Walter.

"Your girl friend's been quiet for the past two days."

"Girl friend?" Walter was very cool.

"Eleven-H," reminded Malcolm with an enigmatic smile.

"Oh. Oh, yeah. Very sad."

Malcolm sat up and asked eagerly, "Is she dead?"

"No, her mother died. She went to Pittsburgh for the funeral. She'll be back tomorrow."

Noiselessly, Malcolm's face fell. "I have to say, Walter, I'm very disappointed in you."

"How's that?" asked Walter, draining his glass and refilling it without invitation.

"I thought we were friends and here you are taking that woman's side against mine all because she's such easy pickings."

Walter felt the blood rushing to his face. "Miss Glunt is a very nice young lady. Okay, so she's got no talent. Okay, so she's giving you a hard time. But all them nasty notes you send her, and screaming out the window at her. And here just now you looked happy when you thought she was dead."

"Hmmm."

"What?"

"Nothing. You can't get her to close those windows?"

"I'm tired of asking her."

Malcolm sighed a very weary sigh and refilled Walter's glass. "You carry so many keys."

"Yeth." The bourbon appeared to be taking effect.

"I suppose they open all the doors in the whole building."

"Jus' this one," said Walter, fingering a particular key. "It's the mashter key."

"The master key?"

"The mashter key, yeah."

"Another drink?" Walter said nothing. Walter had passed out. "Another nice drink of your favorite bourbon laced with something special by yours truly?" Malcolm removed the master key from the ring attached to Walter's belt and carried the bottle of bourbon and Walter's glass to the kitchen. He poured the remainder of the bottle down the sink and threw the bottle into the trash He scoured the glass until it belonged in a television commercial, then he returned to the living room, sat back down opposite Walter, glanced at his wristwatch, and waited.

The handyman found Walter's body in the courtyard in a grotesquely contorted position. The police, finding his toolbox open under the water tank, deduced he had fallen from the roof while doing some repairwork.

The next day Tansy Glunt returned from Pittsburgh, heard the tragic news about Walter from the doorman, and with a theatrical sob fled into an elevator. Entering her apartment, she found a note on the floor. This one was in a sealed envelope. With an unpleasant epithet, she tore it open, crossing to the piano by force of habit. "Welcome home," the note read. "I've been waiting anxiously. Look behind you."

Tansy spun around, but not quickly enough.

When her body was found in the courtyard half an hour later, it was widely assumed that grief over her lover Walter Midzik's death had driven her to suicide.

Two weeks later, Malcolm sat at his desk, the phone familiarly placed between chin and shoulder, staring up at the windows of 11-H. At the other end of the wire, Andy asked, "Do I hear drums and cymbals?"

"Yes," said Malcolm, his fingers counterpointing the percussion with an ominous succession of rat-a-tats on the desk. "The new tenants in Eleven-H."

"Cheer up, Malcolm," said Andy, "perhaps they'll commit suicide, too."

The blood drained from Malcolm's face as he thought, I wish he hadn't said that.

"Q"

Charlotte Perkins Gilman

The Yellow Wallpaper

It is very seldom that mere ordinary people like John and myself secure ancestral halls for the summer.

A colonial mansion, a hereditary estate, I would say a haunted house and reach the height of romantic felicity—but that would be asking too much of fate!

Still, I will proudly declare that there is something queer about it.

Else why should it be let so cheaply? And why have stood so long untenanted?

John laughs at me, of course, but one expects that in marriage.

John is practical in the extreme. He has no patience with faith, an intense horror of superstition, and he scoffs openly at any talk of things not to be felt and seen and put down in figures.

John is a physician, and *perhaps*—I would not say it to a living soul, of course, but this is dead paper and a great relief to my mind—*perhaps* that is one reason I do not get well faster.

You see, he does not believe I am sick!

And what can one do?

If a physician of high standing, and one's own husband, assures friends and relatives that there is really nothing the matter with one but temporary nervous depression—a slight hysterical tendency—what is one to do?

My brother is also a physician, and also of high standing, and he says the same thing.

So I take phosphates or phosphites—whichever it is—and tonics, and journeys, and air, and exercise, and am absolutely forbidden to "work" until I am well again.

Personally I disagree with their ideas.

Personally I believe that congenial work, with excitement and change, would do me good.

But what is one to do?

I did write for a while in spite of them; but it *does* exhaust me a good deal—having to be so sly about it or else meet with heavy opposition.

I sometimes fancy that in my condition if I had less opposition and more society and stimulus—but John says the very worst thing I can do is to think about my condition, and I confess it always makes me feel bad.

So I will let it alone and talk about the house.

The most beautiful place! It is quite alone, standing well back from the road, quite three miles from the village. It makes me think of English places that you read about, for there are hedges, and walls and gates that lock, and lots of separate little houses for the gardeners and people.

There is a *delicious* garden! I never saw such a garden—large and shady, full of box-bordered paths, and lined with long grape-covered arbors with seats under them.

There were greenhouses, too, but they are all broken now.

There was some legal trouble, I believe, something about the heirs and co-heirs; anyhow, the place has been empty for years.

That spoils my ghostliness, I am afraid; but I don't care—there is something strange about the house, I can feel it.

I even said so to John one moonlight evening, but he said what I felt was a *draft*, and shut the window.

I get unreasonably angry with John sometimes. I'm sure I never used to be so sensitive. I think it is due to this nervous condition.

But John says if I feel so, I shall neglect proper self-control; so I take pains to control myself—before him, at least, and that makes me very tired.

I don't like our room a bit. I wanted one downstairs that opened on the piazza and had roses all over the window, and such pretty, old-fashioned chintz hangings, but John would not hear of it.

He said there was only one window and not room for two beds, and no near room for him if he took another. He is very careful and loving and hardly lets me stir without special direction.

I have a schedule prescription for each hour in the day; he takes all care from me, and I feel so basely ungrateful not to value it more.

He said we came here solely on my account, that I was to have perfect rest and all the air I could get. "Your exercise depends on your strength, my dear," he said, "and your food somewhat on your appetite, but air you can absorb all the time." So we took the nursery, at the top of the house.

It is a big, airy room, the whole floor nearly, with windows that look all ways and air and sunshine galore. It was nursery first and then playground and gymnasium, I should judge, for the windows are barred for little children and there are rings and things in the walls.

The paint and paper look as if a boys' school had used it. It is stripped off—the paper—in great patches all around the head of my bed about as far as I can reach and in a great place on the other side of the roof low down. I never saw a worse paper in my life. One of those sprawling flamboyant patterns committing every artistic sin.

It is dull enough to confuse the eye in following, pronounced enough to constantly irritate, and provoke study, and when you follow the lame, uncertain curves for a little distance they suddenly commit suicide—plunge off at outrageous angles, destroy themselves in unheard-of contradictions.

The color is repellent, almost revolting—a smoldering, unclean yellow, strangely faded by the slow-turning sunlight.

It is a dull yet lurid orange in some places, a sickly sulphur tint in others.

No wonder the children hated it! I should hate it myself if I had to live in this room long.

There comes John, and I must put this away—he hates to have me write a word.

We have been here two weeks and I haven't felt like writing before, since that first day.

I am sitting by the window now, up in this atrocious nursery, and there is nothing to hinder my writing as much as I please, save lack of strength.

John is away all day, and even some nights when his cases are serious.

I am glad my case is not serious.

But these nervous troubles are dreadfully depressing.

John does not know how much I really suffer. He knows there is no *reason* to suffer, and that satisfies him.

Of course, it is only nervousness. It does weigh on me so not to do my duty in any way. I meant to be such a help to John, such a real rest and comfort, and here I am a comparative burden already!

Nobody would believe what an effort it is to do what little I am able—to dress and entertain, and order things.

It is fortunate Mary is so good with the baby. Such a dear baby!

And yet I *cannot* be with him, it makes me so nervous.

I suppose John never was nervous in his life. He laughs at me so about this wallpaper. At first he meant to repaper the room, but afterward he said that I was letting it get the better of me, and that nothing was worse for a nervous patient than to give way to such fancies.

He said that after the wallpaper was changed it would be the heavy bedstead, and then the barred windows, and then that gate at the head of the stairs, and so on.

"You know the place is doing you good," he said, "and really, dear, I don't care to renovate the house just for a three months' rental."

"Then do let us go downstairs," I said. "There are such pretty rooms there."

Then he took me in his arms and called me a blessed little goose and said he would go down cellar if I wished, and would have it whitewashed into the bargain.

But he is right enough about the beds and windows and things.

It is as airy and comfortable a room as any one need wish, and of course I would not be so silly as to make him uncomfortable just for a whim. I'm really getting quite fond of the big room—all but that horrid paper. Out of one window I can see the garden, those mysterious deep-shaded arbors, the riotous old-fashioned flowers and bushes and gnarly trees.

Out of another I get a lovely view of the bay and a little private wharf belonging to the estate. There is a beautiful shaded lane that runs down there from the house. I always fancy I see people walking in these numerous paths and arbors, but John has cautioned me not to give way to fancy in the least. He says that with my imaginative power and habit of story-making, a nervous weakness like mine is sure to lead to all manner of excited fancies and that I ought to use my will and good sense to check the tendency. So I try.

I think sometimes that if I were only well enough to write a little it would relieve the press of ideas and rest me.

But I find I get pretty tired when I try.

It is so discouraging not to have any advice and companionship about my work. When I get really well, John says we will ask Cousin Henry and Julia down for a long visit, but he says he would as soon put fireworks in my pillowcase as to let me have those stimulating people about now.

I wish I could get well faster.

But I must not think about that. This paper looks to me as if it *knew* what a vicious influence it had!

There is a recurrent spot where the pattern lolls like a broken neck and two bulbous eyes stare at you upside-down.

I got positively angry with the impertinence of it and the ever-lastingness. Up and down and sideways they crawl, and those absurd, unblinking eyes are everywhere. There is one place where two edges didn't match, and the eyes go all up and down the line, one a little higher than the other.

I never saw so much expression in an inanimate thing before, and we all know how much expression they have!

I used to lie awake as a child and get more entertainment and terror out of blank walls and plain furniture than most children could find in a toy store.

I remember what a kindly wink the knobs of our big old bureau used to have, and there was one chair that always seemed like a strong friend. I used to feel that if any of the other things looked too fierce I could always hop into that chair and be safe.

The furniture in this room is no worse than inharmonious, however, for we had to bring it all from downstairs. I suppose when this was used as a playroom they had to take the nursery things out, and no wonder! I never saw such ravages as the children have made here.

The wallpaper, as I said before, is torn off in spots, and it sticketh closer than a brother—they must have had perseverance as well as hatred.

Then the floor is scratched and dug out here and there, and this great heavy bed, which is all we found in the room, looks as if it had been through the wars.

But I don't mind it a bit—only the paper.

There comes John's sister. Such a dear girl as she is, and so careful of me! I must not let her find me writing.

She is a perfect, an enthusiastic housekeeper, and hopes for no better profession. I verily believe she thinks it is the writing which made me sick!

But I can write when she is out, and see her a long way off from these windows.

There is one that commands the road, a lovely, shaded winding road, and one that just looks off over the country. A lovely country, too, full of great elms and velvet meadows.

This wallpaper has a kind of sub-pattern in a different shade, a particularly irritating one, for you can only see it in certain lights, and not clearly then.

But in the places where it isn't faded, and where the sun is just so, I can see a strange, provoking, formless sort of figure that seems to sulk about that silly and conspicuous front design.

There's sister on the stairs.

Well, the Fourth of July is over! The people are all gone and I am tired out. John thought it might do me good to see a little company, so we just had Mother and Nellie and the children down for a week.

Of course, I didn't do a thing. Jennie sees to everything now.

But it tired me all the same.

John says if I don't pick up faster he shall send me to Dr. Weir Mitchell in the fall.

But I don't want to go to him at all. I had a friend who was in his hands once, and she says he is just like John and my brother, only more so!

Besides, it is such an undertaking to go so far.

I don't feel as if it is worthwhile to turn my hand over for anything and I'm getting dreadfully fretful and querulous. I cry at nothing, and cry most of the time.

Of course, I don't when John is here, or anybody else—only when I am alone. And I am alone a good deal just now. John is kept in town very often by serious cases and Jennie is good and lets me alone when I want her to.

So I walk a little in the garden or down that lovely lane, sit on the porch under the roses, and lie down a good deal.

I'm getting really fond of the room in spite of the wallpaper. Perhaps *because* of the wallpaper. It dwells in my mind so!

I lie here on this great immovable bed—it is nailed down, I believe—and follow that pattern about by the hour. It is as good as gymnastics, I assure you. I start, we'll say at the bottom, down in the corner over there where it has not been touched, and I determine for the thousandth time that I *will* follow that pointless pattern to some sort of conclusion.

I know a little of the principles of design, and I know this thing was not arranged on any laws of radiation, or alternation, or repetition, or symmetry, or anything else I ever heard of.

It is repeated, of course, by the widths, but not otherwise. Looked at in one way, each width stands alone, the bloated curves and flourishes—a kind of debased Romanesque with *delirium tremens*—go waddling up and down in isolated columns of fatuity.

But, on the other hand, they connect diagonally, and the sprawling outlines run off in great slanting waves of optic horror, like a lot of wallowing seaweeds in full chase.

The whole thing goes horizontally, too—at least it seems so—and I exhaust myself in trying to distinguish the order of its going in that direction.

They have used a horizontal width for a frieze and that adds wonderfully to the confusion.

There is one end of the room where it is almost intact, and there, when the cross-lights fade and the low sun shines directly on it, I can almost fancy radiation, after all—the interminable grotesques seem to form around a common center and rush off in headlong plunges of equal distraction.

It makes me tired to follow it. I will take a nap, I guess.

I don't know why I should write this.

I don't want to.

I don't feel able.

And I know John would think it absurd. But I *must* say what I feel and think in some way—it is such a relief!

But the effort is getting to be greater than the relief. Half the time now I am awfully lazy and lie down ever so much.

John says I mustn't lose my strength, and has me take cod-liver oil and lots of tonics and things, to say nothing of ale and wine and rare meat.

Dear John! He loves me very dearly, and hates to have me sick. I tried to have a real earnest reasonable talk with him the other day and tell him how I wished he would let me go and make a visit to Cousin Henry and Julia. But he said I wasn't able to go, nor able to stand it after I got there; and I did not make out a very good case for myself, for I was crying before I had finished. It is getting to be a great effort for me to think straight. Just this nervous weakness, I suppose.

And dear John gathered me up in his arms and just carried me upstairs and put me on the bed and sat by me and read to me till he tired my head.

He said I was his darling and his comfort and all he had, and that I must take care of myself for his sake, and keep well. He says no one but myself can help me out of it, that I must use my will and self-control and not let my silly fancies run away with me.

There's one comfort: the baby is well and happy and does not have to occupy this nursery with the horrid wallpaper.

If we had not used it, that blessed child would have! What a fortunate escape! Why, I wouldn't have a child of mine, an impressionable little thing, live in such a room for worlds.

I never thought of it before, but it is lucky that John kept me here, after all. I can stand it so much easier than a baby, you see.

Of course, I never mention it to them any more—I am too wise—but I keep watch of it all the same.

There are things in that paper that nobody knows but me, or ever will.

Behind that outside pattern the dim shapes get clearer every day. It is always the same shape, only very numerous.

And it is like a woman stooping down and creeping about behind that pattern. I don't like it a bit. I wonder—I began to think—I wish John would take me away from here.

It is so hard to talk with John about my case, because he is so wise, and because he loves me so.

But I tried it last night.

It was moonlight. The moon shines in all around, just as the sun does.

I hate to see it sometimes—it creeps so slowly, and always comes in by one window or another.

John was asleep and I hated to waken him, so I kept still and watched the moonlight on that undulating wallpaper till I felt creepy.

The faint figure behind seemed to shake the pattern, just as if she wanted to get out. I got up softly and went to feel and see if the paper *did* move, and when I came back John was awake.

"What is it, little girl?" he said. "Don't go walking about like that—you'll get cold."

I thought it was a good time to talk, so I told him that I really was not gaining here and that I wished he would take me away.

"Why, darling!" he said. "Our lease will be up in three weeks, and I can't see how we can leave before. The repairs are not done at home and I cannot possibly leave town just now. Of course, if you were in any danger I could and would, but you really are better, dear, whether you can see it or not. I am a doctor, dear, and I know. You are gaining flesh and color and your appetite is better. I feel really much easier about you."

"I don't weigh a bit more," said I, "nor as much, and my appetite may be better in the evening when you are here, but it is worse in the morning when you are away."

"Bless her little heart!" said he with a big hug. "She shall be as sick as she pleases. But now let's improve the shining hours by going to sleep, and talk about it in the morning."

"And you won't go away?" I asked gloomily.

"Why, how can I, dear? It is only three weeks more and then we will take a nice little trip of a few days while Jennie is getting the house ready. Really, dear, you are better."

"Better in body, perhaps—" I began, and stopped short, for he sat up straight and looked at me with such a stern, reproachful look that I could not say another word.

"My darling," said he, "I beg of you, for my sake and for our child's sake, as well as for your own, that you will never for one instant let that idea enter your mind. There is nothing so dangerous, so fascinating, to a temperament like yours. It is a false and foolish fancy. Can you not trust me as a physician when I tell you so?"

So of course I said no more on that score, and we went to sleep before long. He thought I was asleep first, but I wasn't—I lay there for hours trying to decide whether that front pattern and the back pattern really did move together or separately.

On a pattern like this, by daylight there is a lack of sequence, a defiance of law, that is a constant irritant to a normal mind.

The color is hideous enough, and unreliable enough, and infuriating enough—but the pattern is torturing. You think you have mastered it, but just as you get well under way in following, it turns a back somersault, and there you are. It slaps you in the face, knocks you down, and tramples on you. It is like a bad dream.

The outside pattern is a florid arabesque, reminding one of a fungus. If you can imagine a toadstool in joints, an interminable string of toadstools, budding and sprouting in endless convolutions, why, that is something like it.

That is, sometimes!

There is one marked peculiarity about this paper, a thing nobody seems to notice but myself, and that is that it changes as the light changes.

When the sun shoots in through the east window—I always watch for that first long, straight ray—it changes so quickly that I never can quite believe it.

That is why I watch it always.

By moonlight—the moon shines in all night when there is a moon—I wouldn't know it was the same paper.

At night in any kind of light—in twilight, candlelight, lamplight, and worst of all by moonlight—it becomes bars! The outside pattern, I mean, and the woman behind it is as plain as can be.

I didn't realize for a long time what the thing was that showed behind—that dim sub-pattern—but now I am quite sure it is a woman.

By daylight she is subdued, quiet. I fancy it is the pattern that keeps her so still. It is so puzzling. It keeps me quiet by the hour.

I lie down ever so much now. John says it is good for me to sleep all I can. Indeed, he started the habit by making me lie down for an hour after each meal. It is a very bad habit, I am convinced, for you see I don't sleep.

And that cultivates deceit, for I don't tell them I'm awake—oh, no!

The fact is, I am getting a little afraid of John. He seems very queer sometimes—and even Jennie has an inexplicable look.

It strikes me occasionally, just as a scientific hypothesis, that perhaps it is the paper!

I have watched John when he did not know I was looking, and come into the room suddenly on the most innocent excuses, and I've caught him several times *looking at the paper!* And Jennie, too. I caught Jennie with her hand on it once.

She didn't know I was in the room, and when I asked her in a quiet, a very quiet voice, with the most restrained manner possible, what she was doing with the paper, she turned around as if she had been caught stealing and looked quite angry—asked me why I should frighten her so!

Then she said that the paper stained everything it touched and that she had found yellow smooches on all my clothes and John's and she wished we would be more careful.

Did not that sound innocent? But I know she was studying that pattern and I am determined that nobody shall find it out but myself!

Life is very much more exciting now than it used to be. You see, I have something more to expect, to look forward to, to watch. I really do eat better, and am more quiet than I was.

John is so pleased to see me improve! He laughed a little the other day and said I seemed to be flourishing in spite of my wallpaper. I turned it off with a laugh. I had no intention of telling him that it was *because* of the wallpaper—he would make fun of me. He might even want to take me away. I don't want to leave now until I have found it out.

There is a week more, and I think that will be enough . . .

I'm feeling ever so much better! I don't sleep much at night, for it is so interesting to watch developments; but I sleep a good deal in the daytime.

In the daytime it is tiresome and perplexing. There are always new shoots on the fungus, and new shades of yellow all over it. I cannot keep count of them, though I have tried conscientiously.

It is the strangest yellow, that wallpaper! It makes me think of all the yellow things I ever saw—not beautiful ones like buttercups, but old, foul, bad yellow things.

But there is something else about that paper—the smell! I noticed it the moment we came into the room, but with so much air and sun it was not bad. Now we have had a week of fog and rain, and whether the windows are open or not the smell is here.

It creeps all over the house.

I find it hovering in the dining room, skulking in the parlor, hiding in the hall, lying in wait for me on the stairs. It gets into my hair.

Even when I go to ride, if I turn my head suddenly and surprise it—there is that smell! Such a peculiar odor, too! I have spent hours in trying to analyze it, to find what it smelled like.

It is not bad at first, and very gentle, but quite the subtlest, most enduring odor I ever met.

In this damp weather it is awful. I wake up in the night and find it hanging over me.

It used to disturb me at first. I thought seriously of burning the house—to reach the smell. But now I am used to it. The only thing I can think of that it is like is the *color* of the paper—a yellow smell!

There is a very funny mark on this wall, low down, near the mopboard. A streak that runs around the room. It goes behind every piece of furniture except the bed, a long, straight, even *smooch*, as if it had been rubbed over and over. I wonder how it was done and who did it and what they did it for. Round and round and round—round and round and round—it makes me dizzy!

I really have discovered something at last.

Through watching so much at night, when it changes so, I have finally found out.

The front pattern *does* move—and no wonder! The woman behind shakes it!

Sometimes I think there are a great many women behind, and sometimes only one, and she crawls around fast, and her crawling shakes it all over.

Then in the very bright spots she keeps still, and in the very shady spots she just takes hold of the bars and shakes them hard.

And she is all the time trying to climb through. But nobody could climb through that pattern—it strangles so; I think that is why it has so many heads.

They get through, and then the pattern strangles them off and turns them upside-down and makes their eyes white!

If those heads were covered or taken off, it would not be half so bad.

I think that woman gets out in the daytime!

And I'll tell you why—privately. I've seen her!

I can see her out of every one of my windows!

It is the same woman, I know, for she is always creeping, and most women do not creep by daylight.

I see her in that long shaded lane, creeping up and down. I see her in those dark grape arbors, creeping all around the garden.

I see her on that long road under the trees, creeping along, and when a carriage comes she hides under the blackberry vines. I don't blame her a bit. It must be very humiliating to be caught creeping by daylight!

I always lock the door when I creep by daylight. I can't do it at night, for I know John would suspect something at once. And John is so queer now that I don't want to irritate him. I wish he would take another room! Besides, I don't want anybody to get that woman out at night but myself.

I often wonder if I could see her out of all the windows at once.

And though I always see her, she *may* be able to creep faster than I can turn!

I have watched her sometimes away off in the open country, creeping as fast as a cloud shadow in a high wind.

If only that top pattern could be got off from the under one! I mean to try it, little by little.

I have found out another funny thing, but I won't tell it this time! It does not do to trust people too much.

There are only two more days to get this paper off and I believe John is beginning to notice. I don't like the look in his eyes.

And I heard him ask Jennie a lot of professional questions about me. She had a very good report to give. She said I slept a good deal in the daytime. John knows I don't sleep very well at night, for all I'm so quiet!

He asked me all sorts of questions, too, and pretended to be very loving and kind.

As if I couldn't see through him!

Still, I don't wonder he acts so, sleeping under this paper for three months. It only interests me, but I feel sure John and Jennie are secretly affected by it.

Hurrah! This is the last day, but it is enough. John is to stay in town overnight and won't be out until this evening.

Jennie wanted to sleep with me—the sly thing!—but I told her I should undoubtedly rest better for a night all alone.

That was clever, for really I wasn't alone a bit! As soon as it was moonlight, and that poor thing began to crawl and shake the pattern, I got up and ran to help her.

I pulled and she shook, I shook and she pulled, and before morning we had peeled off yards of that paper. A strip about as high as my head and half around the room. And then when the sun came and that awful pattern began to laugh at me I declared I would finish it today!

We go away tomorrow, and they are moving all my furniture down again to leave things as they were before.

Jennie looked at the wall in amazement, but I told her merrily that I did it out of pure spite at the vicious thing. She laughed and said she wouldn't mind doing it herself, but I must not get tired.

How she betrayed herself that time!

But I am here and no person touches this paper but me—not *alive!*

She tried to get me out of the room—it was too obvious! But I said it was so quiet and empty and clean now that I believed I would lie down again and sleep all I could; and not to wake me even for dinner—I would call when I woke.

So now she is gone, and the servants are gone, and the things are gone, and there is nothing left but that great bedstead nailed down, with the mattress we found on it.

We shall sleep downstairs tonight and take the boat home tomorrow.

I quite enjoy the room now that it is bare again.

How those children did tear about here! This bedstead is fairly gnawed!

But I must get to work.

I have locked the door and thrown the key down to the front path. I don't want to go out, and I don't want to have anybody come in till John comes. I want to astonish him.

I've got a rope up here that even Jennie did not find. If that woman does get out and tries to get away, I can tie her.

But I forgot I could not reach far without anything to stand on!

This bed will *not* move! I tried to lift and push it until I was lame, and then I got so angry I bit off a little piece at one corner—but it hurt my teeth.

Then I peeled off all the paper I could reach standing on the floor. It sticks horribly and the pattern just enjoys it! All those strangled heads and bulbous eyes and waddling fungus growths just shriek with derision!

I am getting angry enough to do something desperate. To jump out of the window would be admirable exercise, but the bars are too strong even to try.

Besides, I wouldn't do it. Of course not. I know well enough that a step like that is improper and might be misconstrued.

I don't like to *look* out of the windows even—there are so many of those creeping women, and they creep so fast.

I wonder if they all come out of that wallpaper, as I did?

But I am securely fastened now by my well hidden rope—you don't get *me* out in the road there!

I suppose I shall have to get back behind the pattern when it comes night, and that is hard!

It is so pleasant to be out in this great room and creep around as I please!

I don't want to go outside. I won't, even if Jennie asks me to.

For outside you have to creep on the ground, and everything is green instead of yellow. But here I can creep smoothly on the floor and my shoulder just fits in that long smooch around the wall, so I cannot lose my way.

Why, there's John at the door!

It's no use, young man, you can't open it!

How he does call and pound!

Now he's crying for an ax.

It would be a shame to break down that beautiful door!

"John, dear!" said I in the gentlest voice, "the key is down by the front steps, under a plantain leaf!"

That silenced him for a few moments. Then he said—very quietly indeed, "Open the door, my darling."

"I can't," said I. "The key is down by the front door, under a plantain leaf!"

And then I said it again, several times, very gently and slowly, and said it so often that he had to go and see, and he got it, of course, and came in. He stopped short by the door.

"What is the matter?" he cried. "For God's sake, what are you doing?"

I kept on creeping just the same, but I looked at him over my shoulder.

"I've got out at last," said I, "in spite of you and Jennie! And I've pulled off most of the paper so you can't put me back!"

Now why should that man have fainted? But he did, and right across my path by the wall so that I had to creep over him every time!

Jean Potts

The Inner Voices

Estrella's first impulse had been to cancel her usual birthday reunion this year; it would be too poignant without her favorite son, Byron. But then—as she pointed out, in her bravest tremolo—an Inner Voice had spoken. They must carry on, in spite of their aching hearts and the mute pathos of the one vacant chair. Dear Byron would not want it otherwise. He who could nevermore be with them in the flesh would be with them in spirit.

There she went, stealing her daughter-in-law's lines again. Completely shameless. After all, Byron's widow, not his mother, was entitled to the starring role. But Mary Ethel could afford to be big about it. "Exactly my feeling," she said in the sincere, spontaneous tones that had come across so well in her television interview. "I'm sure Byron wouldn't want his mother's sixtieth birthday to pass unnoticed."

"Fifty-ninth," said Estrella. "I knew you'd understand, my dear."

Then she called Tennyson, who of course questioned the advisability. As the one son left to her, he took his responsibilities seriously. "Are you sure you're up to it, Mother? We all know how hard this has hit you, in spite of the way you've borne up so wonderfully. Not that I'm trying to dictate or anything, you understand—I realize you're the best judge—"

"Then I'll see you on the fifteenth," said Estrella, who was sometimes circumspect about overruling Tennyson's objections and sometimes not, depending on how busy she was. "I can't decide about inviting Carol. What do you think?"

"Carol? Oh. Well, Mother, I hardly know what to say. I mean—"

There was a pause. Then Estrella said gently, "Yes. I think Byron would want her to be with us."

So it was settled. They would meet, but they would miss him.

Indeed they would; indeed they did; it was their own business how and for what reasons.

In one of the more moving passages of her forthcoming book, Mary Ethel described (with certain basic modifications) the incredulity that still seized her at times, oftenest on her return to the empty apartment, just before she turned her key in the lock. It can't be true, she would think; when I open the door Byron will be there.

No doubt all widows had such heart-stopping moments, even those who had actually looked into their husbands' dead faces. But Byron's body had never been recovered from the Everglades swamp where his little plane had crashed six months before. He remained incorrigibly alive in Mary Ethel's memory—and, sometimes, in her imagination.

This was one of the times, this glum February afternoon, the day before the scheduled birthday reunion. She had lunched, at delightful length, with her editors. It was spitting sleet; mindful of her new feather hat (what a grand piece of luck that black was so becoming to her), she dashed from the cab to the street door of the reconverted brownstone where she stayed on, and started up the stairs that led to her second-floor apartment.

Here it was, the familiar inner quaver, like the delicious self-induced shivers that children feel when they tell each other ghost stories. Only a dream, she thought: Byron was not dead. When she opened the door he would come toward her, smiling his doggedly hopeful smile. *There you are, honey,* he would say, and there she would be, thudded back into reality. Not Byron's widow. His wife.

She unlocked the door and stepped into the dusky hall. Everything was just as she had left it. Of course. On her way to the living room she drew a tremulous sigh.

"There you are, honey," he said. "How's tricks?"

The parquet floor under her feet lurched and tipped upward like a ship in a heavy swell. Her hand groped for the wall and found it. Solid, real. No sound now but the click of sleet against the living-room windows. The room itself was already so dark, on this sunless day, that she could not distinguish swarming shadow from impossible substance.

He switched on the table lamp. There he stood, alert, nimble-looking, head tilted in the characteristic way. He risked a smile, but not a step toward her.

"I couldn't get you on the phone," he explained. "So I thought I'd drop by and leave a note in the mailbox. But I still had the door key, and—hey. Hey, Mary Ethel, you're not going to faint, are you?"

She shook her head. Sat down, carefully, on the edge of the wing-back chair. Closed her eyes. Opened them again. He was still there.

"The crash," she whispered. "They told us you couldn't possibly have survived."

"I damn near didn't." He spoke with jaunty complacence. "Wouldn't have, except these Indians came along and fished me out of the swamp. The last thing I remember is thinking, This is it, boy, you've had it, and when I came to it was two months later and the alligators hadn't eaten me, after all. By that time all I had to worry about was a bad case of malaria. Too mean to die, I guess." He paused, but she made no comment. "Would you like a brandy?"

"Please," she said. He had a pronounced limp, she noticed as he crossed to the liquor cabinet. He had always been thin; now he was like a contraption of wire coat hangers and twine, with a piece of parchment for a face. The malaria. Which hadn't killed him, either. "You might at least have called from down there. Or written. You might have given me some warning."

"Yes. I didn't intend to shake you up like this. But somehow I—" He limped over with her brandy. "You look great, Mary Ethel," he said shyly. "Beautiful." He stayed there in front of her, carefully not touching her. "All right, I'll tell you the truth. I didn't call or write because I couldn't make up my mind about whether to come back or not."

"Not come back?"

"Not come back," he repeated. "Let Byron Hawley stay as dead as everybody—including me, for a while there—thought he was. Who needed him? It makes you stop and think, a narrow squeak like that. I couldn't help wondering, for instance, whether you— Well, you've got to admit we weren't doing so hot, you and I, when I took off on that last trip."

"It wasn't my fault," she reminded him bitterly. "You were the one. You and that cheap little stenographer of yours. Carol. Don't blame me for the way we were doing."

"But I never would have gotten mixed up with Carol if—ah, skip it. We've been through this too many times already."

"Yes, we have." She resisted the temptation to add that, to Carol at least, it was now ancient history. Let him find out for himself. "I suppose you've seen her?"

"No," he said shortly. "You're the only one who knows I'm back."

"You haven't even seen your mother? Or Tennyson?" She felt an inner whirring, as if an antenna were beginning to vibrate. *You're the only one who knows I'm back. The only one who knows I'm alive.*

"Not yet. I wanted to see you first. I suppose Tenny's taken over at the office?"

She nodded. "I haven't seen much of him lately. We've both been busy. Your mother's having her birthday do tomorrow. You came back just in time." No vacant chair, after all. "She's very busy these days, too, trying to get through to you in The Great Beyond. She and Dr. Mehallah. He's her latest discovery."

He gave a whoop of laughter. "No! Have they had any luck?"

"Don't be ridiculous," said Mary Ethel, who saw nothing funny about Estrella's fitful dabblings in the deeper mysteries. This time especially it was no laughing matter, as Byron would find out when—if—he talked to his mother. The whirring inside her grew and grew.

"What a pity for me to turn up now and spoil the fun!" The laughter faded from his eyes. "Brings us right back to what I was saying. I couldn't help wondering whether you wouldn't rather be my widow than my wife."

"That's a terrible thing to say!" Not so terrible, though, as the thing vibrating inside her. Her eyes darted away from his.

"Oh, I don't know. I wasn't too sold on Byron Hawley myself. What had he ever done except inherit his father's business and get married and learn how to fly his own plane? The business ran itself. Probably still does, with Tenny in charge. The marriage was damn near on the rocks. Even the plane was smashed up. I kept thinking what a good chance it was to get rid of Byron Hawley, just shuck him off and start from scratch."

She laughed scornfully. "What would you have used for money? Or didn't you worry about that?"

"Not very much. I'm a good mechanic, an expert bartender, an inspired dishwasher. Besides, I had a sizable chunk of cash with me—still have most of it. No, what worried me was whether or not Byron Hawley was worth resurrecting."

"And you decided he was."

"Not exactly," he said. "I decided I had to come back and find out for sure. Mary Ethel, look at me. Please—"

She struck out, in a panic, at his hand. But there was no escape from his unwavering gaze; slowly and relentlessly it forced her head up until he was looking into her eyes, until he was seeing what must be blazing in them. "Somebody else. Is that it? Some other guy?"

She began to laugh, in gusts like sobs. "No," she gasped. "Here, let me show you." She crossed to the desk and came back with the advance copy of her book, *How To Be a Widow: A Testament of Love and Courage.*

Tick-tick-tick went the sleet against the window while he read the blurb. Which she knew by heart: the inspiring, true story of a young woman's battle against sorrow and her victory over despair. The photograph of Mary Ethel on the dust jacket was artfully misty, a face seen through a blur of tears, shadowed with tragedy, lit with hard-won tranquility.

Byron's own face remained blank as he studied it. He flicked through the pages, pausing here and there. Which part might he be reading now? The description of their idyllic life together? The heartbreaking memories that attacked without warning? (They had moved her editor to tears; he had said so, only today at lunch. Thick-skinned cynic that he was, he had said.)

Tick-tick, till at last he closed the book.

"Is it a bestseller?" he asked.

"It isn't out yet officially. They've been giving it a big play—"

Her voice threatened to break. To have so much within her grasp—the recognition, the fame, rightfully hers, but denied her until now; and then to have it snatched away. Byron's return would transform her and her book into a household joke. Even if the publishers withdrew it—and could they, with the release date only a week away?—word would get around. There would be snickering little innuendoes in the columns that were plugging it even now; all the publicity, so flattering, so thrilling, would boomerang into derision.

"Do I congratulate you?" said Byron. "Or do I apologize? Yes, I guess so. Excuse me for living." He picked up his trenchcoat. "I didn't realize you had such a nice career going as a professional widow."

She faced him unabashed, too absorbed in hating him to mind the sneer in his voice. All right. A career. Why not? He himself admitted he had considered not coming back, had wondered if she might not rather be his widow than his wife. Well, now she knew.

Ah, but so did she. *You're the only one who knows I'm back.* And there was no need for anyone else ever to know—if she were quick enough, bold enough, strong enough, clever enough, lucky enough. So many ifs. And so little time. Because it had to be now; she must act first and plan later. She must dare to take the chance while it was still hers.

"You're leaving?" she asked in a voice muffled, in her own ears, by the thick beating of her heart, and as he started across the room she followed. The poker, she thought as she passed the fireplace, but already it was too late—he was glancing back.

Something in the hall, then. The bronze nymph on the table. Her hand closed over its smooth weight convulsively. One blow, struck from behind while he was opening the door. It might be enough—just the one blow. But it did not have to be. She foresaw that her arm, once released, would go on pounding like an automatic hammer; at this moment it was tensing with the force of those potential blows.

She had fallen a little too far behind. Now she must hurry so as to be close enough when he reached the door, just before he turned. Two more steps, and then, and then—

And then—too soon, before she was ready—he turned, so nimbly in spite of his limp, and his hand shot out and closed on her wrist. There was a flash of pain in her arm, a thump as the bronze nymph fell to the carpeted floor.

"Better luck next time," he said.

He was smiling, but not in the doggedly hopeful way she remembered. Now his eyes were stony. Now he knew her.

Just before he slid through the door he added, "So long, Mary Ethel. See you at Mother's reunion."

"Not a manifestation?" Estrella repeated wistfully. "But we were so hoping for one. It would have meant so much to Dr. Mehallah—"

"Sorry to disappoint you." Sorry, indeed! Byron was grinning all over his face. Now he planted a noisy, juicy smack in the slope of her neck. "There. Does that feel like a manifestation?"

She had to admit that it did not. And while spirits were sometimes prankish, she had never heard of one who smelled of brandy or left wet footprints on the rug. Byron in the flesh, no doubt about it, and of course she was overjoyed. Her son, her favorite son—which probably wasn't fair; Tennyson was so much more agreeable, so restful, and she never had any trouble getting her own way with Tenny. Whereas Byron could be difficult.

"Sit down, dear." She sat down herself, with the rattling, clashing sound effects that accompanied all her movements. The long strands of beads and multiplicity of bracelets were as much a part of her as her dimples and the fluttery voice and big blue eyes that gave her such a guileless look.

She wiped away her tears and fluffed her hair. "I'll be all right in a minute. I just can't quite—Indians, you said? You must tell me again—I want to hear the whole story. My poor boy! I suppose you've seen Mary Ethel?"

He did not answer at once, and when he did it was ambiguously.

"That can wait." Then he launched into the whole story she had asked for.

But as he talked, her mind kept straying to Dr. Mehallah. Would it be better to plunge in and get it over with—the element of surprise might work wonders—or to coast into it gradually? Byron would notice, though: he wasn't like Tenny. Either way, her Inner Voice informed her, he was going to be difficult. And then Mary Ethel. Did he mean *seeing* her could wait? Or—*How To Be a Widow!* ha!—did he mean *talking about* her could wait?

"So here I am," he was finishing, "just in time for your birthday party. The bad penny that always turns up."

"Nothing of the sort!" she cried—extra heartily, on account of the pang of disappointment she had just felt: she would have to disinvite Dr. Mehallah to her party. It simply wouldn't do, not with Byron here. "This is the most wonderful birthday present anybody ever dreamed of. Let me see, did you say you have seen Mary Ethel? Because if you haven't—"

"First tell me what's with this Dr. Whatshisname, the manifestations fellow. Was I supposed to rap on tables, or write on slates, or what?"

"Dr. Mehallah relies on his own powers in attaining the mystic state, not on any of the usual trappings," said Estrella stiffly. Then she flashed her dimples at him. "Shame on you for making fun of me. I only did it because I missed you so. I would have given anything for a sign from you."

She had grieved, really. Why, that first night she was beside herself. Tenny had to call the doctor to give her a sedative. Someone had suggested travel as a therapeutic agent, so she had signed up for a cruise, any cruise. And that was where she met Dr. Mehallah.

Strange, strange how fate had woven its pattern; she had felt from the first that Dr. Mehallah's coffee-brown eyes were piercing to her very soul and drawing it out of her body, had heard in his high-pitched voice the cadence of unearthly music, had known beyond all question that in the furtherance of his work she had found her true mission in life. But how explain this to Byron? She sighed.

"Never mind, Mother. There must be plenty of other bona fide spirits for Dr. Mehallah to concentrate on now that I'm out of the running. No need to drop the guy on my account."

Her temper snapped. That indulgent, superior smile of his! "I have no intention of dropping Dr. Mehallah. Ever. Naturally you wouldn't understand what it means to me to be able to help a man of his gifts. Neither does Mary Ethel, not that it's any of her business—"

He straightened up, alert now, a hound on the scent. "Help? What kind of help were you planning to give him?"

"I'm still planning it! And you can't stop me!" But he could. She jumped to her feet, in clattering, chattering agitation. "Tenny's agreed to it—oh, I know you've always belittled him, but at least he doesn't close his mind the way some people I could mention; and another thing, he's got a little feeling for his mother, and if your father were alive he'd be the first to say go ahead. So it's three against one—four, counting Dr. Mehallah—so what right have you to stop us?"

"Stop you from doing what?"

"It's not as if there weren't other institutions for those delinquent boys every bit as good as Hawley Farm. Better, in fact, and bigger. Your father admitted himself that it's only a drop in the bucket. Why, there's only room for twenty. What's the good of a place that small? It's not worthwhile."

"Dad thought it was," said Byron, in an ominously mild voice. "So do quite a few other people. Mother, are you planning to turn Hawley Farm over to Dr. Mehallah?" He was on his feet now, too; he actually took her by the shoulders and gave her a little shake.

"I have a right," she wavered. "It's in my name."

"It's in your and Tenny's and mine. And you may have conned Tenny into making hash of what Dad wanted, but you won't con me. You know as well as I do that Dad would never in the world consent to any such deal. And neither will I. Believe me, if you hand over Hawley Farm to this phony mystic of yours, it'll—"

"He's not! You take your hands off me!"

"—be over my dead body."

The words throbbed, eerily amplified, echoing and reechoing. *Over his dead body.* She had thought that was how it was. Yes. She had believed she was safely beyond the reach of his voice that would not agree, his hand that would not sign, his will that would not bend to hers. Not of course that she had ever wished him dead—

She did now. For once in her life, Estrella looked truth in the eye. It wasn't fair for him to be alive when they said he couldn't be. It was as if he had played a monstrous practical joke on her, pretending to give her freedom only to pull her up sharp just when she was making the most of it. He was her favorite son—and she wished the swamp had swallowed him. She did not want him alive, with the power to block her.

She wanted him dead. Dead.

Horror-struck, she stared into his haggard face.

"Over my dead body," he repeated, and released her—just let his hands drop and abandoned her. He picked up his trenchcoat and slung it over his shoulder. "Unfortunately, I'm still alive. I'll be back for your party. Try to bear up until then."

"Byron! Don't leave me—" she wailed, and she burst into the more or less genuine sobs that had stood her in such good stead so many times in the past. But the door was already closing behind him. Her breath caught in a spasm of shock and fury. The nerve of him! To drop this bombshell on her and then simply walk away from the wreckage, simply stroll calmly off to—to whoever was next on his list. Mary Ethel? Or had he already seen her?

Oh, she didn't know. She didn't know what to *do*. She covered her face with her plump little hands and whimpered.

Once he recovered his power of speech, Tennyson said, with such vehemence that he hardly recognized his own voice, "No, not at a bar. Come on back to the office. We can talk there."

"Okay," said Byron cheerfully. He, Byron, didn't sound any different. His greeting had been so nonchalant, and the way he had swung into step, so poised and easy, as if only a fusspot like Tenny would see anything momentous about this meeting—typical of him, typical. His limp (which women would like as not think romantic) was new, and he was skinny as a stray cat. Otherwise he was the same old Byron, and Tenny was the same old—

No. Absolutely not. He had changed, and Byron was, by gad, going to find it out. He was going to have to get used to playing second fiddle himself, for a change. Tenny lifted his solemn, fleshy face to the wind-driven sleet, squared his shoulders, and inwardly pledged allegiance to the new man he had become, was now, and forever would be, world without end, amen.

"I figured you'd probably still be at the office," Byron was saying. "You always were a great one for overtime."

"And still am. More so, in fact. What I say is, a real executive can't expect to stick to a nine-to-five schedule. He's got to forget about watching the clock and concentrate on getting the job done. Personally, I find I accomplish more after five than during office hours. You don't get the interruptions. No phone calls, et cetera. You can buckle right down and think a problem through."

"That's the spirit," said Byron, whose own attitude toward his executive responsibilities had been light-hearted, to say the least. They would get around to that little matter, among others, before they were through.

The lobby of the office building was deserted except for the elevator starter, new since Byron's time, so they were spared a goggle-eyed reunion scene. Tenny gave the man a preoccupied nod, as became the head of Hawley Enterprises; and after the self-service elevator had borne them smoothly upward, he led the way, keys in hand, past the switchboard where a night light glowed and into the hushed darkness of the president's office.

To Tenny's secret relief, Byron sat down on the green-leather couch, leaving the chair behind the massive desk for its rightful owner. Not that Tenny would have insisted on making an issue of it, but this way the question did not arise.

Ensconced in the security of his big chair, Tenny felt in control of himself and of the situation. His legs stopped their nervous trembling now that they were planted firmly under the desk, which stretched like a bulwark between him and his brother.

But then Byron reached over and slid open the right-hand door of the bookcase. "Ah! Glad to see you still file the bourbon in the same place. Join me?"

"Here, let me. I'm sorry, I should have offered—" Yes, he should have. It disturbed the balance to have Byron pouring out the drinks as if he owned the place. It put Tenny at a subtle disadvantage. Why hadn't he thought of it! Inwardly fuming, he sipped and listened, with half an ear, to Byron's account of his hairbreadth escape. He was rather flippant about it. Trust Byron.

Of course he was not dead. It seemed to Tenny that—without ever admitting it, least of all to himself—he had known it all along. For the past six months he had been waiting for some such moment as this; tonight when Byron fell into step beside him he had felt not so much the throb of astonishment as the thud of suspense ended.

He straightened his glasses and cleared his throat. "I'd like to query you on your plans," Tenny announced. "Is it your intention to pick up where you left off here at the office?"

"I haven't thought much about it. You seem to be doing okay."

"I like to think so. It hasn't been easy, let me assure you." He let that sink in and wound up significantly, "Under the circumstances."

"Which circumstances would those be? I suppose I did leave a loose end or two, if that's what you mean—"

"I mean that Carol—Miss York—found it impossible to continue covering up your little manipulations. And I'd like to go on record right here and now, Byron. You may be able to rationalize the fund juggling to your own satisfaction. But not to mine. Let me assure you. Not to mine. With Miss York's assistance I was able to adjust the matter without its becoming common knowledge, and as far as I'm concerned there's no necessity for ever mentioning it again. I simply wanted to go on record. One more point. If you have any idea of penalizing Carol—Miss York—for exposing what not even she, loyal as she was, could no longer hide, if you have any idea— Well. You will have me to deal with." He leaned back, flushed with triumph.

"I see," Byron said at last. No denial or defense. Just the mild, thoughtful statement, followed—as might have been expected—by the irrepressible grin. "How is Carol, anyway? Miss York?"

"Very well, thank you. As you may already have heard, Miss York has consented to be my wife."

"You're kidding. Carol and you?" Byron exploded into laughter.

And Tenny, having carried everything off so well (except for the drink business), with such dignity and force, now Tenny had to spoil it all by squeaking, "What's so funny?" No other word for it. Squeaking. He couldn't stop, either. "I fail to see—funny, is it? You think just because—shut up!"

He was on his feet, gripping the desk that was no longer a bulwark, quivering with rage and despair at this foolish, flustered, familiar fellow who was his old self—the self he had presumed was gone forever but of course was no more dead than Byron. They were inseparable, this old self and Byron—like Siamese twins; there was no getting rid of the one as long as the other lived.

"Sorry, Tenny." Byron swallowed another guffaw. "I'm sorry—I think it's very nice. Congratulations."

"Thank you for nothing. I know what you're thinking."

It was the basic, galling thing between them, the root that had produced silly old Tenny in the first place. And why? What was there about Byron that drew women to him? Oh, he didn't always come out ahead—Mary Ethel, for instance—but there had to be an exception to prove the rule.

All his life Tenny had bitterly watched the rule in operation: Byron could pick and choose, while he himself must scramble and scrabble for nothing better than a wallflower. If that. Why? It wasn't as if Byron were tall, dark, and handsome. Far from it. He had never bothered much about clothes or the little gestures—corsages, jewelry, et cetera—that were supposed to be so important. Tenny had spent more lavishly, had sweat through dancing lessons, had observed all the fine points of etiquette—and it didn't make a bit of difference; if he got a girl to date him it meant she was really from hunger.

Except Carol. No shortage of men in Carol's life; and if that fact now and then cost Tenny an uneasy pang—well, that was the price you paid for winning such an attractive girl. But his heart contracted in sudden pain. Would he have won her, even as a secretary, if Byron had stayed on the scene? The gossip about her and Byron was only gossip, according to her; surely Tenny knew her better than to believe she would take up with a married man! He most assuredly did. And yet, and yet—

He could not help remembering that she had never so much as glanced his way while Byron was around, any more than he could suppress the thought of what she might do now that Byron was back. The thought that flared up, intolerable and uncontrollable as fire: one wave of Byron's hand was all it would take to bring her running, one flick of his finger could flatten Tenny's house of cards.

No wonder Byron had laughed. No wonder he sat there now with that unconcerned air, as much as to say, There it is, Tenny my boy. What are you going to do about it?

Kill him. It clicked into Tenny's mind, precise as a shot. He was supposed to be dead. Carol thought he was dead. Let her go on thinking so. Kill him and along with him his Siamese twin, the old silly Tenny.

For one dazzling moment it was that uncomplicated—no qualms, no fear of consequences to hold him back. With his hands planted on the desk, he leaned forward giddily, staring down at his brother's bent head. Then he remembered the others. Mother. Mary Ethel. Even if by some fluke Byron had come here first and they still thought he was dead—even then, there was the elevator starter who had seen them come back together; there were all the little potential slip-ups gathering now in a gnatlike pestering swarm.

And there was Byron himself. He was looking straight up at Tenny now, no longer smiling or unconcerned. His eyes were inexpressibly sad and knowing, like a monkey's. "Relax, Tenny. I'm not out to grab anything away from you. I don't know why it is, we always wind up in some kind of a hassle. Well, time I shoved off."

"Where are you—I suppose you've already seen Mary Ethel and Mother. You'd go to them first, I suppose."

"Do you?" Byron cocked his head, grinning a little in the old way. "Why don't you check with them, Tenny? You can't take my word for anything. You know that. I'm dishonest."

"It's Carol, then. Isn't it? I'm warning you, Byron, if you try to—"

"I just want to thank her for her loyalty, that's all. And naturally wish her happiness. So long, Tenny. See you at Mother's reunion."

The door sighed shut behind him. Tenny's knees buckled; but though he sagged in his chair, inert as a sack of flour, inside he still spluttered and raged. Every rankling word came back to him, every gesture, and always in the background was the contemptible squeak of his own voice. Except for that one exalted moment when he hadn't *cared* who knew of what slip-ups he made. That one moment—lost forever, he had let it go by—when he could have done it, should have done it.

But Mother. Mary Ethel. The elevator starter.

He made a strangled sound and put his head down on the desk.

"Now wait a minute," Carol said into the cream-colored telephone in her bedroom. "Sure you sound like him, but Byron Hawley's dead. D-e-a-d. So you *can't* be him. Or if you are you've got to do more than sound like him to prove it to me."

"Okay. Remember last Decoration Day in Atlantic City? It rained so hard there wasn't anything to do but—" He elaborated, in vivid detail.

"Oh, Byron, it *is* you!" Her heart leaped. Then it swooped. "Listen, where are you? I can meet you. Unless you'd rather come up here. I've got to see you. We can't talk over the phone."

"We can try."

"Well, of course if you don't want to see me—" She sat down on the avocado bedspread and reached for a cigarette. Her hand was trembling.

"I don't think Tenny would approve. Do you?"

"So you've seen him." She decided against the cigarette. Her hand, still trembling, began a little pleating project on her black net petticoat. Pleat, smooth. Pleat, smooth. "Listen, Byron, look at it from my point of view."

"I am. It's very educational."

"Don't be such a dog in the manger. After all, a girl's got to think of her future. I never noticed you breaking your neck to make me any offers. I mean, any that were going to get me any further than a rainy weekend in Atlantic City. Tenny may not look like such a bargain—"

"No? From your point of view I'd say he was just about perfect. Especially now that he's moved up into my old spot. I know, money isn't everything, but Tenny has other assets. He's so nice and unsuspecting. You can have your future, plus all the fun on the side that comes along."

"I don't have to take that from you," she said icily. Pleat, smooth. Pleat, smooth. "And to think I *bawled* when they said you were dead! Oh, Byron, please, if only I could see you I'm sure I could explain—"

"I know how persuasive you can be, dear. So I'm not taking any chances."

"You mean you don't trust yourself?" She stretched her legs and smiled.

"I don't trust you, that's for sure. How long had you been dipping into the till before I passed to my reward?"

She stopped smiling. She said, too quickly, "I don't know what you're talking about."

"Oh, come on, Carol. You're talking to me, not to Tenny. I've got to hand it to you, you saw your chance and grabbed it. It would have worked, too, if only I'd had the decency to stay d-e-a-d."

"You think Tenny's going to take your word instead of mine? You can't prove it. Couldn't even if it was true. Why, he'll laugh in your face!"

"He wasn't laughing when I left him," said Byron.

"You rat! Wait. Just wait. Don't think you can barge in like this and louse me up—out of spite, that's all, nothing but spite—"

"Oh, I don't know. I might just possibly want to clear my name."

"Your name," she screeched. "Your name is mud! And not just in my book, either. What about your precious wife? Oh, brother, would I like to listen in on that little reunion! Even your mother—"

She stopped for breath. Well, what was he waiting for? Why didn't he say something? Silence. Not a word out of him.

"Byron? Byron, you there?"

"I'm here," he said. He didn't sound angry, or even upset. Just tired. "That's the whole problem, isn't it? I'm here. Okay, Carol. I'll be seeing you. That is, if you're going to Mother's party." And just like that, he hung up on her.

Presently she remembered to hang up, too. But her hand remained curved around the phone, as if waiting for a signal. Call Tenny? Not now, not yet. She was too churned up, she needed time to pull herself together. And anyway, why hadn't Tenny called her? Only one reason, she thought, and shivered. Proof. Byron must have some actual proof that had convinced Tenny.

She had been so sure, had figured out every possible angle except this impossible one: it had never crossed her mind that Byron might not be dead, that he might come back. The whole scheme grew out of his death. Depended on it. And collapsed without it.

Oh, she knew the fix she was in—she wasn't one to kid herself. That was why she had latched onto Tenny while she had the chance. There weren't going to be too many more chances—never mind how persuasive she might still be at moments. And now—she could forget about being Tenny's secretary, let alone his wife. She'd be lucky if she stayed out of jail.

But to make a run for it now—even if she had anyplace to run to—would be to admit her guilt. And Tenny might not be absolutely convinced, after all. So he wasn't laughing when Byron left him. Naturally not; Carol or no Carol, he would be seeing the end of his lovely little fling as a bigshot. Poor old Tenny. He might still call her. It was worth a gamble. Wasn't it? Was it?

Yes, no, yes, no, in the same compulsive circle that kept her fingers busy with their pleat, smooth. Oh, if only she knew what Byron had on her! If only she knew where to find him.

I'd kill him, she thought with cold certainty. I wouldn't care what it cost me. I'd kill him for this—and enjoy it.

No one expected Estrella's birthday reunion to be anything less than an ordeal. But in the end no one was quite brave enough—or cowardly enough, who knew?—to risk staying away. By the same token, they had all decided against sounding out the others on the question of Byron's return. There had been no inquiries, however tentative, no exchange of information. Each had hung back, waiting for someone else to take the first step—until now it was too late for anybody to budge. Byron alone could break the deadlock.

Itching with curiosity (do the others know? how much do they know?), aching with anxiety, burning with their secret yet mutual knowledge, they sat in Estrella's living room and waited for Byron to liberate them. They waited.

And waited. And waited.

His name remained unmentionable, his chair vacant. (Not literally, since it was a buffet supper; Estrella was grateful for that one small favor.) All the same, the sense of vacancy clamped down on them like a mercilessly tightening vise. The bursts of desperate chatter, even Estrella's, grew fewer and farther between. The silence itself lost its flavor of expectancy as one by one they abandoned waiting—he would not come now, he would never come—and turned into a speculation that was even more tense than the waiting.

There was a constant, furtive exchange of glances among them, each pair of eyes seeking to catch another pair unawares, instantly shifting to avoid being caught. The very air seemed to thrum with the question that obsessed them all: Why isn't he here? And the answer: Because someone, someone else—

Not I, thought Estrella. I only wished, and only for that one moment, and I didn't mean it then. Not really. Why, he's my favorite son! Certainly not I. But then who? I never did trust Mary Ethel—you mark my words, I said, but he wouldn't listen.

And Carol's another. She's got her hooks into Tenny now, but it used to be Byron—yes, she's capable of anything. Even Tenny—the temper tantrums he used to have as a child. He's always been jealous—

What am I thinking?

What am I going to do about Dr. Mehallah?

Not I, thought Tenny, my conscience is perfectly clear. Which is more than can be said for some other people. Not mentioning any names. I knew she wouldn't show up at the office today—that's why I stayed home myself. And I had no intention whatever of escorting her here tonight. She could have saved her ridiculous story about, don't bother, she'd be in the neighborhood anyway, et cetera. I can make excuses, too. I'll make one tonight when we both leave. If we ever do. I wish I could believe it was the fund-juggling they quarreled about. Maybe he blamed her, threatened her. No, of course not. I know what it was, all right. He told her it was Mary Ethel he wanted, not her. That's why she did it, the only reason.

Oh, Carol, Carol, you said you loved me!

Not I, thought Carol, I didn't even see him. That's all that stopped me. Okay. But I didn't see him. No skin off my nose who did. It gives me the creeps, though, not to know for sure.

The old lady's not the sweet little featherbrain she's cracked up to be. A whim of iron, if I ever saw one.

Mary Ethel would get my vote except I know good and well he'd head straight for her, the rat, the minute he hit town. Before he called me, that's for sure. So she couldn't have—wait a minute, they could have made a date for later.

Same thing goes for Tenny, I suppose. For all I know, that's why he stayed away from the office today. He hated Byron enough. And now he hates me. I get the message, I know when I'm getting the old heave-ho. Well, I can take it. Damn, just when I thought I had it made.

Not I, thought Mary Ethel, I only tried and failed. As at least one of them must know, because one of them must have tried and succeeded. Don't tell me he wouldn't be here otherwise—he'd have been in his glory, watching everybody wriggle—and don't tell me they didn't have as much reason as I to want him dead. So who are they to be sneaking looks at me?

It could just as easily have been one of them. Any of them. Or—or all of them.

Is that it? They've always hated me—they'd dearly love to hang it on me if they could. No one of them alone would have the nerve, but all of them together—a solid block of three against one, all telling the same story and sticking to it, backing each other up, planting evidence against me—

He must have told them I tried. That would give them the idea, the ready-made frame. And I've been away from my apartment since noon. Plenty of time and opportunity. They're waiting now for me to go back there and find—whatever it is.

I won't go back. I can't. But if I don't go back it will look even worse.

No way out? There has to be, because I'm not guilty! I failed, I failed! I only tried and failed!

Once across the bridge and on the thruway, the big bus settled down to a steady, purposeful purr. Very soothing. Byron stretched his legs and leaned back comfortably, at peace with the world—the ex-Byron Hawley, traveling light and liking it.

He had fully intended to show up at his mother's party, had in fact been on his way to it when all at once there was the bus station, the bus waiting for him, the space available, the irresistible urge to do everybody a favor and get rid of the old Byron Hawley once and for all.

No doubt about its being a favor to all of them—he had found that out for sure. There hadn't been time for a telephone call before the bus left. And maybe that, too, was just as well, though of course someday he would probably, someday he might—

He yawned hugely. Then again he might not. The bus purred, lulling him to sleep.

William O'Farrell

Over There—Darkness

Everything that Miss Fox owned was of the finest quality. She was a middle-aged woman with delicate features and soft, greying hair who lived alone in self-contained elegance. She dressed beautifully, spending a great deal of thought and money on her clothes. Her only companion was a dog named Vanessa, a pedigreed black poodle who, unlike her mistress, was a little overweight.

Miss Fox was as graceful and slim as she had ever been. She had a sizable income from a trust fund and her own lovely furniture in a four-room apartment. The apartment was in a huge, well managed building which was located, incongruously, in a rowdy neighborhood of the Chelsea district in New York.

She was hardly aware of the neighborhood. She had signed a long-term lease during the housing shortage, and the management had considerately insulated her from any outside crudeness from the day she had moved in. There was a supermarket on the ground floor of the building. There was also a rental library, a beauty salon, and an excellent restaurant.

Theoretically, she could have remained inside the apartment house indefinitely, and in effect that is what she did. But twice a day she walked the poodle along West Twenty-third Street and six times a week her favorite elevator boy took the dog for longer walks at night.

Once, in the spring of 1943, a captain in the Quartermaster Corps had asked Miss Fox to marry him. He had given her the ring of her selection, and two weeks later he entered a hospital in Virginia. The captain had died there of a kidney complaint, and she had not seen him again before his death.

Wartime travel was difficult and Miss Fox preferred to remember him as he had been, unwasted by illness. She had telegraphed flowers, relying on her florist to send something suitable. He was a member of the American Florists Association and had excellent taste.

The ring was exquisite—a diamond solitaire surrounded by emeralds—and Miss Fox still wore it. Her ring, her dog, and Eddie McMahon—the last in a different way and on a lower level—were the only things capable of stirring in her more than casual interest. All three were beautiful, and Eddie McMahon was very useful, too. Eddie was the nighttime dog walker. He was young—not tall, but well proportioned—and he had long-lashed blue eyes and wavy brown hair that turned black under the dim lights of the elevator. He wore a neat navy-blue uniform with a gold stripe down the trousers and he had good manners. As men go, he was nice.

She paid him five dollars a week. That was above the going rate for dog walking, but she did not begrudge the extra money. The arrangement might have continued for as long as he kept his job and she stayed on in the apartment—if she had not made one small mistake.

That happened just before Christmas, and at the time she did not recognize it as a mistake. As in past years, she handed the doorman an envelope containing money to be divided among the other employees and himself; but in a separate envelope on which Eddie's name was written she put a twenty-dollar bill. It seemed to her that from that time on his attitude changed sharply.

He was as respectful as ever, but in early January he asked for his five dollars before it was due. The same thing happened in March, and although she gave him the money on both occasions Miss Fox was disturbed. She lived within her income and expected other people to be as provident as herself.

Then, about the middle of April, he appeared unexpectedly at her apartment on his day off.

There was a knock on the door. She opened it and Eddie came in without being asked. Such a thing was unprecedented. It was necessary occasionally to admit a repairman or an employee of the gas company, but their visits were always preceded by a call on the house telephone and Miss Fox kept the door open while they were inside.

Eddie closed the door. He also leaned against it, breathing heavily. "Climbed the stairs," he explained. "Fourteen flights. Not supposed to hang around the building on my day off."

It was the first time she had seen him out of uniform. His suit was clean, but badly cut. It changed his whole appearance. He seemed older and heavier—a stranger, and an unprepossessing one.

"Then what are you doing here?" she asked.

"Miss Fox"—his breathing was a little easier—"I have to talk to you. Just a minute, please?"

He was almost pleading, and Miss Fox felt distaste. She walked through the small foyer into the living room.

"Come in," she said. Then, hearing his footsteps following her too closely, on impulse she called, "Vanessa!"

The poodle lay in its basket in a corner. It looked at her and immediately went to sleep again. Miss Fox walked to the windows overlooking the avenue and stood there with her back turned to the room.

"Yes, Eddie?" She had always been proud of her gentle voice. It was a relief to hear it now, in perfect control.

Eddie took two more forward steps. When next he spoke, she judged that he was standing beside the coffee table on which she had just placed a cup of tea. The tea was getting cold and that annoyed her. She liked it steaming hot.

"Miss Fox, will you let me have fifty dollars? I need it bad. I'll pay you back. It'll take three, four weeks, but today I have to send this money order—"

His voice dwindled into silence. Miss Fox stood quietly, unshocked by the preposterous request. She felt, rather, an odd sense of satisfaction, as though having known that something like this was bound to come; she was glad to have it in the clear at last.

"You say this money is important to you?"

"Yes, ma'am. Very important."

"Why come to me?" she asked.

"Because I've already tried everywhere else. My watch is in hock. The union gave me a loan, but that's all gone. You couldn't unscrew an advance from the management here with a Stillson wrench. And because"—he hesitated—"because you're kind."

She turned. "Sit down, Eddie." She waited until he was sitting stiffly on the couch. "Why is it necessary to send a money order in such a rush? To whom?"

"To my girl." He saw her lips tighten and added quickly, "She's in this sanitarium. The state pays half the expenses, see, and I promised to pay the other half. I done it so far, too, but now there's this extra—"

"You're engaged?"

"I guess you could call it that," he said.

But there had been a pause before he spoke and obviously the idea was new to him. New and strange. Miss Fox glanced at the ring on her left hand. Her own romance had not been conducted in so casual a manner. There had been the short but proper courtship, the proposal, the betrothal kiss. Marriage would have been the next orderly step if tragedy had not intervened.

She sighed and shook her head. "I can't lend you fifty dollars, Eddie. Don't you earn a good salary?"

"Seventy a week," he said morosely, "but that's not take-home pay."

"No matter how little you actually take home, it's merely a question of planning, Eddie. I live on a fixed income and every cent is budgeted. Fifty dollars?" She shrugged. "I couldn't possibly spare an amount as large as that."

Eddie was no longer listening. His eyes were fixed on something behind her back. She looked over her shoulder and saw her white gloves and alligator bag.

They were lying on the living-room table. Miss Fox grew hot, then cold—which was ridiculous, because there was no earthly way for Eddie to have learned that she had cashed a fairly large check only a few hours before.

"I'm sorry," she said firmly. "It's impossible."

His eyes had left the table. They were focused on her ring. For a moment he was silent. Then he rose.

"Yes, ma'am. My fault for asking. Excuse me, please."

He went out and closed the door.

A vague unrest covered the remainder of her day. She couldn't read. The laundry was delivered at four o'clock, and after she had put it away there was nothing more to do until six. At two minutes before the hour she turned on the television.

The program was a good one, but this evening nothing could have held her interest. The memory of Eddie's bland presumption kept creeping back into her mind. She snapped off the television and poured a glass of sherry. It was infuriating to think that because he was vulgarly good-looking and a few years younger than herself the boy had actually believed that he could take her in.

She drank her sherry, went into the bedroom. When she came back, she had changed her dress and was wearing a light spring coat. A bright scarf was tied around her head. It was a fetching ensemble and made her look ten years younger, but she hardly glanced at the mirror as she picked up her bag and pulled on her gloves.

She went downstairs to dinner a full three-quarters of an hour earlier than she usually did. She had a delicious dinner, which she did not enjoy, and was back in her apartment before eight o'clock.

At a quarter to ten, when the dog whimpered to go out, Miss Fox attached a leash of shocking pink to the poodle's matching collar and once more she pulled on her gloves and picked up her alligator bag.

The weather was freakishly warm for April, so warm that the doorman had propped open the front doors of the apartment house. It had rained earlier and the street lamps were reflected from the still-wet pavement like little moons put there to guide her feet.

There was an exhilarating quality about the night. It called for adventure and Miss Fox responded to it. She walked west instead of, as she usually did, in the direction of the well lighted avenue toward the east.

On her right, as she strolled along, were the amber windows of her own apartment house. These extended west for a hundred yards. The building ended there and was succeeded by a long row of old brownstone fronts—respectable once, but fallen now into almost sinister disrepair. The demarcating line was like a frontier between light and darkness, and she determined to go only as far as the end of the building and then turn back.

Reaching the predetermined spot, she pulled gently at Vanessa's leash. But the poodle had scented something beyond the dark frontier and strained forward. After a token struggle, Miss Fox let the dog have her way.

"Oh, very well," she said aloud, "but only as far as the next tree, dear."

They never reached the tree. Halfway there, a rough arm encircled Miss Fox's throat. She was bent over backward and a hand was clasped across her mouth.

Blood pounded in her ears as above her she saw, for just an instant, a man's shadowed face. She tried to scream and couldn't, and the last thing she heard was Vanessa's frantic yelp. Then the black world tilted up on end and slid away.

When she regained consciousness she was lying on the sidewalk. The doorman from the apartment house was kneeling beside her; the glove had been stripped from her left hand and her diamond-and-emerald ring was gone.

So was her alligator bag containing $180, but as she explained to Detective Sergeant Kirby in her apartment a half hour later, the money wasn't important. What she wanted—what she demanded, in fact—was the immediate return of her ring.

Sergeant Kirby assured her that everything possible would be done. "We don't have a lot to work on, though. You say you wouldn't know the man if you saw him again?"

Miss Fox thoughtfully fingered the bandage around her throat. The policeman was trying to be helpful, but he was going about it in such a plodding way. The fact that she had glimpsed her assailant only for an instant and in deep shadow meant very little. He had brutally manhandled her. She would be able to pick him out of any crowd.

"I did say that," she admitted, "but now I'm beginning to remember how he looked."

"Description?"

"He had dark hair and—let me think—he was strong, but not especially tall."

"Clothes?"

"I didn't notice. His sleeve was of some coarse material."

"Did he say anything?"

"No. I heard nothing but the dog. Now that I think of it," Miss Fox said, "it's odd that she didn't bark until after the attack."

"I've thought of that." Kirby got up from his chair. "Another point is that the mugger only tore the glove off your left hand. It's almost as though he knew about the ring."

Eddie! The abrupt revelation caused Miss Fox no surprise. It was only logical. That afternoon he had tried to borrow fifty dollars. Refused, he had stared at her ring—as now it came to her quite clearly—with unconcealed cupidity. There could be no doubt about it. Eddie was the thief.

But she said nothing. If, employing their own means, the police found and arrested him, that was their business. Her business was to get the ring back. That, she believed, she knew how to do.

Sergeant Kirby was leaving and she rose to say goodbye. "Thank you so much. I may expect to hear from you?"

"Probably very soon. If it isn't soon, it may be never. That's how these things work." He rubbed Vanessa's ears. "You can thank your dog for spreading the alarm, Miss Fox."

"Yes. Good night, Sergeant."

She went to bed, but could not fall asleep. After a tortured half hour, she had to take a capsule. It worked, but just as she was dozing off she was aroused by the ringing of the telephone.

"Hope I didn't wake you," Sergeant Kirby said. "We've picked up a man who may have done the job. Can you come down?"

Miss Fox was half doped and thoroughly exasperated. There was no reason why this unpleasant business of identification could not have been postponed until the morning. "At this hour? Come down where?"

He gave her the station-house address. "It's only one o'clock."

"Does he have my ring?"

"Not on him. But if you make a positive I.D., I'll get it back."

"Very well. As soon as I can find a taxi, I'll be there."

The station house was only a few blocks away. The taxi rounded a corner and pulled up at the curb. Miss Fox saw a dreary-looking building with a green light beside its wide front door. "Here you are, lady," the taxi driver said.

Then she was in a functionally furnished room and Sergeant Kirby was telling her that the suspect had been arrested in a Tenth Avenue bar. "Within a block of where it happened and only twenty minutes later. He was half drunk and flashing a wad of bills he can't account for. Bad record, too. Looks like we wound this up in record time."

"If you have," Miss Fox said, "no one will be happier than I, Sergeant Kirby."

But she was disappointed. The man shoved through the doorway by a uniformed policeman was not Eddie. He was Eddie's height and had dark hair, but there was no resemblance otherwise. His hands were filthy. It was unthinkable that she had been touched by such grimy hands.

"No." She shook her head. "It is not he."

"You're sure?" Kirby sounded disappointed.

"Quite sure," she said, avoiding the man's eyes.

His eyes were insolent. He wore a flashy suit, black shirt, and yellow tie, but Miss Fox paid no attention to his clothes. She was too agitated by his dirty hands and bullying stare.

"Well, thanks for coming," Kirby said.

Miss Fox went home and slept until ten the following morning. Eddie's shift on the elevator started at noon. She took the dog out at eleven and told the doorman that she wanted to see Eddie as soon as he came in.

He knocked on her door a few minutes before twelve.

She opened it. "Come in."

"Say, Miss Fox, I heard about what happened!"

"Come in, Eddie, and sit down," she said.

His expression, as he obeyed, was one of puzzled innocence. It was a pity, she thought, that so handsome a face should conceal a mind so devious. She stood erect, steeling herself to a distasteful task.

"So you've heard."

"Yes, ma'am. I always said this neighborhood ain't safe."

"You know I was robbed of some money and my ring?"

"That's what they say."

"Very well. Now listen carefully. I want to be quite sure you understand. I don't care about the money, but I want my ring. Its description has been circulated. Trying to sell it would be dangerous."

"That's right. It's plenty hot."

"So it might as well be returned to me. Particularly if I promise to forget the hundred and eighty dollars that I've lost and say no more about the matter. Don't you agree?"

Eddie appeared to be thinking deeply. "Well, I don't know. This guy that mugged you—there's a couple of things he could do. He could break the ring up and get rid of the stones that way. Or he could wait until the heat's off and sell it somewheres out of town."

"He would still be taking a risk. I have a better idea. I'm prepared to pay five hundred dollars for the ring's return. Five hundred dollars, Eddie—and no questions asked."

He got up slowly. "I sure hope you get it back. Excuse me—I got to go to work." He walked toward the door, but stopped before he reached the foyer. "Look, Miss Fox, don't count too much on that plan of yours. What would you do—advertise? Chances are the guy would never see your ad, and if he did he'd be dumb to stick his neck out."

"You don't think I'll get my ring back?" There was an edge to Miss Fox's normally soft voice.

"No, ma'am. Not that way, I don't."

"You may go, Eddie," Miss Fox said.

The doorman announced Sergeant Kirby an hour later. He entered briskly and came directly to business.

"You have an arrangement with an elevator boy named McMahon to walk your dog. Yesterday was his day off, but he was seen leaving your apartment about two in the afternoon. Is that correct?"

Miss Fox walked to the window and stood with her back turned, as she had done the day before. "Why do you ask?"

"Routine. McMahon has a good record and he's a steady worker. On the other hand, he needs money. Why did he come here?"

She did not move. Her voice was cool and impersonal as she replied. "You seem to have ferreted out almost everything. You might as well know the rest. He wanted me to lend him fifty dollars."

"Did you do it?"

"Of course not."

There was a silence. Then Kirby asked quietly, "Was it Mc-Mahon?"

She turned and looked directly into the detective's eyes. "I had hoped it wouldn't come to this. I gave him his chance. I even offered him money to return the ring. He refused."

"You positively identify him?"

Unconsciously, she had already passed her own personal line of demarcation between light and darkness. "Yes, it was Eddie," Miss Fox said.

She did not look at Eddie during the trial. She kept her eyes averted as she testified. It was a short trial. He had no alibi. They brought him in and tried him and sent him to prison for three years.

Or maybe it was for one year with the other two suspended. Miss Fox wasn't sure. She had her own problems now that Eddie was no longer on the elevator. She had to find someone else to walk Vanessa, and the other boys had suddenly become very busy. They seemed curiously indifferent as to whether or not they made extra money every week.

Eventually she was forced to hire a professional. He was unsatisfactory. The third night he called, Miss Fox smelled liquor on his breath. From then on she took the dog out every night herself.

At first she shunned the sidewalk west of the apartment house. She never even approached it until, in the heat of summer, the streets became more crowded and consequently safe. Then she found that her dread of the dark frontier had lessened greatly.

Fear was now no more than a rather pleasurable titillation of her senses. She sometimes permitted Vanessa to pull her right up to the line, and she would stand within inches of it, peering into unexplored darkness.

Summer passed and was succeeded by the fall, and in all that time she had no news of her ring. Sergeant Kirby told her that Eddie still insisted he was innocent—but of course Eddie would do that. She telephoned Kirby several times and he was always courteous, until one day in November two policemen came to her apartment and brusquely told her that the sergeant wanted to see her at the station house.

She was indignant. "Why doesn't he come here?"

"Couldn't tell you, lady. Just said he wanted to talk to you."

Kirby met her in the bare room she had been in once before. He looked grim. "We've found your ring," he said.

She displayed none of the emotion she was feeling. "I knew that sooner or later Eddie would tell the truth."

"McMahon never had it." The grimness in the detective's face was reflected in his voice. "Remember the man you *didn't* identify? We got him on another charge and the ring was in his room. He confessed."

Something was wrong. Something was so drastically wrong that Miss Fox couldn't absorb it immediately. "But I saw him! I saw Eddie!"

"Did you?"

"Well, I thought I did. I was so sure!"

"You certainly succeeded in giving that impression. As a result, I look like a fool and an innocent man's in jail."

Miss Fox said angrily, "I may have made a mistake, but it was an honest one. I believe it's the duty of the police to check these things. Could it have been that you were so anxious to arrest someone that you didn't care whether or not he was guilty?"

Kirby shrugged, looking past her at a blank space on the wall.

"If you have nothing further to say, give me my ring."

He wouldn't do it. He showed it to her, and there was no question about it being hers, and he said it would be returned to her in due time. Meanwhile, it was evidence and must be held. He wouldn't even tell her when Eddie would be released.

"I don't know," he said. "Why should you care?"

Miss Fox did care. She foresaw a period of strain when and if Eddie returned to his old job, and she wanted to avoid that by finding another apartment first. She disliked friction of any kind, and so she bought a box of expensive cigars and sent them to Sergeant Kirby. After that she was able to dismiss the detective from her mind.

During the weeks that followed, she inspected a number of apartments, but none of them met her fastidious standards. She flinched from the ordeal of moving, and at last was forced to the realization that she was better off where she was.

Having accepted this, she made a generous gesture. She spoke personally to the manager of the apartment house and was surprised to learn that her request had been anticipated. He had already written to Eddie, offering to take him back.

"But it's thoughtful of you, Miss Fox," he said. "I must say I'm relieved."

She left his office satisfied he would tell Eddie what she'd done. Eddie would be grateful. What might have been a tense situation had been eased.

Eddie came back to work the week before Christmas. One morning she buckled on Vanessa's leash and pushed the elevator bell. With a minimum of delay, the elevator door slid open, and there he was. Everything was as it had been, including his respectful smile.

"Good morning, Miss Fox."

"Eddie!" she said. "I can't tell you how happy I am."

He took her down to the lobby. By the time she had walked the dog, riding up in the elevator again, she had recovered from her surprise.

"Hold the car a moment," she said, stepping out on the fourteenth floor. "There's something I must say to you."

He held the door open, waiting. She turned in the softly lighted corridor to study him. He had changed. His smile was fixed and meaningless and there was a glassy quality in his eyes.

Never mind. It was in her power to change that, and she would. "I want you to know that it wasn't easy for me to testify against you, Eddie. I only told the court what I believed to be the truth."

"Sure, Miss Fox."

"It was a terrible experience for both of us. I think the best thing we can do is to forget it and start afresh."

"Yes, ma'am."

"Good," she said. "Vanessa will be waiting when you finish work tonight." She started down the corridor.

He stopped her. "Miss Fox, I won't be walking your dog any more."

She turned, incredulous and a little piqued. "You want more money, I suppose?"

"It isn't that," he said. "It's just that I can get along now on my pay. I don't have any extra expenses now."

"How about your fiancee?"

"She died," he said.

The elevator door slid shut. Miss Fox was alone.

She let herself into the apartment, sat down, and thought about it rationally. Everything had worked out for the best. The girl had been ill. Eddie would have found her an intolerable burden. He would get over her death.

She herself had gone through the same natural sequence of suffering and recuperation when the captain died. She told herself these things, but still remained unsatisfied, sensing that somewhere there was something she had overlooked.

At two o'clock, she put on her coat again, walked to an elevator at the far end of the building, and went down to her bank.

When she returned, she told the doorman that she wanted to see Eddie during his coffee break.

He came to her apartment at four o'clock. Miss Fox did not invite him to come in.

"I've been thinking about you," she said. "I want to help you—well, to rehabilitate yourself. As I once told you, I was prepared to pay five hundred dollars for my ring. I had the money set aside, and I can think of no better use for it than to give it to you."

She handed him an envelope.

"Shall we call it a Christmas present, Eddie? Five one-hundred-dollar bills."

There was a long moment while he stood holding the white envelope and looking at the floor. Then he put the envelope in his pocket.

"Thank you very much, Miss Fox," he said.

Miss Fox was greatly relieved as she shut the door. It was a pity that Eddie had not accepted the $500 when she'd offered it to him eight months before. It would have been so simple. He could have taken the money and returned her ring—

But Eddie had not stolen the ring, she suddenly remembered. She shrugged. Anyway, it was finished now. She drank a cup of steaming tea and had a nice, long nap.

When she went out with the dog at ten that night, Eddie had already gone off duty. It was snowing, and she had always enjoyed the first snowfall of the season. Vanessa pulled to the right and Miss Fox humored her by walking west, mildly exhilarated by the drifting flakes.

She came to the end of the lighted apartment house and stood, as she had often stood before, on the very edge of darkness. A few yards ahead was the spot where the man had thrown her down.

She smiled nervously, telling herself that she was glad now it had happened. It was rather thrilling to look back from her present security to a danger safely passed.

"Let's go home, dear," she told Vanessa, and turned back.

A man blocked her way. He had come up behind her silently. Miss Fox gasped. Then her shrill scream echoed down the street.

He raised his arm. His open palm found and covered her face. He pushed. Miss Fox staggered backward, tripped, and fell. She had time to scream once more before he stopped the noise at its source. The last thing she heard was the far-off yelping of her dog.

This time when the doorman found her, he was too late. She lay on her back, snowflakes falling in her open eyes. Between her rapidly stiffening fingers were five one-hundred-dollar bills.

William Bankier

In the House Next Door

"Were they arguing again today?" Lily Norton asked when she arrived home from work at six o'clock.

"Hammer and tongs," Sam Norton said. "Or, rather, breakers and beach. There's something definite in the image of hammer and tongs—the job gets done. But Mercy and Clive will go on pounding against each other forever."

"If she doesn't end up murdering him first."

The Nortons did not even know their neighbors' last name. Clive had come around on the day they moved into the little terrace house six months ago and kindly asked them next door for a drink. Lily and Sam accepted and spent a not very comfortable hour over beer and tea and biscuits discussing local politics, which seemed to be Clive's and Mercy's bag.

They were the steam that drove a civic action group determined to keep down municipal taxes. Determined to prevent truck traffic from using their street. Determined to stop the house on the corner from becoming a hairdressing salon. Determined.

Mercy was large-boned and clear-eyed with old-fashioned hair and a loud voice. Clive was tall and ivory-colored with sparse grey hair. He looked at a person as though he knew dreadful things about him which he was ready to forgive.

The Nortons repaid that unpromising hospitality by waiting a week and then asking Mercy and Clive in for dessert and coffee after dinner. The session was a little longer but no more rewarding. Host and hostess dredged up conversation about their Canadian origins while the guests refused to be drawn into responses about their childhood in England. They told, instead, about plans to force British Rail to extinguish a bright light high over the Wimbledon yards. It shone into Mercy's bedroom at night and she was determined to be rid of it.

What followed was a tacit agreement that the two couples were not each other's kind of people and that in the future a simple greeting on the street would suffice.

Then summer came, long, hot, unheard-of in England, and windows hung open day and night as the tiny houses gasped for air.

And gradually the pattern of life in the house next door was revealed to Sam and Lily; it was one long, articulate, self-sustaining argument. The bickering seemed to have a life of its own and it never ran out of material.

Clive: *(slightly singsong and pedantic)* The bottle was in the refrigerator when I left this morning and now it's on the table, empty.

Mercy: *(rounded tones, the voice of student actress)* I am always very careful to be sure of my facts before I accuse.

Clive: I'm perfectly sure of my facts. There's the bottle. It's empty now, isn't it? You don't seem to understand what I'm trying to tell you.

Mercy: I'm not interested in arguing with you. All I'm trying to say is—

In the kitchen next door Sam would turn down the radio and he and Lily would raise their eyebrows, practically holding their breath. Sometimes the argument was about a third person who was never named.

Clive: He's lying to you, don't you see? He's been pulling the wool over your eyes for years and you let him get away with it.

Mercy: You should try to have a little more trust. It wasn't that way at all. Three of us were in the car at the time. Ask anyone else and see what they say.

Clive: *(mildly hysterical)* Lying and cheating for years but you're too blind to see it. He wouldn't dare do it to me!

Mercy: It has nothing to do with you.

Sometimes the dialogue was like a Harold Pinter play, tantalizingly obscure and mined with ominous pauses.

Clive: There were three of them. One was over here, another by the plate, and one was under the counter.

Mercy: I'd rather take his word for that.

Clive: But I tell you I saw the packages in the dustbin. *(pause)* Would you believe me if I showed you the packages?

Mercy: *(a longer pause)* You're the one who leaves it open so they get out in the first place.

Clive: *(ready to kill)* I can *not* seem to *make* you under*stand* that it's a *sim*ple matter of *looking* at the empty *packages.*

The Clive and Mercy dialogues became an important topic of conversation between Sam and Lily. They said it was a deplorable state and they could not understand why two people who so obviously disliked each other did not simply split and go their separate ways.

Sam said, "One thing about it is the way they seem content to keep the argument going, never to resolve it."

"We're never like that," Lily said, helping him make his point.

"Right. If we have a fight, we may say terrible things, but we hate it and we want to get it over with."

"We want to get back to normal."

"Right. But I heard Clive this morning starting up the same subject they were going on about last night."

Sam Norton, writing his radio scripts at home and only driving in to the BBC studios once a week for a recording session, had the advantage of access to the neighbors' private life during the day. Thus he was able to report to Lily over supper.

"I think Clive must be depressed. I heard her say to him today she was tired of his silent self-pity. If he couldn't find a job, there were plenty of things that need doing around the house."

"That's bad." Lily restated her prediction of impending doom. "I'm sure somebody is going to get killed."

And there was no denying, as the Kalahari summer baked the English landscape brown, that a pressure was indeed building up to some sort of violent release in the house next door.

That evening Sam got up and turned down the television sound when the familiar voices began to echo from the brick recess between the houses. He went to stand sideways with one ear to the open louvers of the dining-room window while Lily sat on the living-room sofa, half watching the miming faces on the color screen, half watching her portly husband in the shadows beyond.

"You'll be lucky to get fifteen thousand for it," Mercy was saying.

"You'll be lucky to get twelve thousand." There was a clatter of crockery and a trickle of running water behind her voice. She was cleaning the dishes while arguing. Life had to go on.

"I don't care how much I get. All I know is I can't put up any longer with this constant lack of—" Clive's voice faded as he left the room.

"You were always the one who looked after the insurance," Mercy boomed. "That was never my responsibility."

Fading back in. "You're trying to blame that on me. I showed you the letter and I said this is important."

"You mentioned it once."

"I never said I told you twice. I said this is important. I said—I said—and now you've lost the letter and you're blaming me."

The reference to selling the house must have touched a sensitive fiber in Sam Norton's bundle of insecurity for that night, as he got ready for bed, he said, "I feel sorry for anybody trying to sell a house in England today. There's no market."

"I wish them luck," Lily said brusquely. She was looking at the quarter inch of silver at the roots of her hair; the whole messy coloring business was overdue. In this heat. "I just wish they'd move the hell out of here."

"Well." Sam sat on the edge of the bed and his paunch rested on his thighs. He was going to have to stop with the beer and the peanuts. "I feel a little sorry for the poor guy. He's got her braying down his neck day in and day out."

"Sorry for *him*. If he'd do some of the things he's supposed to do around the house, she wouldn't have to keep after him so much. Have you any idea how long he's been saying he'll paint the living room?"

"She could pitch in and help him, for heaven's sake. It wouldn't break her arm to pick up a paint roller."

"She happens to have a job, Sam. A woman works all day in an office and then comes home and has to wash dishes and clean house, it isn't easy. I'm here to tell you."

Sam felt the mounting pressure in his chest and throat. He worked to keep his voice level. "I don't know. I see pictures of housewives with big happy smiles on their faces, painting walls. In the paint ads in those glossy magazines you keep bringing home at a pound a copy."

Lily turned slowly on the vanity stool. "I *like* buying an occasional magazine and I intend to keep on doing it. With the money *I* earn." She narrowed her eyes and the look she gave her husband was pure malevolence. "As for wasting money, when was the last time I had my hair done at Sassoon's where they do it right? Instead I color it myself in the bathroom sink, breaking my back and ruining my nails."

This was dangerous ground for Sam. The image of his wife, aging and going to seed, and the sound of her bitter voice, was confused in his mind with memories of his mother, the angry recluse of his childhood who embarrassed him by looking tired and poor and who frightened him with her screaming tirades. "Big deal," he said. "Lots of women do their own hair and they don't act like bloody martyrs about it."

"Lots of women have husbands who care about how they feel." Lily was struggling with her sense of worthlessness, implanted during a childhood spent with a tyrannical father and a stoical mother who refused to side against him, both parents so proud of two clever sons they had little time for an equally intelligent and much more sensitive daughter. All she wanted was to be told, "Go spend a little money on yourself, you're worth it." But she did not say anything like this. She said, "You're supposed to be a writer but you have no idea of other people's feelings."

Sam, suspecting there was truth in this, began to get ready to flee. He struggled into his trousers, scuffed shoes onto his bare feet, clutching the bureau for support, knocking his plexiglass paperweight to the floor.

"That's right, coward," Lily taunted him. "Run away, run out into the street. Anything to avoid talking." Then as he said nothing, she came and seized the shirt he was trying to put on.

"Don't prevent me," he groaned, dragging the shirt away and feeling it rip between their hands. He dropped it and took a pullover from the drawer, hauling it over his head, his eyes wild.

"You're not leaving this house," Lily said, her voice cold and flat as ice. "You're going to stay and talk."

"It isn't talking, it's arguing. And you're impossible to argue with."

"You're not leaving." She took his wrist and ground her nails into it, breaking one of them. As she let go, Sam saw little tracks ending in tiny mounds of rolled up skin, the grooves beginning to fill with blood. An overpowering sense of freedom to retaliate engulfed him. His foot struck the paperweight and he bent to pick it up, the plexiglass cube fitting well into his fist, the heavy brass base protruding.

Lily saw what he was doing and helped him by cowering in the posture of the victim about to be struck.

Sam Norton brought the weight down seven times in all. The coroner was to say that the first two were enough.

The real-estate agent showing prospective buyers through the house avoided mentioning the recent crime of violence in the bedroom. The Norton effects had been taken away and sold while the carpet with the rusty stains on it had been replaced. The affair itself had not been widely publicized, so knowledge of it was not a barrier to sales.

The difficulty in sustaining interest arose when the prospects inevitably inquired about the neighbors. No sooner would the agent finish a testimonial to their civilized behavior than the people next door would begin arguing. It never failed. They seemed to argue ceaselessly.

"She was too good for him," the pedantic singsong would fade in. "I knew it the first time I laid eyes on her. An angel married to a vicious brute."

"He never stopped working," the plummy voice would override. "I heard his typewriter going at all hours. The trouble was she never appreciated what a hard-working man he was."

"There you go, making the same old mistake. There are other worthwhile contributions besides work."

"I should have expected you to hold that opinion."

The agent would let his prospects out of the house, hearing them agree that they would have to be crazy to move in next to a couple who were obviously going to kill each other one day.

Jack Ritchie

The Third-Floor Closet

When A. E. Williams discovered that Bertha Malloy was dead, he phoned the police.

I cut the siren of our squad car as Jennings and I turned up the long winding driveway and drove past the large, well tended lawn. We parked in the oval in front of the big house behind two vans, both of which had *A. E. Williams Estate Services* lettered on their sides.

A covey of men and women, all of them in tan work uniforms, were waiting and Williams was their spokesman. "I just didn't know what to do in a situation like this," he said. "It's never happened to us before. And as far as I know, Mr. Hudson is in Europe or someplace. Maybe I should have called a doctor, but I don't know who Mrs. Malloy's doctor is and I don't know if it's appropriate to call in a strange doctor. And besides, Mrs. Malloy is quite dead, so a doctor couldn't have done anything anyway." He dabbed at his forehead with a handkerchief. "I imagine she died of a heart attack."

He led us into the house and through a huge kitchen to a small suite at its far end.

Bertha Malloy reclined in an easy chair, staring sightlessly ahead. She was a large woman, perhaps five foot ten and close to two hundred pounds. I estimated her age at about forty.

Williams was at my elbow. "Mrs. Malloy is—was—Mr. Hudson's housekeeper." And then he explained his own presence. "I am Andrew E. Williams, of A. E. Williams Estate Services. We come here periodically to clean the house from top to bottom. Not that there's really much to do, what with Mr. Hudson gone all the time and the house empty. And we see to it that the grass is cut, hedges trimmed, and so on.

"This morning when we showed up at eight, Mrs. Malloy met us at the door like always and we went to work. At noon, when we take our lunch break, we all go to the kitchen where Mrs. Malloy always has coffee waiting. We supply our own food, but freshly brewed coffee is always welcome.

"Only this time there wasn't any coffee. And the door to her suite was open and she was just sitting there. So I spoke to her; but she didn't answer, and I saw how her eyes were open and her jaw sagging and—" He shuddered. "Well, she was dead."

I agreed. "Could anyone give us the names of some of Mrs. Malloy's relatives? I suppose one of the regular servants might have that information?"

"There are no other servants. Just Mrs. Malloy. She's sort of a housekeeper and caretaker in one, you might say. No household staff at all. That's probably because Mr. Hudson does so much traveling and he couldn't see any point in having a full staff of servants just standing around with nothing to do but collect wages."

"So Mrs. Malloy had the whole place to herself?"

"Yes. I once asked her if she didn't get lonely or afraid being the only one here. But she said she liked being alone and there was nothing to be afraid of. Besides, she had that big revolver."

"Revolver?"

"In that drawer over there. She opened it once to get something and I saw it and asked her about it. She said it was for protection."

I pulled open the drawer. A Colt .38 lay inside. I broke it open and found that one of the cartridges had been fired. I put the gun back. "How long have you been doing cleaning here?"

"Over three years now."

"And you don't know whether Mrs. Malloy has any relatives or where they could be found?"

"I'm afraid not. We used to talk over coffee sometimes, but she was always close-mouthed about some things. Like Mr. Hudson, for instance. But she did mention once that her husband was dead. Fell down some stairs and broke his neck. And she has no children. If she has any relatives at all, I don't think they'd be from around here. She had quite a New England accent."

I moved over to a small desk near the window. On its blotter lay two checks. A large house key, evidently used as a paperweight, lay on top of them.

I studied the checks. One was made out to the Municipal Electric Company, apparently in payment of the monthly bill, and the other to Bertha Malloy in the sum of four thousand dollars. Both of them were dated yesterday and both of them were signed *Jacob Hudson*.

I turned back to Williams. "Are you positive that Hudson isn't in this house?"

"Well . . . I didn't see him anywhere. Neither did any of my people. I just assumed that he was off on a trip again."

"Could he be in the house without you knowing it?"

"I suppose so." Williams frowned. "There's the locked room."

"What locked room?"

"On the third floor. It's always locked. Mrs. Malloy said it was used for storage and we shouldn't ever bother with it."

"What does Hudson look like?"

"I've never seen him in the flesh. Neither has any of my people. But there are photographs around the house. He appears to be a rather small frail man nearing forty."

I picked up the key on the desk. "Let's see if this fits the lock to that third-floor room."

Williams led the way. On the third floor he stopped in front of a door at the end of the corridor. "This is it."

I tried the doorknob and verified that the door was locked. I rapped several times and then said, "This is the police. Is there anyone in there?"

We waited, but there was no answer.

I found that the key I'd brought along did fit and I unlocked the door. We stepped into a small bedroom.

Jennings sniffed the air. "Stale. I'll bet nobody's slept in that bed in years." He glanced around. "It sure doesn't look like a storeroom to me. Why would she want to keep it locked?"

I found that one door on the side of the room led to a bathroom. I tried the door of what I assumed must be the closet. It was locked. I tried my key again, but this time it didn't work.

I spoke to Williams. "Would you have any idea where the key to this closet might be found?"

"Not the faintest."

I studied the closet door for ten seconds and then made up my mind. "Do you have a hammer and a screwdriver in one of those vans of yours?"

Williams nodded and hurried downstairs. He returned almost immediately with a hammer and a screwdriver.

I used them to tap the hinge pins out of their sockets and Jennings and I pulled the closet door out of its frame.

We found Jacob Hudson.

He lay on a mattress on the floor, a small man under a blanket. His eyes were closed. His sallow complexion indicated plainly that he hadn't seen the sun in some time.

Jennings stared wide-eyed. "Is he alive?" Then he knelt down. "He's breathing, but he looks unconscious. Maybe drugged. We'd better radio for an ambulance."

When the medics arrived, two orderlies lifted Hudson onto a stretcher and carried him down the stairs.

Jennings watched the ambulance pull away. "How long do you suppose she kept him in there? The whole three years nobody's seen him? Why didn't she just kill him?"

I didn't have the answer. "Maybe she just couldn't bring herself to go that far. Or maybe she needed him to sign the checks."

While Jennings radioed headquarters, I went back upstairs with a flashlight and examined the closet. It was just big enough to hold the mattress. The light socket overhead contained no bulb.

Had it been pitch-black in here, or had there been at least a sliver of light from under the door? What had it been like to lie here day after day in the darkness?

I directed the beam of my flashlight around the small room, pausing at a spot above the door frame.

I found something.

When I signed out at headquarters at the end of my shift, I went back to my apartment to make my supper. I detest eating out.

I have been with the Police Department for almost ten years, all of that time in squad cars. My record is good. I am diligent, prompt, and dependable, and I will undoubtedly be promoted to plainclothes in another year or so. And in fifteen years more I will retire, probably as a detective-sergeant.

Both of my grandfathers were policemen and one of them retired as a precinct captain. My father was a sergeant when he was killed in the line of duty while attempting to arbitrate a domestic quarrel.

I have a brother and a sister. Both of them are with the department and I would not be at all surprised if Emily became the first female police chief in the history of our city. She is hard-working, driving, and dedicated.

In short, I come from a police family.

To my brother and my sister, police work is more than a job. It is a way of life. On the other hand, I chose police work because of family pressure and our liberal retirement system.

I had, of course, been thinking about Hudson all day. As far as Jennings and I were concerned, he was no longer our concern. The men in plainclothes would take over the case.

Had they questioned Hudson already? Or had the doctors at the hospital told them they would have to wait? Had Hudson opened his eyes yet?

When I finished eating, I stacked the dishes in the sink. Usually—during the warm months—I spent the waning hours of the day in my garden.

It is really not much of a plot, certainly not in size. It is twelve by twenty feet and the space was reluctantly allowed to me by my building superintendent. It is bounded on the west by a graveled parking lot and receives a great deal too much shade from surrounding buildings. However, I have made do. The garden has become my place of refreshment, the center of my day.

Today, however, I would do no gardening. Instead I went down to my car and drove to the County General Hospital.

At the main desk I identified myself and Hudson's room number was given to me without hesitation.

I took the elevator to the fourth floor and found room 446. I paused in the open doorway.

Hudson lay on the bed, the coverlet almost up to his chin. His eyes were open and he frowned as he stared at the ceiling.

When he saw me, alarm flashed in his eyes.

"It's all right," I said. "There's nothing to be afraid of." I moved to a chair beside his bed. "Have you been questioned yet?"

He shook his head. "No. I've been too weak to answer any questions." But he had one of his own. "Mrs. Malloy?"

"She's dead. Possibly a heart attack."

He blinked. "Heart attack? She was only in her late thirties. One wouldn't expect someone that young to die of a heart attack."

"No," I said. "One wouldn't."

He put a hand over his eyes and I thought that he wasn't going to speak again, but then he said, "She let me out of that closet just twice a day. For a few minutes. To go to the bathroom and to give me my food. And sometimes she would make me sign blank checks. And letters that she'd type. To my relatives to make them think that I was traveling abroad. I suppose she had some kind of a mail-forwarding arrangement so that they would arrive at their destinations with foreign postmarks on them. Checks, letters, even holiday cards. She forced me to sign them all."

"Forced?"

"Yes. She always had a revolver with her." He put his hand over his eyes for a moment again. "It all started about three years ago when I fired her. She was so inefficient and insolent that one day I just gave her notice. Told her that she was fired."

"But the firing didn't take?"

"No. She simply refused to go. She grabbed me bodily and flung me into that closet and locked the door."

"Didn't you try to escape?"

"Of course. But the closet has a solid oak door. I was never able to get hold of tools or implements of any kind. And even when she let me out, by no stretch of the imagination could I have overpowered her. You've seen her, haven't you? Really a big woman."

I nodded again. "About once a month she had some cleaning people come into the house. If you'd made some noises, they might have heard you."

He rubbed his neck. "I never heard them. She must have drugged me when she expected them to come to the house. I remember that sometimes I'd go to sleep and wake with the impression that I had slept a long, long time."

I studied him. "Mr. Hudson, you tell an interesting story."

He brightened. "Really?"

"Unfortunately it isn't a true story."

He eyed me warily.

I pulled two keys from my pocket. "I found these lying on the top of the door frame *inside* the closet. One of them fits the closet door and the other the door to the hallway. In other words, Mr. Hudson, you could get out of that closet—and the house, for that matter—anytime you wanted to."

His face lost what little color it had.

"Somehow you got hold of those two keys. When or where I don't know. You could have gotten out, but you didn't. Why not? Did you have other plans? Revenge, perhaps? For what Mrs. Malloy had done to you? Did you sneak out and maybe drop something into her food? Something that would kill her?"

He sat up in quick protest. "But that's absolute nonsense. I would never poison anyone. Certainly not Mrs. Malloy. I insist that you perform an autopsy. On Mrs. Malloy, of course. I'm positive that you will find that she died of something perfectly legal." He thought for a moment and then covered another base. "But *if* she died of poisoning or by some other foul means, I certainly had no part in it."

Funny, but I believed him. I thought there was some other answer to his being in that closet. Something different. Something private. That was why I hadn't shown those keys to anyone else, why I had come here alone. "Why don't you just tell me the truth now, Mr. Hudson? The whole truth."

He closed his eyes to regroup his thoughts and then said, "She was insane."

"Mrs. Malloy?"

"Oh, no. Not Mrs. Malloy. She was in perfect possession of her senses. Very dependable and conscientious. I was referring to my mother. She died six years ago."

He decided to make himself more comfortable by adjusting the hospital bed so that he could sit up with back support. "It all began when I was nine years old. My father was killed in an automobile accident while driving me to a cub scout meeting. I received only superficial bruises. My mother took his death extremely hard and she blamed me for it. After all, it had been my idea to join the cub scouts.

"She had never been the most stable personality to begin with, but now she began having spells. Violent spells during which she would beat me. Thoroughly.

"I tried to keep away from her as much as possible, especially since there was no way to anticipate when one of these spells would occur. And when they did and I wasn't immediately available, she would come looking for me. Literally search the house and usually she found me. I tried hiding place after hiding place without much success until one day I happened on that third-floor bedroom and saw the closet door with the key in the lock. I hid inside the closet, locking the door from the inside.

"Her search brought her into the room. She even tried the closet-door knob, but apparently she assumed that because it was locked, I couldn't have gotten in there in the first place. And she went off searching other places until the spell finally wore off."

He sighed. "Of course, I couldn't avoid her entirely. There were times when she would catch me unawares and give me a beating. Once she came into my bedroom in the middle of the night. After that I couldn't sleep in my bed at all. So I moved a mattress and a pillow into the third-floor closet and spent my nights there.

"I tell you, it was a relief to be sent to boarding school. How I dreaded coming home for holidays and vacations, but my mother insisted. And then, after I graduated from college, I was home and available to her at all times."

I interrupted. "You mean that she was still beating you even when you were an adult?"

He smiled faintly. "As you can see, I am barely five feet tall and weigh less than one hundred pounds. My mother was quite a large

woman, about the size of Mrs. Malloy. The last time she managed
to catch me before I could get to my closet, I was thirty-two years
old. That was a month or so before her death. She was run down by
a delivery truck in the parking lot of a supermarket."

"Why did you stay here? Why didn't you leave?"

"Frankly, I am psychologically incapable of coping with the outside world. I suppose the beatings had something to do with that.
And I had no money in my own name. So I remained here and tried
to keep alert."

He smiled again. "I'm ashamed to admit it, but I was elated at
her death. I was now *free*. Yes, completely elated. For perhaps two
or three days. And then I became—well, restless. So I went upstairs,
just to *visit* the closet. And the mattress was still there, and the
pillow, and I thought, why don't I just take a nap? As long as I was
there anyway, and I *was* a little sleepy. And so I entered the closet,
locked the door, and went to sleep."

He shook his head. "Eventually I had to admit that even though
my mother was now dead, the only place where I felt any degree of
security was in that closet."

"You should have tried psychiatric help."

"I did. Immediately. And I continued trying for three years. But
finally I came to the conclusion that they could not help me. I simply
wasn't going to be 'cured.' As the twig is bent, so grows the tree,
and I was too old to be rebent. So I said the hell with the psychiatrists."

"And you retreated into the closet?"

"It wasn't quite that simple. You see, there were the servants. I
had been quite circumspect and secretive about my closet, but now
that I had decided to make my occupancy full time, so to speak, they
would certainly learn about it. And that could lead to all kinds of
complications. Word would certainly get out, especially to my relatives. It would be a good bet—more likely a certainty—that they
would, out of the kindness of their hearts, see to it that I was committed to an institution. They would also very likely volunteer to
administer my estate. No, no. Disappearing into a closet isn't at all
as easy as it appears at first glance."

"You discharged the servants?"

"Yes. But I saw to it that all of them got generous severance
payments and I also got them other commensurate employment.
And to allay suspicions, if they had any, I told them that I had

decided to travel extensively and that therefore I did not think it economically sound to retain a full staff."

"But you kept Mrs. Malloy?"

"Actually she wasn't one of the regular staff at all. I had to go looking for her. I wanted someone who could be trusted to run things around here and keep her mouth shut. After all, it was still necessary to keep up the physical appearance of the estate. I couldn't have the grounds going to ruin, with weeds growing tall and that type of thing, because inevitably that would lead to questions and investigations.

"So I went to a detective agency out East and had a search conducted. I interviewed a number of prospects and Mrs. Malloy appeared to be the most suitable. A splendid woman with no relatives. I paid her a handsome salary to run things here and especially to keep her mouth shut."

"And so you spent these last three years in that closet? Coming out only a few minutes a day to take care of some basic functions?"

"In reality, I was out more than that. I'd say that I daily averaged about four hours out and twenty in. I would go downstairs and watch television or read, because a mind unfed is a mind dead. And sometimes on moonlit nights I would stretch my legs by going for a stroll on the back grounds." He chuckled. "One night I forgot to inform Mrs. Malloy that I was going out and she mistook me for an intruder. She took a shot at me with her revolver. She was quite a watchdog, though a poor shot."

I still found the story a bit difficult to believe. "You spent twenty hours a day just lying there in the dark?"

"I would close my eyes and search the universe for the kernel of existence. It's very elusive, you know. And, of course, I suppose that I *did* do an awful lot of sleeping, or trying to. After all, the human brain isn't geared for too much or too severe thinking."

He sighed. "When you began tapping the hinge bolts out of the door, I was utterly terrified. I suspected that something drastic must have happened to Mrs. Malloy. How could I explain my presence in the closet? I had never even *anticipated* that such an occasion might occur. And I didn't dare tell the truth. So I quickly hid those two keys, because I thought that if anyone searched me, the keys would be embarrassing to explain, and then I just went limp."

"Limp?"

"Yes. I thought that was about the most intelligent thing to do under the circumstances. Go limp. Close my eyes and pretend to be unconscious. Play for time until I could find out what was going on and think of some explanation the world could accept. And so, lying here, I put together the story about Mrs. Malloy imprisoning me. I hope, wherever she is, that she will forgive me."

He closed his eyes. "Now I'll be the subject of newspaper stories and magazine articles and I'll be committed to a mental institution."

The eyes opened for a moment of hope. "You don't suppose they'll let me have my own closet?"

It was a beautiful Sunday and I worked in the garden until nearly noon. Then I went inside, washed my hands, and made myself a sandwich.

When I finished eating it, I made another, poured a glass of milk, and put them both, along with three apricots and some vitamin tablets, on a tray.

I took the tray upstairs to the third-floor bedroom and put it on a small table next to the closet door. I rapped twice to let Hudson know that his lunch was ready and the milk cold.

I picked up the two checks he'd signed—one to cover a payment to his book club and the other my salary for the month of July.

It has been nearly a year since I resigned from the Police Department and, as far as Hudson's relatives—or the world, for that matter—are concerned, he is now in India and Sri Lanka.

I would probably see Hudson at ten-thirty tonight. The late TV movie was going to be a Western and he was rather partial to John Wayne.

I went back outside into the warm garden.

My closet, I suppose.

John Dickson Carr

The Crime in Nobody's Room

Bands were playing and seven suns were shining; but this took place entirely in the head and heart of Mr. Ronald Denham. He beamed on the car-park attendant at the Regency Club, who assisted him into the taxi. He beamed on the taxi driver. He beamed on the night porter who helped him out at his flat in Sloane Street, and he felt an irresistible urge to hand banknotes to everyone in sight.

Now, Ronald Denham would have denied that he had taken too many drinks. It was true that he had attended an excellent bachelor party, to celebrate Jimmy Bellchester's wedding. But Denham would have maintained that he was upheld by spiritual things; and he had proved his exalted temperance by leaving the party at a time when many of the guests were still present.

As he had pointed out in a speech, it was only a month before his own wedding to Miss Anita Bruce. Anita, in fact, lived in the same block of flats and on the same floor as himself. This fact gave him great pleasure on the way home. Like most of us, Denham in this mood felt a strong urge to wake people up in the middle of the night and talk to them. He wondered whether he ought to wake up Anita. But in his reformed state he decided against it, and felt like a saint. He would not even wake up Tom Evans, who shared the flat with him—though that stern young businessman usually worked so late at the office that Denham got in before he did.

At a few minutes short of midnight, then, Denham steered his way into the foyer of Medici Court. Pearson, the night porter, followed him to the automatic lift.

"Everything all right, sir?" inquired Pearson in a stage whisper. Denham assured him that it was, and that he was an excellent fellow.

"You—er—don't feel like singing, do you, sir?" asked Pearson with some anxiety.

"As a matter of fact," said Denham, who had not previously considered this, "I do. You are full of excellent ideas, Pearson. But let us sing nothing improper, Pearson. Let it be something of noble sentiment, like—"

"Honestly, sir," urged Pearson, "if it was me, I wouldn't do it. *He's* upstairs, you know. We thought he was going to Manchester this afternoon, to stay a week, but he changed his mind. He's upstairs now."

This terrible hint referred to the autocrat of Medici Court, Cellini Court, Bourbon Court, and half a dozen other great hives. Sir Rufus Armingdale, high khan of builders, not only filled London with furnished flats which really were the last word in luxury at a low price; he showed his pride in his own merchandise by living in them.

"No special quarters for me," he was quoted as saying, with fist upraised for emphasis. "No castle in Surrey or barracks in Park Lane. Just an ordinary flat; and not the most expensive of 'em, either. That's where I'm most comfortable and that's where you'll find me."

Considering all the good things provided in Armingdale's Furnished Flats, even his autocratic laws were not much resented. Nor could anyone resent the fact that all the flats in a given building were furnished exactly alike, and that the furniture must be kept in the position Rufus Armingdale gave it. Medici Court was "Renaissance," as Bourbon Court was "Louis XV": a tower of rooms like luxurious cells, and only to be distinguished from each other by an ornament on a table or a picture on a wall.

But Sir Rufus's leases even discouraged pictures. Considering that he was something of an art collector himself and had often been photographed in his own flat with his favorite Greuze or Corot, some annoyance was felt at this. Sir Rufus Armingdale did not care. You either leased one of his flats or you didn't. He was that sort of man.

Otherwise, of course, Ronald Denham's adventure could not have happened. He returned from the bachelor party; he took Pearson's advice about the singing; he went up in the automatic lift to the second floor; and he walked into what the champagne told him was his own flat.

That he went to the second floor is certain. Pearson saw him put his finger on the proper button in the lift. But nothing else is certain, since the hall upstairs was dark. Pushing open a door—either his key fitted it or the door was open—Denham congratulated himself on getting home.

Also, he was a little giddy. He found himself in the small foyer, where lights were on. After a short interval he must have moved into the sitting room, for he found himself sitting back in an armchair and contemplating familiar surroundings through a haze.

Lights were turned on here as well: yellow-shaded lamps, one with a pattern like a dragon on the shade.

Something began to trouble him. There was something odd, he thought, about those lampshades. After some study it occurred to him that he and Tom Evans hadn't any lampshades like that. They did not own any bronze bookends, either. As for the curtains . . .

Then a picture on the wall swam out of oblivion and he stared at it. It was a small dull-colored picture over the sideboard. And it penetrated into his mind at last that he had got into the wrong flat.

Everything now showed itself to him as wrong: it was as though a blur had come into focus.

"Here, I'm sorry!" he said aloud, and got up.

There was no reply. The heinousness of his offense partly steadied him. Where in the name of sanity was he? There were only three other flats on the second floor. One of these was Anita Bruce's. Of the others, one was occupied by a brisk young newspaperman named Conyers, and the other by the formidable Sir Rufus Armingdale.

Complete panic caught him. He felt that at any moment a wrathful occupant might descend on him, to call him a thief at worst or a snooper at best. Turning round to scramble for the door he almost ran into another visitor in the wrong flat.

This visitor sat quietly in a tall chair near the door. He was a thin, oldish, well dressed man, wearing thick-lensed spectacles, and his head was bent forward as though in meditation. He wore a soft hat and a thin oilskin waterproof colored green: a jaunty and bilious-looking coat for such a quiet figure. The quiet light made it gleam.

"Please excuse—" Denham began in a rush, and talked for some seconds before he realized that the man had not moved.

Denham stretched out his hand. The coat was one of those smooth, almost seamless American waterproofs, yellowish outside and green inside; and for some reason the man was now wearing it inside out. Denham was in the act of telling him this when the head lolled, the smooth oilskin gleamed again, and he saw that the man was dead.

Tom Evans, stepping out of the lift at a quarter past one, found the hall of the second floor in complete darkness. When he had turned on the lights from a switch beside the lift, he stopped short and swore.

Evans, lean and swarthy, with darkish eyebrows merging into a single line across his forehead, looked a little like a Norman baron in a romance. Some might have said a robber baron, for he carried a briefcase and was a stern man of business despite his youth. But what he saw now made him momentarily forget his evening's work. The hall showed four doors, with their microscopic black numbers, set some distance apart. Near the door leading to Anita Bruce's flat, Ronald Denham sat hunched on an oak settle. There was a lump at the base of his skull and he was breathing in a way Evans did not like.

It was five minutes more before Denham had been whacked and pounded into semiconsciousness and to such a blinding headache that its pain helped to revive him. First he became aware of Tom's lean, hook-nosed face bending over him and Tom's usual fluency at preaching.

"I don't mind you getting drunk," the voice came to him dimly. "In fact, I expected it. But at least you ought to be able to carry your liquor decently. What the devil have you been up to, anyway? Hoy!"

"He had his raincoat on inside out," was the first thing Denham said. Then memory came back to him like a new headache or a new explosion, and he began to pour out the story.

"—and I tell you there's a dead man in one of those flats! I think he's been murdered. Tom, I'm not drunk; I swear I'm not. Somebody sneaked up behind and bashed me over the back of the head just after I found him."

"Then how did you get out here?"

"Oh, God, how should I know? Don't argue; help me up. I suppose I must have been dragged out here. If you don't believe me, feel the back of my head. Just feel it."

Evans hesitated. He was always practical, and there could be no denying the bruise. He looked uncertainly up and down the hall.

"But who is this dead man?" he demanded. "And whose flat is he in?"

"I don't know. It was an oldish man with thick glasses and a green raincoat. I never saw him before. Looked a bit like an American, somehow."

"Nonsense! Nobody wears a green raincoat."

"I'm telling you, he was wearing it inside out. If you ask me why, I'm going to bat my head against the wall and go to sleep again." He wished he could do this, for he couldn't see straight and his head felt like a printing press in full blast. "We ought to be able to identify the flat easily enough. I can give a complete description of it—"

He paused, for two doors had opened simultaneously in the hall.

Anita Bruce and Sir Rufus Armingdale came out in different stages of anger or curiosity at the noise.

If Evans had been more of a psychologist he might have anticipated the effect this would have on them. As it was, he stood looking from one to the other, thinking whatever thoughts you care to attribute to him. For he was an employee of Sir Rufus, as manager of the Sloane Square office of Armingdale Flats, and he could risk no trouble.

Anita seemed to take in the situation at a glance. She was small, dark, plump, and fluffy-haired. She was wearing a negligee and smoking a cigarette. Seeing the expressions of the other three, she removed the cigarette from her mouth in order to smile. Sir Rufus Armingdale did not look so much formidable as fretful. He had one of those powerful faces whose features seem to have run together like a bulldog's. But the old dressing gown, fastened up at the throat as though he were cold, took away the suggestion of an autocrat and made him only a householder.

He breathed through his nose, rather helplessly, until he saw an employee. His confidence returned.

"Good morning, Evans," he said. "What's the meaning of this?"

Evans risked it. "I'm afraid it's trouble, sir. Mr. Denham—well, he's found a dead man in one of the flats."

"Ron!" cried Anita.

"A dead man," repeated Armingdale, without surprise. "Where?"

"In one of the flats. He doesn't know which."

"Oh? Why doesn't he know which?"

"He's got a frightful bump on the back of his head," said Anita, exploring. She looked back over her shoulder and spoke swiftly. "It's quite all right, Tom. Don't get excited. He's d-r-u-n-k."

"I am not drunk," said Denham, with tense and sinister calmness. "May I also point out that I am able to read and write and that I have not had words spelled out in front of me since I was four years old? Heaven give me s-t-r-e-n-g-t-h! I can describe the place."

He did so. Afterward there was a silence. Anita, her eyes shining curiously, dropped her cigarette on the autocrat's hardwood floor and ground it out. The autocrat seemed too abstracted to notice.

"Ron, old dear," Anita said, going over and sitting down beside him, "I'll believe you if you're as serious as all that. But you ought to know it isn't *my* flat."

"And I can tell you it isn't mine," grunted Armingdale. "There certainly isn't a dead man in it. I've just come from there, and I know."

If they had not known Armingdale's reputation so well they might have suspected him of trying to make a joke. But his expression belied it as well. It was heavy and lowering, with a suggestion of the bulldog.

"This picture you say you saw," he began. "The one over the sideboard. Could you describe it?"

"Yes, I think so," said Denham desperately. "It was a rather small portrait of a little girl looking sideways over some roses, or flowers of some kind. Done in that greyish-brown stuff; I think they call it sepia."

Armingdale stared at him.

"Then I know it isn't mine," Armingdale said. "I never owned a sepia in my life. If this man is telling the truth there's only one flat left. I think I shall just take the responsibility of knocking, and—"

His worried gaze moved down toward the door of the flat occupied by Mr. Hubert Conyers, of the *Daily Record*. But it was unnecessary to knock at the door. It opened with such celerity that Denham wondered whether anyone had been looking at them through the slot of the letterbox, and Hubert Conyers stepped out briskly. He was an unobtrusive, sandy-haired little man, very different from Denham's idea of a journalist. His only extravagance was a taste for blended shadings in his clothes, from suit to shirt to necktie, though he usually contrived to look rumpled. He was always obliging, and as busy as a parlor clock. But his manner had a subdued persuasiveness which could worm him through narrower places than you might have imagined.

He came forward drawing on his coat and with a deft gesture he got into the middle of the group.

"Sorry, sorry, sorry," he began, seeming to propitiate everyone at once. "I couldn't help overhearing, you know. Good evening, Sir Rufus. The fact is, it's not my flat, either. Just now the only ornaments in my sitting room are a lot of well filled ashtrays and a bottle of milk. Come and see, if you like."

There was a silence, while Conyers looked anxious.

"But it's got to be somebody's flat!" snapped Sir Rufus Armingdale, with a no-nonsense air. "Stands to reason. A whole confounded sitting room can't vanish like smoke. Unless—stop a bit—unless Mr. Denham got off at some other floor?"

"I don't know. I may have."

"And I don't mind admitting—" said Armingdale, hesitating as everyone looked at him curiously. The autocrat seemed worried. "Very well. The fact is, *I've* got a picture in my flat something like the one Mr. Denham described. It's Greuze's *Young Girl with Primroses*. But mine's an oil painting, of course. Mr. Denham is talking about a sepia drawing. That is, if he really saw anything. Does this dead man exist at all?"

Denham's protestations were cut short by the hum of an ascending lift. But it was not the ordinary lift in front of them; it was the service lift at the end of the hall. The door was opened and the cage grating pulled back, to show the frightened face of the night porter.

"Sir," said Pearson, addressing Armingdale as though he were beginning an oration. "I'm glad to see *you*, sir. You always tell us that if something serious happens we're to come straight to you instead of the manager. Well, I'm afraid this is serious. I—the fact is, I found something in this lift."

Denham felt that they were being haunted by that phrase, "the fact is." Everybody seemed to use it. He recalled a play in which it was maintained that anyone who began a sentence like this was usually telling a lie. But he had not time to think about this, for they had found the elusive dead man.

The unknown man lay on his face in one corner of the lift. A light in the roof of the steel cage shone down on his grey felt hat, on an edge of his thick spectacles, and on his oilskin waterproof. But the coat was no longer green, for he was now wearing it right-side-out in the ordinary way.

Anita, who had come quietly round beside Denham, seized his arm. The night porter restrained Tom Evans as the latter bent forward.

"I shouldn't touch him, sir, if I was you. There's blood."

"Where?"

Pearson indicated a stain on the grey-rubber floor. "And if I'm any judge, sir, he died of a stab through the heart. I—I lifted him up a bit. But I don't see any kind of knife that could have done it."

"Is this the man you saw?" Armingdale asked Denham quietly.

Denham nodded. Something tangible, something to weigh and handle, seemed to have brought the force back to Armingdale's personality.

"Except," Denham added, "that he's now wearing his raincoat right-side-out. Why? Will somebody tell me that? Why?"

"Never mind the raincoat," Anita said close to his ear. "Ron, you don't know him, do you? You'll swear you don't know him?"

He was startled. She had spoken without apparent urgency and so low that the others might not have heard her. But Denham, who knew her so well, knew there was urgency behind the unwinking seriousness of her eyes. Unconsciously she was shaking his arm. His wits had begun to clear, despite the pain in his skull, and he wondered.

"No, of course I don't know him. Why should I?"

"Nothing! Nothing at all. Ss-t!"

"Well, I know him," said Hubert Conyers.

Conyers had been squatting down at the edge of the lift and craning his neck to get a close view of the body, without touching it. Now he straightened up. He seemed so excited that he could barely control himself and his mild eye looked wicked.

"I interviewed him a couple of days ago," said Conyers. "Surely you know him, Sir Rufus?"

" 'Surely' is a large word, young man. No, I do not know him. Why?"

"That's Dan Randolph, the American real-estate king," said Conyers, keeping a watchful eye on Armingdale. "All of you will have heard of him: he's the fellow who always deals in spot cash, even if it's a million. I'd know those spectacles anywhere. He's as nearsighted as an owl. Er—am I correctly informed, Sir Rufus, that he was in England to do some business with you?"

Armingdale smiled bleakly.

"You have no information, man," he said. "And so far as I'm concerned you're not getting any. So that's Dan Randolph! I knew he was in England, but he's certainly not made any business proposition to me."

"Maybe he was coming to do it."

"Maybe he was," said Armingdale, with the same air of a parent to a child. He turned to Pearson. "You say you found him in that lift. When did you find him? And how did you come to find him?"

Pearson was voluble. "The lift was on the ground floor, sir. I just happened to glance through the little glass panel and I see him lying there. So I thought I'd better run the lift up here and get you. As for putting him there—" He pointed to the *Recall* button on the wall outside the lift. "Somebody on any floor, sir, could have shoved him in here, pressed this button, and sent him downstairs. He certainly wasn't put in on the ground floor. Besides, I saw him come into the building tonight."

"Oh?" put in Conyers softly. "When was this?"

"Might have been eleven o'clock, sir."

"Who was he coming to see?"

Pearson shook his head helplessly and with a certain impatience. "These ain't service flats, sir, where you telephone up about every visitor. You ought to know we're not to ask visitors anything unless they seem to need help or it's somebody who has no business here. *I* don't know. He went up in the main lift, that's all I can tell you."

"Well, what floor did he go to?"

"I dunno." Pearson ran a finger under a tight collar. "But excuse me, sir, may I ask a question, if you please? What's wrong exactly?"

"We've lost a room," said Ronald Denham, with inspiration. "Maybe you can help. Look here, Pearson: you've been here in these flats a long time. You've been inside most of them—in the sitting rooms, for instance?"

"I think I can say I've been in all of 'em, sir."

"Good. Then we're looking for a room decorated like this," said Denham. Again he described what he had seen, and Pearson's expression grew to one of acute anguish. He shook his head.

"It's nobody's room, sir," the porter answered simply. "There's not a sitting room like that in the whole building."

At three o'clock in the morning a somber group of people sat in Sir Rufus Armingdale's flat and did not even look at each other. The police work was nearly done. A brisk divisional detective-inspector, accompanied by a sergeant, a photographer, and a large amiable man in a top hat, had taken a statement from each of those concerned. But the statements revealed nothing.

Denham, in fact, had received only one more mental jolt. Entering Armingdale's flat, he thought for a second that he had found the missing room. The usual chairs of stamped Spanish leather, the refectory table, the carved gewgaws greeted him like a familiar nightmare. And over the sideboard hung a familiar picture—that of a small girl looking sideways over an armful of roses.

"That's not it!" said Anita quickly.

"It's the same subject, but it's not the same picture. That's in oils. What sort of game do you suppose is going on in this place?"

Anita glanced over her shoulder. She had dressed before the arrival of the police; and also, he thought, she had put on more makeup than was necessary.

"Quick, Ron, before the others get here. Were you telling the truth?"

"Certainly. You don't think—?"

"Oh, I don't know and I don't care; I just want you to tell me. Ron, you didn't kill him yourself?"

He had not even time to answer before she stopped him. Sir Rufus Armingdale, Conyers, and Evans came through from the foyer and with them was the large amiable man who had accompanied Divisional-Inspector Davidson. His name, it appeared, was Colonel March.

"You see," he explained, with a broad gesture, "I'm not here officially. I happened to be at the theater, and I dropped in on Inspector Davidson for a talk and he asked me to come along. So if you don't like any of my questions just tell me to shut my head. But I do happen to be attached to the Yard—"

"I know you, Colonel," said Conyers, with a crooked grin. "You're the head of the Ragbag Department, D-3. Some call it the Crazy House."

Colonel March nodded seriously. He wore a dark overcoat and had a top hat pushed back on his large head; this, with his florid complexion, sandy mustache, and bland blue eyes, gave him something of the look of a stout colonel in a comic paper. He was smoking a large-bowled pipe with the effect of seeming to sniff smoke from the bowl rather than draw it through the stem. He appeared to be enjoying himself.

"It's a compliment," he assured them. "After all, somebody has got to sift all the queer complaints. If somebody comes in and reports, say, that the Borough of Stepney is being terrorized by a blue pig, I've got to decide whether it's a piece of lunacy or a mistake or a hoax or a serious crime. Otherwise, good men would only waste their time. You'd be surprised how many such complaints there are. But I was thinking, and so was Inspector Davidson, that you had a very similar situation here. If you wouldn't mind a few extra questions—"

"As many as you like," said Sir Rufus Armingdale. "Provided somebody's got a hope of solving this damned—"

"As a matter of fact," said Colonel March, frowning, "Inspector Davidson has reason to believe that it is already solved. A good man, Davidson."

There was a silence. Something unintentionally sinister seemed to have gathered in Colonel March's affable tone. For a moment nobody dared ask what he meant.

"Already solved?" repeated Hubert Conyers.

"Suppose we begin with you, Sir Rufus," said March with great courtesy. "You have told the Inspector that you did not know Daniel Randolph personally. But it seems to be common knowledge that he was in England to see you."

Armingdale hesitated.

"I don't know his reasons. He may have been here to see me, among other things. Probably was. He wrote to me about it from America. But he hadn't approached me yet, and I didn't approach him first. It's bad business."

"What was the nature of this business, Sir Rufus?"

"He wanted to buy an option I held on some property in—never mind where. I'll tell you in private, if you insist."

"Was a large sum involved?"

Armingdale seemed to struggle with himself. "Four thousand, more or less."

"So it wasn't a major business deal. Were you going to sell?"

"Probably."

Colonel March's abstracted eye wandered to the picture over the sideboard.

"Now, Sir Rufus, that Greuze—*Young Girl with Primroses*. I think it was recently reproduced, in its natural size, as a full-page illustration in the *Metropolitan Illustrated News?*"

"Yes, it was," said Armingdale. He added, "In—sepia."

Something about this afterthought made them all move forward to look at him. It was like the puzzle of a half truth: nobody knew what it meant.

"Exactly. Just two more questions. I believe that each of these flats communicates with a fire escape leading down into the mews behind?"

"Yes. What of it?"

"Will the same key open the front door of each of the flats?"

"No, certainly not. All the lock patterns are different."

"Thank you. Now, Mr. Conyers—a question for you. Are you married?"

Hitherto Conyers had been regarding him with a look of watchful expectancy, like an urchin about to smash a window and run. Now he scowled.

"Married? No."

"And you don't keep a valet?"

"The answer to that, Colonel, is loud and prolonged laughter. Honestly, I don't like your 'social' manner. Beston, our crime news man, knows you. And it's always, 'Blast you, Beston, if you print one hint about the Thing-gummy case I'll have your hide.' What difference does it make whether I'm married or not or whether I have a valet or not?"

"A great deal," said March seriously. "Now, Miss Bruce. What is your occupation, Miss Bruce?"

"I'm an interior decorator," answered Anita. She began to laugh. It may have been with a tinge of hysteria, but she sat back in a tall chair and laughed until there were tears in her eyes.

"I'm terribly sorry," she went on, holding out her hand as though to stop them, "but don't you see? The murder was done by an interior decorator. That's the whole secret."

Colonel March cut short Armingdale's shocked protest.

"Go on," he said sharply.

"I thought of it first off. Of course, there's no 'vanishing room.' Some sitting room has just been redecorated. All the actual furnishings—tables and chairs and sideboards—are just the same in every room. The only way you can tell them apart is by small movable things—pictures, lampshades, bookends—which could be changed in a few minutes.

"Ron accidentally walked into the murderer's flat just after the murderer had killed that old man. That put the murderer in a pretty awful position. Unless he killed Ron, too, he was caught with the body and Ron could identify his flat. But he thought of a better way. He sent that man's body down in the lift and dragged Ron out into the hall. Then he simply altered the decorations of his flat. Afterwards he could sit down and dare anyone to identify it as the place where the body had been."

Anita's face was flushed with either defiance or fear.

"Warm," said Colonel March. "Unquestionably warm. That is why I was wondering whether you couldn't tell us what really happened."

"I don't understand you."

"Well, there are objections to the redecoration. You've got to suppose that nobody had ever been in the flat before and seen the way it was originally decorated. You've also got to suppose that the murderer could find a new set of lampshades, pictures, and bookends in the middle of the night—haven't you got it the wrong way round?"

"The wrong way round?"

"Somebody," said March, dropping his courtesy, "prepared a dummy room to begin with. He put in the new lampshades, the bookends, the copy of a well known picture, even a set of new curtains. He entertained Randolph there. Afterwards, of course, he simply removed the knick-knacks and set the place right again. But it was the dummy room into which Ronald Denham walked. That, Mr. Denham, was why you did not recognize—"

"Recognize what?" roared Denham. "Where was I?"

"In the sitting room of your own flat," said Colonel March gravely. "If you had been sober you might have made a mistake; but you were so full of champagne that your instinct brought you home after all."

There were two doors in the room and the blue uniform of a policeman appeared in each. At March's signal, Inspector Davidson stepped forward. He said, "Thomas Evans, I arrest you for the murder of Daniel Randolph. I have to warn you that anything you say will be taken down in writing and may be used in evidence at your trial."

"Oh, look here," protested Colonel March, when they met in Armingdale's flat next day, "the thing was simple enough. We had twice as much trouble over that kid in Bayswater who pinched all the oranges. And you had all the facts.

"Evans, as one of Sir Rufus's most highly placed and trusted employees, was naturally in a position to know all about the projected business deal with Randolph. And so he planned an ingenious swindle. A swindle, I am certain, was all he intended.

"Now you, Sir Rufus, had intended to go to Manchester yesterday afternoon, and remain there for a week. Mr. Denham heard that from the night porter, when he was advised against singing. That would leave your flat empty. Evans telephoned to Randolph, posing as you. He asked Randolph to come round to your flat at eleven o'clock at night and settle the deal. He added that you *might* be called away to Manchester; but, in that event, his secretary would have the necessary papers ready and signed.

"It would have been easy. Evans would get into your empty flat by way of the fire escape and the window. He would pose as your secretary. Randolph—who, remember, always paid spot cash even if it involved a million—would hand over a packet of banknotes for a forged document.

"Why should Randolph be suspicious of anything? He knew, as

half the newspaper-reading world knows, that Sir Rufus lived on the second floor of Medici Court. He had seen photographs of Sir Rufus with his favorite Greuze over the sideboard. Even if he asked the hall porter for directions he would be sent to the right flat. Even if the hall porter said Sir Rufus was in Manchester, the ground had been prepared and Randolph would ask for Sir Rufus's secretary.

"Unfortunately, a hitch occurred. Sir Rufus decided not to go to Manchester. He decided it yesterday afternoon, after all Evans' plans had been made and Randolph was due to arrive. But Evans needed that money; as we have discovered today, he needed it desperately. He wanted that four thousand pounds.

"So he hit on another plan. Sir Rufus would be at home and his flat could not be used. But, with all the rooms exactly alike except for decorations, why not an *imitation* of Sir Rufus's flat? The same plan would hold good, except that Randolph would be taken to the wrong place. He would come up in the lift at eleven. Evans would be waiting with the door of the flat open and would take him to a place superficially resembling Sir Rufus's. The numbers on the doors are very small and Randolph, as we know, was so nearsighted as to be almost blind.

"If Evans adopted some disguise, however clumsy, he could never afterwards be identified as the man who swindled Randolph. And he ran no risk in using the flat he shared with Denham."

Anita interposed. "Of course!" she said. "Ron was at a bachelor party and ordinarily it would have kept him there whooping until two or three o'clock in the morning. But he reformed and came home early."

Denham groaned. "But I still can't believe it," he insisted. "Tom Evans? A murderer?"

"He intended no murder," said Colonel March. "But, you see, Randolph suspected something. Randolph showed that he suspected. And Evans, as a practical man, had to kill him. You can guess why Randolph suspected."

"Well?"

"Because Evans is colorblind," said Colonel March.

"It's too bad," Colonel March went on sadly, "but the crime was from the first the work of a colorblind man. Now, none of the rest of you could qualify for that deficiency. As for Sir Rufus, I can think of nothing more improbable than a colorblind art collector—unless it is a colorblind interior decorator. Mr. Conyers here shows by the blended hues of brown or blue in his suits, shirts, and ties that he has.a fine eye for color effect; and he possesses no wife or valet to choose them for him.

"But Evans? He is not only partially but wholly colorblind. You gave us a spirited account of it. Randolph's body was sent up in the lift by Pearson. When Evans stepped forward, Pearson warned him not to touch the body, saying that there was blood. Evans said, 'Where?'—though he was staring straight down in a small brightly lighted lift at a red bloodstain on a grey-rubber floor. Red on any surface except green or yellow is absolutely invisible to colorblind men.

"That was also the reason why Randolph's waterproof was put on inside out. Randolph had removed his hat and coat when he first came into the flat. After Evans had stabbed him with a clasp-knife, Evans put the hat and coat back on the body previous to disposing of it. But he could not distinguish between the yellow outside and the green inside of that seamless oilskin.

"You, Mr. Denham, let yourself into the flat with your own key—which in itself told us the location of the 'vanished' room, for no two keys are alike. I also think that Miss Bruce could have told us all along where the vanished room was. I am inclined to suspect she saw Randolph going into your flat and was afraid you might be concerned in the murder."

"Oh, well," said Anita philosophically.

"Anyway, you spoke to a corpse about his coat being inside out; and Evans rectified the error before he put the body in the lift. He had to knock you out, of course. But he genuinely didn't want to hurt you. He left the building by way of the fire escape into the mews. He disposed of his stage properties, though he was foolish enough to keep the money and the clasp-knife on his person, where they were found when we searched him. When he came back here, he used the main lift in the ordinary way as though he were returning from his office.

"And he was genuinely concerned when he found you still unconscious on the bench in the hall."

There was a silence, broken by Armingdale's snort.

"But colorblindness! What's that got to do with the solution? How did you come to think the murderer must have been colorblind to begin with?"

Colonel March turned to stare at him. Then he shook his head, with a slow and dismal smile.

"Don't you see it even yet?" he asked. "That was the starting point.

We suspected it for the same reason Randolph suspected an imposture. Poor old Randolph wasn't an art critic. Any sort of colored daub, in the ordinary way, he would have swallowed as the original *Young Girl with Primroses* he expected to see. But Evans didn't allow for the one thing even a nearsighted man does know: color. In his effort to imitate the decorations of Sir Rufus's flat the fool hung up as an oil painting nothing more than a sepia reproduction out of an illustrated weekly."

Lilly Carlson

Locked Doors

November 1982

I'm writing at my desk. It's 7:00 P.M. and I've broken my schedule again. I need a schedule. Three hours writing in the morning, three pages completed. One hour of reading. Six days a week, every week. But I cheat. I write three hours, then three more. I'm not supposed to work at night. I should relax then, take a bath. But here I am. Work controls fear.

Locked doors.

Through the window facing my desk the rising moon is almost full.

I live on a small island in Puget Sound, in a whitewashed, shuttered town by the sea. A writer, I'm divorced, with two boys. Ezra is ten, Sammy nine. We have a parakeet named Sondheim and a shepherd called Dog.

The children are upstairs, waiting for me to come read to them. Ezra is on the phone to his father in Los Angeles. Sammy is taking a shower.

Locked doors.

It's 7:30. I sit on my big bed, a child on each side of me. We're reading *Treasure Island*. As I read, I think about tomorrow's lunch. The adoption-homefinder is coming over from the mainland. Sitting at the round oak table in my sunny kitchen, she will question me as she chews her quiche: How much money do you have? Do you date? How do you manage alone? Why do you want to adopt this child?

I'll answer with enthusiasm and candor. Inside, I'll be screaming: Who are you? What allows you to question me? I saved this child, not you. For the first five years of his life, the people here saw what was going on and did nothing. Why? In my first conversation with a social worker, she asked me, "Do you know what you're getting into? The people here take care of their own. *And* she's rich."

121

No one would have anything to do with them.

The first time Sammy called me he was five. Ezra and I had just moved here from Los Angeles . . .

He called at midnight, asking if he could spend the night with me and Ezra (they'd met in the playground). I heard his mother laughing in the background, then a glass breaking . . .

From that call to the others:

"Marta? This is Sammy," he'd say. "Can I come over, please?"

"Marta? This is Sammy. I was wondering if I could come over for the night."

"Marta? This is Sammy. Do you think I could spend the weekend with you?"

Again and again I said no. But after a few weeks I began to question people. I asked the principal. I asked the pediatrician. I asked everyone I met: Who are Sammy and Christine?

And everyone said: Stay away from them. Don't. Do *not* get involved.

But the phone kept ringing. "Marta? This is Sammy . . ."

Locked doors.

I began to get to know them. Ezra invited Sammy over for his birthday. When Christine came to pick him up, she was drunk. She invited me to her house. We all spent time together. Later, I drove her around when her license was revoked.

It took over a year, but late one December evening two and a half years ago I went with a social worker, two policemen, and a Court Order to Christine's house on the cliffs. When I left, Sammy was with me.

He got into the car and said, "I never want to see her again."

That night the phone kept ringing: Thank God you did something, we've known for years . . . The stories I could tell you . . . Why, even before he was born . . . Let us know if there's anything we can do to help.

Oh, there was a lot they could have done to help, but they didn't. Not before. Not after.

Locked doors.

The Court ordered visits between Sammy and Christine. Christine arrived drunk. She broke furniture, slapped Ezra. She slugged a social worker, breaking her wrist. The worker didn't press charges. She attacked her plumber with a knife. He didn't press charges, either. We've gone to Court nine times in thirty months. We go again in two weeks.

Christine writes to Sammy that she is spending a lot of time with her dead father.

Our doors are locked.

She has made two kidnaping attempts. She threatens to burn down the house. I carry a knife in my hip pocket. I don't think about what I might do with it. I just carry it.

8:30. I have finished reading to the children and sent them to bed. I search my diaries, looking for the entry right before the doors had to be locked.

November 24, 1979

Christine called early this afternoon.

"Sammy sleeps with me," she said. "What do you think of that?"

"I think it's a bad idea."

"Oh? Well, maybe by next year it'll be a bad idea, but he's only seven. And I'd never sleep with him unless I had really thick pajamas on. I mean, if your Ezra spent the night over here, I'd never have *him* in bed with me, except . . . well, Sammy gets embarrassed if he sees me naked. He sleeps with his back to me. *You* know. He doesn't throw his arms or legs around me like a lover or anything. I'm not like my *damned* mother. She had him in *her* bed. She wants to steal him from me. She was seducing him. I mean, she slept in the same *bed* with him! She always has to have every man she sees. She has to have them all."

Her speech was slurred.

This evening she called back.

"Guess who wants to come visit you?" she shouted.

"Sammy." No surprise there. She always dumps him with me when she wants to go out. Last time she left him here for five days.

"You got it!" she crowed.

Going down the narrow tree-lined driveway to Christine's beach house was nearly impossible. Two bikes, first hers, then Sammy's, lay in the road. I drove around them and got out. I couldn't smell the ocean for the stench of rotting food. I walked past the overturned garbage pails, through trash spilled over the steps. I knocked.

Inside, I heard her yelling. "Tell her to wait! Goddammit, tell her to effing *wait!*"

I opened the door. "Can I come in?"

"Sure, sure." She smiled at me. "Come in."

The door opened into what should have been the living room. Though the house had nine other rooms, this room served as kitchen, living room, dining room, and bedroom for both Sammy and Christine. There was no couch—only a small double bed with an ornate brass headboard pushed against the far wall under plastic-covered windows.

The one chair, a mahogany Chippendale with a threadbare seat, was piled with clothes. Pots were all over the floor, a chicken carcass half out of one, grease puddled around it.

Christine was on the bed. She was tickling Sammy, a drink in one hand, skirt hiked to her hips. She wore high-heeled red-leather boots. Sammy was naked.

"Hi," she said, toasting me.

Sammy grabbed at the sheet, trying to wrap it around himself.

"Don't cover yourself up!" his mother yelled. "Your body is beautiful! *Everybody's* body is beautiful! Isn't everybody's body beautiful, Marta?" She winked at me. "Hi," she whispered.

"Hi. Sam, get ready."

"I don't know where my pants are." He pushed his mother's hand away from him.

"Well, find some," I said.

He got off the bed and began plowing through the pile of clothes on the chair. He pulled on a pair of brown corduroys, torn at one knee, and a tie-dyed purple T-shirt, two sizes too small. He pushed his bare feet into tattered green sneakers.

Dressed, he walked over to me and rubbed the side of his face along my arm, making mewling sounds. Then he looked up, his bright-blue eyes half hidden under untrimmed bangs.

"Ma-ma-ma-ma-ma," he crooned to me. "Can I bring my sleeping bag, Ma-ma-ma?"

"Go get it."

He disappeared into the unused dining room.

Christine hunched over her drink.

"Will you do me a favor?" she asked. "Take me someplace? I want to go out."

"Where would you like to go?"

"The Copacabana! El Morocco!" She stood up, tottered. "Caesar's Palace!"

She sat back down.

"Sure. And for your second choice?"

"I had a call from a man I used to know. He once asked me to marry him."

"Mom!" Sammy had come back into the room, dragging his sleeping bag and carrying a record.

"I mean it, Weasel. Imagine that! Someone once wanted to marry your mother. Wasn't your father, though. Whoever he was."

"Don't mind her," Sammy said. "She's just depressed." He held the record up to me. "Look at this. This is my *Kiss* album. Ezra likes *Kiss*. He told me so. I want to bring it. Can I? I want to listen to it with Ezra. Can I bring it? Ezra will like it. I'm sure he will. Maybe I'll give it to him. Do you think he'd like that?"

Before I could answer, Christine began talking. "Called Mummy today. I'm giving Sammy to her. I'm giving him away. Maybe I'll give him to you."

Sammy took the record and balanced it on the back of the chair. He smashed his hands down on either side of it in karate chops, over and over.

"You'll break the record, Sam," I told him.

"I'll give him to you, Marta," Christine called from the bed. "You can have him. For keeps. Who'd want him, anyway? Clumsy little—"

Sammy ran around in a tight little circle. He ran up to the refrigerator and kicked the door. Then he kicked the wall.

His mother said, "El Morocco!"

Sam kicked again. I grabbed his arm. "Stop it!"

He bent over and examined the dent he'd made. "Wow!" He was impressed.

"Well," I said. "What did you think would happen?"

"Come on!" Christine shouted.

I was resigned to taking her. If I didn't, she'd appear at my door later and try to spend the night with me.

"Let's go," I said. "Sammy, get in the car."

"My purse!" she cried. "I need my purse!"

I found it. She'd been using it as an ashtray.

"Thank you." She bowed her head to me. "I'll just finish this drink."

"What is it?"

"What is it? I don't know what is it."

"You can get a better one when we go out."

"Right!" She stood up again. Her long thin arms and legs stuck out of a grossly bloated body. She smoothed her silk dress. Its side seam had opened, showing a patch of fat white hip. She staggered. "Hee-hee," she giggled, reaching for me. The inside of her mouth was black. I looked away quickly, looking down at her hand where it grabbed my arm. Her wrist was tattooed with the face of an electrified cat.

I held her hand down the steps and got her into the car. Sammy sat in back, alternately purring and whining.

I backed around the bikes and turned onto Main Street. I looked at Christine. "Where do you want to go?"

"Huh?"

"Tell you what," I offered. "I'll take you to the Belly-Up."

Silence. Then: "Okay! OKAY! You *do* that! Do that to me! Take me to the Belly-Up!"

When we got there, it hadn't opened yet. Sammy began kicking the back of my seat.

"I'll get out!" Christine yelled. "Just leave me here!"

"I'm not going to leave you here in the street at night in the cold with no coat. We'll go to the Ship Ahoy."

By the time we arrived, she was slumped in her seat.

I nudged her. "We're here."

"Where?"

"Ship Ahoy."

"I want to go to the Belly-Up."

"It's closed."

Sammy howled in my ear and kicked harder.

"Already?" Christine asked. "For the season?"

"Until later tonight."

"I thought you meant it was *closed*."

"Marta?" Sammy asked. "Can you take me to your place before you take my mother to any more bars?"

"I'd like to go to the Tower Rubble," Christine said.

"The Tower of Babel *is* closed."

"Marta?" Sammy whined. "Marta? Could you—"

Christine threw her arms out and shouted, "The Copa! I want to go to The Copa!"

"I know. Tell you what. I'll drop Sammy off at my place and then we can decide what to do . . ."

So we drove back to my house. Sammy came inside with me.

Ezra was sitting at the kitchen table, his feet tucked under him. He was making an illustrated list of armaments carried by Allied planes, referring to an open copy of *Aircraft of World War II*.

"What took you so long?" he demanded.

"Say hi to Sam."

Ezra made pistols of his hands, held them one behind the other to indicate a machine gun, and sprayed Sammy with bullets.

"Thirty caliber," he said between rounds. "Small shot."

I sent them upstairs to get into pajamas.

As I set a bag of Oreo cookies next to the TV, I heard Sammy saying, "I brought you my *Kiss* album. Want to hear it? It's real good. Maybe your mom'll let us listen to it when she gets back. Whaddaya think? Huh, Ezra?"

"What do you mean, when she gets back? Mom! You just got in!"

"Just for a minute!" I called up. "I'm taking Christine home—she's not feeling well!"

"She's drunk," Sammy said.

"I've left some Oreos by the TV. You can watch until I get back."

"Oreos! You never let me eat Oreos!"

"I'll be right back."

I climbed into the car. Christine's eyes were closed, but she roused when I slammed the door.

"Where's Sammy? Where's my bear?"

"Inside. Listen, I'm going to drive you home."

"Where's Sammy?"

She asked that several more times on the way back to her place, then nodded out as we turned into her driveway. I dodged the bikes again.

"Christine, we're here."

"Where?"

"Your house."

I got out and opened the door for her. She cracked her head, said she was all right, stumbled up the steps and into the house. She leaned against the sink.

"Where's . . . What's his name? Oh, yes. Sammy. Where's Samuel?"

"At my house."

She reeled. Caught herself on the edge of the sink.

"How is he? Marta. My friend. How-is-he? . . . How is who? . . . How's Sammy? How's my Nudie Bear, my Worm?"

She crashed across the room and fell on the bed, passed out. I covered her up. Tried to get the boots off but couldn't. I turned the light off and left.

At 1 A.M., my phone rang. Christine.
"Is Sammy with you? I can't remember what I did with him. Did I give him away again?"

Two weeks later, I went and got Sammy for the last time.
He said, "I never want to see her again." But every night for months he woke up screaming. He dreamed she'd been kidnaped. He'd try to save her. Every night he failed and woke up shrieking. I'd run to comfort him and he'd tell me the dream, beating himself in the face with his fist. I'd hold him, whispering forgivenesses until his fist opened and he stroked his own forehead back to sleep.
And every night I woke shaking. I dreamed I was Christine. I dreamed the police had come and taken Ezra away. I saw him at a great bleak distance, standing in a dusty field with a Gypsy family. In my sleep, I heard the social workers condemn *me*, the judge order *my* rehabilitation. I promised to do better, all the while knowing that it was hopeless, that I would never have Ezra back, never see or speak with him again.
When I woke, I'd go to the bathroom and vomit.
"Morning sickness," I'd mutter to the toilet. "Just another kind of morning sickness."
                    November 1982

Locked doors.

It's 9:30 P.M. The children are asleep. I go to the kitchen. I have a little notebook there. Blue. I take it out of the drawer and add up all the calories I've eaten today: 645.
I go upstairs and weigh myself. A hundred nine and a half with jeans and sneakers. I get on and off the scale twice to make sure it still works.
The phone rings. My baby-sitter's mother tells me Christine is on-Island. She's seen her hitchhiking from the wharf toward town. She says her daughter can't sit for me now. It's too dangerous.
I take off my clothes and weigh myself again. Five-seven and a hundred and seven. That's too much, I think, too much. It's all just too much.

Locked doors.

I pull on my white terry bathrobe, put my knife in the right pocket, and go downstairs to make my rounds. Front door, locked. Garage door, locked. Back door, locked. Cellar door, locked. Dog inside.

I sit at my desk, editing today's work. I cross out and rearrange, cheating my schedule some more. Then I go to the kitchen and organize the refrigerator shelves: glass jars to the left, cardboard containers to the right, produce in the middle. Before I put the vegetables away, I weigh each bunch twice on the kitchen scale to make sure it still works. I add up the calories.

Locked doors.

I check each door again. I give Dog a bowl of water, cover Sondheim's cage.

I look in on the children. Ezra drowses over *Ivanhoe*. Sammy, curled against Ez's back, sucks his thumb. I carry him to his own bed and tuck him in.

I pour myself a glass of wine and get into bed, placing my knife on the radio alarm. I want to weigh myself again. Instead, I pick up the book I'm reading, Nina Schneider's *The Woman Who Lived in a Prologue*.

The phone rings.

"This is Chris," she whispers. "I'm here."

Georges Simenon

Le Château de L'Arsenic

He hesitated a moment. Then he stood on tiptoe and rang the bell. He was a small man and the bell was situated in an abnormally high position. The Little Doctor knew that he was being watched — not only from inside the château but from the houses in the village, where they must be wondering who, at such a time, would dare to ring this bell.

He was in a village in a clearing in the forest of Orléans, but the clearing was rather small for the château and the few surrounding cottages. The forest seemed to overflow, stifling the village, and you felt that the sun had difficulty in getting through the thick branches. A few thatched roofs, a grocer's shop, an inn — all low, narrow houses — and then the château, too large, too old, falling to ruin and looking like an impoverished aristocrat in rags, but rags which had once been well cut.

On the first floor a curtain moved. A pale face appeared for a moment at one of the windows.

Finally, a servant came to the door. She was a girl of about twenty to twenty-five, pleasant-looking, prettier than you would have expected to find in such a place.

"What do you want?" she asked him.

"I want a word with Monsieur Mordaut."

"Have you an appointment?" she asked.

"No."

"Are you from the Public Prosecutor?"

"No, but if you would be good enough to give him my card —"

She went away. A little later she came back with another servant, a woman of about fifty with a forbidding face.

"What do you want with Monsieur Mordaut?"

Then the Little Doctor, despairing of ever passing this closely guarded gate, spoke frankly. "I have come about the poisonings," he said, with the same charming smile he would have used to give someone a box of chocolates. The face had reappeared behind the first-floor window. Probably Monsieur Mordaut.

"Come in, please," he said. "Is that your car? You had better drive it in, too, or the children will soon be throwing stones at it ..."

The drawing room, like the exterior of the château, was sad and dusty. So also was Monsieur Mordaut in his long, old-fashioned jacket, and with his sunken cheeks covered by a lichenlike, short, dirty grey beard.

"Good morning, sir," said the Little Doctor. "I must apologize for having almost forced an entry, particularly as you have probably never so much as heard of my name."

"No, I haven't," said Monsieur Mordaut with a shake of his head.

"Well, sir, as others are interested in handwriting or palmistry, I have a passion for human problems — for the puzzles which, in their early stages, are nearly always crimes."

"Pray continue."

"I have been extremely interested in the rumors which have been current for some time about you and this château. I came here to discover the truth; that is to say, to find out whether you murdered your aunt Emilie Duplantet; then your wife, who was Félicie Maloir before you married her; and lastly your niece, Solange Duplantet."

It was the first time that the Little Doctor had addressed such a speech to another human being, and his nervousness was aggravated by the fact that he was cut off from the world by a long corridor, with innumerable doors leading off it.

Monsieur Mordaut had not stirred. At the end of a long piece of black cord he swung an old-fashioned eyeglass; his expression was infinitely sad.

"You were right to speak frankly . . . Will you have something to drink?"

In spite of himself, the Little Doctor shivered. It is somewhat disconcerting to be offered a drink by a man you don't know, and whom, in a slightly indelicate fashion, you have just accused of being a poisoner.

"Please don't be afraid. I'll drink out of the bottle before you. Did you come by the village?"

"I stopped at the inn for a minute to book a room."

"That was unnecessary, Monsieur — Monsieur —"

"Jean Dollent."

"I would be honored, Monsieur Dollent, if you would stay here."

Monsieur Mordaut uncorked a dusty bottle of an unusual shape. Almost without thinking, the Little Doctor drank one of the best wines he had ever tasted.

"You must stay here as long as you please. You must have the run of the château, and I will answer all your questions to the best of my ability. Excuse me a moment."

He pulled a long woolen cord and somewhere in the building a reedy bell sounded. Then the old servant who had opened the door to Dollent appeared.

"Ernestine, please lay another place at the table. Also prepare the green room for monsieur. He is to be treated here as if it were his own house, and you must answer any questions he puts to you."

Once more alone with Dollent, he sighed. "You are probably surprised by this reception. But there are, Monsieur Dollent, moments when one jumps at no matter what chance of salvation. If a fortune-teller, a fakir, or a dervish offered to help me, I would treat him in the same way."

He spoke slowly, in a tired voice, fixing his eyes on the worn carpet while, with exaggerated care, he wiped the lens of the eyeglass which he never used. "I am a man who has been pursued from birth by ill luck. If there were competitions of bad luck, championships for bad luck, I would be certain to win. I was born to attract unhappiness, not only to myself, but to all those around me.

"My grandparents were extremely rich. My Grandfather Mordaut built a large part of the Haussmann area in Paris and was worth millions. The day I was born he hanged himself because of some political scandal in which he was involved. As a result of the shock, my mother developed puerperal fever and died within three days. My father tried to make good his father's losses — but of his whole fortune only this château remained. I came here when I was five. Playing in the tower I accidentally set fire to a whole wing, which was destroyed, and with it many objects of value."

This was becoming too much. It was almost comical.

"I could continue the list of my misfortunes indefinitely."

"Excuse me," interposed the Little Doctor, "but it seems to me that up to now those misfortunes seem to have fallen more on others than on yourself."

"Ah! Don't you think that it is just that which is the greatest misfortune? Eight years ago my aunt Duplantet, recently widowed, came to live with us, and six months later she was dead of a heart attack."

"They say that she had been slowly poisoned by arsenic. Hadn't she taken out a life-insurance policy in your favor, and didn't you come into a considerable sum of money through her?"

"A hundred thousand francs — scarcely enough to restore the south tower which was crumbling away. Three years later my wife—"

"Died in her turn, and again of a heart attack. She also had taken out a policy which brought you —?"

"Which brought me the accusations you know of, and a sum of two hundred thousand francs."

"Finally," said the Little Doctor, "a fortnight ago, your niece Solange Duplantet, an orphan, died here, at the age of twenty-eight, of a heart attack, leaving you the Duplantet fortune, which is nearly half a million francs."

"But in property and land — not cash," corrected the strange man.

"This time tongues were really loosened, anonymous letters poured into the Préfecture, and an official investigation was set on foot."

"The police have already been three times and found nothing. On two other occasions I was called to Orléans for questioning. I think I would be lynched if I dared appear in the village."

"Because traces of arsenic were found in the three corpses."

"It seems they always find some."

"You have a son?" asked the Little Doctor rather abruptly.

"Hector, yes. You must have heard of him. As the result of an illness in childhood, the growth of his brain was arrested. He lives here in the castle. At twenty-two he has the body of a man and the intelligence of a child of nine. But still, he's harmless."

"The person who showed me in—Ernestine — has she been here a long time?"

"Always. She was the daughter of my father's gardener. Her parents died and she stayed on."

"She never married?"

"Never."

"And the young woman?"

"Rose," said Monsieur Mordaut with a slight smile, "is Ernestine's niece. For nearly ten years now she has worked here as a maid. When she first came she was a schoolgirl of sixteen."

"Have you any other servants?"

"None. I am not rich enough to live in great style. I live among my books and my works of art. Incidentally, Ernestine hasn't got cancer," said Monsieur Mordaut, "but she talks of nothing else. Since her sister, Rose's mother, died of cancer, she has an unshakable belief that she has also got it. At one moment it's in her back, another in her chest, another in her stomach. She spends half her time consulting doctors, and she's furious that they can't find anything. If she consults you, I advise you —"

But a furious Ernestine now appeared before them.

"Well, are you going to have any lunch or not?"

Monsieur Mordaut turned to the Little Doctor and said sadly: "Please fear nothing. I will eat from each dish and drink out of each bottle before you touch them. It no longer means anything to me. You should know, Doctor, that I am also suffering with my heart. For the last three months I have felt the same symptoms that my aunt, my wife, and my niece all complained of at the beginning of their illnesses."

It really required a very good appetite to eat that meal. The Doctor wondered if he wouldn't have done better to eat and sleep at the inn. Hector ate gluttonously, like a badly brought-up child. It was alarming to watch this large youth with the face of a cunning urchin.

"What do you want to do this afternoon, Doctor?" asked Monsieur Mordaut. "Can I be of any help?"

"I would really like to be free to come and go as I please. I'll look round the grounds. Perhaps I'll ask the servants one or two questions."

And that is where he started. He moved off towards the kitchen where Ernestine was washing the dishes.

"What's he been telling you?" she asked immediately, with the habitual distrust of the peasant. "Did he tell you about my cancer?"

"Yes."

"Ah. He told you it wasn't true, didn't he? But he swears his heart is bad. Well, I'm certain that it's nothing of the sort. He's never had a bad heart. There's nothing wrong with him."

She talked on without stopping her work, and one was conscious of her health and strength. She must once have been a lovely girl, buxom as her niece.

"I wanted to ask you, Doctor. Can cancer be given to people by arsenic or other poisons?"

He didn't want to say yes or no, because it seemed more profitable to play on the old servant's fears.

"What do you feel?" he replied.

"Pains. As if something was being driven into me. Mostly in the bottom of my back, but sometimes also in my stomach."

He mustn't smile. It would make him an enemy.

"I'll examine you, if you like."

"As soon as I've finished the washing up," she replied with alacrity.

The examination had lasted a good quarter of an hour, and each time the Little Doctor showed signs of abandoning it Ernestine called him firmly to order.

"You haven't taken my blood-pressure."

"What was it last time?"

"Minimum nine, maximum fourteen on the Pachot apparatus."

"Well, well!" laughed the Little Doctor. "I see you know your medical terms."

"Indeed I do," she retorted. "You can't buy health, and I want to live to be a hundred and two like my grandmother."

"Have you read any medical books?"

"Gracious, yes. I had some sent from Paris only a month ago."

"I suppose your books mention poisons?"

"Of course, and I won't conceal the fact that I've read every word about them. When there have been three cases under your nose, you learn to look out. Especially when you're in a similar position.

"What did they find when Madame Duplantet died?" she went on. "That she had taken out a life insurance in favor of monsieur. And when his wife died? Another insurance. Well, I'm insured, too."

"And the money goes to your niece, I suppose?"

"No. To Monsieur Mordaut. And it's no small matter. A hundred thousand francs!"

"Your master insured your life for a hundred thousand francs! When was this?"

"At least fifteen years ago. A long time before Madame Duplantet's death so I thought nothing of it at the time."

It was before Madame Duplantet's death. This fact was immediately catalogued in a corner of the Little Doctor's mind.

"Has your master always lived in such a secluded way? Hasn't he ever had any love affairs?"

"Never."

"Er — your niece Rose is young and pretty. Do you think —"

She looked him straight in the eye before replying. "Rose would never allow it."

She had been dressed for some time and had again become the stern old cook. She seemed comforted. Her whole expression proclaimed: "Now you know as much as I do. It was my duty to tell you."

It was a strange home. Built to house at least twenty people, with an endless succession of rooms, corridors, and unexpected staircases and corners, it now sheltered only four inhabitants. And these four people, instead of living close together as would have been expected — if only to give themselves the illusion of company — seemed to have used an extraordinary amount of ingenuity in isolating themselves as much as possible. Ernestine's room was on the second floor at the farthest corner of the left wing.

The Little Doctor went in search of Rose.

He had just made a rapid calculation. Rose had been in the house for about a year when Madame Duplantet had died from arsenic — or from a weak heart. Could one conceive of a poisoner sixteen or seventeen years old?

He listened at the door of Rose's room, heard no sound, and softly turned the handle.

"Well, come on in," she said impatiently. "I've work to do."

It was obvious that she had expected him to come. She had prepared his reception. The room had been tidied and some papers had been burned in the fireplace.

"Monsieur Mordaut gave me permission to question everyone in the house. Do you mind?"

"Go ahead. I know already what you're going to ask me. My aunt told you I was Monsieur Mordaut's mistress, didn't she? The poor thing thinks of nothing else; that's because she's never been married or had a sweetheart."

The Little Doctor looked at the ashes in the fireplace and asked more slowly, "Haven't you a lover or a fiancé?"

"Wouldn't that be natural at my age?"

"Can I know his name?"

"If you can find it out . . . Since you are here to look, look. Now, I must go downstairs, because it's my day to polish the brass. Are you staying here?"

"Yes, I'll stay here if you don't object."

She was annoyed, but she went out and he heard her going down the stairs. She probably didn't know that it is possible to read the writing on burned paper. She hadn't bothered to disperse the ashes and there was an envelope which, being of thicker paper, had remained almost intact. At one corner the word "restante" could be made out, which led him to suppose that Rose fetched her mail from the village post office. On the other side the sender had written his address, of which the words "Colonial Infantry Regiment" and, lower down, "Ivory Coast" could be deciphered.

It was almost certain that Rose had a follower, a fiancé or a lover, who was at present stationed with his regiment in the tropics.

"I'm afraid I'm disturbing you once more, Monsieur Mordaut. You told me this morning that you felt pains from time to time. As a doctor I should like to make sure, above all, that there's no question of slow poisoning."

Without protest and with the trace of a bitter smile the master began to undress.

"For a long time," he sighed, "I have been expecting to suffer the same fate as my wife and aunt. When I saw Solange Duplantet die in her turn . . ."

The consultation lasted half an hour, and the Little Doctor became more and more serious.

"I wouldn't like to say anything definite until I had consulted some colleague with more experience. Nevertheless, the discomfort you have been feeling could be caused by arsenical poisoning."

"I told you so." He was neither indignant nor even afraid.

"One more question. Why did you insure Ernestine's life?"

"Did she tell you about it? Well, it's quite simple. One day, an insurance salesman called. He was a clever young man with a persuasive manner. He pointed out that there were several of us in the house and all of us getting on in years."

"I know exactly the arguments he used. Someone was bound to die first. It would be sad, of course, but why shouldn't it at least help you to restore the castle? If all your family died . . . But, excuse me," the Little Doctor interrupted himself. "Is Hector insured, too?"

"The company won't insure mental deficients. Anyhow, I allowed myself to be persuaded, and I insured Ernestine in spite of her wonderful health."

"Another question. Did you insure yourself?"

This idea seemed to strike him for the first time.

"No," he said in a reflective voice.

Should one treat him as an inhuman monster, or just pity him? Or should one read the greatest cunning into everything he said? Why had he so willingly given the Little Doctor a free hand? Wouldn't a man who was capable of poisoning his wife and two other women also be capable of swallowing poison himself, but in insufficient quantities to do any real harm?

The Little Doctor, overcome by a kind of disgust which his curiosity only just succeeded in dominating, wandered round the château and the grounds. He was standing by the gate, wondering if a stroll to the village wouldn't be a good thing — if only for a change of atmosphere — when sounds of confusion reached him, followed by a loud cry from Ernestine.

He ran round a corner of the château.

Not far from the kitchen was an old barn containing some straw and milking utensils. Inside this building Hector lay dead, his eyes glassy, his whole face contorted. The Little Doctor did not even have to bend down to diagnose.

"A large dose of arsenic."

Near the corpse, stretched out on the straw, lay a bottle with the inscription "Jamaica Rum."

Monsieur Mordaut turned slowly away, a strange light in his eyes. Ernestine was crying, while Rose, standing a little to one side, kept her head lowered.

Half an hour later, while they were waiting for the police who had been summoned by telephone, the Little Doctor, his brow covered in a cold sweat, was wondering whether he would live to see the end of this investigation.

He had just elucidated, in part at least, the story of the bottle of rum.

"Don't you remember the conversation I had with Monsieur Mordaut after lunch?" asked Ernestine. "You were there. He asked me what there was for dinner and I said, 'A vegetable soup and a cauliflower.' "

She was quite right. The Little Doctor remembered vaguely having heard something of the sort.

"Monsieur Mordaut replied that as you were staying here it wasn't enough, and asked me to make a rum omelette."

"When you need rum," asked Dollent, "where do you get it from?"

"The cupboard in the dining room, where all the spirits are kept."

"Have you a key?"

"No, I ask for it when I want it."

"Did you return the key?"

"Yes, to Monsieur Mordaut."

"What did you do with the rum?"

"Put it on the kitchen mantelpiece, while I cleaned the vegetables."

"Did anyone come into the kitchen? Did you see Hector wandering round?"

"No."

"Did you leave the kitchen?"

"Only for a few minutes to feed the dogs."

"Was Hector in the habit of stealing drinks?"

"It has been known to happen. Not only drinks. He was terribly greedy; he stole anything he could lay his hands on and went off, like a puppy, to eat it in a corner."

What would have happened if Hector hadn't found the bottle of arsenic and suposed it to contain rum?

Ernestine would have prepared the omelette. Would anyone have noticed an unusual taste? Wouldn't any bitterness have been put down to the rum? Who would have managed not to eat the omelette — an omelette made in the kitchen, served by Rose, with Monsieur Mordaut, Hector, and the Little Doctor in the dining room?

There was no dinner at the château that evening. The police were in possession, and two of them stationed at the gate had difficulty in restraining the crowd, which was becoming noisy.

In the dilapidated drawing room Monsieur Mordaut, white and haggard, tried to understand the questions which were flung at him by the police. When the door opened after the interview, he was handcuffed. He was led into an adjacent room to remain in custody of two policemen.

How often had Dollent said to himself: "A solid fact, even one, and then, if you're not sidetracked, if you don't lose the thread, you must automatically arrive at the truth."

Solid facts. They were:

1. Monsieur Mordaut had placed no obstacle in the way of the Little Doctor's investigation and had insisted on his staying at the château.

2. Ernestine was strong and healthy. She counted on living to be a hundred and two like her grandmother, and everything she did was with this single aim in view; and she was haunted by the idea of cancer.

3. Ernestine said that her niece was not Monsieur Mordaut's mistress.

4. Rose was healthy, too, and had a lover or fiancé in the Colonial forces.

5. Rose also said that she was not Monsieur Mordaut's mistress.

6. Monsieur Mordaut showed all the symptoms of the beginnings of slow arsenical poisoning.

7. Like the three dead women, Ernestine had a life insurance which would be paid to her master.

"Would you like to know what I really think?" It was Ernestine's turn to be questioned in the ill-lit drawing room.

"Well, my idea is that my master has gone slightly mad — and when he knew that he was being found out, he preferred to finish with it all. But, as he was unbalanced and not like other people, he didn't want any of us to survive him.

"If poor Monsieur Hector hadn't drunk that rum, we should all be dead by now, including the Doctor."

This thought gave Dollent shivers down his spine.

"Monsieur," he murmured to the Police Superintendent, moving towards the door, "I'd like to have a word with you in private."

They spoke in the corridor, which was as gloomy as everywhere else in the house.

"I suppose — I hope that you have the necessary powers," the Little Doctor concluded. "There is still time — if you send an officer by car."

His work was over. The mystery was solved, and as usual it had been in a single flash. Diverse facts, little points of illumination in the fog, and then, suddenly . . .

The only way in which the Superintendent and the Little Doctor had managed to escape public curiosity was to take the banqueting chamber on the first floor of the little inn.

After an omelette, made not with rum but with *fines herbes,* they had ordered stewed rabbit, which they were now eating.

"Until we hear from the solicitor, all that I can tell you, Monsieur, is simply hypothesis.

"Well, I was struck by the fact that a man who took out a life insurance for everyone else didn't take one out for himself. If the man is a murderer, and if his object is to get the money from all those policies, what would he do to conceal his intention? First and foremost, take out a policy for himself, so as to avert suspicion . . . Monsieur Mordaut has no life insurance. For some time also he has been suffering from the effects of slow arsenical poisoning, just like the previous victims. So I ask, who will inherit on his death? Which is why I asked you to send an officer to the solicitor.

"Follow me closely now," said the Little Doctor. "It would seem that the person who inherits from Monsieur Mordaut must almost inevitably be the murderer."

"And the murderer is?"

"A moment. Do you want to know who I think is Monsieur Mordaut's heir? Rose."

"So that —"

"Not so fast. Let me follow my fantasy, if I can use such a word, until your officer returns from the solicitor. I came to the conclusion that at some time, years ago no doubt, Mordaut and Ernestine were lovers. The years went by. He married to restore his fortunes, and Ernestine didn't oppose the match.

"She just killed his wife, slowly, as she had killed the aunt whose death brought in so much money. For she was more than Mordaut's mistress, she was his heir. She knew that one day everything he possessed would come to her.

"I am sure it was she, and not some insurance agent, who was behind that long series of policies. And she had the splendid idea of making him take one out for her, so that she would appear, when the time came, as a potential victim.

"You don't understand all this? It's because you don't live, as I do, in the country, and you are not familiar with long-term schemes. Ernestine intends to live a long time. It hardly matters that she wastes twenty or thirty years with Mordaut. Afterwards she'll be free, and rich. She'll have the house of her dreams and live to be as old as her grandmother.

"That's why she's so frightened of illness. She doesn't want to have worked so hard for nothing. But the fortune she is eventually to inherit must be big enough. Emilie Duplantet, Madame Mordaut, Solange Duplantet. One by one they die, and their fortunes go to Monsieur Mordaut — and finally to Ernestine.

"What's the risk? No one will suspect her because nobody thinks she is the beneficiary of all these deaths. No one knows that she made her lover draw up a will leaving everything to her in default of direct heirs.

"She kills without any danger to herself. If anything happens, he will be the one to go to prison, to be condemned. She only starts worrying the day that she feels that her niece, whom she unwillingly brought into the house, is beginning to exert some influence. For Rose is young and pretty, and Mordaut —"

"It's disgusting," interpolated the Superintendent.

"Alas, it's life. His passion for Ernestine is transferred to her niece. Rose has a lover or a fiancé, but what does it matter to her? Rose has something of her aunt's character. She'll wait a few years. She'll wait for the inheritance her master has promised her. She doesn't have to kill anyone. Did she have any suspicions about these murders? She could ignore them, because, in the end, they fare to her benefit."

"It's been a long business, Messieurs," sighed the police officer who had had no lunch and was now confronted with the remnants of the feast.

"Apart from the son," he continued, "all Monsieur Mordaut's property is left to Mademoiselle Rose Saupiquet."

The Little Doctor's eyes shone.

"Is there no other will?" asked the Superintendent.

"There was another, in which everything was left to Mademoiselle Ernestine Saupiquet, but it was altered nearly eight years ago."

"Did Mademoiselle Ernestine know?"

"No, the change was made in secret."

The Little Doctor laughed. "So now you see it all? Ernestine didn't know about the new will. She was certain, one day, of profiting from her crimes, but she wouldn't kill Mordaut until he had amassed enough money."

"And Rose?"

"Legally she's certainly not an accomplice. But still, I wonder if she hadn't guessed what her aunt was up to."

Another bottle was placed on the table, ostensibly for the police officer. But it was the Little Doctor who helped himself first and who, after a gulp, said:

"Do you know what put me on the right track? It was when Ernestine affirmed her niece's virtue, because to doubt that would be to doubt Mordaut's virtue, and if I became suspicious of this, I might begin to suspect other things.

"In fact, we interrupted her in the middle of her work. She only killed Hector by chance in her attempt to get rid of the poison and to incriminate Mordaut. He had ordered the rum omelette for dinner. What better way to throw suspicion on him than to poison the rum? I'm sure that the rum wouldn't in fact have been poured over the omelette, but how easy to say afterwards that it seemed to have a funny smell — and so lead to the rum-bottle being examined!

"Little more would have remained to be done. And then the pretty home in the country and forty years of life lived according to her dreams."

The Little Doctor replenished his glass once more and concluded:

"There are still people, especially in the country, who make their plans far ahead. Which is why they need so desperately to live to a great age."

Joyce Harrington

My Neighbor, Ay

It all started the day the old man on the top floor next door emptied his spittoon out the window and the wind was blowing from the east. It wasn't what you might call an elegant antique of a spittoon. More like an old coffee can, and I caught the flash of tin up there in the fifth-floor walkup out of the corner of my eye as I was crouched over my tenderly cherished Christian Dior rosebush inspecting for aphis with a banana peel at the ready.

My wife, Brenda, who was flaked out on the garden chaise in her green bikini promoting a city suntan, caught more than a flash of tin.

"Rats! It's raining," she muttered before she opened her eyes. When she finally did get them open and adjusted to bright-blue sky and dazzling August sunshine and a case of instant full-length freckles, she screamed.

"What is it? Damn, what is it? Who did that?"

She scrambled off the chaise and the freckles began to slither in streaky rivulets toward her belly button and down her incredibly long and slender legs. A few dripped off her chin and fell into her well proportioned cleavage.

"It's not tea leaves, honey."

I must confess that the sight of lissome, fastidious Brenda spattered from head to toe with second-hand chewing tobacco brought out the snide side of my character, and I had difficulty gulping down a fit of guffaws. For my pains I was rewarded with a fit of hiccups.

"Will you stop that stupid noise and *do something!*" she shrieked. Have you ever seen anyone turn red with rage all over? That was Brenda. Bright pink actually, overlaid with lengthening stripes and scattered specks of mahogany, the whole girl trembling and angrier than I'd ever seen her.

I turned away, ostensibly to deposit my banana peel at the foot of Christian Dior, and managed to subdue the grin that was quirking at the corners of my mouth. It crossed my mind that someone had once told me tobacco, like banana peel, was good for roses, but I couldn't remember why. It definitely wasn't good for Brenda.

"A shower, perhaps?" I suggested. "I'll scrub your back."

144

"A shower! A disinfecting is what I need! Don't just stand there. Call the police!"

"What'll I tell them? My wife has been spat on wholesale? I'll get you some paper towels." I started for the kitchen door.

"Don't leave me here like this. Do something! If you won't call the police, I will. I will, I will, I will!" Tears were beginning to add to the mess on Brenda's face and the shocked rigidity was leaving her outflung arms. She was making an awful lot of noise.

"Do you want to stay like that so the police can see the evidence?" I grabbed the real-estate section of the Sunday *Times* and began tentative mopping-up operations, at the same time trying to steer her indoors.

"Stop that, you nit! You're just making it worse."

She was right. Heads were beginning to appear at the rear windows of the surrounding brownstones. Brenda came to her senses long enough to realize that she was the star of this backyard melodrama, and then fled howling to the bathroom.

"I'll speak to Guttierez," I called after her.

When the shower had been drumming satisfactorily for at least five minutes and I had subdued my hiccups, I put on a clean shirt and a stern manner and marched next door. Guttierez owned this next-door brownstone, outwardly an identical twin of ours, and lived in the basement apartment with his silent, round-faced, brown-eyed wife, and four not-so-silent young sons. Upstairs, Guttierez rented rooms. The house was a mini-U.N. and the sounds that flowed out through the open windows were the normal sounds of people living loudly in Spanish, Haitian French, West Indian lilted English, with an occasional bright thread of Pakistani or Chinese. It was microcosmic Brooklyn in the summer of the brownstone generation.

I rang the bell. Somewhere inside a buzzer zapped and there was instant quiet. I waited a few moments. Then a flowered plastic curtain at the barred basement window twitched. I hit the buzzer again. Pretty soon an inner door rattled, an outer door rattled, and a miniature Guttierez materialized inside the iron gate of the basement entrance.

"Hi," I said masterfully.

Young Guttierez masterfully non-replied and stared absolutely without blinking for a year-long minute before I tried again. This was really a job for Brenda, who used to boast of having read *El Cid*

in the original during her Hunter College days. I sighed and spoke
again.

"Um, hi there. Is your father home?"

Reinforcements arrived in the shape of an even smaller and more
solemn Guttierez sporting a T-shirt lettered *Puerto Rico Encanta*.
Double-barreled silence for another minute, then the curtain twitched
again. I was about to leave, defeated by this one-sided confrontation,
when the two small brown bodies erupted into noise and action.
They pounded away back into their lair squealing, *"Mama, Mama!
Mira, Mama, un hombre!"*

The squeals receded into a distant interior chattering, and I stood
with my nose pressed to the iron grille, trying to decide whether it
was worthwhile waiting around for someone over the age of five to
come to the door. My whole attention was riveted through those
open inner doors, listening to the rapid incomprehensible chatter,
breathing in the fumes of something cooking vaguely connected in
my sensory apparatus with Brenda's superb *paella,* and hoping for
the sound of adult footsteps to head in my direction.

My concentration on the Guttierez interior was such that I failed
to notice the adult footsteps coming up behind me. I whirled at the
sound of the voice and almost fell into the lidless garbage can beside
the door.

" 'Ello, 'ello. What you wan' here?"

I suspected Guttierez of being slightly deaf. He always spoke in
a modified roar. In the circumstances it was a bit unnerving, and
I felt like the notorious neighborhood mailbox burglar caught in the
act. Add to this the fact that although Guttierez and I were about
the same height, I was standing one step down in the entrance to
his castle. He towered over me with a six-pack of beer in each hand.
It was difficult to remember that as Guttierez always roared, he
always glowered even when playing stick ball with his kids, and I
had no desire to get beaned with the *cerveza fria.*

"Hello there. Um, I was just looking for you. Nice day, isn't it?"

I'm ashamed to say that my voice came out somewhat higher than
its normal range, and suspicion flamed all over Guttierez' face. He
took a firmer grip on his six-packs.

"You lookin' for me? What you wan'?"

"Well, Mr. Guttierez, I'm Jack Rollins. I live next door, you know?"

I got my voice back down into its normal range, but I was having
difficulty getting to the point. I scrambled up out of the entryway
and felt a little better facing Guttierez at eye level.

"*Si*, I know. What you wan'?"

He was obviously impatient to get inside to whatever was cooking that smelled so good. Whispers and giggles came from behind the twitching curtain, and I caught an occasional "Americano" between the giggles.

"Well, Mr. Guttierez, the old man on the top floor, you know?"

"*Si?*"

"Well, he throws things out the window."

"*Si?*"

"Well, he empties his spittoon out the window."

"*Si?* What is this 'spittoon'?"

I sighed, inaudibly I hoped, and tried again.

"Well, he chews tobacco, you know? And he spits it in a can. And then he throws it out the window."

"Oh, *si!* He is one filthy old man, him."

I squared my shoulders and prepared to do battle for my wife's honor. The guy's machismo was beginning to rub off on me.

"Well, see here, Guttierez. It's got to stop. It landed on my wife today."

"Oh, *lastima!* You wife! she with the bathing suit? In the back-yard?"

It was the first time I had ever seen Guttierez smile. He was grinning. He was positively leering.

"That's right. My wife. And I want something done about it." I hoped I was scowling at least as fiercely as Guttierez normally did.

"What you wan' to do? You wan' to fight him? He is *muy viejo*, very old. An' he have one leg. You wan' to fight him?"

"No, I don't want to fight him! He's your tenant. You should speak to him. Tell him it's against the law to throw things out the window. Tell him I'll call the police."

"You called police?" Guttierez was beginning to bristle and his grin vanished.

"No, not yet. But if he does it one more time I will. You tell him that."

"Okay. I tell him. No more out the window."

A young Guttierez, who had been lurking just inside the gate throughout our exchange, now opened the gate and took the beer from his father's hands. Guttierez went through the gate, and as he turned to close it he grinned once more.

"Tell you wife she is very pretty."

The gate slammed and the chatter and giggles reached a crescendo.

Back in my own renovated townhouse, I settled into my black-leather Eames chair and sought solace with the Sunday *Times* crossword puzzle. The shower was still splashing, so I was safe from vengeance until Brenda got her hair dry. Before attacking square one across, I sat back and admired for perhaps the hundredth time the restored beauty of my front parlor.

Brenda and I had scraped and Red Deviled and polished the woodwork, plastered and spackled and painted, replaced missing bits of molding. We had labored mightily and with love, and the result was a gleaming, pristine Victorian mansion with all mod cons, a duplex apartment upstairs, which rented at a price that paid the mortgage, and our own lower duplex with garden. Our piece of the city.

I shook my head over Brenda's rage, decided it was justified, and clicked my ballpoint pen into action. The air conditioner hummed gently, producing just the right amount of refrigeration, and I lost myself in the wiles of the puzzle which bore the theme of "The Last Resort." I puzzled away for perhaps twenty minutes and was somewhat nearer sleeping than waking when Brenda stalked into the room.

"Well?" she demanded. The shower had cleaned her up but had not cooled her off.

"Uh, what's a ten-letter word for African animal ending in 'u'?"

"Lesser Kudu. What happened?" Brenda was always very good at natural history.

"Thanks. Aren't you cold?"

She had exchanged her spattered green bikini for a pair of shocking-pink short shorts and a purple scarf intricately tied to allow maximum bare skin and freedom of motion.

"No, I'm not cold. It's ninety-two degrees outside. Did you call the police?"

"Well, no. It's very cool in here. The air conditioner is on high." I settled deeper into my chair to give the impression of extreme comfort and immovability.

"If you didn't call the police, what did you do?"

"Well, I spoke to Guttierez. You aren't going outside again, are you? Like that?" I knew I was doing this all wrong. Brenda wasn't the sort of girl you could safely practice machismo on.

"Of course I am. It's my backyard, isn't it? What did Guttierez say?"

"He said you were very pretty. He asked if I wanted to fight the old guy."

"Oh, damn, you're impossible!" She dropped onto the blue-velvet Victorian chaise longue which was her pride and joy, and she almost laughed. "Did you ever get to the point?"

"Oh, yes. Point Number One, Guttierez will speak to the old guy. And Point Number Two, your sunbathing gives great visual pleasure to the surrounding natives. Does Mrs. G. ever sunbathe?"

"Of course not. She's always pregnant. There's a steak for the barbecue. Shall I light the fire now?"

During the week following "L'Affaire Tabac" the heat wave was still melting Madison Avenue. Brenda and I shuttled between our air-conditioned jobs and our air-conditioned bedroom, ducking in and out of air-conditioned restaurants along the way. Neither one of us felt much like cooking or even eating with the thermometer pushing 100 day after day, and the humidity making my best Brooks Brothers young-executive-on-the-rise wash-and-wear blue-and-white stripe look like a much worn and seldom washed suit of the latest in limp dishrag.

The management of the aggressive young ad agency where Brenda wrote copy had considered going on a four-day week for the summer, but had decided that there were too many Goliaths abroad on the Avenue to leave the slingshots unmanned (or unwomanned) for even one day. So Brenda hammered away at producing bright, clever words designed to sell bras and all-in-ones to the overfed female population of the nation, while I sweltered and accounted for the bookkeeping vagaries of an endless roster of small-business clients of the mammoth accounting firm where I C.P.A.'d. We both regretted our decision to save our vacation time for a January ski tour of Europe.

If we noticed Guttierez and company at all it was only in passing on the evening drag from subway to cool haven. A clutter of brown humanity, stoop-sitting, hoping for a breeze from the bay or even from the Gowanus Canal, and tossing Malta Hatvey cans languidly toward the garbage cans and just missing. Occasionally we heard a guitar and plaintive island songs, and saw the kids trundling second-hand plastic tricycles up and down the sidewalk. Mrs. Guttierez had tried to brighten the small front yard with a few marigolds, but the heat and pounding children's feet had left only a few yellow tatters among the popsicle wrappers on the packed earth.

We passed without acknowledgment, either of overtures toward mutual understanding or mutual hostility. It was too darned hot. One night, though, we were forced to take notice.

The heat had lifted slightly and the air was electric with premonitions of a storm. Despite the threat of rain Brenda and I decided to take a chance on Shakespeare in the Park. We did it in style: Brasserie box lunches (paté, *ratatouille,* cold chicken) and chilled champagne (New York State) while waiting in line; a rather fine *Macbeth* with distant thunder obligingly produced on cue by the great Stage Manager in the Catskills; and afterward a taxi home across the Brooklyn Bridge with the lights of our town, ships in the Narrows, and the Verrazano Bridge crowning the evening with the spectacle which never palled.

We pulled up outside our house and paid off the driver, adding a generous happy-time tip. A gale-force wind was blowing off the bay and up our street, bending the newly planted plane trees into fragile arcs. Above the clatter of the frantic leaves and the din of the wind playing Frisbee with the garbage-can lids, the roar of Guttierez was heard. The stoop-sitters were energized, plugged into the crackling atmosphere. The children, not yet in bed, huddled smear-faced and wide-eyed on the top step.

Mrs. Guttierez wept loudly in the arms of a broad full-bellied Indian-faced woman who shrieked imprecations to the tops of houses. Armed with a saw-toothed bread knife, Guttierez bellowed and stabbed the air. The opposition, small, thin, dark, and very drunk, whirled a baseball bat above his head with both hands. The two men circled each other on the sidewalk, slowfooted, eyes aglint with the adrenalin of battle, searching for the deadly opportunity and shouting macho insults at each other.

Brenda stared, breath held, her body stiff with shock and rooted to the pavement.

"Inside!" I shouted. "Get inside!"

She didn't move. She didn't hear. She was hypnotized.

"My God!" she breathed at last. "They'll kill each other."

The wind plastered her long hair across her face, and a single fat raindrop fell on my hand as I tried to drag her away.

"Get into the house, Brenda." I spoke as calmly as I could. "The rain will stop it."

Her fascination broke abruptly and she whirled on me, her eyes wild with near-hysteria.

"Police!" she screamed. "They'll kill each other! Call the police! I'll do it!"

She bolted for the entrance to our fortress and began scrabbling in her purse for keys. I had mine ready, but the seconds necessary for manipulating the double locks seemed like hours with Brenda shivering impatiently behind me and the shouts and weeping continuing unabated on the sidewalk.

I flung the gate open and Brenda charged through, rattling the double doors and racing down the hall to the telephone. I went back for another look at the combatants. They were still circling, still brandishing their weapons, still shouting, There was not another soul to be seen on the block—no late dog-walkers, no midnight loiterers at the corner bodega, no curious heads at windows.

Lightning flashed somewhere over Staten Island, coming closer, and raindrops spattered the sidewalk. I felt fairly sure that Guttierez and enemy would continue their Mexican stand-off until the deluge, then put down their armaments and go inside for another beer. But you never could tell. When the thunder rolled I went inside and relocked the double locks.

Brenda, at the kitchen phone, was just concluding her conversation with 911. In a tight, edgy voice she gave her name and address. "Please hurry," she added. "I'm afraid they'll kill each other."

I could imagine the laconic voice on the other end of the wire giving assurance that law and order were on the way, lady. Brenda hung up the phone and dug a cigarette out of her bag, lighting it at the gas range.

"Jack—" she slumped in the telephone chair and surveyed the chrome and terra cotta tile, electronic oven and massive freezer, the ranks of custom-built walnut cabinets—"Jack, we've done all this, and it's beautiful. I love it." She dragged deeply on her cigarette. "But I want out. I don't want to live next door to *that* any more."

"Where do you want to go, honey?"

I began to massage her tight shoulders, her rigid neck. But she pulled away.

"How do I know? The damn suburbs. Westchester! Nyack! Bloody Australia! The farther the better."

"Brennie, you know you'd hate the suburbs. Those guys are just showing off for their women. They're enjoying every minute of it, and nobody's going to get hurt."

I had some small faith in my words and the flamboyant nature of our neighbors. Still, it was unnerving and not very neighborly to come home to brandished bread knives and baseball bats.

Brenda brooded unhappily.

"Come on, honey." I took her hand. "Let's go be spectators and see how long it takes the police to get here."

We took up stations at the darkened front-parlor window to find that one patrol car had already arrived, while another was flashing its way up the street.

"Well," I commented. "Nobody can say the fuzz doesn't respond in this neighborhood."

Guttierez, leaning indolently against the front fender of the police car, was answering the young officer's questions with expressions of sublime innocence and gestures of incredulity.

"Who, me?!!!" seemed to be the substance of his replies.

Mrs. Guttierez and the bread knife had disappeared. One child remained on the sidewalk, idly swinging the baseball bat. The small thin man and the Indian-looking woman leaned against the railing sipping from cans of liquid clothed in brown paper bags.

The wind had died. The trees stood expectantly, their leaves hanging limp and exhausted. A flash of lightning lit the scene in blue-white relief, and the rain crashed down.

The young policeman ducked inside his car with a final admonition to Guttierez, who nodded, tried to shake hands, then dashed for his house, picking up the boy and the baseball bat on the run. He was joined by the paper-bag drinkers, the woman laughing widely from her round belly and raising her face to the downpour. I could see her gold teeth.

After a few moments the police cars drove away, undoubtedly to respond to another crisis on another block. We watched the rain punish the empty street.

"Come on, Brennie." I hugged her. "It's bedtime."

We never found out what the argument had been about, but the next evening when we came home from work we found our backyard thoroughly inundated with garbage. There seemed to be about a ton of assorted chicken bones with fragments of yellow rice clinging stickily, dozens of the ubiquitous Malta Hatvey cans, watermelon rind and orange peel, coffee grounds, tea bags, and, yes, even the tobacco chewer of the fifth floor was represented.

"They must have taken up a collection." I tried to laugh, but it didn't come off very well. "What do you think, Brenda? The police again?"

Brenda seemed to have shrunk. Her eyes glazed over as she viewed the unexpected landfill.

"No, Jack," she said quietly. "I think the shovel and hose."

Our neighbors remained invisible and inaudible during the clean-up operation. Brenda remained silent and tight-lipped, wielding her shovel with a tense energy which augured ill for the dispensers of the odiferous revenge. Side by side we shoveled and hosed. All my attempts to point up the ridiculous side of the great kitchen-midden caper fell decidedly flat.

"You should maybe get her recipe for *arroz con pollo*."

Brenda shoveled.

"We could toss it all back with a little contribution of our own. Make it a real classy garbage war. *Coq au vin* bones, congealed quiche, rind of brie, and shell of clam. Just think how we could expand their horizons."

Brenda swept, and looked determined.

"This may be the answer to the city's disposal problem. Just keep tossing it back and forth. You keep it one day, I'll keep it the next."

"Just shut up and shovel!"

Brenda had the hose in her hand, I shut up and shoveled.

An hour and many plastic bags later Brenda was once again showering away rage and refuse. The refuse would go down the drain. The rage I was not too sure about. Brenda's usual form was an explosion of mildly profane wrath, followed by tremulous laughter or at the very least a self-conscious smirk. This was different. This was cold fury, silent and calculating. Brenda was up to something. And I didn't like it.

I made her a drink, gin and tonic in equal proportions with two wedges of lime, and took it into the bathroom.

"Hey, Bren. Here's a drink."

"Thanks." Steam billowed out of the shower and frosted the mahogany-framed mirror over the sink. I wrote *Bren & Jack 4ever* inside a lopsided heart.

"How about dinner at Gage and Tollner?"

"No, thanks."

"How about dinner at Peter Luger's?"

"No."

"How about dinner?"

"I've lost my appetite."

Brenda without an appetite was like bagels without cream cheese. Unnatural. And for her to turn down a Peter Luger steak was worse than unnatural.

The shower shut off abruptly and Brenda emerged dripping, a pale bikini shape outlined against rosy sunburn.

"Dry you off, lady?"

"Just hand me that towel."

She snatched the towel from the rack before I could reach it, dried off in a frenzy of flapping terrycloth, and slid into her no-nonsense button-to-the-chin nightgown.

"If you can bear to think about food, there must be something in the fridge. I'm going to bed."

Sweating drink in hand, she long-legged it into the bedroom. I followed. "Great idea. I could use a little nap myself. And then we can go to Peter Luger's."

Brenda whirled on me, sloshing her drink all over herself and the red shag bedroom rug.

"Beat it, Jack. Just bug off. I'm getting in that bed. And I'm going to drink this drink. Or what's left of it. And then I'm going to sleep, sleep, sleep! And I hope I never wake up! I want to be alone. Understand?"

"Okay, Garbo. Okay. All right. Pleasant dreams."

I slouched downstairs to the kitchen where I found sufficient material for a hero sandwich which, along with a couple of beers and my newest old Teddy Wilson records, induced a state of hopeful nirvana. Tomorrow would be better.

When I tiptoed into the bedroom around midnight, Brenda was asleep, asleep, asleep.

Tomorrow came right on schedule, and Brenda woke up. But refused to get out of bed. I brought her coffee, but she still refused to budge.

"Call the office around nine-thirty, Jack. Tell them I'm sick. I *am*." She buried her face in the pillow and moaned unconvincingly.

"It's Friday. You can't call in sick on Friday."

"Oh, yes, I can. Anyway you're going to do it for me. Tell them I've got scurvy, beri-beri, jungle rot, anything. Garbage poisoning, that's what I've really got. Please, Jack. I really need a day off to pull myself together after last night. I'll be all right. I promise. Tell them I have a bad case of hives."

"Look, Brenda, you'd be better off to go to work and forget all about last night. It's over. Let it end."

"Hives, dear. In fact, I think I feel one blossoming on my left kneecap right now."

She sat up and scratched energetically and then piled all the pillows together into a cosy sickbed nest. Smiling and sipping coffee, she seemed altogether more like a normal Brenda. Last night's cold and silent fury must have been dissipated by ten hours of sleep on an empty stomach.

"Well," I wavered. "I hate to leave you like this."

"Don't worry. I just want to spend the day in bed with a good book. Haven't done that in a long time."

She settled in more snugly and pulled the covers up to her chin. She looked helpless and vulnerable, even though I knew better, and I really did hate to leave her.

"Shall I bring you something to eat?"

"No, thanks. I'll get up and boil an egg in a little while."

I guess that's what convinced me that all would be well. Soft-boiled eggs were convalescent food for Brenda. Whenever she was recovering from any kind of upset, physical or emotional, soft-boiled eggs appeared on the menu, and disappeared as soon as things were back to normal.

"Well." I knotted my tie. "I guess I'd better be going."

"All right, dear. Don't forget to call in for me. And don't worry." She was already thumbing through a magazine.

"You won't—uh—I mean, you'll stay away from—" I still was not entirely convinced that Brenda's intentions ran solely to bed rest and literature. "You won't start anything with Guttierez, will you?"

"No, dear. I won't start anything. I promise."

I left.

I spent a usual kind of Friday closing out the previous month's books in the supermod offices of a team of graphic designers. The bookkeeper, a minuscule and meticulous Japanese girl, drew graphically perfect numbers and persistently covered up her errors by adding or subtracting a totally fictitious petty-cash amount at the end of each month. Each month Sumi and I engaged in a polite skirmish in which errors were routed, the books balanced, and I laid down anew the simple rules of double entry. Each month Sumi accepted my edicts with apologetic and suitably flattering awe, and I felt like a samurai of the statistics. Until the next month.

I tried to reach Brenda several times during the day, but each time the line was busy.

By mid-afternoon I had settled Sumi's accounts and decided to knock off the rest of the day. It was one of those rare summer days in New York. The unsmogged sky was actually blue and gentle breezes meandered along the cross streets. The storm of the night before had washed away heat, humidity, and dog droppings. and as I walked the six blocks to the Grand Central subway station, the city and its people gleamed as dwellers in an iridescent and fantastic mirage.

The subway put an end to fantasy with its congealed heat and the smell of generations of doomed hot dogs sweating out their grease on eternally rotating grills. On the train, sparsely populated with Alexander's shopping bags and noisy groups of day-camp kids, I welcomed the dank wind that swirled through the cars and wondered if this might not be a good weekend to take advantage of an open invitation to visit friends on Fire Island. There was plenty of time to catch an evening ferry, and two days of beachratting in congenial company would bring Brenda out of the garbage dumps.

She met me at the door suppressing manic laughter. Her eyes gave her away. Wild and triumphant, they sparkled with discharged venom. She grabbed my arm and before I could unload my attaché case or broach my Fire Island plan she dragged me to the window.

"Look, Jack." She was almost incoherent. "The gas company. It's the gas company."

"Well, sure. It's the gas company." It was not unusual to see a blue-and-yellow gas-company truck parked outside. I failed to comprehend Brenda's elation over this one.

"Oh, Jack! You don't get it. It's too fantastic! I reported a gas leak!"

I turned to sniff the air.

"Where is it? In the kitchen?" I headed for the stairs. "Did they find it yet?"

"No, dummy. You still don't get it. Next door. I reported a gas leak next door. And exposed wiring. And fire hazards in the halls. The fire inspectors have already been there. I'm still waiting for the housing department. You know, illegal roominghouse. He doesn't have a license. Overcrowding and rats. Plumbing violations, sewer smells. Rent gouging. Everything. Everything I could think of. I even called the Mayor's office, but he was off inspecting snowplows."

"In August?" I was stupefied. No adequate comment came to mind, and I stared out the window as two purposeful men in gas-company uniforms emerged from next door. "They're leaving now."

"Okay. Now what's next?" Brenda paced excitedly up and down the living room. "Child abuse! That's it. I'm sure he beats his kids. Where do you report child abuse?"

"Brenda! Knock it off. That's harassment. It's illegal. He could sue you, for God's sake."

"Harassment! What do you call garbage in our backyard? I'll sue *him*. I'll put him out of business. I'll close down that rat trap. Where's the phone book?"

Brenda's erratic pacing and arm waving came dangerously close to putting my blue Tiffany tablelamp out of business. I pulled her onto the sofa and held both her hands. She squirmed and fidgeted.

"Look, kid. You've done enough for one day. What do you say we call Jenny and Charley and spend the weekend on Fire Island?"

"Oh, no, Jack. We can't do that. We have an appointment tomorrow morning to look at houses in Westchester."

On Saturday we took an early train to wild and wooly Westchester to view real estate. We saw cathedral ceilings and three-car garages, pseudo-salt-boxes and split-level bathrooms, cosy cottages nestled into careful foliage allowed to grow just so wild and no wilder, rambling ranches designed from the same general all-purpose scheme for storing a standard quota of children in standard-sized boxes with a standard number of windows.

Mrs. Handiford, the real-estate saleswoman, efficient and motherly, graciously hauled us around winding tree-lined roads in her late-model battleship-on-wheels station wagon, pointing out local amenities and landmarks: stables here, swim club there, home of notable this and pillar of the community that.

"And of course the public school system is one of the finest in the state, although if you prefer private—"

"We haven't any children." Brenda was terse, bordering on rude, but Mrs. Handiford patted her neatly waved silver-grey coiffure and bravely pressed on.

"Ah, well, you're young and there's noplace better for starting a family. I'm sure you'll find many activities here to interest you. There's the Arts and Crafts Guild. They have exhibits twice a year. And a very active chapter of the League of Women Voters. We have the Garden Club. They've done those very lovely plantings we saw in the village. Do you play bridge? We have several informal bridge groups, always looking for new members. Tennis and golf, of course. Oh, I'm sure you'll find lots to do, Mrs. Rollins."

"Yes. Well, I have a job. In the city." Brenda was obviously hating every minute of this grand tour of suburban glories.

Dammit, I thought. This was your idea. Let the poor woman get on with her spiel. And glared at her behind Mrs. Handiford's neat and businesslike navy-blue back.

Only momentarily dampened, Mrs. Handiford rallied swiftly and tried another tack.

"Well, if you're both going to be commuting, perhaps you'd like something closer to the station. I have a sweet little place, walking distance. Not much land, so it's easy to maintain."

The sweet little place near the station materialized as a Swiss chalet, replete with kitsch, cuckoo clock, and a grotto in the rear where recirculated water trickled over imitation moss on plastic rocks. Miraculously there were no gnomes. But I fully expected Shirley Temple as Heidi, or at the very least a nanny goat, to come bounding out of the garage-cum-cowshed exuding Alpine charm and the fragrance of edelweiss or emmenthaler, take your pick. A tour of the interior offered us eaves to bump our heads on, which Brenda did, bottle-glass windows reducing the entrance of daylight to a minimum, low beamed ceilings, and endless square feet of dark and intricately carved woodwork.

Brenda was breathing hard by this time, not saying much. Just breathing. And nursing the bump on her head. It was the bathroom that really finished her off. She opened the door, quickly closed it, and tried to choke back a despairing "Oh, no!"

She was not to be let off so easily. Mrs. Handiford bustled through the door, taking Brenda's arm as she went. I followed in horrified fascination. There were the gnomes—frolicking on the vinyl wallpaper, in a landscape featuring distant cows and Matterhorns.

"Of course, it's all custom-designed," stated Mrs. Handiford, eyeing Brenda with grim satisfaction.

Indeed it was. The usual facilities were all encased in as much wood carving as possible without interfering with function. The tub-shower enclosure resembled a confessional and the toilet-paper roll, when activated, tinkled "The Sound of Music."

Revenge must be sweet to real-estate ladies spending unprofitable Saturdays with obviously unsuitable clients.

"Sweet," gasped Brenda. "Utterly too sweet. But not my—" She broke off, headed for the front door at an ungainly gallop, and narrowly missed impaling herself on the staghorn doing duty as a coat rack in the tiny foyer.

Regrouped on the sidewalk, we all three tried to conceal our eagerness to split.

"We've seen so much . . . it's hard to decide."

"It's been a pleasure taking you around."

"We'll have to think it all over."

"If something new comes in—"

"Yes, please do give us a call."

"I'll drive you to the station."

"Oh, thanks. We'd like to walk. It's so close."

"Goodbye then. If I can be of help, don't hesitate—"

"Thanks again. Yes, we can find the station."

"Goodbye."

"Good grief!" snorted Brenda as Mrs. Handiford piloted her dreadnaught off to whatever suburban utopia she called her own, which I devoutly hoped included a well earned double Scotch on the rocks.

"You were right, Jack. Absolutely right. I could never hack this. Not in a million years. Where's that train schedule?"

By the time the train reached 125th Street, Brenda was enthusiastically discussing plans for the erection of a ten-foot-high solid redwood fence to take the place of the post-and-wire affair currently separating our turf from Guttierez'.

Back home again, the late Saturday afternoon Brooklyn streets basked in a golden glow. We bought Good Humors from Maxie outside the subway station and walked home munching and kicking prickle balls fallen from the huge old chestnut tree at the corner.

"It's okay, isn't it, Jack?" Brenda mouthed around a chunk of chocolate-chip ice cream.

"Sure it is," I replied from the midst of my toasted almond.

"I don't really want to leave," she went on. "And I'm sorry I made all those stupid phone calls. Maybe I should try to talk to Mrs. Guttierez."

"Maybe you should just leave the whole thing alone."

We let ourselves into the house, dim and cool and quiet. Quiet, except for the muffled sound of a radio voice—the unmistakable voice of the WHOM announcer blasting out an Hispanic hard sell, exhorting his listeners to buy Vitarroz. Suddenly the penetrating commercial message was drowned, obliterated by a frantic frightened animal squealing. The squeals continued rising in pitch, interrupted only by an inhuman snuffling, a snorting attempt to breathe. In the next moment this hair-raising noise was overridden by cheers and laughter, quite definitely arising from human throats. "Jack, what's going on?" Brenda whispered. Her words were normal, but her eyes had gone unfocused as she listened intently. "It's them again. I know it. What are they doing?"

"Stay here, Bren. I think it's coming from the yard. I'll go take a look."

I strode off toward the back door, hoping Brenda would not follow. I didn't like the way she looked. Anything could set her off again.

The cheers and squeals had subsided, and WHOM had taken over with a burst of Latino music when I opened the door and stepped out into my garden. The first thing I saw was people. The neighboring yard was full of people, young, old, and in-between, sitting on kitchen chairs and boxes, lying on blankets, leaning against the fence. One enormous old matriarch sat enthroned on a plastic-covered armchair. Guttierez was having a party.

All conversation stopped and thirty pairs of piercing black eyes turned full on me as I advanced to the center of my yard. Inquiry into the source of the frightful squealing was clearly unthinkable. A quick and furtive survey of Guttierez' yard disclosed a shallow trench filled with charcoal and a young man seated in a corner industriously whittling the end of a long wooden pole. The other end had already been shaped to a tapered point.

I turned to my rosebushes; Christian Dior was definitely drooping and I knelt for a closer look. Across the fence chatter and laughter resumed.

I didn't hear Brenda come out. I heard her gasp.

"My God! It's a pig!"

I turned. A pig it was. A small pig, not quite a suckling but not yet fully grown. I had missed it, lying under the hedge at the back of the yard, eyes closed and panting. A boy wandered over and began poking it with a stick. The pig gave a half-hearted squeal of protest, rose clumsily to its feet, and trotted around the perimeter of the yard to escape its tormentor.

The boy trotted after the pig, and other children joined him. Several of the men rose and stationed themselves attentively around the yard. An anticipatory hush fell among the people; the radio was the only sound. The children stalked the pig; the men waited; we watched.

Guttierez marched out of his house, a gleaming, finely honed machete held lovingly in both hands. The waiting circle of guests tensed for the moment of truth. The children began to run. The pig scrabbled and galloped, turning to one side and then the other, seeking escape where there was none. And then the squealing began again.

The pig ricocheted off chair legs and people legs; the children shrieked and tumbled in the dust. The waiting stone-eyed man lunged and missed and lunged again. Guttierez stood motionless at the hub of the pig chase, the machete held ritually across his body. His moment would come. And rising above the shrieks and laughter of the children, the grunts and muttered comments of the men, the pig squealed its mortal terror.

In the corner of the yard the stake sharpener set down his whittling knife. On light feet he moved, a thin sensitive-faced young man. Slowly and quietly, almost casually, he moved to a position some six feet behind the exhausted animal.

The pig stood at bay, its small wary eyes fixed on Guttierez and his shining blade. It did not sense the danger creeping up from behind. Suddenly the young man tensed, sprang, and soared across the intervening space. The full weight of his falling body flattened the protesting pig, splaying its slender dainty legs in four directions and cutting off its lament in mid-squeal.

A cheer rose from the spectators and the men and children crowded around the pair wrestling in the dusty arena. Guttierez flexed his sword arm and thumbed the edge of his blade. Two men struggled out of the writhing group on the ground, carrying the pig belly up. Its eyes rolled frantically as the men deposited it at Guttierez' feet, holding it immobile, throat exposed.

Guttierez imperiously motioned all others to stay behind him. The seated women drew in their feet and prepared to cover their eyes. The stroke, when it came, was almost anticlimactic. The machete swung upward, flashed once in the sun, and swung down. The hot pig blood spurted in a perfect arc and formed a puddle on the dried earth.

The women forgot to cover their eyes, but groaned instead in a kind of communal sensual satisfaction. The children capered around the carcass whose wound pumped a few smaller and smaller ribbons of blood, which finally subsided to a trickle. The smallest boy explored the puddle and squished his toes in the reddish mud.

The execution of the entire pigsticking must have taken no more than five minutes, but I felt as if I had been holding my breath for an hour. I sucked in a lungful of air, still heavy with the smell of fear and blood, and muttered to Brenda, "I wonder who's going to be awarded the pig's ear."

There was no reply. At some time during the slaughter Brenda must have fled indoors, unnoticed. I thought I'd better do the same. I found her, tears streaming down her face, hysterically mouthing into the telephone.

"... killing a pig ... oh, God, the blood ... all over the yard ... come quick, he's got a machete."

I grabbed the phone from her hand and slammed it down.

"What have you done?" I demanded. "Not the police again?"

She was shaking uncontrollably, and now her head began a rhythmic nodding while the tears welled and splattered.

"Brenda. Brenda, they're having a barbecue. That's all it is. Brenda, snap out of it. Where do you think pork chops come from?"

I couldn't reach her. She would not be comforted. But while I was trying, thinking of calling a doctor, the sirens came. We stood at the center of a storm of sirens, more sirens than I thought existed coming from every direction. In moments the doorbell shrilled, fists pounded at the door, voices demanded that we open up.

I ran to the door and opened it to a surge of blue uniforms with guns drawn, emitting a staccato battery of questions.

"Where is it? Where's the body?"

"Next door? Which side?"

"Is he armed? Is he still there?"

"How many are there?"

"You reported the cop killing?"

"One side. Let us through."

Cop killing! I ran after them, trying to explain. They raced through the kitchen out into the yard.

"It was a pig! Only a pig!" I shouted after them. Brenda, in the kitchen, was trying to stop one of them, held onto his arm, and was swept out into the yard. I followed, still hoping to explain the colossal mistake.

In his yard Guttierez stood facing the pig now strung head down from a low-hanging ailanthus branch. The blood-streaked machete was still in his hand; he was preparing to disembowel. The charcoal in the trench was flaming and the double-pointed stake stood ready to impale its victim.

Scores of policemen were swarming into all the neighboring gardens up and down the block, vaulting the fences, converging on the big party. Cop killing is not taken lightly in this town.

Brenda had not loosened her grip on the arm of the law. She clung, and with her free arm pointed to the hung pig; she chattered, gasped, and shook. Her words tumbled out in an incoherent stream. The policeman looked stunned; all the policemen looked blank and chagrined, their drawn pistols hung superfluous and obscenely naked at their sides. They had come to do battle for a brother and found only a barbecue.

In that momentary hiatus before explanations and recriminations must be made, in the silence before the full weight of embarrassment descended, understanding came to Guttierez. And with it fury. It swelled his chest and added inches to his height. His narrowed eyes sought Brenda, and the fury erupted from his throat. "A-a-y-y! *Pig!*" he screamed.

And the machete flashed in the sun once more. It left his hand in a graceful arc, crossed the fence, and seemed suspended in the still evening air for endless ages before it came to rest.

At almost the same instant a policeman standing near Guttierez fired once. He later said he was aiming for the upswung arm but was too close and a split second too late. Guttierez lay beneath the hanging pig, the wreckage caused by the bullet in the brain mingling with the slow drip from the draining carcass.

Brenda sprawled at the foot of Christian Dior, the machete still quivering in her chest. The slowly spreading stain on her blouse matched the roses that drooped over her.

Somebody turned the radio off. And then the screaming began.

Charles B. Child

The Dwelling Place of the Proud

Chafik J. Chafik, a policeman of Baghdad with many duties, entered his office in a well guarded building on upper Rashid Street early in the morning of a very hot day. He complained to the uniformed sergeant who attended him with the night's reports, "Is it ordained that I must sit in dust?" and took a feather whisk from the lower drawer of a filing cabinet. When he had brushed his chair, he sat with proper care for the creases that his wife had pressed into the trousers of his white linen suit.

"Proceed," he said to the sergeant.

"Sir, there are corpses—"

"A day without corpses in Baghdad will be a day when our streets are perfumed with roses."

The sergeant, a very large man, whose bulk contracted the small office, recognized domestic symptoms. His mahogany-colored face was proofed against expression, but his tiger's eyes were sad. He made a prayer for himself and others, said, "May God will it!" in answer to the Chief Inspector's reference to roses, and went on, "About the corpse, sir—"

"So? Corpse singular? Why then bother me with corpses plural?"

"All clay robbed of souls demands our attention," the sergeant said severely.

Inspector Chafik stood up. He was a small man with high, bony shoulders, delicate feet and hands. His head was large for his body, his face thin, his nose long, his lips full under the ghost of a moustache. Large dun-colored eyes, flat as the land of his birth, were animated by the shadows of his thoughts. In profile he had the likeness of a Babylonian king.

He salaamed humbly to his assistant. "Forgive me, my dear Abdullah—I brought personal troubles to the office. How rightly you correct me in pointing out that all corpses once had souls!"

"We are liable to forget," Sergeant Abdullah said in a forgiving voice.

"Please continue about the singular corpse." Inspector Chafik reached for cigarettes, changed his mind, restlessly tapped the desk with his fingertips. He had nicely manicured nails and there was a signet ring set with a red intaglio on the small finger of his left hand.

"The corpse is named Hamid Babur," Sergeant Abdullah began his recitation of the facts. "Age, about sixty. Address, Mohamed-bin-Ali Street, Kademein—"

Chafik interrupted, "Holy Kademein has been in various reports recently—an epidemic of stomach troubles probably due to over-indulgence in broken glass, scorpions, and the other delicacies they eat up here."

He was a religious man but he had an intellectual's scorn for the conjurers who infested the great shrines of his faith. Kademein, a town four miles from Baghdad, was a glory of Islam and a police-man's nightmare; in its twisting alleyways were born the mobs that sometimes terrorized Baghdad. The Shrine was particularly sacred to the Shia denomination, which for centuries had opposed the caliphate of the orthodox Sunni majority. Thus the Christians, too, had shed each other's blood for dogma.

Inspector Chafik, a middle-of-the-road man, straddled the schism of his Church.

"How did Hamid Babur die?" he asked Sergeant Abdullah.

"Death by poison, sir."

"A woman's weapon. How many wives? How many concubines?"

"Deceased had one wife and no known concubines. A cobbler by trade. No fortune except his sweat. Upright. Devout. He habitually rose at dawn to make his prayer at the Shrine—"

"Death was sudden?"

"Within the holy precincts, sir. Preliminary medical reports suggest a narcotic poison—"

"Probably a hashish addict. We all have our vices." Inspector Chafik took a cigarette from the box on his desk, tapped it on a thumbnail, frowned, and dropped it unlit into the king-size ashtray. "Recite the history of the other corpses," he said brusquely.

The patient sergeant obeyed.

First, the Inspector pondered a knifing of the Alwiyah district where the body of a bedouin girl had been found ripped in the belly. She had been a brothel inmate. "Look for her father or a brother—she disgraced her family and the tribal law is strict," he said.

He was considering the case of a male corpse taken from the river, a strangler's cord around the neck, when he was interrupted by a call from the Police Chief of Kademein. "A moment, my dear *mu-*

fawwadh." Chafik made a bow to the telephone and said to Sergeant Abdullah, "Find out if the knot was a fisherman's knot. If so, hold for interrogation Hassan Asak, who moors his boat near the old Beit Malek Ali. That one moonlights odd jobs for the gangs.—I am now at your disposal," he said into the telephone.

"My concern is the death of Hamid Babur—"

"It has been brought to my attention—"

"I would be gratified, Chief Inspector, if you would give it priority. You know we have an epidemic of sickness up here?"

"Is that unusual in a drainless jungle?"

"The one who died—a poor shoemaker—was much loved for his saintly works. And the sick are all religious men. And we are at the eve of Muharram—"

Somber shadows moved across the screen of Inspector Chafik's drab eyes. The festival was the opening month of the Moslem year, a time of mourning for the Shia, a time when those rigid dissenters flagellated themselves to achieve a condition of religious ecstasy. Rumor, howling like a wolfpack through the labyrinth of Kademein, could bring out the mobs.

The little man reached for a cigarette and then with an impatient gesture swept the box from the desk.

"How bad is the situation?" he asked the Chief of Police.

"We require reinforcements—"

"I come."

Sergeant Abdullah drove the car. They followed the left bank of the Tigris, passing the Abdul Kadir palace and the burial ground of Iraq's short-lived monarchy. They crossed the river at the site of the old Bridge of Boats and went through groves of date palms and cemeteries; the bodies of the devout, brought from Persia and beyond, once by camel train, now by General Motors trucks, were a richer investment to landowners than the trees.

The streets of Kademein, unchanged from the days of Turkish domination, were attic-hot where the sun struck and cellar-cold where the sun could not reach. Houses with shuttered windows leaned on one another as they seemed to reel in drunken oblivion. An odorous place, and silent, but Chafik was not fooled.

"A policeman's knock would shake out the bedbugs of ancient hates," he said to Abdullah.

"Holy men live here, sir."

"Accept my apologies."

They came to the *midan,* the great square in front of the Shrine, and a view of the forty-foot pillars of the Rose Gate, covered with glazed tiles of pink and turquoise-blue arabesque. There were seven gates to Kademein—all but the Rose Gate were closed on the eve of the time of mourning.

A chain hung between the pillars at the level of a tall man; it was caught up in the center and gracefully looped.

The sanctuary was encompassed by grey walls. There were many beggars—the halt, the blind, and the conjurers. Chafik noticed a crouched figure in a doorway opposite the Shrine; a pale face, a boy, a cripple, and Chafik paused to thank God for blessing him with a healthy son.

He cricked his neck as he strained to look up at the golden towers and cupolas of Kademein. The Gate, earth-level for mortals, was easier to see. He watched the worshippers pull down the chain to bless it as they entered.

"A symbol—just a symbol!" he grumbled. "Chains—prisons—martyrs!"

Sergeant Abdullah, who was of the Shia persuasion, ground his gears as he stopped at police headquarters.

The *mufawwadh* was an old friend, a tall thin man whose professional ulcers gave him a melancholy expression. When they had ritually greeted one another, Chafik said, "I am flattered by your request for my help, but you are as competent as me to investigate this mystery."

"The Assistant Director does not think so."

Chafik shrugged. "That little rooster has to crow twice to make himself heard."

"He will crow more than twice if the death of Hamid Babur is not cleared up on a non-religious basis," the Kademein Chief of Police said grimly.

He beckoned Chafik to the window. Below was the courtyard of the Shrine, beautifully paved, the ablution tanks crystal, the doors and archways graciously proportioned and patterned. The two major domes of Kademein were golden shields turning to the blazing sky; communities of doves clustered and occasionally rose in clouds when disturbed by the chanting of the worshippers. There were four slender towers, each girdled with anachronistic strings of electric lights, which sent their nightly beams over the desert land. Once fires had blazed on these gilded minarets to guide pilgrim travelers. Kademein was a tree tap-rooted in yesterday. Inspector Chafik kissed his hand in respect.

He took his friend's binoculars and examined the scene. "Who is the one in the doorway?" he asked, remembering the boy he had noticed from the police car.

Not a boy, he saw now; not even a wizened child. The head was too large, the body somehow truncated. The legs were lost under the hem of a ragged gown such as street urchins wore—the whole squatting on a crude platform mounted on wheels. Enormous eyes were fixed on the towers and domes of Kademein.

"Yusif, son of Ahmed Fadil," the Chief of Police said. "Not so young as you might think—one detained in childhood."

"Speechless?"

"Yes."

"But his eyes talk. How they plead! Why is he not taken into the Shrine? Sometimes in moments of ecstasy the sick become whole— No miracle!—even psychiatrists do not claim magic for their gods."

"His father forbids it. Ahmed Fadil hates God."

Inspector Chafik played with a cigarette. "No, no!" he said when his friend reached for matches. "My wife," he explained with a nervous laugh. "She is a visiting lady at the hospital and concerns herself with those who cough themselves to death. Why does Ahmed Fadil hate God?"

"Clearly, because he was given an incomplete son. He is a proud man."

"Pride is like perfume—pleasant to inhale but revolting to swallow. The blasphemy is in his bile, not in his heart."

"May that be true," the Chief of Police said piously. He went on, "The man has had many troubles. In his youth he wished to be a doctor but failed to pass the examinations. He is employed as an attendant in the mental ward of the State Hospital. Last month his wife died. He is pockets-down with debts and furthermore has trouble with the Qadhi."

Chafik raised his eyebrows. The Qadhi sat in judgment in the religious courts, which, among other matters coming under Kóranic law, dealt with family problems. "What is Ahmed Fadil's offense?" he asked.

"He neglects his son."

The little inspector sighed. "And foolishly he thinks he can punish God?" He adjusted the binoculars to watch the worshippers as they entered the Shrine. Each man reached for the chain looped across the doorway, pulled it down with a rattle of links, pressed it to forehead and lips. A father bearing a boy of circumcisional age on his shoulders paused to permit the small one to grasp the tattered handgrips and sturdily raise himself for the ritual. A cloud of tumbler doves obscured the view and Chafik turned from the window.

"You referred to the sickness as an epidemic. Describe the symptoms."

The Chief of Police took medication for his ulcers. "Well," he said, as he put down the glass. "First, the victim becomes immobilized. In some cases the heart is affected. He collapses. Later there may be vomiting. Normally, the condition clears within twenty-four hours. According to the medical authorities, there are traces of a poisonous substance in the vomit. Its nature has not yet been determined."

"But more important, what causes such an epidemic? A germ? A virus?"

"It has not been determined."

A disturbance at the Shrine drew Chafik's attention. A fanatic who shrieked, "Ali!—Hussein!—" clung to the chain and covered it with kisses. He was removed by the attendants whose duty it was to keep order within the sacred walls.

Tension thrummed like a drawn bowstring as others cried, "Ali! Hussein! Ali-Hussein! Hussein-Ali!" naming their martyrs with a frenzied mourning chant. Soon the flagellants and head slashers would begin grisly demonstration and madness would reign in Kademein.

Time to mourn. Time to hate. Time to transfuse the ancient schism with the fresh blood of self-inflicted wounds.

"They begin early this year," said the Chief of Police.

"Because of the sickness?"

"Yes. There were the usual smoldering rumors and Hamid Babur's death added fuel. He was a devout man and, as I have said, the people think this evil comes from the Sunni—that the sickness strikes only the very devout Shia, those who say *Fajr* at Kademein—"

"You mean that only those who attend the early morning prayer are inflicted with the sickness?"

"Mainly so. There have been a few mild cases during the afternoon prayer, but the majority occur at the dawn hour. Hamid Babur was always of the congregation and he had previously had the sickness.

This time he died—at the foot of the sepulcher of Musa-bin-Tafar. Excuse me." The Chief of Police answered the telephone.

The little color in his face faded; the look he gave Inspector Chafik was expressive.

"It has happened. A Sunni knifed a Shia in a cafe brawl. The mobs are out. If more are taken sick at *Fajr* tomorrow, we will need troops."

Chafik left his friend and joined Sergeant Abdullah, who had waited with the car. The big man was watching the crowds. "Trouble brews," the sergeant announced.

"You croak like the bird of ill-omen."

"Trouble brews," repeated Abdullah. He pointed with his chin at the gathering mob. "There are doorways which we should sandbag for machine-gun posts—"

"There is a doorway with a fine view of the Gate and at present it is occupied by a cripple."

"Previously noted and under surveillance, sir."

"Oh, most perfect of policemen! Your light runs before you!" Inspector Chafik at once apologized for his testiness. "If only I could smoke I would not be so fretful," he confessed, and gave the crumpled cigarette to a whining beggar.

It was before the hour of *Zuhr;* the open place fronting the Shrine would soon fill for the afternoon prayer. Chafik went to the doorway where the son of Ahmed Fadil crouched, small and frail and lonely. The hands, used to propel the wheeled platform, were calloused; the legs under his gown were withered.

Unblinking pain-wracked eyes were fixed on Kademein. Yusif paid no attention when the Inspector spoke to him.

"Don't waste your time. He neither hears nor speaks," said a bitter voice at Chafik's elbow.

The man was tall and thin. A pharaoh's mummy out of its wrappings, Chafik thought, and the description was apt; the man had the hawk nose and long skull of a yesterday's Egyptian, the same delicate hands and feet, the same high cheekbones and sensuous lips. And the same pride. He looked down at the Inspector as a god at a mortal.

Chafik noted the cleanliness of the white-linen trousers and short-sleeved tunic and recognized the uniform of a hospital worker. "You are Ahmed Fadil?"

"Does it concern you?"

"I am concerned when a father neglects his son."

"You call *that* a son?" The man pointed to the cripple in the doorway. He shrugged with contempt as he uncovered a small basket, took out a bowl of scraps, a round of unleavened bread, a crock of soured milk, and put them within reach of the silent youth. Thus food was given to a kenneled dog. "I do my duty," the man said in his bitter voice. He picked up the basket.

"God asks more than duty—He asks you to give your son love." It stopped Ahmed Fadil as he turned to go. His chin jerked up and he declared in a voice harsh with anger, "There is no God!"

He spat in the direction of the golden domes of Kademein.

Sergeant Abdullah, who loomed behind the Inspector, took a step forward, his hand hovering near the worn leather of his holstered gun. A glance from Chafik stopped him.

"If there is no God, why do you hate that which does not exist?" Chafik asked softly.

"I hate all those who mouth prayers to a myth, who degrade their bodies by flagellation."

"But some men, Mr. Fadil, scourge themselves mentally. Do you? Because of him?" Chafik pointed at the mute in the doorway.

The man looked at his son for the first time. There was a moment when his face softened; then he turned his back and said savagely, "That is what your God gave me! Surely there will be a reckoning!"

"There is a time of reckoning for all of us."

Ahmed Fadil's eyes blazed. "The time has come for *them!*" he said, pointing to the great gate of the Shrine where the devout were gathered for prayer. "They corrupt even this husk of a thing you call my son! Look at him—how he longs to be with them! I forbid it! Look at him—look—"

Yusif's small body was rigid, but his lips moved soundlessly, shaping the words in unison with the chanting of the worshippers.

The father spat in disgust and went away with long strides.

"Let him go," Chafik told Sergeant Abdullah. "Pride and hatred blind him. Poor fool—one day his eyes will open."

Inspector Chafik sat in his small office which overlooked the busy thoroughfare of Rashid Street. He had been sitting there since his return from Kademein and the pile of crushed and unsmoked cigarettes in his ashtray was evidence of wrestling with a priority problem. Subordinates who brought routine problems were treated to a blank look and extraneous snatches of conversation.

He said in a sleepwalker's voice to an officer reporting a confession from the father of the bedouin girl found with slit belly: "But how was it administered to so many?" And to another who came to confirm that Hassan the Fisherman had indeed knotted the cord about the neck of the man found in the river: "How can I weave with broken threads?"

When Sergeant Abdullah arrived with the autopsy report on Hamid Babur, the Inspector was quoting the twenty-ninth verse of the sixteenth chapter of the Koran, "Evil is the dwelling place of the proud." The understanding sergeant crisply interrupted, "Permit me, sir, to advise you that you talk to yourself," and tapped the report for attention.

Chafik shuddered like a man coming out of a nightmare. "Ah, that habit—can I ever break it?" He was in the act of lighting a cigarette when he remembered the promise to his wife and said glumly, "Now I have two habits to plague me." He studied the report.

Hamid Babur had an organic heart condition and it had killed him. But there were also traces of the powerful drug found in the vomit of the more fortunate victims of the Kademein sickness. Analysis mentioned curare, and the Inspector called the police laboratory.

"Oh, Father of Intestines!" he said to the pathologist in charge. "Enlighten me about this drug you found within the corpse I sent you. It was my understanding that curare is used by South American natives to poison their arrows."

"In a crude form, yes, Inspector. It causes immobilization of the animal struck by the arrow. Then the creature's throat can be cut at leisure."

"But I understood—"

"—that the scratch would kill, Father of Ignorance?" The medical man laughed merrily. "You have been reading detective stories. Hamid Babur would not have died if it had not been for his heart condition."

"Does the drug work if taken orally?" asked Chafik.

"It might cause vomiting, but not seriously. If, however, there was a cut on the mouth—an abrasion—"

"And the condition of the mouth of Hamid Babur?"

Papers rustled. Then the pathologist said, "There was a jagged cut on the lower lip."

Inspector Chafik reached for a cigarette, then angrily discarded it. "Tell me," he rasped. "Tell me, Father of Hearts and Livers, did those who did *not* die of the Kademein sickness also have abrasions near their mouths?"

"I must look. I have the reports of the health officer."

The small policeman cradled the telephone under his chin; his hands wove spider's webs as he waited. When the doctor came back he greeted him harshly, "Well?"

"Examinations made by the health officer of the more serious cases do include mouth sores—"

"So!" The Inspector chose and toyed with another cigarette and then asked in a deceptively gentle voice, "My dear Doctor, about this curare thing and my ignorance—what is it in substance?"

"Well, it is defined as coming from a loganiaceous vine or tree—a resinous extract, dark brown in color—an aromatic, tarry odor—um, not unpleasant—"

"Used medically?"

"Beneficially so. We use it in conjunction with shock treatment to bring patients out of deep depression. Curare keeps them from hurting themselves. These mental cases require—"

Chafik slammed down the telephone and rose tiptoe, balanced on the balls of his feet to give himself stature. His thin sharp face was a mask cast in bronze newly drawn from the furnace. Shadows swirled in the flat drab eyes; so kite-hawks gather in the desert sky above a kill.

"Tomorrow we say *Fajr* at the Shrine of Kademein," he said to Sergeant Abdullah.

And added, "Petition God for a miracle."

The stars were still the bright eyes of the night when Inspector Chafik rose from beside his sleeping wife. He appreciated her as he dressed; they had been twenty years married and her dark hair spread over the pillow brought to his mind words of an old love song, "Your ringlets are daggers in my heart." He went to look at his son.

Faisal had ten years. Perhaps more. He was an elfin-eared boy born without name in the labyrinth of the Baghdad bazaars where the Homeless Ones ran. Chafik had chosen Faisal, and Leila, his wife, had given him rebirth.

They were very happy with their adopted son.

The Inspector removed the plastic machine gun that the boy cuddled, replaced it with the schoolbooks that had fallen from the bed, kissed Faisal lightly, and went away.

Sergeant Abdullah was waiting outside. They drove from the

Street of the Scatterer of Blessings, where Chafik lived, to Kademein. They passed through a city that slept uneasily; it was already tomorrow and Muharram, but too early for religious fervor to mount the mobs.

The police car crossed the Tigris into the area of date palms and tombs. Pre-dawn silence cloaked the land and Inspector Chafik shivered as he toyed with the new inevitable unlit cigarette. "The cold is in my soul," he said to the solicitous sergeant.

"Prayer will warm you, sir."

"I overflow with prayer. Also I ooze fear—my body has the odor of a freshly killed chicken."

The diadems on the towers of Kademein had scattered the stars when Chafik halted the car. They went on foot through the winding sewers of the streets into the freshness of the *midan*. At this hour the Shrine was black-walled and the Rose Gate a splash of ebony.

Aloft, where the dawn now challenged the night, a lark prematurely greeted the day.

"The Crier, fortunately, still sleeps," said Inspector Chafik as he looked up at the muezzin's tower.

Unsleeping was the son of Ahmed Fadil. Yusif was couched in the doorway, hunched in his rags, the pale oval of his face turned to the sky. Sergeant Abdullah raised him with a scoop of bear's paws and lowered him to the Inspector's shoulders, crotch hooked about Chafik's neck, the withered legs tucked under his armpits.

He was as light to carry as a confessed sin.

The Inspector walked with Yusif across the open place to the Gate of the Shrine.

A yawning Crier adjusted the microphone on the east tower of Kademein as the lark's song soared to meet the rising sun. The call to prayer, a sobbing chant, went out over the sleeping city, its faith a song to God.

"Allah-u Akbar!"

Four times repeated.

A many padding of feet as those roused by the call ran to the Gate. There they were halted by lines of police who rose from lurking places.

"Ash-hadu al-la-ildha ill-Allah!"

As the voice pronounced the creed, Chafik approached the doorway. There was now light in the land and he could see the dangling chain. His frail burden raised himself and reached for the loop.

"Hayya 'alas-salah!"

The appeal to come to prayer was sung with all the emotion of faith. Then, suddenly, the mute on Chafik's shoulders echoed it. Sound burst from a throat too long silent. Harsh, yet singing. And ended in the wail of a disappointed child as Chafik stopped short of the Gate.

Extended hands. Pleading eyes.

"God the Merciful! God the Loving-Kind!" prayed Inspector Chafik, shaken with wonder.

He had directed the police to permit one man to pass the barrier, and now he came, tall, thin, crying without pride: "No! No! Do not let him touch it!"

Ahmed Fadil dropped to his knees between the Gate of Kademein and the man who carried his son.

"Is there then a barrier between Yusif and his God?" asked Chafik.

"The chain—"

"Chains are made to break or to bless if they have been worn by martyrs." The Inspector spoke with calculated impatience and moved forward, wishing he could move back.

The man rose and barred the way. He looked not at Chafik, but eye-level with the Inspector's burden.

Yusif did not see his father, but reached for the chain, as a child reaches for the unknown world beyond the cradle.

Ahmed Fadil struck down his son's hands, shouting, "It is poisoned!"

He tore off his neckcloth and wiped the links. "See?" he cried. The cloth was soiled with a brownish substance sweet with the odor of honey.

There was blood on his hand.

"So you also roughened the links to cut the mouths of the devout before you applied the curare?" said Inspector Chafik.

"Yes."

"You stole the extract from the mental ward, came at night, put the curare on the chain?"

"Yes, yes."

"You planned an epidemic for Kademein to incite the mobs, to put man against man, sect against sect?"

"But I did not intend a man should die—that Hamid Babur—"

"You did all this because you have been given an incomplete son? Because you hated God?"

"Yes—yes."

"You confess?" Inspector Chafik asked the question as a policeman

concerned only with secular law. In this moment he towered, dominated the Gate of Kademein. Then he said in a humble voice, "May I be forgiven. Your crime is against God, and in His Court you will find justice."

He signaled Sergeant Abdullah to remove Ahmed Fadil. And sensitive to the voices of the worshippers, he heard the calm as they streamed to the Gate, answering the call to prayer.

"La-ildha ill-Allah!"

"Do you hear?" Chafik asked the burden that he bore lightly on his shoulders.

The Inspector kicked off his shoes and walked into the promise of the Shrine.

Helen Hudson

The Thief

Mrs. Marvell sat at the kitchen table, steaming her nose inside the coffee cup, watching the birds in her feeder and getting quite worked up over the jay. She had a strong sense of law and order and a devotion to detail. Her iced-tea spoons were exquisite and her diet balanced. She was sixty-eight with blue eyes and a fragile little face, round as a cup and beautifully preserved, as though it had been wrapped in tissue and used only on special occasions.

She still saved ribbon and paper and rubbed her furniture with lemon-oil polish to preserve the wood. She wore her glasses on a chain around her neck like a second pair of eyes on her bosom ("Too vain to put them where they belong," Josephine Hooker had said), and kept two appointment books, one upstairs, one down, thus keeping a double check on time, though most of the pages were blank.

Through the windows she could see the sandbox and the swing and the jungle gym next door where Margaret Witherspoon's roses had once waved little white gloves over the fence. On the other side, at the old Brewster place, the flowerbeds were sinking into a sea of grass and an empty washline swayed in the breeze. Her own garden was neat as ever, with rows of tulips at the back and petunias on their knees along the borders.

She watched the jay swoop down on the feeder, scattering the sparrows and the chickadees, a plump, arrogant fellow in a blue suit. He reminded her of the policeman who had filled her kitchen after the last robbery, a big clumsy man whose hands stumbled and tripped among her china. They had been increasing steadily, these robberies, ever since Lewis went to the nursing home.

They were not really robberies, though, since nothing ever seemed to be taken—nothing, that is, that she missed. And they never happened when she was home. But they were beginning to frighten her all the same, and she was very careful now about locking up—double bolts on all the doors, curtains open, lights on, and the burglar alarm switched up. She was thinking of getting a dog and an electric fence.

"It's just a bunch of kids, Amy," Josephine Hooker told her. "After your liquor. I can't think why you don't leave it out where they can get at it easily. It would be cheaper in the long run." She rubbed her nose with the back of her hand like a child who won't carry a handkerchief, though she was sixty-five and born to one of the oldest families in Newburyport, Massachusetts. She had read so much poetry through the years that her face had begun to resemble a page of free verse, all dots and dashes and irregular lines.

Mrs. Marvell shook her head carefully, as though she still had a mass of blonde curls on her neck. "They're after my *things,* of course," she said. "That's why they always choose *my* house. I have *lovely* things." And she thought of her fine old silver bundled in its flannel jackets and the china and the pair of Venetian-glass decanters she kept clean and empty on the sideboard.

She pushed the coaster under Josephine's highball and stirred her own tea. "The liquor will stay where it belongs," she said firmly. But she didn't expect Josephine to understand. For Josephine kept extra hairpins in an ashtray on the mantel and pencils in mayonnaise jars all over the living room. Her hair always looked as if it were about to slide down over one ear like a wig, though she kept it skewered on dozens of pins and bunched up under a net. Mrs. Marvell's hair, all white now, stood up in soft little wisps as though she were being constantly—and gently—fanned.

Yet it seemed only a few years ago that her hair was still bright and shiny as the day Lewis first saw it from the lecture platform, like a golden spray in that sea of bent heads. He had married her at the end of the term, taking her home to a large white house with a driveway that swept past the front door and a grape arbor and a birdbath behind, and Valerie to cook and clean and draw the curtains so Mrs. Marvell never had to see the end of a day or the coming of night, dripping silently through the trees.

Lewis was an associate professor by then, with tenure stretched out comfortably beneath him and an adoring family high on Nob Hill, a continent away. He was a mild, courteous man, with a hint of the cutaway about him: a conciliator, a moderator, much in demand at college debates and faculty meetings. He brought to his new wife the love he had been saving up for years, like water in a bowl, and rubbed the back of her neck with tender hands. But he went on living most of his life in his study at home and in the office at the college, with the long walk between for exercise and reflection. Josephine Hooker said he was the only married bachelor she had ever known.

But Mrs. Marvell just smiled and ran a finger down the smooth silver curve of her teapot. She had her Wednesday reading group and the Sunday art lectures and long naps when she was bored. Sometimes she put a piece of black-velvet ribbon in her hair and went out to lunch. But on the whole she preferred her garden, where the demands were simple and the responses predictable.

Occasionally she gave dinner parties for six or eight, with two maids to serve. "She really does it for her things," Josephine Hooker said. "To lay a new tablecloth or light up her Cellini candlesticks." But Mrs. Marvell had been content. Her days had opened and closed like paper fans without even the pain of childbirth to cause the tiniest tear. And only Lewis to say, in his mildest manner, "I don't believe I would if I were you, Amy. I really don't."

Oh, I was spoiled, Mrs. Marvell thought now, sitting alone at her kitchen table with the jungle gym on her right and an old rope swinging slightly at her left and that fat jay lording it over her feeder. Terribly, terribly spoiled. She stared into the empty coffee cup and sucked one end of her glasses.

Yet even away back then the robberies had begun. The first one came about a year after her marriage. Lewis had just left for a conference. "Do come," he had said the night before. But she had an appointment with her garden man the next day and she hated trains and cigarette smoke and Lewis's middle-aged, academic friends, who gave her admiring smiles but kept the conversation to themselves. She much preferred to stay behind and watch Douglas Fairbanks, strong and silent in the dark, and wait for Lewis to come back with his memories of Chicago strung on a chain or a locket for her.

But when she got home that night, for the first time, standing all alone outside the dark and silent house, she suddenly felt frightened. And when she stepped inside, she had the strange feeling that some-one had been there—someone who did not belong. She stood just inside the back door with the feeling that he was standing right behind her. She could almost feel his breath on her neck.

She saw a burnt matchstick in the little enamel ashtray, a dish-cloth in a heap on the counter beneath the rack, and the liquor cabinet slightly open. She turned and ran around the corner to where Josephine Hooker lived with Alden, her new husband, who did all the cooking while his wife read poetry aloud.

Josephine put her arms around her and Mrs. Marvell sobbed into the wool on Josephine's shoulder that still smelled of camphor though it was mid-January. "Stay here tonight," Josephine said. But Mrs. Marvell remembered that the Hookers had no real guest room, just a lumpy cot in Alden's study with Alden's music stand at the head and Alden's swivel chair at the foot and smudges on the spread where Alden's feet had been.

The Hookers took her back home and saw her inside. She left most of the lights on and put chairs behind the doors. But she lay awake a long time wondering about him, whoever he was, who had watched the house so carefully, whose fingers had violated her possessions, and who even now, she felt sure, was still out there beneath the trees or under the arbor, with his hands restless in his pockets and his eyes fixed on her windows.

Lewis came home the next morning. The police came; also a carpenter in overalls, looking ready to cope, with a hammer and a rule sticking out of his back pocket. They examined the locks and the windows and the doors. They searched the cupboards and the closets. But they found nothing gone and nothing added.

Lewis put his arms around her. "Are you sure you didn't just imagine it?"

"He must have had a key," she said.

The liquor cabinet was closed, the dishcloth hung up, and the ashtray washed. They had new locks put on all the doors. The days became smooth again, with Rowena, this time, closing the curtains and Lewis pouring the tea and carving. There was nothing to remember except, for a while, a small hole, a jagged slit where something ugly had forced its way in.

Mrs. Marvell had forgotten all about it when, three years later, Lewis had to go West to his mother's funeral. "I really think you should come with me this time, Amy," he said. She was in bed with a headache and symptoms that might have meant the early stages of pregnancy.

She held out her hand. "I'm so sorry. I know I shouldn't let you go alone. But I'm afraid to take chances. And funerals upset me so."

He took her hand. "Funerals upset me, too," he said. "Especially this one."

She stayed in bed long after he had gone, thinking how glad she was not to be going with him: the chapel smelling of hothouse flowers and dusty hymnals and old men waiting in the pews. She had a long bath and a slow breakfast and spent the afternoon in the garden with a book on her lap, admiring the bright, shiny faces of her jonquils. She went to the Hookers' for dinner.

"Good God!" Josephine said. "Of course you should have gone."

She rubbed her nose and glared. "Really, Amy, you're getting more selfish by the minute."

"I know, dear," Mrs. Marvell said mildly. "But Lewis does spoil me so." She smiled at Alden. No one, she thought, would ever want to spoil Josephine, that outcropping of New England granite in a plaid skirt.

But when she got home that night, standing at her back door, fumbling for the key, Mrs. Marvell suddenly remembered the last time she had come home alone in the dark. And when she stepped inside, she knew at once that someone had been there, stirring the air in that locked house. She saw one of the kitchen drawers slightly open and the liquor cabinet unlatched. She turned and ran back to the Hookers'.

"Well," Josephine Hooker said, pressing Mrs. Marvell's face against her cardigan. "Any bottles missing?"

Mrs. Marvell shook her head. "How can I tell? You know I never touch liquor. And I don't pay any attention to the supply."

"Pity," Josephine Hooker said. "Part of your unfinished education, not learning to drink. Now you'll have to go through life never knowing whether or not you're being robbed."

But Mrs. Marvell remembered the sight of that slightly gaping cabinet and the kitchen drawer hanging down like a greedy little mouth, and she shuddered. It was a long time before she got over the feeling that something or someone was waiting just outside the house, with his shoulder against the door.

The housebreaking continued, but only when Lewis was away, and so seldom and sporadically through the years that each intrusion came as a surprise. She had time, in between, to get angry. She refused to move the liquor. She refused to spend the night with the Hookers. She would not take down the arbor or put up an ugly electric fence or get a dog to chew her furniture and make messes on the rugs. She would go on doing as she pleased. Like the burglar.

She built a new little sitting room for herself with French windows, in spite of the burglar, and insisted that Lewis keep the liquor supply well stocked, perhaps *because* of him. But mostly she lived without reference to him. She pulled up her lawn in half a dozen places and moved the flowerbeds around like furniture. She hired a squadron of maids, one after the other, and fired them when they forgot to wash the empty decanters or put the sofa cushions back upside down. They all seemed to have fancy names and she dressed them in white.

"Like hospital nurses," Josephine Hooker said. "They even walk on their toes. So as not to disturb the jade ashtrays, I suppose."

"We're happy," Mrs. Marvell said. "I've made Lewis happy. Without poetry. At least he doesn't have to do the cooking."

"Alden loves to cook," Josephine said. "And he never washes up."

It was true. Mrs. Marvell had seen her with her arms in the dishpan and her face soft, the lines running together, and Alden practicing scales on the violin near the drainboard.

"Lewis has never had to do either," Mrs. Marvell said. "I've been a good wife. I've made him happy."

She wondered now, sitting at the kitchen table smoothing the place mat, if this were true. But it was too late to ask him. Lewis was dying, inch by inch, in a nursing home twenty miles away tucked discreetly between the pleats of the surrounding hills. It was where all the aged middle class of the town were sent when death loitered too long on the doorstep.

Lewis was suffering from a circulatory disease.

"Tired blood," Josephine Hooker told her husband.

"There's no such thing."

"Bored blood, then. After forty years with Amy anybody's blood would get sluggish."

But Lewis was letting go very slowly, beginning with his little toe at one end and his mind at the other and his heart holding the balance between them. It was as though, mild and moderate as he was, he could not accept anything so extreme as death and was temporizing still, keeping it at arm's length with his voice low. Every day when Mrs. Marvell went to see him, he looked at her sadly and asked why she hadn't come the day before.

Yet when he had forgotten everything else, he remembered his manners and his sense of propriety. Whenever they brought him a tray or a drink or a pill, he would raise solicitous eyes to his wife and ask, "Where's yours? Why aren't they bringing yours?" And when the nurse said, "Did you sleep well?" or "Did you have a movement?" he would raise his voice slightly and answer, "Did you?"

But he had no defenses. A gentle man, he could not stay for the final battle but had moved out, looking in only occasionally, shocked to discover how far the invasion had advanced. He sat in the big chair in pajamas and robe with his hair long around his ears and barely enough strength to turn his head from the raised spoon.

The nurses stood about in the halls, big and white as plaster casts, and they often complained of Lewis to his face. "Keeps trying to pull the catheter out all the time," they told Mrs. Marvell. She would cry all the way home, remembering Lewis as he had been, tall and elegant in dark suits and so polite that just winding his watch seemed an act of courtesy.

In the garage she would sit in the car for a moment, drying her eyes and wondering if Lewis would ever come home again. And then she remembered the burglar who came only when Lewis was away. She would go quietly up the back steps and stand inside the kitchen door, over against the wall, waiting for someone to brush past her in the narrow hall. And then she would look for the evidence. She found it more and more often, penetrating farther and farther into the house: a used glass in the sitting room, a broken stem on the begonia plant in the study, the tops of the decanters crooked in the dining room, and, just the other night, a dead leaf in the hall at the bottom of the stairs.

She had had the burglar alarm installed then, and all the locks changed once more. She kept all the inside doors sealed permanently, living only in the kitchen and the bedroom and the upstairs bathroom. But she locked even these behind her.

Now she put on her glasses to watch the birds, but the jay had chased them all away. Only he was left, fat and cocky with his head in her feeder. Soon he, too, flew behind a tree and disappeared. The garden was suddenly quiet. She took off her glasses.

Behind her, the house was quiet, too, with that terrible silence which had been seeping in ever since Lewis left. She was down to just the Wednesday reading group now and a Thursday maid (called simply Gussie), and they made no sounds that carried through the week. The phone almost never rang, or the doorbell. Everyone else seemed dead or busy or away.

Besides, she had never encouraged callers. She had never really developed any tolerance for people, any more than for alcohol, and she could not start now, could not listen to their prattle of husbands and grandchildren and the party at the Binghams'—not now while Lewis sat in a nursing home with his hands in his lap, waiting for the blood in his veins to stop flowing.

And so she lived in silence, while the plants around her grew without a sound and measured the weeks with a length of green. Shy little flames burned unheard in the stove, scorching, at regular intervals, small holes in her day that were breakfast and lunch and dinner. Even the clocks were quiet, electric clocks that marked the time in silence, their hands sliding or sticking at will. She longed for the regular, dependable tick of her youth when she could hear the passing of time and it had a serene and soothing sound.

She was all alone in a silent house with a thief who came more and more often. Should she move to an apartment in town? Make certain, once more, that the tops were straight on the decanters and the sofa cushions right side up and call the auctioneer? There was no one to tell her—no one to advise or command or say, simply, "You're wrong." There was not even Lewis's mild "I don't believe I would." They said only, "Do whatever you want." Like shutting a drawer. Even Josephine Hooker had gone up to Boston when Alden died, to read poetry to her grandchildren.

Mrs. Marvell got up at last and washed and dried her cup and saucer.

Then, locking the kitchen door behind her, she went slowly upstairs, holding her glasses flat against her breast.

Lewis was much worse that afternoon. He lay on his back in bed. His white hair almost covered his ears now and his beard was sprouting like new grass around his mouth. His words came out in a mere trickle that she could not understand. Until she got up to go.

"Goodbye, Lewis," she said softly.

He clung to her hand.

"I really think you should come with me this time, Amy," he said distinctly. "I really do."

She drove home with the hand he had held on her lap tucked carefully under her coat.

At home she found her bathroom window open. Her housebreaker had come again, but it was the first time he had ever dared come upstairs. He must have climbed up the arbor. Now she would have to tear it down. Maybe put up an electric fence and get a dog. From now on she would even have to leave the car outside where he could see it *all the time.*

She called the police and sat down in the kitchen to wait. She could see the liquor cabinet in the pantry. It was open just a crack, making a thin gash in the smooth surface of the wall. She got up suddenly, pulled out a bottle, and poured herself a drink.

After the police had gone, she turned on all the lights and checked all the doors, including the inside ones—the dining room and the sitting room and the living room and the study.

Whenever, however he came, there would be many sealed doors between them.

Then she picked up the bottle, locked the kitchen door behind her, and went softly up the stairs. She bolted the bedroom door, put the bottle on the dressing table, and sat down to wait.

She knew that sometime soon, very soon, tomorrow or the next day or the next, he would come again. And she knew that next time he would come when she was there. She would sit waiting for him in the locked bedroom, staring at the oak panel of the door, listening to the sound of his steps on the stair—strange, irregular steps like a man's with a limp.

She put on her glasses and poured herself a drink and stared at her bedroom door. It was a lovely door, all smooth, with a rich, dark grain and an old-fashioned brass keyhole. It would be a shame to have it all smashed and splintered. Sipping her drink and staring at the door, she wondered suddenly if she shouldn't unlock it for him. Hadn't he been her most constant caller?

Edmund Crispin

The Name on the Window

Boxing Day—the first weekday after Christmas—snow and ice, road surfaces like glass under a cold fog. In the North Oxford home of Gervase Fen, the University Professor of English Language and Literature, the front doorbell rang at exactly three minutes past seven in the evening.

The current festive season had taken toll of Fen's vitality and patience. It had culminated, that afternoon, in an exceptionally tiring children's party, amid whose ruins he was now recouping his energies with whiskey, and on hearing the bell he jumped inevitably to the conclusion that one of the infants he had bundled out of the door half an hour before had left behind some such prized inessential as a false nose or a bachelor's button and was returning to claim it. As it turned out, however, and despite his premonitory groans, this assumption proved to be incorrect. His doorstep was occupied not by a dyspeptic, overheated child with an unintelligible query but by a neatly dressed greying man with a red-tipped nose and woebegone eyes.

"I can't get back," said the apparition. "I really can't get back to London tonight. The roads are impassable and such trains as there are are running hours late. Could you possibly let me have a bed?"

The tones were familiar, and by peering more attentively at the face Fen discovered that that was familiar, too. "My dear Humbleby," he said cordially, "do come in. Of course you can have a bed. What are you doing in this part of the world, anyway?"

"Ghost-hunting." Detective-Inspector Humbleby, of New Scotland Yard, divested himself of his coat and hat and hung them on a hook inside the door. "Seasonable but not convenient." He stamped his feet violently—thereby producing, to judge from his expression, sensations of pain rather than warmth—and stared about him. *"Children,"* he said with sudden gloom. "I daresay that one of the Oxford hotels—"

"The children have left," Fen explained, "and will not be coming back."

"Ah. Well, in that case—" And Humbleby followed Fen into the drawing room, where a huge fire was burning and a slightly lopsided

Christmas tree, stripped of its treasures, wore tinsel and miniature witch-balls and a superincumbent fairy with a raffish air. "My word, this is better. Is there a drink, perhaps? I could do with some advice, too."

Fen was already pouring the whiskey. "Sit down and be comfortable," he said. "As a matter of interest, do you believe in ghosts?"

"The evidence for *poltergeists*," Humbleby answered warily as he stretched out his hands to the blaze, "seems very convincing to me. The Wesleys, you know, and Harry Price, and so forth. Other sorts of ghosts I'm not so sure about—though I must say I *hope* they exist, if only for the purpose of taking that silly grin off the faces of the newspapers." He picked up a battered tin locomotive from beside him on the sofa. "I say, Gervase, I was under the impression that your own children were all too old for—"

"Orphans," said Fen, jabbing at the siphon. "I've been entertaining orphans from a nearby Home. But as regards this particular ghost you were speaking of—"

"Oh, I don't believe in *that*." Humbleby shook his head decisively. "There's an obscure sort of nastiness about the place it's supposed to haunt—like a very sickly cake gone stale—and a man *was* killed there once, by a girl he was trying to persuade to certain practices she didn't relish at all, but the haunting part of it is just silly gossip for the benefit of visitors." Humbleby accepted the glass Fen held out to him and brooded over it for a moment before drinking. "Damned Chief-Inspector," he muttered aggrievedly, "dragging me away from my Christmas lunch because—"

"Really, Humbleby—" Fen was severe "—you're very inconsequential this evening. Where is this place you're speaking of?"

"Rydalls."

"Rydalls?"

"Rydalls," said Humbleby. "The residence," he elucidated laboriously, "of Sir Charles Moberley, the architect. It's about fifteen miles from here, Abingdon way."

"Yes, I remember it now. Restoration."

"I daresay. Old, in any case. And there are big grounds, with an Eighteenth Century pavilion about a quarter of a mile away from the house, in a park. That's where it happened—the murder, I mean."

"The murder of the man who tried to induce the girl—"

"No, no. I mean, yes, *that* murder took place in the pavilion, cer-

188 THE NAME ON THE WINDOW

tainly. But then so did the other one—the one the day before yesterday, that's to say."

Fen stared. "Sir Charles Moberley has been murdered?"

"No, no, no! Not *him*. Another architect, another knight—Sir Lucas Welsh. There's been quite a large houseparty going on at Rydalls, with Sir Lucas Welsh and his daughter Jane among the guests, and it was on Christmas Eve, you see, that Sir Lucas decided he wanted to investigate the ghost."

"This is all clear enough to you, no doubt, but—"

"Do *listen*. It seems that Sir Lucas is—was—credulous about ghosts, so on Christmas Eve he arranged to keep vigil alone in the pavilion and—"

"And was murdered, and you don't know who did it."

"Oh, yes, I do. Sir Lucas didn't die at once, you see: he had time to write his murderer's name in the grime of the windowpane, and the gentleman concerned, a young German named Otto Mórike, is now safely under arrest. But what I can't decide is how Mórike got in and out of the pavilion."

"A locked-room mystery."

"In the wider sense, just that. The pavilion wasn't actually locked, but—"

Fen collected his glass from the mantelpiece where he had put it on rising to answer the doorbell. "Begin," he suggested, "at the beginning."

"Very well." Settling back in the sofa, Humbleby sipped his whiskey gratefully. "Here, then, is this Christmas houseparty at Rydalls. Host, Sir Charles Moberley, the eminent architect. Have you ever come across him?"

Fen shook his head.

"A big man, going grey. In some ways rather boisterous and silly, like a rugger-playing medical student in a stage of arrested development. Unmarried. Private means—quite a lot of them, to judge from the sort of hospitality he dispenses. Designed the Wandsworth power station and Beckford Abbey, among other things. Athlete—a simple mind, and generous, I should judge, in that jealous sort of way which resents generosity in anyone else. Probably tricky, in some respects—he's not the kind of person *I* could ever feel completely at ease with. A celebrity, however—unquestionably that. And Sir Lucas Welsh, whom among others he invited to this houseparty, was equally a celebrity, in the same line of business. Never having seen Sir Lucas alive, I can't say much about his character, but—"

"I think," said Fen, "that I may have met him once, at the time when he was designing the fourth quadrangle for my college. A small, dark person, wasn't he?"

"Yes, that's right."

"And with a tendency to be nervy and obstinate."

"The obstinacy there's evidence for, certainly. And I gather he was also a good deal of a faddist—Yogi, I mean, and the Baconian hypothesis, and a lot of other intellectual—um—detritus of the same dull, obvious kind. That's where the ghost vigil comes in. Jane, his daughter and heiress—and Sir Lucas was if anything even better off than Sir Charles—is a pretty little thing of eighteen, of whom all you can really say is that she's a pretty little thing of eighteen. Then there's Mórike, the man I've arrested—thin, thirtyish, a Luftwaffe pilot during the war, and at present an architecture-student working over here under one of these exchange schemes the universities are always getting up, which accounts for Sir Charles's knowing him and inviting him to the houseparty. Last of the important guests—important from the point of view of the crime, that is—is a C.I.D. man (not Metropolitan, Sussex County) called James Wilburn. He's important because the evidence he provides is certainly reliable. There has to be a *point d'appui* in these affairs, and Wilburn is it, so you mustn't exhaust yourself doubting his word about anything."

"I won't," Fen promised. "I'll believe him."

"Good. At dinner on Christmas Eve, then, the conversation turns to the subject of the Rydalls' ghost—and I've ascertained that the person responsible for bringing this topic up was Otto Mórike. So far, so good: the Rydalls' ghost was a bait Sir Lucas could be relied on to rise to, and rise to it he did, arranging eventually with his rather reluctant host to go down to the pavilion after dinner and keep watch there for an hour or two. The time arriving, he was accompanied to the place by Sir Charles and by Wilburn—neither of whom actually entered the pavilion. Wilburn strolled back to the house alone, leaving Sir Charles and Sir Lucas talking shop. And presently Sir Charles, having seen Sir Lucas go into the pavilion, retraced his steps likewise, arriving at the house just in time to hear the alarm bell ringing."

"Alarm bell?"

"People had watched for the ghost before, and there was a bell installed in the pavilion for them to ring if for any reason they wanted help. This bell sounded, then, at shortly after ten o'clock and a whole party of people, including Sir Charles, Jane Welsh, and Wilburn, hastened to the rescue.

"Now, you must know that this pavilion is quite small. There's just one circular room to it, having two windows, both very firmly nailed up, and you get into this room by way of a longish, narrow hall projecting from the perimeter of the circle, the one and only door being at the outer end of this hall."

"Like a keyhole," Fen suggested. "If you saw it from the air it'd look like a keyhole, I mean—with the round part representing the room and the thin part representing the entrance hall, and the door right down at the bottom."

"That's it. It stands in a clearing among the trees of the park on a very slight rise—inferior Palladian in style, with pilasters or whatever you call them. Something like a decayed miniature classical temple. No one's bothered about it for decades, not since that earlier murder put an end to its career as a love nest for a succession of squires. What is it Eliot says—something about lusts and dead limbs? Well, anyway, that's the impression it gives. A *house* is all right, because a house has been used for other things as well—eating and reading and births and deaths and so on. But this place has been used for one purpose and one purpose only, and that's exactly what it feels like.

"There's no furniture in it, by the way. And until the wretched Sir Lucas unlocked its door, no one had been inside it for two or three years.

"To get back to the story, then. The weather was all right—you'll remember that on Christmas Eve none of this snow and foulness had started. And the rescue party, so to call them, seem to have regarded their expedition as more or less in the nature of a jaunt. I mean that they weren't seriously alarmed at the ringing of the bell, with the exception of Jane, who knew her father well enough to suspect that he'd never have interrupted his vigil, almost as soon as it had begun, for the sake of a rather futile practical joke, and even she seems to have allowed herself to be half convinced by the reassurances of the others.

"On arrival at the pavilion, they found the door shut but not locked, and when they opened it and shone their torches inside they saw a single set of footprints in the dust on the hall floor leading to the circular room. Acting on instinct or training or both, Wilburn kept his crowd clear of these footprints, and so it was that they came—joined now by Otto Mórike, who according to his subsequent statement had been taking a solitary stroll in the grounds—to the scene of the crime.

"Fireplace, two windows, a crudely painted ceiling—crude in subject as well as in execution—a canvas chair, an unlit electric torch, festoons of cobwebs, and on everything except the chair and the torch *dust*, layers of it. Sir Lucas was lying on the floor beneath one of the windows, quite close to the bell-push, and an old stiletto, later discovered to have been stolen from the house, had been stuck into him under the left shoulderblade. No damning fingerprints on it, by the way, or on anything else in the vicinity. Sir Lucas was still alive, and just conscious. Wilburn bent over him to ask him who was responsible. A queer smile crossed Sir Lucas's face and he was just able to whisper"—here Humbleby produced and consulted a notebook—"to whisper: '*Wrote it—on the window. Very first thing I did when I came round. Did it before I rang the bell or anything else, in case you didn't get here in time—in time for me to tell you who—*'

"His voice faded out then. But with a final effort he moved his head, glanced up at the window, nodded, and smiled again. That's how he died.

"They had all heard him and they all looked. There was bright moonlight outside and the letters stood out clearly.

"Otto.

"Well, it seems that then Otto started edging away, and Sir Charles made a grab at him, and they fought, and presently a wallop from Sir Charles sent Otto clean through the telltale window, and Sir Charles scrambled after him, and they went on fighting outside, trampling the glass to smithereens, until Wilburn and company joined in and put a stop to it. Incidentally, Wilburn says that Otto's going through the window looked *contrived* to him—a deliberate attempt to destroy evidence—though, of course, so many people saw the name written there that it remains perfectly good evidence in spite of having been destroyed."

"Motive?" Fen asked.

"Good enough. Janie Welsh was wanting to marry Otto—had fallen quite in love with him, in fact—and her father didn't approve, partly on the grounds that he thought the boy wanted Jane's prospective inheritance rather than Jane herself. To clinch it, moreover, there was the fact that Otto had been in the Luftwaffe and that Jane's mother had been killed in nineteen forty-one in an air raid.

Jane being three years under the age of consent—and the attitude of magistrates, if appealed to, being in the circumstances at least problematical—it looked as if that was one marriage that would definitely not take place. So the killing of Sir Lucas had, from Otto's point of view, a double advantage—it made Jane rich and it removed the obstacle to the marriage."

"Jane's prospective guardian *not* being against it."

"Jane's prospective guardian being an uncle she could twist round her little finger. But here's the point." Humbleby leaned forward earnestly. "Here is the point: windows nailed shut, no secret doors—emphatically none—chimney too narrow to admit a baby, and in the dust on the hall floor only one set of footprints, made unquestionably by Sir Lucas himself. If you're thinking that Otto might have walked in and out *on top* of those prints, as that page-boy we've been hearing so much about recently did with King Wenceslaus, then you're wrong. Otto's feet are much too large, for one thing, and the prints hadn't been disturbed, for another. So that's out.

"But, then, how on earth did he manage it? There's no furniture in that hall whatever—nothing he could have used to crawl across, nothing he could have swung himself from. It's a long, bare box, that's all, and the distance between the door and the circular room—in which room, by the way, the dust on the floor was all messed up by the rescue party—is miles too far away for anyone to have jumped it. Nor was the weapon the sort of thing that could possibly have been fired from a bow or an air gun or a blowpipe or nonsense of that sort, nor was it sharp enough or heavy enough to have penetrated as deeply as it did if it had been thrown. So, ghosts apart, what *is* the explanation? Can you see one?"

Fen made no immediate reply. Throughout this narrative he had remained standing, draped against the mantelpiece. Now he moved, collecting Humbleby's empty glass and his own and carrying them to the decanter, and it was only after they were refilled that he spoke.

"Supposing," he said, "that Otto had crossed the entrance hall on a tricycle—"

"A tricycle!" Humbleby was dumfounded. "A—"

"A tricycle, yes," Fen reiterated firmly. "Or supposing, again, that he had laid down a carpet, unrolling it in front of him as he entered and rolling it up again after him when he left—"

"But the dust!" wailed Humbleby. "Have I really not made it clear to you that apart from the footprints, the dust was undisturbed? Tricycles, carpets—"

"A section of the floor at least," Fen pointed out, "was trampled on by the rescue party."

"Oh, that. Yes, but that didn't happen until *after* Wilburn had examined the floor."

"Examined it in detail?"

"Yes. At that stage they still didn't realize anything was wrong, and when Wilburn led them in they were giggling behind him while he did a sort of parody of detective work—throwing the beam of his torch over every inch of the floor in a pretended search for blood-stains."

"It doesn't," said Fen puritanically, "sound the sort of performance which would amuse me very much."

"I daresay not. Anyway, the point about it is that Wilburn's ready to swear that the dust was completely unmarked and undisturbed except for the footprints. I wish he weren't so ready to swear to that," Humbleby added dolefully, "because that's what's holding me up. But I can't budge him."

"You oughtn't to be trying to budge him, anyway," retorted Fen, whose mood of self-righteousness appeared to be growing on him. "It's unethical. What about blood, now?"

"Blood? There was practically none of it. You don't get any bleeding to speak of from that narrow type of wound."

"Ah. Just one more question, then—and if the answer's what I expect, I shall be able to tell you how Otto worked it."

"If by any remote chance," said Humbleby suspiciously, "it's *stilts* that you have in mind—"

"My dear Humbleby, don't be puerile."

Humbleby contained himself with an effort. "Well?" he said.

"The name on the window." Fen spoke almost dramatically. "Was it written in *capital* letters?"

Whatever Humbleby had been expecting, it was clearly not this. "Yes," he answered. "But—"

"Wait." Fen drained his glass. "Wait while I make a telephone call."

He went. All at once restless, Humbleby got to his feet, lit a cheroot, and began pacing the room. Presently he discovered an elastic-driven airplane abandoned behind an armchair, wound it up, and launched it. It caught Fen a glancing blow on the temple as he reappeared in the doorway, and thence flew on into the hall where it struck and smashed a vase. "Oh, I say, I'm sorry," said Humbleby feebly.

Fen said nothing.

But after about half a minute, when he had simmered down a bit: "Locked rooms," he remarked sourly. "Locked rooms. I'll tell you what it is, Humbleby: you've been reading too much fiction, you've got locked rooms on the brain."

Humbleby thought it politic to be meek. "Yes," he said.

"Dr. Gideon Fell once gave a very brilliant lecture on the locked-room problem in connection with that business in the Hollow Man, but there was one category he didn't include."

"Well?"

Fen massaged his forehead resentfully. "He didn't include the locked-room mystery which *isn't* a locked-room mystery—like this one. So that the explanation of how Otto got in and out of that circular room is simple: he *didn't* get into it and he *didn't* get out of it at all."

Humbleby gaped. "But Sir Lucas can't have been knifed before he *entered* the circular room. Sir Charles said—"

"Ah, yes. Sir Charles saw him go in—or so he asserts. And—"

"Stop a bit." Humbleby was much perturbed. "I can see what you're getting at, but there are serious objections to it."

"Such as?"

"Well, for one thing, Sir Lucas *named* his murderer."

"A murderer who struck at him *from behind*. Oh, I've no doubt Sir Lucas acted in good faith. Otto, you see, would be the only member of the houseparty whom Sir Lucas *knew* to have a *motive*. In actual fact, Sir Charles had one, too—as I've just discovered—but Sir Lucas wasn't aware of that. And in any case, he very particularly didn't want Otto to marry his daughter after his death, so that the risk of doing an ex-Luftwaffe man an injustice was a risk he was prepared to take. Next objection?"

"The name on the window. If, as Sir Lucas said, his *very first* action on recovering consciousness was to denounce his attacker, then he'd surely, since he was capable of entering the pavilion after being knifed, have been capable of writing the name on the *outside* of the window, which would be nearest and which would be just as grimy as the inside. That objection's based, of course, on your assumption that he was struck before he ever entered the pavilion."

"I expect he did just that—wrote the name on the outside of the window, I mean."

"But the people who saw it were on the *inside*. Inside a bank, for instance, haven't you ever noticed how the bank's name—"

"The name Otto," Fen interposed, "is a palindrome. That's to say, it reads backwards as well as forwards. What's more, the capital letters used in it are symmetrical—not like B or P or R or S, but like A or H or M. So write it on the outside of a window and it will look exactly the same from the inside."

"My God, yes." Humbleby was sobered. "I never thought of that. And the fact that the name was on the *outside* would be fatal to Sir Charles after his assertion that he'd seen Sir Lucas enter the pavilion unharmed. So I suppose that the 'contriving' Wilburn noticed in the fight was Sir Charles's, not Otto's: he'd realize that the name *must* be on the outside, Sir Lucas having said that the writing of it was the very first thing he did, and he'd see the need to destroy the window before anyone could investigate closely. Wait, though. Couldn't Sir Lucas have entered the pavilion as Sir Charles said, and later have emerged again and—"

"One set of footprints," Fen pointed out, "on the hall floor. Not three."

Humbleby nodded. "I've been a fool about this. Locked rooms, as you said, on the brain. But what *was* Sir Charles's motive—the motive Sir Lucas didn't know about?"

"Belchester," said Fen. "Belchester cathedral. As you know, it was bombed during the war and a new one's going to be built. Well, I've just rung up the Dean, who's an acquaintance of mine, to ask about the choice of architect, and he says it was a toss-up between Sir Charles's design and Sir Lucas's, and that Sir Lucas's won. The two men were notified by post, and it seems likely that Sir Charles's notification arrived on the morning of Christmas Eve. Sir Lucas's did, too, in all probability—but Sir Lucas's was sent to his home, and even forwarded it can't, in the rush of Christmas postal traffic, have reached him at Rydalls before he was killed. So only Sir Charles knew, and since with Sir Lucas dead Sir Charles's design would have been accepted—" Fen shrugged. "Was it money, I wonder? Or was it just the blow to his professional pride? Well, well. Let's have another drink before you telephone. In the hangman's shed it will all come to the same thing."

Suzanne Blanc

The Hump in the Basement

In the days before the pounding in his head began, Alec Fenton used to like to sit with Colette in front of the living-room fire and think of Marion. Particularly on wintry days, just when the pale-pink traces of the sunset were being swallowed up by night, he would think of her. He would remember how, at the very same hour, he had called her to the basement to see where the plaster was peeling, how she had grumbled on the way down, as she always did when he asked her to do anything.

He would remember how her pale, near-sighted eyes had peered into the dimness, how the naked overhead bulb had accentuated the brassiness of her hair and gilded the nervous thinness of her face. Then he would hear the acid of her voice asking, "What do you want now?" and recall with pleasure the scream that followed when he pushed her and her barbed tongue and her interminable complaints into the old disused well.

That part was very pleasant to remember, like an accomplishment long strived for and finally achieved. What happened in the silence afterward was less pleasant to remember. But having gone this far, Alec would make himself think of it all—the emptiness of the house around him, the unidentified creaks and rustlings in the walls, the metal of the furnace that glimmered in the shadows like watching eyes, the unforeseen panic that threatened to undermine his purpose.

In spite of all his careful planning, he had thrown her clothes—the fur coat, the diamond watch, her best shoes, the blue suitcase, a pile of frothy lingerie—into the well after her without stopping to make certain they were everything she would have taken. He had replaced the well cover, cemented it over, and stepped back to examine his work.

That was when panic seized him. The wet circle of cement humped noticeably in the dimness. Anyone coming down the basement stairs could detect it instantly. Sweating with fear, he tried to move the fruit cupboard to cover the hump but, filled with fruit jars, it was too heavy for him to budge.

He had been so paralyzed with fright that it took him several minutes to solve the problem. Then, in what seemed to be a frantic race against time, he emptied the cupboard, moved it, then replaced the jars.

As soon as that was finished, his fright receded. Moving the cupboard proved, indeed, to be a stroke of genius: beneath it the wet cement was barely visible.

Still he was not fully assured. He kept feeling that he had forgotten something and he wandered through the house like a restless ghost searching for things he might have overlooked in his hasty accumulation of Marion's possessions. It was fortunate he did. He found her new gloves, her cloth purse, her black hat with the white feather lying on the hall table, her nylon dressing gown hanging on the bathroom door. Only after he had burned them all was he able to relax.

Now when he sat near Colette watching the fire he could recall just how slowly they had seemed to burn—the hat especially, holding its shape long after the other objects had disintegrated, a round, thin black shell that slowly, very slowly collapsed. Sometimes he would almost imagine he could see it again shriveling in the flames, the final, distasteful trace of Marion vanishing from his life. And he would experience the same transition from uneasiness to contented relaxation.

At such moments his face must have betrayed him, for Colette would invariably interrupt. "A penny for your thoughts, Alec," she would say in her sweet young voice. "Share them with me. They must be happy ones."

He would turn from the flames to find her dark velvety eyes beaming at him above her embroidery.

"They are," he would answer. "I'm thinking of you, my dear."

Frequently, when he said that, she would put aside her embroidery and come to nestle at his feet, lay her dark silken head on his lap, and rub against his legs like an affectionate kitten. But often she would just smile happily at him, then go into the kitchen and fix them both some tea. She would return to her needlework and Alec would continue to stare at the fire, trying to pick up the broken thread of his reminiscences.

For some reason, he never seemed able to resume exactly where he had left off. His mind might shift ahead to the weeks after Marion's death or quixotically back to the period of careful preparation before he had killed her. He would, perhaps, dwell on the method he had used to seed the idea that Marion was interested in other men. He had chosen Mrs. Ryan, whose acre adjoined his, as the logical person to help him. Whenever Marion was at a club meeting or out shopping, he would call on the gossipy old lady. "Do you know when my wife left?" he would inquire. And then, with shamefaced embarrassment ask, "Did she leave alone?"

He could not have lived next to Mrs. Ryan for all these years without being aware of the constant and twisted clattering of her tongue. He recognized the dawning suspicion in her rheumy eyes, reinforced it subtly, knew when it was fully formed, and when every casual male visitor to his house automatically assumed the identity of one of Marion's lovers. He could tell from the pitying manner in which his neighbors greeted him that Mrs. Ryan was doing her work, and doing it well.

The scandal must have reached major proportions for the minister to visit him at the office and sympathetically inquire, but not too subtly, "How is everything at home, Alec?"

Mrs. Ryan had proved herself a master. The results of his worried innuendos far exceeded his original expectations, and after Marion's death Alec treated the old lady with cautious respect. Whenever he thought of how dangerous she could be, his eyes would leave the fire and dart in the direction of her house, where, usually, the windows blazed long into the night.

And whenever he did that, Colette would be reminded to pull the drapes. "That nosy old woman is probably spying on us again," she would say, as if with some sixth sense she was tuned into the channel of his thoughts. "I don't see why you tolerate her so, Alec."

"I've known her all my life," Alec would say. "She's not a bad old soul."

Colette would shake her head fondly and lean over to kiss him. "You're the kindest man I've ever known, Alec. You always have a good word for everyone."

No doubt because she lived so close, Alec thought more often of Mrs. Ryan than he did of the policeman who had investigated Marion's disappearance. The officer was just a large blue figure whose opinion, already formed by inquiries among the neighbors, was that Marion had obviously run away with another man.

"You say she's taken her clothes," he had said as if that clinched it.

Alec, who had been sitting on the sofa with his head buried in his hands, looked up despondently. "You've seen her closet. Some of her things are still there."

"Nothing left but house dresses, Mr. Fenton. You've got to face it. Even her suitcase is gone."

"Then the police won't help me find her?"

The policeman was patient, understanding. "What good would it do, Mr. Fenton, if she doesn't want to come back?"

After the officer had left, Alec went down to the basement and examined the light spot edging out beyond the fruit cupboard—just to make certain Marion would never come back. Already the cement had darkened and was blurring into anonymity with the rest of the floor.

There was an endless variety to the incidents he could recall during those quiet hours in front of the fire, flickering images that came and went, each in its own way delightful and satisfying—the wonderful peace that followed his freedom from Marion, the subdued kindness of the men in his employ, the unaccustomed invitations to dinner, the frequent consoling visits of the minister. Alec even had pleasant memories of his trip to Reno where, after a suitable stay, he was granted a divorce by default. No one appeared to contest the action. No one would ever appear to set the decree aside, for the only complainant was Marion and she was very, very dead.

Alec's single regret was that his memories must remain forever unshared. He could select a fragment of the experience at random, reexplore each nuance with the pride of accomplishment, yet be unable to display his ingenuity to anyone—not even to Colette.

On the occasions that she would curl on the floor at his feet and lay her glossy head on his lap he was often tempted to tell her about his cleverness. But, of course, he never did. He would stroke her hair and think instead about their first meeting, less than a year after he had returned from Reno.

He had grown tired of eating alone and decided to take his evening meals out. Lucky chance led him to select the restaurant in which Colette worked. She was so much younger than he, such a pretty little woman, that it did not occur to him in the beginning that her welcoming smile represented more than courtesy. He always sat at her table, however, and if she was not busy they chatted together.

He realized that her interest in him was more than casual when an unexpected business appointment delayed him and he arrived at the restaurant later than usual.

Colette's face brightened when she saw him. "I was afraid you weren't coming," she said. "I saved you a piece of chocolate pie."

"That was kind of you. Would you really have missed me if I hadn't come?"

With a charming blush she nodded.

He waited until she had finished work and drove her to the apartment she shared with a married sister. They sat outside talking for several hours and he told her about Marion—how one wintry afternoon he had returned home to find his wife gone.

"Without a word she simply packed her best clothes and left. Apparently there was another man," he commented sadly. "I never suspected it."

Colette's large soft eyes shimmered. "How terrible it must have been for you."

"It was hard," he said. "I kept thinking she'd come back, but she never did. After a while I accepted it. You can get used to anything. I divorced her finally."

Less than a month later, he and Colette were married. He was very happy. Colette was such a quiet, gentle person that in retrospect Marion seemed brassier, more shrewish than ever. Colette fussed over him, catered to him, rarely expressed an opinion of her own. She was almost like a child in her eagerness to please; yet, before they had been married very long, he discovered that she could be unpredictably willful.

She developed a sudden illogical aversion to the house. "It's so old, Alec," she said unexpectedly one evening. "Why don't we sell it and buy a newer place?"

He could feel the color bleed from his face. He had an immediate vision of strangers prowling through the cellar, moving the fruit cupboard, and seeing the uneven ring of cement in the floor.

Instantly he recovered his composure. Colette had only made a suggestion. He parried it deftly. "This is my home, Colette. I was born here. I wouldn't be happy anywhere else."

As far as he was concerned, that settled the matter. But it was not settled for Colette. Periodically she would complain about how old the house was. Intermittently she would suggest moving. She took to wandering through the building developments mushrooming up all around them. He could always tell when she had been househunting, for she would sit through dinner with a dreamy expression and sooner or later she would describe the places she had seen.

"They're all glass, Alec—great big windows. Everything is so shiny and new. Please, Alec, let's sell this old barn."

Even if he had wanted to please her, he wouldn't have dared. He was tied to the house by more than the hump in the basement. The memories that were so enjoyable here would not be quite the same elsewhere.

He was patient with Colette. "The value of this place, my dear, is mostly in the land. The house, as you say, is old. But it is comfortable. We wouldn't get enough out of it and it's foolish to go into debt for a new one."

It was not until she actually called in a realtor to have the house appraised that he took Colette's whim seriously. When he learned that a stranger had been prowling through the cellar he was furious. He raised his fist and shouted at her.

"No more realtors! I'm not selling. I want to hear no more about it. I had one nagging wife and that's enough. If you want a new house you'll wait till I'm dead."

Colette had wept unconsolably and he had finally apologized for his outburst. Still, a coolness came between them until he became certain that she had really given up her dream. Then their relationship reverted to what it had been before the quarrel, and the tenor of their days became the same.

Perhaps not quite the same. Alec dwelt ever increasingly in the past. He worked shorter hours at the office so that he could spend more time in front of the fire sorting through his memories. His images of Marion were frequently so vivid that momentarily he would sense her presence in the room. He would brace himself against the acid of her voice and glance apprehensively at her favorite chair, almost expecting to see the brassy waves of her hair glistening in the firelight. Instead he would find Colette bent over her embroidery.

Then with relief he would remember that Marion was safely dead, buried in the basement well, and she was going to stay there.

Then one afternoon, he returned from the office to have Colette greet him at the door with cheeks flushed from excitement. Her dark eyes danced with delight. She threw her arms impulsively around his neck.

"Alec! Alec! The most wonderful thing has happened. I'm going to have my new house after all. And we'll be able to afford it."

So she hadn't forgotten about selling the place, hadn't become reconciled to living here. He wondered what she had committed them to. He stiffened angrily and pushed her arms away. At that instant he hated her as much as he had hated Marion.

"I told you, Colette, we're not selling. No matter what you promised anyone, I won't agree to sell. Nothing you can say will change my mind."

Rebuffed, her enthusiasm faded. "But, Alec, I have nothing to do with it," she protested. "It's not my idea at all. A man was here today, an assessor from the state. He says the new highway is going right across this property. They'll pay you top dollar. But whether we like it or not, the house will have to be pulled down."

Her voice—like the echo of Marion's scream resounding in the well—left a vacuum of silence behind it, a silence in which he heard the crash of ancient timbers being felled by bulldozers. He saw the cellar stretch before him, exposed and naked, with the telltale bulge of cement in the corner. He pictured giant hammers smashing into the floor.

And then the terrible pounding in his head began.

Donald McNutt Douglass

The Ghost of Greenwich Village

I was involved in a murder case one time. I was even one of the suspects. It was before I was married. I was living with Mac-Pherson Smith and we had this two-room basement apartment on Eleventh Street. It was dirty and down-at-the-heel but it had a garden in back. Rather, it had space for a garden. There was a brick terrace and the rest of the area was covered with something that looked like soil. We tried grass, annuals, perennials, and a rose bush and it was sudden death for all of them. But we did have enough garden furniture on the terrace to make it seem pretty elegant for a couple of bachelors. It also had its own private entrance, which was an added attraction in our eyes.

The apartment on the first floor, just over us, was occupied by a man and his wife and a kid about eight or nine years old. The name was Foster. The man had one leg shorter than the other and he walked with a bad limp. Being a traveling salesman, he was away a good deal. The wife was not bad-looking at all, a bleached blonde with a definite invitation in her eye, and both Mac and I entertained ideas from time to time. But we never did anything about it on account of that kid. He was, without a doubt, the most objectionable child I ever knew. I won't try to describe him. Just think of any bad trait—he had it. He was constantly pestering us for a nickel, and if we didn't give it to him he would set up a howl and run to his mother, saying, "The man hit me, the man slapped me, the man knocked me down." What a character! We never laid a hand on him, but it wasn't because we didn't want to.

He got plenty of punishment from his parents, though, especially from his father, and of course when he did get a spanking it sounded as though he were being skinned alive. One night his cries were so anguished we thought he was being boiled in oil. Windows went up all over the block and people who lived on Tenth Street and didn't know the little brat threatened to call the police. The father cussed the neighbors back and it had all the makings of a community wingding. The only ones who thoroughly enjoyed the evening were Mac and me.

The second-floor apartment was occupied by an old couple named Hogan who owned the house, and on the third floor were two old-maid artists. That, plus the various cops and detectives, is the cast of characters.

I've got to explain the layout of our apartment because the setting is important to the story. Our living room was in the back, on the garden side, and the bathroom was on that side, too, opening off the living room. To enter the house, you went through an iron gate on the sidewalk. This gate clanged. Then you went down a few steps under the stoop and through a door that didn't fit very well and had to be jerked and slammed to open and close. Then along a corridor past the bedroom and kitchenette to the door of the living room. The living-room door had a Yale lock. The bedroom door to the corridor was nailed shut. The outside door was never locked.

I have good enough reason to remember the date. It was June 21, 1927, about 11:30 P.M. It had been a hot day, all the windows were open, and Mac and I were getting ready for bed. We had had three or four beers during the evening and were stone-cold sober.

I had my shirt and shoes off when we heard the iron gate open and clang shut. Then three steps down and the front door being manhandled and slammed. Either Mac or I said, "Who the hell is barging in at this hour?" and we heard this guy's footsteps along the corridor. You could hear them as though they were in the same room. He stopped at our door and we sat there in that state of suspended animation in which you wait for a knock or a hail.

But no sound came. No rattling at the knob, nothing.

I went into the living room and listened. There was a half inch crack under that door and you could have heard a person breathing. Only I didn't hear a person breathing. I called out, "Who's there?" and got no answer. I guess I needed a little moral support because I called Mac and asked him if he had heard what I heard.

He said, "Sure, it's Foster." The minute Mac said that, I knew he was right. Those footsteps were the limping steps of Foster, the guy that lived upstairs. We had heard them over our heads a thousand times. But why didn't he knock or something?

Well, Mac and I opened the door and nobody was there. I tell you it makes the chills run up my spine just writing about it.

Mac and I, both being of sound mind and not given to hallucinations, had heard Foster open and close the iron gate, open and shut the front door—neither operation physically possible without loud noises—and we had heard his unmistakable steps along the uncarpeted corridor. There was noplace he could have gone, but he was not there. Nobody was there. It wasn't a big corridor, you understand, maybe twenty or twenty-two feet long and four feet wide. I went to the outside door and pulled it, shudderingly, open. It was the only way it ever would open. We had heard it all. Foster had come in and disappeared.

I'll repeat. It was utterly, completely impossible.

But there were two things that proved the two of us weren't suffering from dual hypnosis or delirium tremens. For one thing, the light was on. A little bare fifteen-watt bulb, with a chain hanging from it, was sending out its feeble rays. That was one thing we just never forgot. It was an automatic reaction. We would always pull the chain to light the light, unlock our door, and pull the chain again. I never knew Mac to leave that light on, and he said the same about me. Second, spaced all along the corridor, about eighteen inches apart, there were spots, about as large as a quarter, of wet, sticky new blood. We had stepped in some of them and they made a bright-red smear.

We went back in our living room and locked the door. I kept looking at Mac for some sort of reassurance, but I didn't get any. He looked just as green as I felt. It wasn't the blood. Both of us had been through a war. It was the fact that Foster wasn't there and yet he still must be. There just was noplace for him to have gone.

We were young and we had a half bottle of bathtub gin, but the experience had been so eerie we almost wanted to hold each other's hands. We discussed calling the police, but it was out of the question. They would say we were crocked. After all, that was the only explanation we could give ourselves.

The gin was a big help and the bars on our bedroom window a great satisfaction, but we did look under our beds before we got into them.

The next morning I opened the living-room door while Mac was brushing his teeth. The blood spots were no longer wet but were still there.

Mac and I sort of mutually shut up. But when I got to the office I told the boys all the lurid details. I was glad, then, we hadn't called the police the night before. The only response I got was skepticism and wisecracks. O.K., we were crocked. Forget it!

That night nothing happened, but I was mighty glad when Mac called up to suggest we meet for dinner and go home together.

The blood spots were still on the floor.

The next night was uneventful, too, but the night after that, the twenty-fourth, was a lulu. It was a Friday, payday, and Mac and I had done ourselves very well at Luigi's with plenty of chianti. When we came out of the restaurant, a beautiful thunderstorm was in progress and by the time we got home we were wet to the skin.

We had just got inside and were matching coins as to who would get the first hot shower when we heard the iron gate creak. We froze in our tracks and listened. The outside door was opened and banged. Tottering footsteps came along the corridor and there was a knocking at our door.

"Who is it?" I called, and only got more knocking. I doubt if we would ever have opened that door without having had the chianti, but we did, and there was our landlord, old Mr. Hogan, looking like a ghost and trembling so that he, literally, couldn't speak.

Right away, we felt better. There is nothing that gives you more courage than to be scared to death and suddenly find someone else more frightened than you are. After all, Mr. Hogan was not only finite and human, we knew him. We paid him rent.

It seems that the spinster ladies on the top floor had smelled a dead rat and had called Mr. Hogan the day before. Today Mrs. Hogan, with a less sensitive nose, had smelled the dead rat, too. And tonight Mr. Hogan, with the least sensitive nose of all, had finally smelled the dead rat and let himself into the Fosters' apartment to investigate. He had not found the dead rat but he had found Mr. Foster. Mr. Foster had his hat on and his throat cut. Mr. Hogan was extremely incoherent but he seemed to be especially shocked that Mr. Foster had had his throat cut *with* his hat on.

Otherwise, the apartment was empty.

It is curious about the human mind. Mac told me afterward that he felt exactly as I had. He was delighted that Mr. Foster had had his throat cut, hat or no hat. Not that we bore Mr. Foster any ill will. Quite the contrary—he spanked efficiently and in the right place. But he had proved himself to be human, even though dead. How he had got out of our corridor and into his own apartment was still a deep mystery, but at least he certainly wasn't the wraith that we had imagined him to be. We thought this at the time and were immensely relieved.

Later, we weren't so sure.

We were still comforting old Mr. Hogan when the police trooped in. Because we had called them, they came into our place first. After they had heard Hogan's story, we all went outdoors and up the front stoop together. He did have an odor. It's funny we hadn't noticed it. I guess a thing like that goes up, not down.

All of a sudden this detective or inspector, the head man on the job, turned to me and said, "You know anything about this, bud?" and I started to tell him, Mac joining in. He looked at us with a very fishy eye and took off his hat. It's a fact that detectives *do* keep their hats on as a rule.

"Clancy," he said to a uniformed policeman, "take these two birds below where we found 'em and sit on 'em." So Clancy and Mac and I went back to our apartment and sat down. We tried to tell Clancy what had happened but he wouldn't listen.

"Save your breath," Clancy said. "I'm just sitting on you."

From what we could hear, the whole police department was upstairs. There were sirens and squad cars and ambulances, and everybody in the neighborhood seemed to be on the street outside.

Finally the activity upstairs quieted down and this inspector, another plainclothes man, another cop, and Mr. Hogan walked in. They didn't pay any attention to us or to Mr. Hogan. They went over the whole place with flashlights, inside and out. In the garden they found that, because our floor level was two or three feet below the level of the garden, a person could go out there, pull himself up quite easily, and get onto the Fosters' porch.

The three of them came back in the living room and sat down, hats still on. The inspector looked at Mac and me and then he turned to me and said, "Where's the babe?"

"What babe?" I said.

"That babe," he said, not taking his eyes off me but tossing over an eight-by-ten photograph. It was Mrs. Foster, without any clothes on. I examined it carefully and handed it to Mac, who examined it likewise.

"Listen, you young punks." The inspector was talking to both of us now. "Hogan tells me this Wilbur Foster was away most of the time and the two old dames upstairs swear they've seen his wife shining up to both of you. With the layout you got here, I don't have to hunt for the guy who stuck him, or wonder why. I just want the details, and where I can find *Mrs.* Foster."

Mac rose to the occasion. He was all dignity.

"Lieutenant," he said, "we are law-abiding citizens who happen to live in the apartment beneath the Fosters, just as Mr. Hogan lives in the apartment *over* them. We have never made any improper advances to Mrs. Foster. We don't even know her first name. I don't deny that, as the kind maiden ladies have told you, she has seemed at times less than unapproachable, and I don't deny that we've discussed approaching her, but we never did. Mrs. Foster has a son who is better protection than a pack of wolves. She and her brat have been gone for about a week and everybody in the vicinity is happy about it. If we never see them again, it will be too soon."

Mr. Hogan nodded vigorously.

"We have no idea where she is," Mac continued, "but we do have a story about Mr. Foster. We'll tell it to you, if you'd like to hear it."

The inspector grunted, so Mac told him our story, ending up with a dramatic exhibition of the bloodstains.

Somehow the very implausibility of our tale seemed to take suspicion from us. They tried opening and closing the front door and made the usual noise with it. The plainclothes man examined the little panel at the end of the corridor which was designed to give access to the plumbing in our bathroom, but that was seen to be nailed to its casing frame and numerous coats of old paint seemed to indicate it had not been opened since being installed. The whole story stumped them, as it had us, but they didn't seem to think it was a lie. After all, what could be the point?

By this time it was after three, the body had been removed, and everybody was bushed, including the inspector. He told us to stay put for further questioning in the morning, they scraped up some of the blood, and they departed. I don't think Mac and I exchanged a word. Our sopping clothing had dried on us without our giving it a thought. I know I was asleep when I hit the pillow.

We slept late in the morning. When we got up, we telephoned our offices and were told they already had been informed. We had our usual bacon and eggs and waited. There were sounds from the apartment upstairs, but it was not until late afternoon that the clang of our gate announced a visitor.

We opened the door to a large, fat, white-haired man of great affability. He introduced himself as Detective Bower, addressed us as "Boys," and asked which was Smith and which Douglass. He asked our permission to inspect our rooms, saying that he had already been upstairs. He wandered about, complimenting us on our furniture and pictures, which was silly but made us like him. Finally he sat down, bidding us do likewise.

Leaning back and putting the ends of his fingers together, he said, "Boys, when I was put on this case at four o'clock this morning I had naturally never heard of either of you. But now I think I know you pretty well. You wouldn't believe how much can be found out about people in a few hours.

"And I want to congratulate you. Aside from a rather nasty little experience with that librarian in Williamstown which, I am sure, Smith, you will not lay entirely to boyishness, you're both pretty clean. I'm sorry to say such a good report is rare. Criminal investigation all too often brings out unpleasant facts. Such as that when a murder is committed and the victim is married, the widow or widower is always suspected and usually guilty."

There was nothing for us to say, so we didn't say it.

"In the specific case of Mr. Wilbur Foster," continued Detective Bower sadly, "we can find no one who would benefit by his death except his wife, Elsie. She benefits to the extent of forty thousand dollars in life insurance. But she has come forth with a statement that makes two important points in her favor. First, she says she had come to dislike her husband to such an extent that she left him on June eighteenth. A letter to that effect was, in fact, written by her and postmarked on that date. This proves only that, if he was alive on June nineteenth, he could have transferred his insurance to another beneficiary."

Mac spoke up.

"We know he was alive on the twenty-first."

"More on that later," Bower said. "It's a point in her favor. Most wives who murder their husbands claim they loved them dearly.

"The second point in her favor is that she has the right kind of alibi. She says she took the child on the eighteenth and traveled by train to the home of her parents in Norwalk, Connecticut. A check shows that she did, in fact, stay with her parents in Norwalk from the nineteenth till today, when she says she read about the murder in the papers. But she doesn't try to *prove* that she took the train on the eighteenth. She just says she did, and her parents say she did. That's a proper as against a so-called ironclad alibi."

Bower got confidential.

"Boys, if this were a case of breaking or confirming a widow's alibi, that would be handled by officers who find such work congenial and who are therefore better at it. The reason I'm here, and the reason I've given you these details, is that I believe the key to this case is your story, and—"

At this point he leaped out of his chair, scowling, and shook two large forefingers at us.

"And I intend to get it!"

He had been so quiet and fatherly that both of us almost fainted. This reaction seemed to satisfy him; Detective Bower smiled and resumed his affable air. He had Mac and me recite our experience of June twenty-first. He had me sit on the bed, where I had been sitting that night, and he and I listened while Mac opened and closed the outside door and walked along the corridor as Foster had done. Then we went into the living room and listened at our door and, by George, we could hear Mac breathing. If he had dropped a pin we could have heard that.

Bower went out in the corridor, examined it carefully, tried the outside door himself, and came back. He asked us politely if we minded his using our phone, and he called police headquarters. He asked them politely to please send up a detective "of small stature" and a two-foot jimmy. Then he leaned back in the chair as though time meant nothing to him and questioned us about our jobs, our girls, our speakeasies. He was all leisure until the squad car drove up and stopped with a squeal of rubber. Then he was on his feet and unscrewing a light bulb, a 100-watt, from our reading lamp.

By the time the detectives of small stature (they had sent two) came in, we were in the corridor to meet them and Bower had me up on a stool changing the little bulb for the big one.

"Boys," says Bower, "there are two, and only two, possibilities. Either you're liars or your invisible visitor of the other night escaped through that access door."

He pointed down to this plumbing gadget which was not over eight inches wide and twelve inches high and which, as I said before, anybody could see hadn't been opened in years. If a midget could have managed to squeeze through that hole, where would he have been? Under our bathtub. I thought Bower must be crazy.

He sat down on the floor, took off his glasses, and substituted another pair, called for a jimmy, and studied the access door. He looked at the bottom and he looked at the top, and then he stuck that jimmy in above the casing frame and gave a little wrench. The access panel had been securely nailed to the frame all right, but the frame wasn't nailed to the wall. The frame was about three and a half inches wide. It had been hinged at the bottom and secured at the top from the inside with a simple hook-and-eye. The jimmy pulled that out easily and we were confronted with an opening, not eight by twelve inches, but fifteen by nineteen. The pipes for our bathtub were in there, but there was room, too.

Bower got to his feet.

"Boys," he said to the detectives, whose names he didn't seem to know, "I think you had better get a fingerprint unit up before you go in there. I doubt if they find any prints but we'll have to check it."

The detectives scurried to the telephone and Mr. Bower turned to us.

"Boys," he said, "I have no children of my own. If I had, they'd be around your age. Your connection with this murder case is finished and so is mine. If you know a good restaurant around here, which I don't, I'll be delighted to buy you dinner."

Of course we took him to Luigi's, and it turned out that Bower and Luigi had known each other years before. But a good dinner and chianti wasn't enough tonight. We wanted some meaty facts.

Mac said encouragingly, "We see now that Foster dived into that hole, making us think he was a ghost. But I don't see *why* he did it, or *how* he got upstairs, or *who* cut his throat. The mystery is solved, Mr. Bower, but the murder isn't."

Detective Bower put the tips of his fingers against each other and looked at the ceiling.

"No," he said, "the murder isn't solved. In fact, it may never be. I only said our connection with it was ended. But you haven't solved the mystery, either."

"But, Mr. Bower—" Mac said.

Bower looked at Mac severely. I think he was remembering Mac and Williamstown.

"Why do you insist it was Foster you heard on the night of the twenty-first? The medical examiner can't fix the time of Foster's death exactly, but it was sometime between the morning of the nineteenth and the morning of the twentieth. On the evening of the twenty-first, therefore, Mr. Foster was too dead to visit you or anybody else. As to how the ghost of Mr. Foster got from your corridor back into his earthly remains upstairs, let me explain."

The chianti had had its effect on Detective Bower.

"In the old days, boys, plumbers plumbed properly. It's true the materials they used weren't as good as you can get today and so had to be replaced more often. But, in those days, when they built an access panel it was to obtain access. Not access to one fixture, or two fixtures, but to *all* fixtures. If for any reason you wished to visit the artistic ladies on the top floor of your building—"

The chianti had hit Mac, too. "Which God forbid!"

Bower nodded gravely. "Amen. But if you did, you could get there through that plumbing stack. All the plumbing in the building can be reached through that one stack. It was plumbers' standard procedure."

"But, Mr. Bower," I said, "who killed Foster?"

"Boys," Bower said, "if my buddies find the fingerprints of Elsie Foster on those pipes, or anywhere within that stack, the case is closed and she'll probably burn."

He paused and stood up.

"Close your eyes and listen."

We closed our eyes and he walked a few steps beside the table. Of course, he was right. A limp is the easiest thing in the world to imitate. He sounded exactly like Foster.

"Boys," said Detective Bower, sitting down comfortably, "you are entitled to my theory. It's a theory which I will propound to my superiors this evening in writing—which I would recite in any court of law. But it's only a theory. Pure supposition, with no legal value whatsoever.

"I believe Mrs. Foster planned this murder, having come to think she preferred forty thousand dollars to Foster. I believe she wrote the farewell note on the eighteenth and waited for her husband to come home on the nineteenth. I believe she was packed and ready and had got her child out of the room when Wilbur sat down to read his paper. The fact that he did so with his hat on does not constitute justifiable homicide. And homicide, with a kitchen knife, is what I think she did. I believe she carried the knife away with her, suitably wrapped, and immediately departed for Norwalk. I believe she had no qualms of conscience but did, seriously, underestimate medical knowledge. I believe she drove a car back to town from Norwalk on the night of June twenty-first and, wearing a pair of men's shoes, pulled the limping-footsteps trick on two young men she had sized up as gullible. This, of course, was to prove her husband was still alive on the twenty-first. She hid in the stack and, after you two were asleep, she must have crawled up the stack, let herself out of her own apartment, and driven back to Norwalk.

"The whole thing was risky, useless, and stupid, but it was also bold and resourceful. That's why I predict my theory will remain only a theory. I predict that neither the knife that killed Foster nor the cat that provided the blood for your hall will ever be found. I predict that her fingerprints will be photographed all over her apartment but will not be discovered anywhere in the plumbing stack. And I predict that, although she will not attempt to *prove* that she didn't come into New York that night, it will be impossible to prove that she did."

Detective Bower smiled sadly again, and nodded his head.

"I have never met this lady in the flesh, but I have seen her photograph ditto. I think my brother officers will do their level best to pin this murder on Elsie Foster but, cynical though it may sound, boys, I don't think they ever will."

His prediction came true. They never pinned that murder on anybody.

Richard A. Selzer

The Dark Place

Ada heard the commotion all the way to her upstairs back-bedroom, where she had gone to escape the afternoon heat. It came through her drowse, subtly at first, then growing, and finally annoying her into wakefulness. A man was shouting and children were whooping and screaming. She tried to hear, but the words were not clear and she was left wondering. Finally, there was an urgency in the voices and in the running feet that made her get up and stand by the front window. She could hear the words clearly now.

"Where?"

"The cave. He was sitting there just inside when they saw him, skinning a possum."

"Who was he?"

"Don't know. The kids said a wild man, thin and white, with wild staring eyes, all dressed in black rags. They hid in the bushes and watched. When they made a sound he turned around to see, then ran into the cave."

"What's going to be done?"

"Well, c'mon, everyone's headin' up there now. They've got ropes, flashlights, and guns—he may be dangerous!"

The voices faded and Ada looked down on the street burnt dry in the sun. She was trembling, and suddenly it was hard to breathe. "Pippo," she whispered. "Oh, my God, it's Pippo, I know it. I'm certain. It's Pippo!"

She ran down the stairs out into the street. It was empty; they had already left. The whole town was just one main street bracketing the old Post Road, with a few extra houses added carelessly on the periphery. The cave was about two miles from town. There were bobcats up there, and bears. And hardly anyone went up in that tangled mess except for an occasional hunter or children exploring the woods.

She could see the line of people moving up the path above. They were following a curve on the hill that threw them into her direct vision. The women in their yellow and blue cotton dresses followed the men who marched determinedly ahead. Behind and alongside, the children fluttered like rags. From the distance it looked gay.

She ran and walked and ran until she had caught up with the stragglers.

"There it is!" a man called. "All right now, everybody, stand back—give us room!"

Lloyd Bascom had taken charge. She watched him as though she hadn't seen him every day of her life, as though he were a stranger, or rather as if she had suddenly become a stranger and was now peering into the rites of an old and mysterious people. These people were wearing new faces—people she had known all her life. She remembered a game she used to play. It was a terrible game in which she would imagine how each person would look if he were insane. It was remarkable, but she felt that she could tell just what they'd do, how they'd look. Some women would wear timid house-dresses, and make their lips go, and once in a while dart a brilliant smile at the far edge of vision. Others, stung with animation, would hop and jump ceaselessly, gesticulating with their skinny arms and legs. And there were those men, private as gorillas, who peered from under great frontal bulges, enraged, dull. She hadn't thought of the game for years, but today it came back to her, and as she looked about at the faces she could see the craziness like an abscess that had pressed its way to just under the skin.

She joined the crowd gathered in an arc in front of the entrance. The children were already climbing trees to get a better view. There were laughter and chattering among the women. Ada stared at the great blank mouth fringed with whiskery shrubs. She shivered in the rank, cold, sour belch which emanated from it. She watched the men knotting and coiling their ropes, slinging them easily over their shoulders. Flashlights were tested one final time and a group of eight men separated itself from the body and flowed unsteadily, awkwardly, into the cave. Light quivered on the lips of the hole for a few moments, and then it was black again. A silence fell on those outside. There were faint callings and shoutings from the cave as the expedition deepened.

Ada stood for a time staring into the blackness. Then in a quick movement she was at the edge of the cave. Without stealth or backward glance, she slipped silently into its shadow, making as much noise as a flower when it closes for the night. It was a relief to be inside, out of sight. She didn't have to hold herself so tightly. She could breathe! And the invisibility that the cave bestowed seemed to expand and free her. If it is Pippo, she thought—yes, it must be.

Far ahead she could see the jumping, swaying lights of the hunters. They were moving slowly.

"Stay close, Bud."

"Where are you, Lloyd?"

"Over here. Look out now. He may be anywhere and we don't know what he's got to throw at us. If there's any question about it, shoot first and find out later."

They had gone about two hundred yards. It seemed like miles to Ada, who followed behind, edging sideways through the darkness and hugging the cold slimy walls. Pippo. My little brother Pippo, she thought. Why? When you didn't come back I went out looking. Didn't you hear me? You said you were going for a walk and then you never came back. The townspeople searched and searched for you, but after a while they gave up. "He must have fallen and hurt himself," they had said. "Must've been took by a bear or a cat." Oh, how I cried!

The men were moving more slowly. Their voices had been harsh, overlapping, reverberating, but now they were strangely hushed, full of hisses and coughs. There was fear in the cave, and, with it, hate. The courage and stamp was now replaced by a clustering, a need to huddle, to back into a safe center where there was no heroism, only a hope that the wild man's blow, when struck, would miss, hit the next man.

It was cool, and Ada wondered at the sweat that ran from her hair onto her neck and temples. It had a thick slimy feel. There were currents of air on her face, and sound, a clicking, sharp and rapid. With a start, she realized its source as a bird flew at her head and swerved off at the last moment. But in the faint light of the nervous men ahead, she saw the red eyes and three-foot wing-spread. Lighter winds touched her, and once she suppressed a scream of surprise at the leathery whisk of a bat across her face. Now and then she could see the undulating carpet of wings and eyes that covered the ceiling. A steady rain of droppings fell to the floor and the stench of ammonia was biting. The slimy wall of the cave sucked at her nape as she pressed against it.

She had caught up with the men and the walking was a bit easier now, despite the sticky mud of the floor. At least she could see to walk. She marveled at her lack of fear. In its place she felt a kind of elation, as though she were on the brink of a great discovery. They had gone about six hundred yards, and abruptly the cave narrowed to a cone. They could go no farther. They were single file and those behind had bumped into the ones in front.

"Watch out! Looks as though it ends here. Unless there's a side path we've missed somewhere."

"No chance. I've covered it all with my light," said Lloyd Bascom. "Where do we go now?"

"Back, I guess. Whatever it is knows this cave better than we do and he's hidin' somewhere. I think we'd better get out now."

There was a general shuffling, a mixture of disappointment and relief.

"Wait!" The call was sharp, authoritative.

"What is it?"

"Here's an opening!"

The light revealed a hole, no more than a foot and a half in diameter, at the level of the floor. Lloyd was kneeling at the opening, peering along the beam of his light.

"It's a few feet long. And narrow. There's empty space beyond—another chamber, looks like. Hey!" he shouted into it. "Come out of there! Come out or we'll block it up!"

"Yeah, block it up, Lloyd!"

"No, let's try to get a look at him first."

They were torn between the need to escape the wild man and his dark place, and the lust, deep and powerful as blood, to see him, prod him, encircle him.

"Let's smoke him out. Here's the tear gas."

"Yeah."

The arm was raised and swung back for an underhanded toss.

"Stop!" Her voice shocked her. It commanded. There was no beggary in it. They wheeled to see her. Ada felt thinner and smaller than she was. She let them assault her with their flashlights, let the beams travel across her body, covering each part and then lingering on her face, blinding her. She stared straight ahead.

"What the hell? Who is it?"

"Ada! Whatcha doin' here?"

"I can get through there," she said quietly. "Give me a flashlight and I'll crawl through."

"No, you won't. Keep out of this, Ada. Now you're here, we won't send you back, but you damn well better stay out of the way."

She headed straight into the nearest beam of light. It narrowed to a burning spot on her breast, and she took it from the lax hand that held it.

"Let her do it, Lloyd. If she can get in, she can always get out."

Ada was already on her knees in front of the hole, then flat on her face, her thin arms stretched in front, one hand scrabbling in the muddy floor. It was tight. For the first foot of the way there was hope, then the passage narrowed. The back of her head hit against the rock, and pebbly mud slipped through her lips and between her teeth. Her shoulders wedged, scraped, then slid an inch, the tunnel biting into her flesh with each push. Abruptly, strength left her and she lay exhausted. Her heaving chest strained against the floor. It was like a vise that clamped ever tighter or in which she had somehow swollen.

Behind, the voices of the men whispered. Their feet shuffled as they waited.

"You makin' it, Ada?"

She forced down the panic. Expelling all the air from her lungs, she sank the fingers of one hand into the floor, pushing with her feet, pulling with her fingers. She burst through the narrows and felt her shoulders spilling out into space. With a final kick, she was inside. It was cool and damp. And still. No currents of air brushed her skin.

Ada rose and turned the flashlight in a tentative circle about her. The floor was covered with dry silt from which no dust rose as she walked. The humidity must have been absolute, for in a few moments she was dripping with sweat and condensation. The walls were a soft sand-color, and here and there a trickle of water ran down, leaving a glistening trail behind. Scurrying out of range of the light were spectral little beasts—white beetles and crayfish and pale-pink salamanders. She wondered how they lived here, what they ate. A recess in the wall coned into a path and she followed it, stooping where the ceiling swooped low above her, stepping around small shallow pools in which little insects plopped.

"Pippo!" she cried softly. "Pippo, it's me, Ada. Don't be afraid. Pippo, please, if you're here let me know. Pippo!"

Her voice became hollow, with metallic echoes fading at the end. "Pippo!" she called, and the name came back to her with ever-increasing frequency, gaining in urgency and mania, then dying off. She came to another chamber, larger than the first, and stopped at the entrance, scanning the walls. A salamander, caught in the glare, stood poised on the wall. She stepped toward it, then felt the shock of another person's presence.

Her heart triggered like a machine gun, shaking her body with its volley. She aimed the light at the wall opposite her, higher and higher, in slow even sweeps. Suddenly it jumped in her hand like a fish. Something large and black hung on the wall high up. She forced the light back with both hands and saw him, hanging from a ridge twenty feet up. Emerging from a tatter of black rags were four sticklike appendages, white as milk. The sinews stood out like rods with the effort of clinging to the wall. A tangle of black hair framed a face whose white skeleton seemed ready to burst through the skin.

"Pippo," she breathed. "It's Ada. I've found you. Come down—don't be afraid. I'm not going to hurt you. Oh, Pippo, I've missed you. Please, please come down."

She had come closer to him and could see the droplets of moisture caught in the cloud of his hair. They glistened and winked as he turned his neck to stare down behind him. The little muscles around his nose twitched, snoutlike, and his dry white eyes reached out for her like suckers. Not the smallest light of recognition warmed them. They were animal eyes that spoke directly, without subtlety, of fright and flight.

She was strangely calm. There was excitement enough to have laid her panting on the ground, but her breaths came slowly, evenly. There was no wild thudding in her chest—it was as if she stood in the eye of a hurricane, unbuffeted for the moment, able to see with such clarity that her vision burned back up into her brain.

She took a few small steps toward him. The dead-white eyes, like picked lilies, never left her. She was close beneath him now and raised her hand toward him with deliberate slowness, until her arm was fully extended, fingers straining.

"Pippo! Reach down. Touch me." If only he would touch me, she thought. It was with a small shock that she recognized parts of herself in that face. There had been a strong resemblance, everyone said—"like two peas in a pod" or "cut from the same cloth." It was like looking into a crazy mirror where lines undulate with each breath. There was the same cleft chin, the same thin oval face, and those unfortunate ears. His nose was thinner, tighter than before, and his mouth hung slightly open. For a single lacerating moment she saw herself up there clinging to the cave wall. It was as though his face had given in grudgingly to the changes of the cave, but still held to its family structure and form.

Even on tiptoe she could not reach him and he made no move

toward her. He clung to whatever tiny crevices and juttings were there. From far behind, she heard the voices of the men.

"Ada!" they called. "Come back! Now-ow-ow!"

Pippo heard them, too, and his eyes never left her.

She turned then, and cupping her hands to her mouth, called back, "I'm coming! There's no one here!"

She turned back to him, and in a voice she had never used before said softly, "Goodbye."

She backed off a few steps, turned the light to the entrance, and walked to the narrow little tunnel. "I'm coming," she said.

"It's about time. Damn you, Ada, what took so long? We had half a mind to leave you here to rot."

The squeeze through was not half as hard as before, as though the cave itself was not anxious to keep her. She stood up on the other side and faced the converging beams of light.

"It's empty."

"The kids must have made it up. Let's go, Lloyd. This place is bad. Those kids will get the beating of their lives when we get back."

Ada submitted passively to their orders and took her place in line. She moved like a sleepwalker, but still she was calm and felt a queer emotion, hard to identify. She was surprised when she finally linked it to a kind of happiness. She caught herself smiling, and as the light at the entrance widened she closed her eyes to hold it out.

The next morning she went to the hardware store and bought a jackknife and a canteen. Mr. Cantrell looked at her for a long questioning moment, then wrapped her purchases and handed her the package in silence. Yesterday he would have asked, "What you want with a knife, Ada? Fixin' to go hunting?" and he would have smiled at any response she gave; but today it was different. Did he suspect her?

Then there was the grocer. She bought cheese and ham and cans of fruit, things she rarely bought, and enough to feed a family. Adam Patterson was a simple man, but that day he asked her, "You layin' in for the winter, Ada, or are you goin' to set up shop in your parlor for competition?" Did he suspect, too?

She had mumbled and smiled and carried home the big brown bag full of food.

Every morning she went to the cave and sat down in the shade of the rock for a few minutes of rest. It was a steep climb and even in the morning the heat and gnats were tiring. Not that she minded, not a bit. In fact, she had developed a certain taste for the exertion, like a long-distance runner who savors the straining of his body. Resting in the shade, she felt a certain peacefulness. She could see the village down below, straddling the road. On the farms, clumsy cows, released from the barns, were stumbling into each other to get to pasture.

Up here on the mountain it was cool and crackling dry and the trees were big enough to hold onto a bit of the night, even in the midst of day. Up here there were no zinnias or roses or asters, no gardens stuffed with hollyhocks—more hollyhocks than people in the town! Only a trillium surprised now and then, or a jack-in-the-pulpit just where it belonged.

After a few minutes Ada would rise, take a deep breath as though gulping air before going underwater, then step into the darkness of the cave. She advanced until she needed to pause and wait for her eyes to accommodate to the darkness, and then walked on. At about twenty yards from the mouth, she knelt and put a brown-paper bag on the ground. With a smile of satisfaction she noted that yesterday's bag was empty, folded neatly and tucked under a corner of the rock. She slipped it out and withdrew, blinking into the daylight.

When she got back to town, there was still no one stirring in the streets. The clock on the kitchen wall said 6:30. The whole trip had taken one hour.

On her thirty-first trip to the cave, the bag which she had left the day before had not been opened. It was exactly as she had left it. She placed the full new bag alongside it and after pausing, as if trying to come to a decision, she abruptly left the cave and went home.

Ada sat for a long time in the chair by the bedroom window. Through dusk she sat, the world filling up with particles of darkness until, with the addition of one more speck, night was realized. At that she rose and walked to the kitchen. She made a tunafish sandwich, wiping the extra mayonnaise carefully from the edges before she wrapped it in waxed paper. Then she selected an apple from a bowl on the table, washed it, and polished it on her apron. Together with a napkin full of cookies, she packed the brown-paper bag. She had always prepared the food the night before.

That night she did not sleep. She lay awake and thought about another, deeper darkness, and about how dark it can get, blacker and blacker, but never reaching perfect blackness. Like infinity, because there would always be a touch of grey in it. And of how they were all living in it, only in different degrees of the blackness, even at noon, and if you thought of it that way it seemed pure and serene.

When she got to the cave, she did not stop to rest from the climb as she usually did but strode immediately in, taking the darkness on her arms like the sleeves of a robe which she then pulled close around her. At twenty yards, she stopped and saw the two bags, untouched, on the floor. She placed the third one next to the others, took the flashlight from her pocket, and, flicking it on, felt her way into the corridor of the cavern.

The slick on the walls sparkled icily in the beam of light. It was as though she had come this way many times, rather than just once before. She knew the juttings and ledges, knew precisely where the soft sound of wings, like that of blankets flapping in the wind, would startle her, precisely when she would have to stop to let her nose adjust to the ammonia smell of the bat droppings. The small black eye of the inner opening gazed gravely up at her, and she knelt, then lay on the slimy floor, her arms outstretched before her.

One hand clutching the light, Ada raked at the ground with the other, pulling herself forward. At first she was able to use her hips and knees and quickly came to the narrow part. There she rested, lying limply for a minute in the clutch of stone. Then, bending her ankles as far as she could, she pushed with her toes, pulling all the while with her free hand.

It was slow, and minutes went by seemingly without a jot of progress. She could feel the pain of scrapes on her shoulders and head, and the hard pressure on her chest. She was afraid for only one moment, when she felt nausea and thought she might throw up. I mustn't, she thought, and slowed her pace, alternating her thrusts with deep exhalations. There was a sudden little give and she heard herself gasp and moan as the rock cut into her skin.

Her head was free, another gasp. A push, a clawing at nothing, then a tiny twist, a wrench so small as to be imperceptible, yet enough. A shoulder was through, then the other. For a long moment she lay there, then mentally gathering her chest, trunk, abdomen, and legs behind her, like the segments of a worm, she flung her body through to freedom. It did not take long to reach the inner vault. She knew the way, each rock and pool.

At the entrance she turned to face the wall where she had first seen him. Her light roved slowly back and forth across the base of the cave, from ceiling to floor. At the bottom, jutting into the circle of light, she saw his foot, white, thin, the delicate toes. Her light moved to include the rest in its pale membrane.

He lay where he had fallen, his moth-white face bent backward, too far back, and twisted on the broken neck. Dark black solid blood surrounded him, pasting his hair to the ground, where white blind beetles and pale salamanders darted and dipped.

Ada took it all in. She had seen it in her mind all day, and felt no surprise or shock. With stately steps she walked to the wall of the cave and ran her hand across it, gathering the slimy mud. She walked to the spot where he lay and descended to one knee. Deliberately, she smeared the mud on his face, while the flashlight flickered and danced like a candle.

Edward D. Hoch

The Problem of the Whispering House

"This time I promised you a story about a real haunted house," old Dr. Sam Hawthorne began, pouring the drinks as he always did. "And that's what I'm going to give you. It happened in February of 1928, and it came darned close to being the last case—either medical or mysterious—that I ever handled. But first I better tell you about the ghost-hunter, because the story really started the day he arrived in Northmont . . ."

The ghost-hunter's name was Thaddeus Sloan (Dr. Sam continued), and with a name like that I suppose I expected to meet a grey-bearded old professor with thick spectacles and a cane. Instead, he proved to be a man in his mid-thirties, not much older than myself, who immediately said, "Call me Thad."

"Then I'm Sam," I said, shaking his hand. He was taller than me, and thin to the point of being gaunt. A tiny beard—almost a goatee—helped to hide a weak chin, and it combined with his deep-set, intense eyes to suggest a sort of benevolent Satan.

"I suppose you know why I'm here in Northmont, Sam."

I scratched my head and smiled. "Well, I can't rightly say. We have our neighborhood haunts, certainly. Some years back there was talk that the bandstand in the town square was haunted, but it turned out to be a human spook. And then there's the—"

"I'm interested in the Bryer house."

"Oh, yes. I should have guessed." A Boston newspaper had recently run a Sunday feature on the old place, telling more than most of Northmont's residents had ever known.

"Is it true that the house whispers? And that it contains a secret room which no one has ever come out of, once they've entered it?"

"To tell you the truth I've never been inside the Bryer place. It's been empty for as long as I've lived in Northmont, and I only go where there are patients who need me."

"But surely you've heard the legends."

"It was just an old empty house to me till I read that feature in the Boston paper. Maybe that reporter used his imagination a bit."

He seemed so dejected by my words that I had to add, "I've heard people say it was haunted, though. And that sometimes the wind makes sounds as if the house is whispering."

That seemed to cheer him up. "I spoke to the reporter about his story, of course. He said he obtained most of his information from former Northmont residents now living in the Boston area."

"That's quite possible."

"Someone mentioned your name as one who has made something of a hobby out of solving local mysteries."

"I wouldn't say that," I demurred. "Things happen here the way they do in any town. Sometimes I help out Sheriff Lens, and if I'm lucky I spot a piece of evidence others have missed."

"Nevertheless, you're the only one who can help me. I need someone who knows the area to act as a guide. I intend to spend a night in the old Bryer house, and I'd like you to join me."

"Ghost-hunting is a little out of my line," I said. "Ghosts don't need doctors."

At that moment my nurse April entered with the morning mail. She smiled uncertainly at Thad Sloan and said, "Dr. Sam, there's a telephone call from Mrs. Andrews. Her son Billy fell out of the hayloft and hurt his leg."

"Tell her I'll be right out." I smiled at my visitor. "Come with me if you'd like. You'll see how a country doctor practices. And Mrs. Andrews lives just down the road from the Bryer place."

He followed me out and climbed into my yellow Pierce-Arrow Runabout. "This is quite a car for a country doctor."

"A graduation gift from my family, seven years ago. It's getting a bit old now, but it still runs well."

I took the North Road, which got us to the Andrews place first. Mrs. Andrews hurried out to meet me, plainly distraught. "Dr. Sam, I'm so glad you came! Billy landed on a pitchfork! He's bleedin' pretty bad."

"Don't you worry, Mrs. Andrews. Just take me to him."

She led the way across the barnyard where vestiges of our February snow still lingered in spots. I could understand the reason for her concern. Her husband, a former carnival pitchman, had died of a heart attack the previous year. The job of running the farm and tending the livestock had fallen on twenty-three-year-old Billy. A serious injury to the only able-bodied man on the place could be fatal to the future of the farm.

I found Billy lying on the barn floor, a crude tourniquet tightened around his left leg. His bloodied coveralls had been torn away from the wound where a prong of the pitchfork had gone clear through the fleshy part of his calf. "That's not so bad," I said reassuringly, after a careful inspection. "The bleeding helped cleanse the wound."

Billy Andrews gritted his teeth. "I was forkin' hay down for the cows when I lost my footing and fell. Damned fork went clear through me."

"Could have been a lot worse." Then I remembered Thad Sloan standing by the barn door and introduced him to Billy and Mrs. Andrews. He nodded a greeting but kept his eyes on me, apparently fascinated by my doctoring.

"Now I'm going to give you a little painkiller," I told Billy. "Then I'll stitch up the hole in your leg." I cleansed the wound with antiseptic and set to work. There was no point moving him to the house till I had him patched up.

To make conversation while I worked, I said, "Mr. Sloan is a ghost-hunter. He's here to see the old Bryer house."

"Oh, there's no ghost in there," Mrs. Andrews said with a flutter of her hand. "Them's just stories."

Thad Sloan was staring off across the fields at a house about a half mile away.

"Is that the place?" he asked.

"That's it," I confirmed. "I'll get you there when I finish with Billy here."

The ghost-hunter turned to Mrs. Andrews once again. "You mean you've never noticed anything strange there? No odd lights at night, or unexplained noises? It's said the house can be heard to whisper."

"Not by me, it can't. Billy used to play around there when he was a boy. Billy, you ever hear the Bryer house whisperin' to you?"

He shifted a bit on the barn floor as I completed my mending job. "Never heard a sound 'cept once when I found some hobos camped there. An' they did more than whisper. They chased me clear across the fields."

"Come on now," I said, helping him to his feet. "Just keep the weight off that leg and you'll be okay. We'll get you up to the house." I walked on his left side, keeping my arm around him as he hobbled along. Up at the house we got him into bed and I told him to stay put. "It'll be painful to walk on for a few days, but there's no serious damage. You'll be back in shape in no time."

Mrs. Andrews saw us to the door. "I can't thank you enough for comin' right out, Dr. Sam."

"That's what I'm here for."

"How much do I owe you?"

"Don't you worry. April will send a bill, and you pay me when you're able."

Back in the car, driving down the bumpy dirt road to the Bryer place, Thad Sloan said, "I thought country doctors like you only existed in books."

"There are a few of us left."

The driveway to the Bryer house, overgrown with weeds in summer, was rutted and muddy from the current thaw. One look at it decided me to leave the car on the road and walk up to the house. From the outside, even close up, it appeared in remarkably good shape for its seventy years. The mostly shuttered windows seemed undisturbed, and though the grey paint was faded, there were no signs of peeling.

"I don't suppose we can get in," I said.

He smiled at me. "We can if the lock's working. I got a key from the real-estate man in Boston who has the property listed."

"Then you're serious about spending the night here?"

"Certainly."

Until that moment I hadn't really believed him. "If the place is for sale, does that mean the last of the Bryer family is dead?"

"There are some cousins, but they want to get rid of it." He inserted the key in the lock and opened the door with ease. I followed him into the darkened house.

"I'd suggest opening some shutters to let the daylight in. There's never been electricity here."

Thad Sloan produced a flashlight from his pocket. "I'd rather use this. You can see there's a good supply of candles here and that should do us. Sunlight isn't conducive to conjuring up ghosts."

Most of the furniture had been removed from the house long ago and I was surprised to see the few pieces remaining. There was a shabby, moth-eaten armchair in the living room, and an empty cabinet standing next to the big old fireplace. There were two straight chairs in what might have been the dining room. In one corner of the kitchen we found a burned-down candle stub and an empty bottle which could have contained bootleg whiskey. "I guess Billy Andrews was right about the hobos," I remarked.

"No recent signs, though. This might have been here for years."

We moved on through the other first-floor rooms, noting occasional pieces of furniture that hadn't been worth carting away. We went up the creaking stairs to the second floor, guided by Sloan's pocket torch and the sunlight that came from some unshuttered upper windows.

"Nothing here," I said at last. "Satisfied there are no ghosts?"

"Spirits hardly sit around welcoming noontime visitors. It's in the night that we'll find them, if there are any."

"I don't hear any whispering, either. And what about that room you mentioned, where no one ever comes out of once they've entered it?"

Thaddeus Sloan sighed. "I don't know. We'll have to come back tonight."

I still wonder why I ever agreed to spend the night with a ghost-hunter in a supposedly haunted house. Now I can only blame it on the folly of youth, though at the time it didn't seem that wild an idea. I suppose I wanted to prove something to Thad Sloan, and maybe to myself. Northmont was my town, if only by adoption, and if there was a ghost to be revealed, I wanted to take part in the exorcising of it.

And so that night, shortly before ten, we drove back out to the Bryer place. Sloan had a good supply of candles and matches, along with some other equipment that puzzled me. "You see," he explained, "there are certain procedures which must be followed. Some ghost-hunters seal the doors and windows with seven human hairs, and wear a necklace of garlic. I don't go quite that far, but I do bring along a revolver—"

"For a ghost?"

He smiled at me. "Just a precaution."

We were in the largest of the downstairs rooms, and Thad Sloan stepped to the center of it with a piece of chalk in his hand. Without saying a word he drew a large circle on the wooden floor, and within it traced a five-pointed star. "A pentacle, you see. One is said to be safe inside it."

"A revolver and a pentacle," I marveled. "You *are* ready for anything."

He had other equipment, too—a camera and flashgun that he mounted on a tripod with a revolving head. "If any ghost comes here tonight, we'll be prepared."

I settled down for a long boring night, wishing I'd brought along the latest medical journal to catch up on.

It was about an hour later, not long before midnight, when we heard the whispering. At first I took it to be the wind stirring through the upper reaches of the old house, but soon it seemed to take on the sound and substance of speech.

"Be gone from here if you value your lives . . ."

"Did you hear that?" Sloan exclaimed.

"I think so. I can't be too sure."

"Be gone from here . . ," the voice whispered again.

"It's some sort of trickery," I decided. "Somebody's trying to fool us."

"Come on, Sam. Let's have a look." He picked up the revolver and stepped outside the carefully drawn pentacle. I followed, a bit reluctantly for all my bravado.

"What do you think?" I asked. "Upstairs?"

"Let's see."

We went quickly up the front stairs and paused at the top to listen once more. Now there did seem to be a wind blowing outside, but we heard no sound of whispering.

Then suddenly the downstairs door opened. We froze in our tracks and Sloan signaled for me to hide. I stepped into one of the open bedrooms.

Someone was coming up the stairs. I saw the glow of a lantern and then I saw a man. A thin bearded man, not too tall, wearing a shabby winter coat and a fur hat. He moved quickly but carefully, holding the lantern high to light his way. Though he seemed familiar with the house, I was certain I'd never seen him before.

And yet, as the figure passed me, not five feet away, there could have been something familiar about it, after all.

I expected Sloan to come out of hiding at any moment, but perhaps like me he was more interested in seeing where this man was going. We found out soon enough. He walked to the end of the hall, where a blank wall faced him, and touched a spot in the frame of an adjoining doorway. Immediately there was a click, and when he pushed the wall it swung open before him. It was the first time I'd ever seen a real secret panel in operation.

The hidden door closed behind him and the upper hallway was once more plunged into darkness. I waited a moment and then stepped back into the hall. Thad Sloan saw me and came out of his hiding place. "What do you think?" I asked.

"I think we've found our secret room," Sloan replied softly.

"The room no one ever comes out of?"

"We'll know soon enough. He went in, and he hasn't come out yet."

We waited for what seemed an eternity, though in truth it was no more than a half hour. At any moment we were prepared to leap back into our hiding places should the secret panel open, but it remained closed.

Finally, Sloan said, "I'm going downstairs for my camera. Then let's open the damned thing and confront him."

"There's always the possibility of another exit," I pointed out.

"But where would it lead to? If he'd come out elsewhere on this floor we'd have seen him." He went down for his camera and tripod and returned in a few moments carrying them on his shoulder. "Did you notice where he pushed to open it?"

I'd been feeling around the door jamb and found a loose piece of molding.

"I think this is it," I said.

Sloan positioned the tripod and camera so that it pointed at the wall. He filled the flashgun with extra powder and gripped the shutter release. "All right," he said. "Open it."

I pressed the molding. The door in the wall gave a click and swung open. I wondered if we would find a startled man or an empty room.

We found neither.

The man was still there, seated upright by a table facing us. But our sudden appearance did nothing to startle him. "I think he's—" I began, stepping into the room and going to him.

"Dead?" Thad Sloan tripped the shutter of his camera and the small secret room was filled with an instant's glare from the flash powder. It was enough to show us there was no other occupant and no other exit.

"He's been stabbed," I said, pulling back the man's coat to reveal a hunting knife plunged deep into his left side, toward the heart. "And here's something." I pointed toward the floor where a small .22-caliber automatic had apparently slipped from the dead man's fingers.

Sloan glanced around at the solid walls. He even looked behind the open door of the secret room. "But there's no hiding place, and no way out of here!"

"Exactly."

"You're saying, Sam, that he was killed by a ghost?"

I straightened up from my examination of the body. "No, what I'm saying is even more fantastic than that. I know quite a bit about rigor mortis and such things. This body is already cold and stiff. He didn't die within the last half hour. He's been dead for probably fifteen to twenty hours."

"But that's impossible! We just saw—"

I nodded. "It wasn't a ghost that killed him, but it certainly seems to have been a ghost that walked into this room tonight."

I stayed with the body while Thad Sloan ran down the road to use the phone at the Andrews house. He called Sheriff Lens as I instructed him, and most of the rest of the night was given over to the police investigation. We learned nothing new from it, except that a great many people entered the secret room during those hours and left it again without anything happening to them.

Sheriff Lens was fascinated with the workings of the secret door. "This place was built in the late 1850s," he said. "They say it might have been a station on the underground railway into Canada—for escaped slaves."

"I suppose that's a possibility," I agreed. We'd been tapping at the walls and floor without finding a thing. I'd even allowed myself to be closed into the room alone while Thad Sloan and Sheriff Lens waited outside. I discovered to my horror that there seemed to be no way of opening the secret door from the inside.

"There you have it," Sloan said, obviously excited by the results of his ghost-hunting. "The room of no return! The room from which no one ever emerges! That's what it means—a secret cell in which someone could starve to death without ever being found."

"I'll admit these walls are thick," I said. "You could be right."

Sheriff Lens was examining the tiny automatic. "This gun has been fired. Looks like he took a shot at his killer."

I remembered a hole I'd noticed in the wooden table leg. "And I'll bet here's where it went. Do you have a pocketknife, Sheriff?" In a few moments I'd extracted the slug from the slender leg of the table. It was mashed a bit, but clearly identifiable as a bullet.

"What does that tell us?" Sloan asked.

"Nothing except that the dead man was a poor shot."

"The bullet would have passed through a ghost."

"Ghosts don't use huntin' knives," Sheriff Lens said. "I never believed in ghosts myself and I ain't about to start now."

"What about the thing we saw?" Thad Sloan asked. "It had to be a ghost!"

Sheriff Lens snorted. "That's your problem, not mine."

"Any idea who the dead man is?" I asked the sheriff.

"Never saw him before, and his pockets are empty. No cash, no identification, nothing."

We could do little more that night, but in the morning I was barely awake when Sheriff Lens was knocking at my door, bringing me some interesting news.

"The coroner backs you up, Doc. Says he died sometime between three and nine yesterday morning. But there's somethin' else, too. The dead man's beard is false."

"What?"

"A fake beard, glued on his face with spirit gum like actors use. What do you make of that?"

"I feel stupid for not realizing it. Did anyone recognize him with the beard off?"

"He looked a little familiar, Doc. I wouldn't want to swear to it, but I might have seen him hangin' around town."

"Funny—when he passed me in that hall I thought he seemed familiar, too."

"You still onto that ghost story of yours?"

"I'm only telling you what we saw."

"How about telling me instead how you could see a dead man walkin'."

I thought about it. "That may not be the real problem, Sheriff."

"It's another one of them impossible crimes you like so much, ain't it?"

"Seems so," I admitted. "It certainly looks impossible."

"What are you goin' to do about it?"

"Go back to that house by daylight and start all over again."

I went alone, parking on the road as I'd done before, and made my way up the driveway to the house. The man last night, whoever he was, had apparently come without a car—or else someone had driven it away. I wasn't even considering the possibility of a ghost. The man I'd seen was flesh and blood, very much alive, and if that only deepened the mystery it was something I'd have to figure out.

I went around to the back of the house, walking over long grass still flattened by the weight of the recently melted snow. I didn't really know what I expected to find, but I had to look anyway.

It was the drainpipe at the rear of the house that finally caught my attention. The spout at its bottom curved out about two feet above the ground, and there was something about it that reminded me of the mouthpiece for a particularly large trumpet. I cupped my hands around it and tried calling through it. My voice reverberated in the distance, but I couldn't tell if it was coming from inside the house.

"Back to the scene of the crime?" a voice behind me asked. I straightened up with a start and saw that it was Thaddeus Sloan.

"Look, I think I've found something. Do you still have the key to the front door?"

"Yes." He produced it from his pocket.

"Go inside the house and stand about where we were standing last night when we heard the whispering. I want to try an experiment."

He followed my instructions, and I discovered I could see him moving about through the window above the drain spout. I tried calling again and he signaled that he heard. Then I lowered my voice to a harsh whisper. He hurried over and opened the window. "That's it, Sam! That's the whispering house! How did you know?"

"Just a guess. Our ghost last night entered the house right after we heard the whispering. That made me think there was some way of causing it from outside."

"Then you're saying our ghost is not a ghost?"

"I'm saying it's someone who knows that sounds from this drainpipe are somehow amplified in the attic and fed through the whole house, probably by way of the chimneys."

"How could that man have whispered into the drainpipe, opened the door, walked upstairs, and gone into the secret room if he'd been stabbed to death almost a full day earlier?"

"I don't know," I admitted. "There is one explanation, but at this point it raises more questions than it answers. It merely substitutes one impossibility for another."

"What's that?"

"Well, if the man we saw was the murderer, disguised as his victim, that would explain a lot."

"It wouldn't explain how he got out of that secret room."

"No, it wouldn't," I agreed.

"I like the idea of a ghost much better. I only wish I'd gotten a picture of him walking."

"Did you develop the photograph of the room and the body?"

He nodded, reaching into a leather case he carried. "Here it is, but it doesn't help."

A photograph of the scene had once helped me solve a mystery, but this time I had to admit it showed me very little. The body at the table, the solid wall behind—that was all. We were still confronted with a nameless ghost.

"I'm going back to the office," I said, handing the picture to Sloan. "You coming?"

He shook his head. "I want to look around some more."

I walked out to the road and climbed into my Runabout. I was just pulling away when there was a sputtering from under the hood, then a sheet of flame shot up, and suddenly the whole car was on fire.

Somehow I managed to jump free and roll around on the cold earth to smother the few flames that had clung to my clothing. But the car was a total loss. I stood and watched it burn as I might keep a vigil at the bedside of a dying patient. There was nothing I could do to save it.

Attracted by the smoke, Thad Sloan finally appeared from behind the Bryer house. He ran toward me. "What happened? Your car—"

"I don't know. There was something like an explosion, I think. I was lucky to get out."

"I'll drive you back to town."

"No, I think I want Sheriff Lens to look at this." I started down the road to the Andrews house. "I'm going to call him."

Mrs. Andrews greeted me at the door. "More trouble, Dr. Sam? Your clothes—"

"Car caught fire. I want to phone the sheriff, if I may."

"Go right ahead."

"How's Billy's leg coming along?"

"Slowly. I wish you'd have a look at it while you're here."

He was up in his room, trying to limp around as best he could. I saw at once that his stitches were a bit inflamed. "You should be in bed," I told him sternly. "It's too soon for you to be up on that leg."

"I feel so helpless when there's chores to be done. Momma can't do everything."

"Just get back in bed and let me put some salve on those stitches. Otherwise I'll send you to the hospital where you belong."

That seemed to scare him and he got back on the bed. "You don't look much better'n me, Doc. What happened?"

"Car burned up."

"Not your Runabout!"

"Yes. Needed a new one anyway, after seven years. Hated to see it go like that, though."

I finished up there and walked back to the car with Mrs. Andrews. The flames had died down and I saw that Sheriff Lens had arrived in answer to my call. He had a couple of our volunteer firemen with him and they extinguished the rest of the fire. "It sure is a shame," Mrs. Andrews said, watching them.

"That was meant to cook your hide, Doc," Sheriff Lens said. "Somebody hid a can of gasoline under the hood, with a rag wick leadin' to the spark plugs. It was like a crude bomb."

"I suspected something like that."

"What do you think it means, Sam?" Thad Sloan asked. "You got any enemies around here?"

"The only enemy I've got is the person who killed our unknown man yesterday. And I guess this rules out a ghost, 'cause ghosts don't go around planting bombs in automobiles."

"The bomb had to be planted while we were out behind the house," Sloan said. "That means the killer must have been watching us."

"Maybe," I said, remembering that I'd been there first, before he arrived.

Sheriff Lens looked sadly at the smoking ruin and shook his head. "It was one beauty of a car, Doc."

"April will be heartbroken. Worse than me." The car had always been a special joy to my nurse.

Sheriff Lens led me aside. "I do have one bit o' news for you, Doc. I got a call this mornin' from the State Police. They managed to identify the dead man."

"Who was he?"

"Fellow named George Gifford. He was involved in some frauds during the Florida land boom a few years back. A grand jury indicted him, but the trial was still pending and he was free on bail. The state cops tell me Gifford was a real land promoter, always sellin' nonexistent oil wells or gold mines to somebody."

"Interesting. I wonder what brought him to the Bryer place."

"Maybe he saw that newspaper article and decided to buy a real haunted house."

"Or to sell one," I said. The news had started me thinking, and on the way back to the office I asked Sloan for the name of the Boston newsman who'd written the story about Northmont's haunted house.

The news about the car had already reached April. "Oh, Dr. Sam!" she cried as I entered the office. "Are you all right?"

"I'm in better shape than the car, April. Any calls?"

"Nothing urgent."

"Good. I want to phone long distance to Boston."

The reporter's name was Chuck Yeager and I could barely hear him on the poor connection. Yes, he remembered the story about the haunted house, and he remembered Thaddeus Sloan asking him about it.

"Sloan came after the article appeared?" I shouted into the mouthpiece. "You didn't see him before?"

"No—I never knew Mr. Sloan."

"Who was the former Northmont resident that told you about the house?"

"Well, it was a man named Gifford. He's in real estate."

"And under indictment for land fraud."

"I don't know about that," the reporter said, taken aback. "But I checked out what he told me. The house used to be a stopping place for runaway slaves, and there was a legend connected with a hidden room from which no one ever came out. You know, that article caused me lots of grief."

"How's that?"

"The family was trying to sell it, and they claimed my story spoiled the deal. Some people don't like ghosts and other people don't like publicity. They especially don't want a house that's the object of curiosity. That's why the owners had to hire Sloan."

"Sloan works for the owners? Are you sure?"

"Sure I'm sure. They hired him to chase away the ghost or something. He promised to let me know what happened and give me an exclusive on the story. *Has* anything happened?"

"Nothing much," I assured him. "You'll hear about it when it does."

I hung up and decided I had things to do. But first of all I had to get out of my scorched clothing.

Late that afternoon I called Sloan at his hotel and told him I was going back to the Bryer house. "It's time I confronted the ghost," I said. "Want to come along?"

"Of course!"

"Then pick me up, will you?"

It was already dark by the time we reached the house, and the weather had turned cold again, bringing a few snow flurries to the brisk February air. I waited while Sloan unlocked the door. "Does Sheriff Lens know you've got that key?" I asked.

"I mentioned it to him, but he didn't ask me for it."

"He should have."

"Then how would we get in?"

That set me thinking about something else, and I didn't answer him right away. Instead I followed him inside and up the stairs to the hidden room.

"There has to be a way out of here," I said. "Those legends about the runaway slaves and the room no one ever comes out of must have a basis in fact. No one comes out because there's another exit, and I'm going to find it."

"How?"

I pressed the door jamb and then pushed in the unlocked panel. "I'm going in here and shut the door. Give me a half hour and then open it."

"Can't I come with you?"

"Then who would let us out if I don't find the other exit?"

He agreed with that and I entered the secret room alone. The panel swung shut behind me and I heard the lock click. I was alone in a room without an exit.

I set the lantern I'd brought along on the table and went to work on the walls first. They were all solid, but the back wall seemed more solid than the rest. I wondered why, and then I remembered that the fireplace would be somewhere below me. This solid stone wall would be the side of the chimney running up through the center of the house. It was the perfect place for a secret passage, but no amount of tapping yielded a clue. I tried the other walls next with the same result. And the wooden floor was just as solid.

But I'd been over all this before with Sheriff Lens. The one place we hadn't touched was the ceiling. It looked solid, and I climbed up on the table to make sure. It was solid. Even where the paint had chipped away here and there, I found no clue.

I climbed down off the table. It was a dead end.

I sat down on the chair, as the late George Gifford had done, and thought about it. Four walls, no windows, a solid floor and a solid ceiling. There wasn't even any ventilation when the door was closed. Had they all died like Gifford, here in this room? Was that why it was a room of no return? I could almost imagine the runaway slaves imprisoned here, dying of suffocation or starvation, whichever claimed them first.

No. No, no, no.

I had proved to myself that the killer left this room while it was locked. I couldn't be wrong about that. There was something I wasn't seeing—a door I wasn't finding.

My pocket watch showed that the half hour was up. I pounded on the locked panel to signal Thad Sloan for my release.

Nothing happened.

I pounded again, louder this time. Still nothing.

Thad Sloan. Had I misjudged him completely? Had I delivered myself into the hands of the murderer himself? I remembered him running down to the burning car, remembered that he was working for the owners of the house, remembered that he'd gone downstairs for his camera after the ghost entered this room.

The camera!

I'd been momentarily blinded by the flash when he took that picture. Could someone have sneaked past me, out of the room, in that instant?

I pounded louder, but nobody came.

It was a moment when all my certainties were called into question. If I'd been wrong, I'd put myself in the hands of a killer who'd already tried to burn me to death.

But I wasn't wrong. No one could have passed unseen in the instant that flash went off. Sloan and I were blocking the doorway. And some trace of him would have shown in the photograph itself.

But if Sloan wasn't in league with the killer, what had happened to him?

I stared at the blank solid walls, looking for the way out that didn't exist, growing more frightened by the minute.

And then I thought of something.

I'd been in here for close to forty-five minutes, yet the air still seemed fresh and the lantern burned brightly.

The room was not as tightly sealed as it seemed.

I removed the glass chimney from the lantern and the flame immediately began to flicker. It took me only an instant to locate the source of the draft. Air was coming up from between the wooden floorboards.

Yet there was no way of lifting them, no trap door or panel. The floorboards extended beneath the solid wall on the chimney side.

And that stopped me. How could the floor run *beneath* the wall, into what I was certain was the chimney itself?

I bent to examine the floor once more and noticed some gouges that could have been caused by the point of a knife. A few looked recent, but many seemed quite old. I took a penknife from my pocket and jabbed it into the floorboard that seemed to have the most gouges. Using it as a lever, I tried sliding the single board toward the chimney wall.

It moved. I tried a second and then a third. They all moved.

Each of the gouged floorboards slid away into the chimney wall, and I could only imagine them extending out into the chimney itself. When I'd moved four of the four-inch boards, there was a space in the floor wide enough for me to squeeze through. I dropped down, taking the lantern with me, and found myself in a crawl space above the first-floor ceiling. It was little more than a foot high, and difficult to negotiate, but I managed. Above me, I found that the wooden floorboards could be slid shut as easily as they'd been slid open.

I knew now there must be a way out of here, and I kept crawling on my stomach until I found it. Along the outside wall I came at last to an opening with a ladder running down to the first floor. I climbed down and found myself in a small pantry at the back of the house. This was the escape route the runaway slaves had used to avoid being trapped in the upstairs room. This was the exit from the room of no return.

I hurried through the house to the front stairs and went back up. Thad Sloan was sprawled on his back in the hallway, alive but unconscious. He'd been hit on the back of the head.

I straightened up and looked around, trying to see into the dark doorways of the other rooms. "You can come out now, Mrs. Andrews," I said. "I know you're in there."

She stepped into the circle of light from my lantern, holding a shotgun pointed at my chest.

"You know too much, Dr. Sam," she said. "I'm real sorry that I'll have to kill you."

The light danced off her face as she spoke, and I felt a chill of fear run down my spine. This was the real evil of the Bryer house, more dangerous than any ghost. "You've finally come out in the open, Mrs. Andrews."

She raised the shotgun an inch. "I didn't think you'd ever find the way out of that room, but I waited to be sure."

"You rigged that gasoline bomb in my car, didn't you?"

"Yes. I was afraid of your reputation for solving mysteries."

"My reputation almost went down to defeat tonight. It was only luck that I found the exit from that room—luck, and my certainty that there had to be an exit."

"How did you know?"

"Gifford's body had no identification. The pockets were all empty. But if the pockets were empty, what happened to the key he needed to enter the house? We saw him come in, pass us, and go into the secret room. Of course, Gifford's body was already in that room and it was you who passed us, wearing the hat and coat and false beard.

"But the absence of the key only added to the evidence of rigor mortis to convince me it was someone else who walked by us. You needed the beard and hat and coat, probably left over from your husband's carnival days, to disguise your own identity—and then you put them on the dead man to heighten the illusion that it was he who walked by us in the hall. Then you escaped through the floorboards as I just did."

"George Gifford deserved to die," she said quietly.

"Why? I haven't quite figured out your motive."

"He came here months ago with some sort of land scheme. He wanted to buy this place and our farm, too, and sell shares in a vacation resort of some kind. I made the mistake of telling him about the legends and the secret room, and he got a Boston reporter to write it up so's the value of the land would fall. When the Bryer family sent this ghost-hunter fella, Gifford hurried out here and started threatening us. We were dreadfully afraid he would take away the farm Billy and I worked so hard at!"

There was no need telling her that Gifford was more interested in bilking investors than in taking away her farm. It was the fear of losing the farm that had caused George Gifford's death. "I can understand that," I said gently. "But there's something else."

"What's that?" Her face was knotted with suspicion.

"Why did you take such a risk coming here last night in your false beard and coat? Why was it important that we see the dead man alive? We might never have found the body. You led us to it, at great risk to yourself. We might have grabbed you or burst into the secret room before you could escape."

She was confused now.

"I—I don't—"

I shook my head sadly. "Out here in the country you don't get to know about things like rigor mortis, do you? You didn't know the police could tell the approximate time of death. You used Gifford's key, taken from his body, to come here in disguise after whispering into the drainpipe. Then you transferred the disguise to the dead man so we'd think he wasn't killed till last night. Tell me now, isn't that true?"

"You think too much, Dr. Sam." She raised the shotgun and I stared down the double barrels, knowing only that I had to keep on talking, keep on making her talk.

"You won't shoot me, Mrs. Andrews. You could plant the firebomb because that was impersonal. You didn't have to see me die. But you won't shoot me because you haven't killed anyone yet and you're not going to start now. It was your son Billy who killed Gifford, wasn't it?"

The sound that came from her throat was all the answer I needed.

"Whispering up a drainpipe to scare people," I hurried on. "Not the sort of thing a mother does, unless her son's told her how to do it. Her son who played here and stumbled on the secret room in his childhood. And found the way out, too. It was Billy all the time, wasn't it?

"You didn't stab that man to death with a hunting knife—Billy did. And when Gifford pulled a tiny pistol during the struggle and shot Billy in the leg, it was your idea to pass the wound off as a barn accident. The small bullet, no bigger than a pitchfork's tine, made a clean wound through his leg and then lodged in the table leg. The fact that it didn't even have the power to go through that table leg hinted that it had gone through something else first.

"Of course Gifford's bleeding covered up the blood from Billy's leg, and I suppose Billy wrapped something around his wound till he managed to hobble home. He had too bad a limp to impersonate the dead man last night, so you did it for him. If we believed Gifford wasn't killed till last night, it gave your son a perfect alibi—in case Sloan and I found Gifford's body and Billy needed an alibi."

"Billy stabbed him in self-defense! The man had a gun! Billy only stole the things from his pockets to delay identification!"

"Then don't make it any worse for Billy than it already is, Mrs. Andrews. Let the jury decide. Sheriff Lens is at your house right now, arresting him."

It wasn't true but she didn't know that. The shotgun wavered for just an instant, but I only needed that instant to take it away from her. . . .

"Terrible case," Dr. Sam Hawthorne concluded, finishing his drink. "I almost lost my life twice over, and I did lose my car. That ghost-hunter fella Thad Sloan got a bump on the head and went back to Boston without his spook. The jury gave Billy the benefit of the doubt and only found him guilty of manslaughter, but the trial was too much for his mother and she died before it was over. And—oh, yes—April went with me the following week to pick out a new car."

He held up the bottle to the light. "Got time for one more small—ah—libation? No? Well, come again soon. Next time I'll tell you about when I went to a medical convention in Boston and found out that impossible crimes can happen in the big city, too!"

Jean L. Backus

A Hearse Is Not a Home

Recently I came face to face with myself, beard and all. The encounter was brought on by a scary crisis in interdependency and masculine responsibility and other nonsense like that, including marital fidelity.

I'd been drifting around the country since my wife was killed, living on a small inheritance, working when I could, scrounging when I had to. Amazing the people you meet on the road these days, willing chicks and a few real innocents whom I didn't touch, those on drugs and those on the health-food kick, those damned and those into a new religion.

So one day I found myself in Berkeley, California, with noplace to stay and a rule on the city books that nobody could sleep in a vehicle parked on the street. Well, I drove around until I saw a GARAGE FOR RENT sign in a cul-de-sac off one of the main boulevards. I parked my old hearse in front, got out, opened the back doors, and went in to slick up, comb my beard, and so on. My jeans were dirty but decent, so I closed the hearse and went to ring the doorbell.

The lady who answered wasn't unattractive exactly, just unkempt. And wary. I asked in my best manner what she wanted to rent the garage and she said a hundred bucks a month. Imagine. I asked how long she'd been asking such a huge sum, and she said a long time, but it kept the undesirables away.

I toyed with the idea of settling for a week just to have a base for mail and going to a launderette, and while I was thinking I took a look at the scabby paint on the porch and the dirty windows and weedy garden. As rundown and unkempt as the lady of the house. Finally I offered to clean up the place if she'd let me use the garage for as long as the work lasted.

She was sharper than I thought she'd be, because she put a time limit on the deal. Two weeks, she said, and either leave or pay thereafter. Well, that was fair and I agreed.

Then she asked my name. Sam, I told her, and what was hers? She was the widow Alma. And finally she asked me in for coffee.

The old house was as rundown inside as out, and I pondered the picture. Here was this woman about my own age, around forty, who hadn't the need or the strength or the inclination to work. She wasn't bad-looking, only slovenly, as if she had no one to dress up for, which of course, being a widow, she hadn't. I wondered what she did in her spare time, and looking around saw some sewing and a television and half-filled coffee cups.

Her hair was dirty blonde, long and straight, and it fell over her pale-blue eyes so she was always pushing at it; her hands were soft and white. Under a grubby dress her bust and hips weren't too bad, but her middle sagged a bit, and her shoes were only old sneakers with holes, as if she scuffed her toes a lot.

Her eyes met mine directly, no side glances or hidden meanings—her whole manner was like that, direct, on the level. A nice lady even if she was lazy. Or maybe she was sick or something. Or still in mourning for her husband. I didn't ask, it being no business of mine—and, anyway, I was wary of involvement. That I didn't need, ever again. With anyone.

In the beginning I played straight with her. I put the hearse in the garage and invited her in to see how well I managed. She looked around and suddenly the old mattress and dirty blankets on the floor, the Coleman camp stove and lantern, and my old record player, even the heaps of books lying about didn't look so hot to me, either.

"But where do you wash?" Alma asked at last.

"Public johns, ma'am. Is there a gas station reasonably close?"

She was silent a moment, and then she said, "There's a lavatory you can use at the back of the garage. It has a shower."

We went to inspect the place. "This is neat," I said. "Thank you."

"My husband always changed here after he worked in the garden," she told me. "He looked a bit like you. Without a beard."

I got the funny feeling she was measuring me against her late husband, thinking perhaps that clean-shaven I might pass. In the dark. I thanked her again and hustled her outside.

"Vandals," Alma said, "you want to watch out for vandals. The neighborhood isn't what it was when we came here fifteen years ago. People were friendly then, and they cut their lawns and kept their houses painted. It was nice."

"Yeah, it must have been. Well, thanks again, Alma. I'll go to work in the morning. See you tomorrow."

When the two weeks were up, the job was nowhere near done, and Alma agreed to another two weeks. She was a reasonable lady—she'd seen me stripped to the waist and sweating. The front lawn was mowed, the borders were weeded, the shrubs and trees in back were pruned, and the roses lush with bloom. The first day I worked in the garden, half a dozen people stopped and asked if Alma was getting ready to sell, and a couple of real estaters drifted by as well. I gathered the property was a bonanza if Alma wanted out.

I took a silly sense of pride in the garden, and it being a warm summer I'd set the Beethoven going loud on my record player and lie out on the grass in the evening. Several times Alma opened a window and sat just inside, but I never invited her to join me.

Then one afternoon when I was puttering with systemic for the roses, I saw her come home pushing one of those heavy grocery carts up and over the step to the front walk.

"For Lord's sake, Alma, how far's the market?"

"Six blocks over and two up."

"You do it this way all the time?"

"How else? You know I haven't a car, and it's too much to bring on the bus. Besides, it gets me out, gives me a little exercise."

"I know but it's heavy. Be my guest next time."

"In the hearse?" She grimaced. "No, thank you."

"All right then. I'll walk along and push the darn thing back."

"That's kind of you," she said, "but no, thank you. I can manage."

I sat down on the lawn, pondering the scratchy independence of women, and how the modern female has messed up the scene for those with gentlemanly hangovers. Still, it had given me a little more insight into Alma. As hard as I was trying to avoid involvement, she was now trying to push me away. I knew almost nothing about her, only things she'd let drop by accident, like the day her monthly check was late in the mail, and how her husband had been killed in an accident four years ago, and that she had no family or old friends.

I had told her only what I didn't care if she knew about me—that I'd been born in Maine, my wife was dead, there were no kids, and I was a wanderer by nature, not necessity.

Three mornings later Alma knocked on the hearse before I was up, and when I spread the back doors wide she looked at me and then quickly away.

"I'm going to market early to beat the heat. Want to come along?"

"Sure. Just give me time to put on pants. I don't own any pajamas."

"Look in the closet beside the lavatory," she said, almost turning her back on me. "There's an old trunk of my husband's in there."

Was there ever. Suits, slacks, shirts, underwear, even handkerchiefs—with monograms yet. And pajamas. Half a dozen pairs. I found everything washed and ironed and neatly folded, too. I used a few safety pins, and the slacks didn't look too bad on me, although I was a lot thinner than her husband had been.

Her eyes widened, but she didn't say anything when we met outside half an hour later. Today her hair was tied back with a pink ribbon; she had on a pretty pink dress, and a little makeup. Finally she said, "If you shaved, you'd resemble my husband a bit more."

"No, thanks, Alma. I'm Sam, and I don't dig the idea of resembling—or replacing—your husband."

"I didn't mean that," she said, and her heels clacked harshly on the sidewalk as she hurried ahead of me.

We did a big shopping, heavy things like flour and sugar and shortening, and I wondered what she was storing up for. When we got back to the house, I helped her put the stuff away, and then she asked me to dinner and suddenly things got a bit too domestic, however unintentionally, and I went out and stayed out until it was time to eat that evening.

After I finished the garden, I began on the house—the sagging floors, the cracked plaster, the leaky drains, the holes in the kitchen linoleum. A wonder Alma hadn't hooked a heel and hurt herself. I patched it all up and laid plastic tiles in the kitchen, and replaced the old electric wiring in the attic, and she never questioned any charge I asked for supplies. Fortunately, honesty had never been a problem with me, but just the same it was nice to be trusted.

And she was feeding me now. A meal a day at night because she couldn't stand to see me so thin, and it was nice to have someone to cook for and company at the table. I didn't tell her I was afraid of getting fat, and didn't like the personal relationship getting closer between us, because when I tasted her cooking I couldn't turn it down. No way. Not for anything.

The work ran on until I'd been there two months, perfectly happy one day, and waking up the next morning knowing I had to get out of the city, away from the traffic and the smog, and the neighbors who greeted me by name but never came to visit, and Alma who cooked like an angel and thought I'd resemble her husband if I shaved my beard.

So I took off, intending to go for good. Just backed the hearse out of the garage without saying anything at all. Three days I was gone. Then I couldn't stand it any longer. When I drove up in front of Alma's house on the third night, I caught her looking out the window just as I set the brake.

I bounced up the steps as if I already owned the place, and before I could ring the bell she opened the door. Her dress was dirty and pinned together at the neck, and her hair hung limp over her forehead.

I swallowed. "Look, lady, I'd like to clean out your attic in trade for parking in your garage for a few days."

She laughed, one of the few times I'd heard her laugh, although it sounded more like a sob. "Sam, you fool! Where have you *been?* Oh, I look so messy. I thought you'd left forever."

"Without saying goodbye?" I couldn't meet her eyes. "Why, I wouldn't do that, Alma girl."

"Well, you didn't say where you were going or if you'd be back, so what else could I think? Tell me where you've been, what you've been doing."

"Collecting," I said, ready with a lie. "I'm going to open a shop. And sell things. You wouldn't have a cup of coffee handy, would you?"

"Oh, Sam, forgive me. Of course. Are you hungry? Come in. I haven't eaten all day. I'll fix us something."

That meal was different from before. I don't know. The dark night outside the windows, the china and silver on the tablecloth, the canned pork and beans because she hadn't been expecting me, and most of all the feeling of welcome, as if I'd been missed. Terribly.

"Now, tell me about this shop," she said, over coffee. "What kind? What will you use for capital, for money?"

"Nothing. I'll see an old house, and I'll say, 'Ma'am, let me clean your attic or basement, and it won't cost you a cent. I won't throw away anything you want to keep, and I'll haul anything you don't want away when I leave.' That's how I'll get my stock."

"Oh," Alma said, brightening. "Antiques."

"Not really. Souvenir spoons and comic books and toy trains and stuff like that. Collectibles, they're called. Below antiques, but above junk."

"Sounds like junk to me," she said. "But you know what you're doing. You always do."

"Well, I try. Only I can't stay here. I'm broke until the first of the month, and you don't need a thing done to the house or garden now. I only came by to say hello."

"Oh, forget it, Sam. I'll stake you until you get settled. You can store what you collect in the garage. Maybe I can help, if you'll let me. Let's go see what you brought back this time."

"Not on your life," I exclaimed in panic. "You think it's junk, so you can just wait until I clean it up so it looks like something people will buy."

"All right. I promise I won't even go near the garage. But you have to make me a promise, too."

"What?" I eyed her, worried about how deep I was getting in.

"Let me know before you go off again to collect."

"Okay. I'll do that. I promise."

"You know, under that shrubbery on your chin, you're a very nice man."

"And you're pretty nice yourself, lady." And then I thought, well, why not? "Time to hit the sack, I guess." I groaned aloud and shook my head. "I can't remember when I last slept in an honest-to-God bed."

"Good night," Alma said. She all but pushed me out the front door.

I went away for the second time a week later, and when I told Alma, she looked so wistful I almost asked her along, except that would have blown the whole thing.

When I returned four days later, she was neatly dressed, her hair was soft and clean, and she had a roasted turkey in the refrigerator. She let me pick a wing while she sliced breast and heated stuffing and gravy.

"I didn't know exactly when to expect you," she said, "so I filled the freezer. And I baked bread and cookies. Next time I'll pack some food for you to take along."

"I gather you missed me," I said, watching her with growing pleasure.

She stopped slicing turkey for a second. "Yes. Well. I think that's enough meat for now. Want cranberry sauce with it?"

"Of course. Turkey's not turkey without it."

She got the jelly and sat down opposite me. "Tell me what you found this time. I've been trying to guess. Old china? Furniture? Oh, and I thought of patchwork quilts. And old shawls are good, either knitted or crocheted. I've seen them in the second-hand shops around Berkeley. I've been browsing for ideas for you."

"Everything you mentioned except quilts," I said grandly. "And old paintings and some silver. Hey, this turkey's marvelous."

"Good. There are quilts upstairs," Alma told me. "My grandmother made some and I made the rest. After I left Utah."

"So that's where you're from. How come a good Mormon girl ends up in Berkeley with no family or friends?"

She gripped her knife as if it were a dagger, and her eyes went stony-hard. "I'm no Mormon now. I was the oldest of fifteen kids, and I brought them all up because my mother was always having another. When the sixteenth was announced, I walked out. It was that, or kill myself." The knife came point down on her plate, and split it.

After a moment Alma got up and took the pieces of plate to the sink and stood there with her back to me. All I could think of was what a rough deal she'd had all the way along.

When she finally turned around, her eyes were normal again. "Forget what I said, Sam. Let's go up and look at the quilts."

There were twenty-four of them in the attic, in a variety of old patterns, all made with tiny stitches, warm and yet lightweight, the kind my mother used to make in Maine when I was a kid.

"Look," I said. "These are valuable. In the East you could get at least a couple of hundred dollars apiece for them, maybe more. You should find a store that'll take them on consignment if you don't want to keep them. Then you could take a trip. Or buy a car."

"But, Sam—?" She stared at me. "Won't you take them for your shop?"

I sat back on my heels and looked at myself, face to face, beard and all. After a second I said, "Alma girl, there isn't going to be a shop. I didn't collect anything. I'm moving on for good tomorrow."

"What!" She looked almost as she had when she broke her dinner plate. "But you said—"

"I lied. I wanted a base. A hearse is not a home, after all, and I like your cooking, but I don't want to get involved."

"We'd better go downstairs now." Her voice was dead. Then she picked up a couple of quilts. "Put these in the hearse, Sam. For when it gets cold. Wherever you are."

For a good long minute we stared at each other. "Thanks. Do I have to leave tonight?"

"Tomorrow. By noon." She turned and went downstairs and I followed and let myself out.

I thought it over during the night, knowing I could start a shop if I wanted to bad enough, only the idea bored me. I could find work, any amount of it, if I wanted. What I couldn't do was get all dressed up and play house with Alma. Or any other woman. On the other hand . . .

Alma knocked on the hearse before I was up, and wearing her husband's pajamas, I stumbled to open the back doors.

"I'm fixing breakfast for you," she said, "and you'd better take the food in the freezer. It's no good to me, and it'll keep for a few days."

"Thanks. Okay. You're being mighty nice about this."

But she was gone.

I took my time washing and dressing, and when I entered the kitchen, Alma caught her breath, but she didn't say anything, just put out juice and toast, set eggs and bacon before me, and filled my coffee cup. Then she sat down to watch me eat.

"Aren't you hungry?" I asked, attacking my plate.

"Not very."

I said nothing more, but I let her refill my cup again and again even after I finished eating. Finally I thought of something to say.

"How was your husband killed?"

She went white and her lips tightened. "He was in an accident . . . an accident. With a girl f-friend. A car accident. They were both killed. They were running away together."

That told me a lot more than I'd already guessed. "Where does your monthly check come from?"

"It's my widow's pension. My husband was a mining assayer for the state. He made good money, and we were still married when he died." She looked at me. "What is this, Sam? You've never pried before."

"Doesn't mean I haven't wanted to. You got any savings?"

"I won't tell you."

I got up from the table. "Okay. So long. Nice knowing you."

"Enough to carry me over emergencies." Her voice was small and sobby. "Does money make all the difference to you?"

"Not really." I sat down. "Tell you what. You sell this house and come away with me. Let's get away from loneliness and memories and all the other pollutants we live with, you and I. Will you do it?"

"Why, how could I?" She looked about to cry. "I've got to think. Don't you—that is, don't you want to live here?"

"Not permanently. Some wanderers are airplane pilots and some are sailors. Me, I'm just a wanderer, period. I can't live in one place."

"But the house, Sam. I don't want to sell the house."

"Then rent it. What good is it with no man, no kids, no friends?" I took a breath. "If you don't come with me, you won't see me again. Ever. And that's no lie. So take five and make up your mind."

"How do I know you won't use my money and strand me somewhere?"

"You don't." Obviously she sensed something of my panic and

revulsion at what I'd just proposed, or she wouldn't hesitate, one way or the other. But what she might think wasn't as bad as it really was. I'd already murdered one wife with my bare hands. In a cold rage at her infidelity. And nothing I learned about her either before or after I was paroled from state prison had ever made me sorry about it. Until now.

"I'll do it, Sam! I'll do it! Is that why you shaved off your beard?"

"Maybe I just didn't like the image of myself."

"Oh, Sam." She leaned against me, and I put my arms around her. "I'm so happy. Only you said yourself a hearse is not a home, so don't ask me to ride in yours. That's all I'll ever ask of you."

"No, I won't do that. We'll take your money and buy a decent camper." As we kissed, I realized how glad and happy I was about what had happened. Of course I could never know for sure how I would handle it if the provocation to kill ever set me off again. But I had a hunch that question was dead and buried now. Along with the sick pleasure I'd taken in driving the beat-up old hearse all over the country.

"You didn't ask," I said, sitting down with Alma on my lap, "but I'll promise just the same. You keep on cooking the way you do, and so help me, I'll never strand you anywhere. Ever."

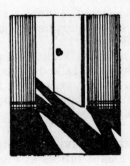

Ellery Queen

No Place To Live

When they entered the flat they were after someone else altogether. But in one of the rooms off the center hall they found a man with half his head blown off, and over him a pretty blonde with a cheap new wedding band on her left hand holding the cannon.

Sergeant Velie took the gun from her by the barrel delicately, and Inspector Queen looked at her ring and said to her, "And you're Mrs. ——?"

"Graham," the girl said. "June Graham."

Ellery caught June Graham as she fell.

Twenty-four hours earlier, Brock was on his unmade bed doping the next day's fourth race when his landlord came to call.

Brock went out and opened the apartment door. He had a broken nose and he was dressed in pink and brown.

"If it ain't Mr. Finger," Brock said, surprised. "You come to investigate my cockroaches personally?"

Mr. Finger stepped into Brock's flat in ominous silence. Brock hustled him into the dirty bedroom and shut the door.

"What's on your mind?" Brock said.

"Rent." Mr. Finger was small and fat and wore a big ruby on his right hand. He owned eight apartment houses on the Upper West Side. "*Their* rent, Mr. Brock."

Brock followed the line of his landlord's fat thumb and it told him the whole sad story. "So Jerky talked," Brock said.

"If you're meaning my super, yeah," Mr. Finger said in a chilling voice. "Look, Brock, you been behind my back renting out three of your five rooms. This is against the law."

"You don't mean it," Brock said.

Mr. Finger began ticking off invisible subtenants. "Mrs. Wodjeska, no husband, two kids, cleans offices at night—some subtenant! A no-good that calls himself Smith. Smith, ha! A G.I. and his wife name of Graham, just back from the service. Brock, those six didn't sign no lease with Harvey Finger."

"Let's talk this over," Brock said, showing his gold-capped teeth.

"So we're talking, ain't we?" the landlord said. "Twenty-five dollars a week per room you're charging. That's a monthly income to you of three hundred. My super you smear forty a month. Me you pay the frozen rent of eighty-five. I didn't even graduate public school, Mr. Brock, but even I can figure your net profit on my apartment is one seventy-five a month. So tell me one reason why I shouldn't report you to the State Temporary Rent Commission?"

"Aw, get smart," Brock said. "So I'm dispossessed. So they let you sign on a new tenant at a great big twelve dollars and seventy-five cents more a month, and you'll maybe have to redecorate, fix the plumbing, check the wiring, and God knows. Mr. Finger, what's the percentage?"

Mr. Finger said softly, "We split it."

Brock got him, all right. "Robber!"

"Can names hurt me?" The landlord shrugged, "It's one hundred a month extra from you or you're out on your ear."

"Fifty. Not a nickel more!"

"Hundred."

"Seventy-five—"

"I'm a one-price landlord," Mr. Finger said, not without humor. "Is it pay, Mr. Brock, or on your way, Mr. Brock?"

Brock kicked the armchair. It was his own chair, so Mr. Finger waited unperturbed.

"The goats ain't been running for me," Brock growled. "I got to have time to scrape it up."

"Scrape fast," Mr. Finger said, smiling. He turned at the door. "You got till eight o'clock tomorrow night."

"Big deal," Brock said bitterly.

He waited till the fat little man was gone and then he stalked up the hall and shoved Mrs. Wodjeska's door open. Mrs. Wodjeska was in bed being fed some soup by a little girl while another little girl applied cold compresses to her mother's head. When the two little girls saw who it was they stopped what they were doing and ran to hide behind the lopsided sofa.

"Can't you ever knock?" the woman said hoarsely.

Brock scowled. "You still sick?"

"It's the virus." Mrs. Wodjeska pulled the covers up to her chin. "What do you want?"

"My rent."

"I'll pay you next week."

"Listen, you, I been kidded by experts. What's the score?"

"Tomorrow I'm promised a job. Will you please go? You're scaring my children."

"Now I scare kids!" Brock said in an injured tone. "Look, Mrs. Social Register, I need this rent, see? You pay up by tomorrow night or bed your kids down on the sidewalk. This ain't the Salvation Army!"

Brock was figuring other angles when Hank Graham, the lanky ex-G.I., burst in on him.

"Okay, Brock," Graham said, glaring. "Where is it?"

Graham was twenty pounds lighter than Brock, but something in the thrust of his jaw made Brock step behind the armchair.

"Where is what?" Brock asked cautiously.

"My money!" Hank Graham said. "And don't play dumb with me, buddy. I want the three thousand dollars you swiped from my room, and I want it now."

"Hold it, hold it," Brock murmured. "You got three grand?"

"Savings. I brought it back from Germany last month and got married on the strength of it. Nobody knew about that money, Brock, not even my wife. I was keeping it for a down payment on a house in Jersey as a surprise to Juney. All of a sudden it's gone from where I hid it in my room and you're the only one with a duplicate key to the lock!"

"First I hear of it," Brock said absently.

Young Graham advanced on the chair. "Give, you crook, or I call the police."

"Keep your shirt on, General. I didn't take your three grand. But I got a pretty good idea who did."

"And who would that be?"

"My experience is you check first and make with the names later," Brock said. "Look, Graham, yell copper and you may never see a cent. But give me time and I think I can get it back for you."

Hank Graham looked him over.

"Tomorrow night," he said grimly. "Then it's either my money back or you'll explain in a police station."

Through a crack in his door, Brock watched the ex-G.I. trudge back to his room. Pretty June Graham was waiting in their doorway. She was in a clinging negligee and Brock saw her ask her husband something in a puzzled way, and Graham's forced smile. Then they went into their room and locked the door.

Brock waited.

He stole up the hall and scratched on the last door.

"Open up, Smith," he said in a soft voice. "It's Brock."

He grinned when he heard the chain rattle. Installing a chain latch had been Smith's own idea.

Smith glanced swiftly down the hall before he motioned Brock into his room and relatched the door. Smith was a dark skinny man with holes for eyes.

"What do *you* want?" He had a nasty voice.

"Graham's three thousand bucks."

"What? What?" Smith said excitedly.

Brock reached down to fix Smith's egg-stained tie. "I know I didn't take it, and it wasn't the Wodjeska number—what crook scrubs floors for a living? So that leaves you, Smitty. No three-buck lock would keep *you* out of the Grahams' room."

"You're on the junk," Smith jeered, trying to back off. "I don't know nothing about no three grand—"

Brock pulled Smith's tie tight, using both hands. Smith's eyes bugged and he began to turn blue, his legs jerking.

"You little punk," Brock smiled, "how long do you think it took me to spot you—a guy who don't stick his nose out from one day to another except for a couple minutes at night sometimes? You're Ratsy Johnson, Frank Pompo's finger man. Inspector Queen's been looking for you since early summer to testify in the case he got up against Pompo for the D.A., and so's Pompo to see that you don't. Do you shell out Graham's three grand or do I tip off Queen *and* Pompo where you're hiding out?"

Johnson pointed frantically to his throat. Brock loosened his hold a little.

"I'll make a deal," the fugitive gasped.

"With what?"

"With a frame, that's with what! Brock, without moola I'll chance the D.A. I'm down to shoe buttons. You hog this bundle and I'll surrender to the law and say you fixed it for me to hide out in your place! See?"

Brock thought. Then he let go.

"Okay, I'll chisel the kid into settling for one grand of his dough, and I'll give you five C's for your end."

Ratsy Johnson fingered his neck. "We split even up, see?"

"You're a hard man," Brock mourned. "Where's the take?"

Johnson produced a cheap cigarette case. From it he extracted a stained king-size cigarette and peeled the paper down. The gap revealed a tuft of tobacco on one end, a filter at the other, and a green paper tube between. He unrolled the tube and it became three one-thousand-dollar bills. Brock snatched them, then looked down at his fingers. The oily stain on the cigarette paper was also on the outer bill.

"What do you smoke, fuel oil?" Brock wrapped the bills in a silk handkerchief and tucked it all carefully away.

Johnson clawed at him. "Give me mine, you chiseler!"

Brock's big hand chopped down and Johnson fell like a clubbed fish. "What's the uproar, Ratsy? You get yours when I con Graham into the deal. Maybe he won't play."

"Okay, okay," the fugitive sniveled from the floor. "But you dou-ble-cross me, Brock, and so help me—"

Brock went out grinning.

That was Tuesday night.

On Wednesday one of Sergeant Velie's regular stoolies had passed the word that Ratsy Johnson was holed up in Apartment 4-A of a tenement on the West Side. Velie had had the house staked out since Wednesday afternoon, waiting for Johnson to show. He was not known to be armed but he was considered dangerous and the street seemed a safer place to take him. Detectives were planted on the roof, the fourth floor, and in the lobby. Because of the importance of the arrest, Inspector Queen showed up to take personal charge, and Ellery tagged along.

At 8:30 P.M., the Inspector decided not to wait any longer and they had entered Apartment 4-A to find not only Ratsy Johnson but the body of Charlie the Chiseler Brock. Brock had been shot with a .45 automatic at close quarters—through one of his pillows used by his killer to muffle the report. His body was still warm.

In the first few minutes, they learned all about Brock's illegal subrentals of three of his five rooms and the events of the night before. Brock's threat to put Mrs. Wodjeska and her children on the street for nonpayment of rent came out in a rush. The theft of Hank Graham's three thousand dollars had been registered by the aggrieved ex-G.I. immediately. Even landlord Finger's ultimatum to Brock twenty-four hours earlier was in Sergeant Velie's notebook, Mr. Finger deciding that candor about a harmless little rent conspiracy was preferable to being mixed up in a murder.

And Ratsy Johnson, found cowering in his room, meekly undid the chain with his own hands and apparently was so overwhelmed by his plight—caught by the police, hunted by boss mobster Frank

Pompo, and now up to his stringy neck in a murder rap—that he confessed his theft of young Graham's money and told all about his Tuesday-night deal with Brock.

It was all very clear—except who was lying about what went on in Charlie the Chiseler Brock's dirty bedroom between 8:00 and 8:30 Wednesday evening.

Landlord Harvey Finger had arrived at the apartment house for his payoff from Brock a few minutes before 8:00 P.M. He had been permitted to enter 4-A, but on coming out a few minutes later he was stopped by detectives—and after Brock's corpse was found at 8:30 when they entered the apartment to arrest Johnson, the little fat landlord insisted he had left Brock alive.

Hank Graham said he had visited Brock's room after Finger's departure, spoken to Brock for five minutes or so, and claimed he, too, had left Brock alive.

Ratsy Johnson said he had not seen Brock on Wednesday evening at all, and Mrs. Wodjeska said the same thing. The hoodlum had no alibi and Mrs. Wodjeska's two little girls could not corroborate their mother's claim, as they had been playing hopscotch all evening in the alley behind the tenement with other children.

So it all came back to the pretty blonde girl found standing over the body, the gun in her hand.

She had been revived by Ellery and her frantic husband and now she was in one of Brock's chairs, pale and trembling.

"Why did you kill this man?" Inspector Queen said to her.

"She didn't kill him," Hank Graham shouted, "and for God's sake cover him up!"

Sergeant Velie obliged with the evening paper.

"I didn't kill him," Juney Graham said, not looking. "I came in here to talk to him and this is what I found."

"And the gun?" Ellery asked gently.

"It was on the floor and I picked it up."

"Why?"

She did not reply.

"Innocent people who walk in on corpses and immediately pick up the gun are common in the movies and on television," Ellery said, "but in real life they'd rather pick up a live rattlesnake. Why did you pick up the gun, Mrs. Graham?"

The girl's hands twisted. "I—I don't know. I wasn't thinking, I guess."

"Did you ever see the gun before?" Inspector Queen asked.

"No."

It went on that way for some time.

"Now, as I get it," Inspector Queen said to Hank Graham's pretty bride, "your husband went to Brock's room to demand the return of his three thousand dollars that Brock had promised to get back. Brock offered him a thousand dollars in settlement, your husband lost his temper and refused, and he came rushing back to your room all set to call the police. And that was when he told you he'd saved three thousand dollars of his overseas pay and it had been stolen from him, Mrs. Graham? That's the first you knew about the whole thing?"

June Graham nodded stiffly.

"Why did you talk your husband out of calling the police?"

"I was afraid Hank would get beaten up or—or something. I never did want to rent this room. I didn't like Brock's looks."

Sergeant Velie had been studying the girl's curves. "Brock ever make a pass at you?"

"No. I mean—well, once, when Hank was out. I slapped his face and he walked out laughing. But he never tried it again."

"You didn't tell me that," Hank Graham said slowly.

Inspector Queen and his son exchanged glances.

"Now, about that gun, Mrs. Graham," Ellery began.

"I've told you about the gun!"

"You talked your husband out of phoning the police and you went to Brock's room to see what you could do," the Inspector said. "Take it from there."

"But I've told you!"

"Tell us again."

"I knocked," June Graham said wearily. "He didn't answer. I tried the door. It opened. I went in. He was lying on the floor all—all messy. There was a gun beside the body. I picked it up and then you all came in."

"Why did you pick up the gun, Mrs. Graham?"

"I don't *know,* I tell you."

"Then suppose I tell you," Ellery said. "You picked it up because you recognized it."

"No!" It was almost a scream.

"Instead of bulldozing the poor kid," Hank Graham muttered, "why don't you find my three thousand dollars?"

"Oh, we found them, Graham. We found them right here in Brock's room, stashed under the arch support of an alligator shoe. The shoe, by the way, was on Brock's foot." Inspector Queen smiled. "But let's not change the subject, Graham. Your wife is lying about that gun."

"I'm not," the girl said despairingly. "I never saw it before."

"Good try, Mrs. Graham," Ellery said, "but not good enough. The fact is it's your husband's gun—an Army .45. When you found it beside Brock's body after Hank had been arguing with him, you naturally thought Hank had shot him. Isn't that it?"

"Hank, no! Don't!"

"No use, honey." Hank Graham shook his head. "Okay, Mr. Queen, it's my gun. But I didn't shoot Brock. I left him alive."

"That's your story," Inspector Queen said sadly, for he was a notorious softie about young love.

But he signaled Sergeant Velie.

"Hank!" The girl flew to him and clung sobbing.

"A story with one chapter missing," Ellery said, eying June Graham tenderly. "You left something out, Graham."

Hank Graham was stroking his wife's hair. He didn't bother to look up. "Did I?"

"Yes. The one fact that clears you, you idiot, and pins this murder where it belongs!"

And Ellery had them bring Brock's killer in.

"You kept saying your money was stolen from where you'd hidden it in your room, Graham, and Johnson admitted he'd been the thief. But what you forgot to tell us, and what Johnson carefully neglected to say, was where in your room the money was hidden."

He requisitioned the official envelope containing the evidence and from it he took Graham's money.

"These three one-thousand-dollar bills were tightly rolled up, and the top bill is oil-stained," Ellery said. "You'd therefore hidden your money, Graham, in something narrow and tubelike whose insides are oily.

"Hank, why didn't you tell us you'd rolled up the bills *and slipped them into the barrel of your .45 for safekeeping?*"

"Holy smokes," Hank groaned.

"Then it wasn't money Ratsy Johnson was after when he went on the prowl in your room, it was your .45. He had no gun and he figured a newly returned G.I. might have one. It was only when he examined the .45 later that he found the three bills in the barrel.

"So the money places the gun that shot Brock in your possession, Ratsy," Ellery said to the suddenly green-faced fugitive. "You sneaked into Brock's room after Graham left tonight, shot Brock, looked for the money he'd hijacked from you, couldn't find it, lost your nerve, and ducked back to your room. June Graham must have just missed seeing you as she went to Brock's room to find him dead." Ellery turned and grinned at the newlyweds. "Any questions?"

"Yes," Hank Graham said, drying his wife's tears. "Anybody know a good real-estate agent?"

Nedra Tyre

A Nice Place To Stay

All my life I've wanted a nice place to stay. I don't mean anything grand, just a small room with the walls freshly painted and a few neat pieces of furniture and a window to catch the sun so that two or three pot plants could grow. That's what I've always dreamed of. I didn't yearn for love or money or nice clothes, though I was a pretty enough girl and pretty clothes would have made me prettier—not that I mean to brag.

Things fell on my shoulders when I was fifteen. That was when Mama took sick, and keeping house and looking after Papa and my two older brothers—and of course nursing Mama—became my responsibility. Not long after that Papa lost the farm and we moved to town. I don't like to think of the house we lived in near the C & R railroad tracks, though I guess we were lucky to have a roof over our heads—it was the worst days of the Depression and a lot of people didn't even have a roof, even one that leaked, plink, plonk; in a heavy rain there weren't enough pots and pans and vegetable bowls to set around to catch all the water.

Mama was the sick one but it was Papa who died first—living in town didn't suit him. By then my brothers had married and Mama and I moved into two back rooms that looked onto an alley and everybody's garbage cans and dump heaps. My brothers pitched in and gave me enough every month for Mama's and my barest expenses even though their wives grumbled and complained.

I tried to make Mama comfortable. I catered to her every whim and fancy. I loved her. All the same, I had another reason to keep her alive as long as possible. While she breathed I knew I had a place to stay. I was terrified of what would happen to me when Mama died. I had no high-school diploma and no experience at outside work and I knew my sisters-in-law wouldn't take me in or let my brothers support me once Mama was gone.

Then Mama drew her last breath with a smile of thanks on her face for what I had done.

Sure enough, Norine and Thelma, my brothers' wives, put their feet down. I was on my own from then on. So that scared feeling of wondering where I could lay my head took over in my mind and never left me.

I had some respite when Mr. Williams, a widower twenty-four years older than me, asked me to marry him. I took my vows seriously. I meant to cherish him and I did. But that house we lived in! Those walls couldn't have been dirtier if they'd been smeared with soot and the plumbing was stubborn as a mule. My left foot stayed sore from having to kick the pipe underneath the kitchen sink to get the water to run through.

Then Mr. Williams got sick and had to give up his shoe repair shop that he ran all by himself. He had a small savings account and a few of those twenty-five-dollar government bonds and drew some disability insurance until the policy ran out in something like six months.

I did everything I could to make him comfortable and keep him cheerful. Though I did all the laundry I gave him clean sheets and clean pajamas every third day and I think it was by my will power alone that I made a begonia bloom in that dark back room Mr. Williams stayed in. I even pestered his two daughters and told them they ought to send their father some get-well cards and they did once or twice. Every now and then when there were a few pennies extra I'd buy cards and scrawl signatures nobody could have read and mailed them to Mr. Williams to make him think some of his former customers were remembering him and wishing him well.

Of course, when Mr. Williams died his daughters were johnny-on-the-spot to see that they got their share of the little bit that tumbledown house brought. I didn't begrudge them—I'm not one to argue with human nature.

I hate to think about all those hardships I had after Mr. Williams died. The worst of it was finding somewhere to sleep; it all boiled down to having a place to stay. Because somehow you can manage not to starve. There are garbage cans to dip into—you'd be surprised how wasteful some people are and how much good food they throw away. Or if it was right after the garbage trucks had made their collections and the cans were empty I'd go into a supermarket and pick, say, at the cherries pretending I was selecting some to buy. I didn't slip their best ones into my mouth. I'd take either those so ripe that they should have been thrown away or those that weren't ripe enough and shouldn't have been put out for people to buy. I might snitch a withered cabbage leaf or a few pieces of watercress or a few of those small round tomatoes about the size of hickory

nuts—I never can remember their right name. I wouldn't make a
pig of myself, just eat enough to ease my hunger. So I managed. As
I say, you don't have to starve.

The only work I could get hardly ever paid me anything beyond
room and board. I wasn't a practical nurse, though I knew how to
take care of sick folks, and the people hiring me would say that since
I didn't have the training and qualifications I couldn't expect much.
All they really wanted was for someone to spend the night with
Aunt Myrtle or Cousin Kate or Mama or Daddy; no actual duties
were demanded of me, they said, and they really didn't think my
help was worth anything except meals and a place to sleep. The
arrangements were pretty makeshift. Half the time I wouldn't have
a place to keep my things, not that I had any clothes to speak of,
and sometimes I'd sleep on a cot in the hall outside the patient's
room or on some sort of contrived bed in the patient's room.

I cherished every one of those sick people, just as I had cherished
Mama and Mr. Williams. I didn't want them to die. I did everything
I knew to let them know I was interested in their welfare—first for
their sakes, and then for mine, so I wouldn't have to go out and find
another place to stay.

Well, now, I've made out my case for the defense, a term I never
thought I'd have to use personally, so now I'll make out the case for
the prosecution.

I stole.

I don't like to say it, but I was a thief.

I'm not light-fingered. I didn't want a thing that belonged to anybody else. But there came a time when I felt forced to steal. I had
to have some things. My shoes fell apart. I needed some stockings
and underclothes. And when I'd ask a son or a daughter or a cousin
or a niece for a little money for those necessities they acted as if I
was trying to blackmail them. They reminded me that I wasn't
qualified as a practical nurse, that I might even get into trouble
with the authorities if they found I was palming myself off as a
practical nurse—which I wasn't and they knew it. Anyway, they
said that their terms were only bed and board.

So I began to take things—small things that had been pushed into
the backs of drawers or stored high on shelves in boxes—things that
hadn't been used or worn for years and probably would never be
used again. I made my biggest haul at Mrs. Bick's, where there was
an attic full of trunks stuffed with clothes and doodads from the
Twenties all the way back to the Nineties—uniforms, ostrich fans,

Spanish shawls, beaded bags. I sneaked out a few of these at a time and every so often sold them to a place called Way Out, Hippie Clothiers.

I tried to work out the exact amount I got for selling something. Not, I know, that you can make up for the theft. But say I got a dollar for a feather boa belonging to Mrs. Bick: well, then I'd come back and work at a job that the cleaning woman kept putting off, like waxing the hall upstairs or polishing the andirons or getting the linen closet in order.

All the same, I *was* stealing—not everywhere I stayed, not even in most places, but when I had to I stole. I admit it.

But I didn't steal that silver box.

I was as innocent as a baby where that box was concerned. So when that policeman came toward me grabbing at the box I stepped aside, and maybe I even gave him the push that sent him to his death. He had no business acting like that when that box was mine, whatever Mrs. Crowe's niece argued.

Fifty thousand nieces couldn't have made it not mine.

Anyway, the policeman was dead and though I hadn't wanted him dead I certainly hadn't wished him well. And then I got to thinking: well, I didn't steal Mrs. Crowe's box but I had stolen other things and it was the mills of God grinding exceeding fine, as I once heard a preacher say, and I was being made to pay for the transgressions that had caught up with me.

Surely I can make a little more sense out of what happened than that, though I never was exactly clear in my own mind about everything that happened.

Mrs. Crowe was the most appreciative person I ever worked for. She was bedridden and could barely move. I don't think the registered nurse on daytime duty considered it part of her job to massage Mrs. Crowe. So at night I would massage her, and that pleased and soothed her. She thanked me for every small thing I did—when I fluffed her pillow, when I'd put a few drops of perfume on her earlobes, when I'd straighten the wrinkled bedcovers.

I had a little joke. I'd pretend I could tell fortunes and I'd take Mrs. Crowe's hand and tell her she was going to have a wonderful day but she must beware of a handsome blond stranger—or some such foolishness that would make her laugh. She didn't sleep well and it seemed to give her pleasure to talk to me most of the night about her childhood or her dead husband.

She kept getting weaker and weaker and two nights before she died she said she wished she could do something for me but that when she became an invalid she had signed over everything to her niece. Anyway, Mrs. Crowe hoped I'd take her silver box. I thanked her. It pleased me that she liked me well enough to give me the box. I didn't have any real use for it. It would have made a nice trinket box, but I didn't have any trinkets. The box seemed to be Mrs. Crowe's fondest possession. She kept it on the table beside her and her eyes lighted up every time she looked at it. She might have been a little girl first seeing a brand-new baby doll early on a Christmas morning.

So when Mrs. Crowe died and the niece on whom I set eyes for the first time dismissed me, I gathered up what little I had and took the box and left. I didn't go to Mrs. Crowe's funeral. The paper said it was private and I wasn't invited. Anyway, I wouldn't have had anything suitable to wear.

I still had a few dollars left over from those things I'd sold to the hippie place called Way Out, so I paid a week's rent for a room that was the worst I'd ever stayed in.

It was freezing cold and no heat came up to the third floor where I was. In that room with falling plaster and buckling floorboards and darting roaches, I sat wearing every stitch I owned, with a sleazy blanket and a faded quilt draped around me waiting for the heat to rise, when in swept Mrs. Crowe's niece in a fur coat and a fur hat and shiny leather boots up to her knees. Her face was beet-red from anger when she started telling me that she had traced me through a private detective and I was to give her back the heirloom I had stolen.

Her statement made me forget the precious little bit I knew of the English language. I couldn't say a word, and she kept on screaming that if I returned the box immediately no criminal charge would be made against me. Then I got back my voice and I said that box was mine and that Mrs. Crowe had wanted me to have it, and she asked if I had any proof or if there were any witnesses to the gift, and I told her that when I was given a present I said thank you, that I didn't ask for proof and witnesses, and that nothing could make me part with Mrs. Crowe's box.

The niece stood there breathing hard, in and out, almost counting her breaths like somebody doing an exercise to get control of herself.

"You'll see," she yelled, and then she left.

The room was colder than ever and my teeth chattered.

Not long afterward I heard heavy steps clumping up the stairway.

I realized that the niece had carried out her threat and that the police were after me.

I was panic-stricken. I chased around the room like a rat with a cat after it. Then I thought that if the police searched my room and couldn't find the box it might give me time to decide what to do. I grabbed the box out of the top dresser drawer and scurried down the back hall. I snatched the back door open. I think what I intended to do was run down the back steps and hide the box somewhere, underneath a bush or maybe in a garbage can.

Those back steps were steep and rose almost straight up for three stories and they were flimsy and covered with ice.

I started down. My right foot slipped. The handrail saved me. I clung to it with one hand and to the silver box with the other hand and picked and chose my way across the patches of ice.

When I was midway I heard my name shrieked. I looked around to see a big man leaping down the steps after me. I never saw such anger on a person's face. Then he was directly behind me and reached out to snatch the box.

I swerved to escape his grasp and he cursed me. Maybe I pushed him. I'm not sure—not really.

Anyway, he slipped and fell down and down and down, and then after all that falling he was absolutely still. The bottom step was beneath his head like a pillow and the rest of his body was spread-eagled on the brick walk.

Then almost like a pet that wants to follow its master, the silver box jumped from my hand and bounced down the steps to land beside the man's left ear.

My brain was numb. I felt paralyzed. Then I screamed.

Tenants from that house and the houses next door and across the alley pushed windows open and flung doors open to see what the commotion was about, and then some of them began to run toward the back yard. The policeman who was the dead man's partner—I guess you'd call him that—ordered them to keep away.

After a while more police came and they took the dead man's body and drove me to the station where I was locked up.

From the very beginning, I didn't take to that young lawyer they assigned to me. There wasn't anything exactly that I could put my finger on. I just felt uneasy with him. His last name was Stanton. He had a first name, of course, but he didn't tell me what it was; he said he wanted me to call him Bat like all his friends did.

He was always smiling and reassuring me when there wasn't

anything to smile or be reassured about, and he ought to have known it all along instead of filling me with false hope.

All I could think was that I was thankful Mama and Papa and Mr. Williams were dead and that my shame wouldn't bring shame on them.

"It's going to be all right," the lawyer kept saying right up to the end, and then he claimed to be indignant when I was found guilty of resisting arrest and of manslaughter and theft or robbery—there was the biggest hullabaloo as to whether I was guilty of theft or robbery. Not that I was guilty of either, at least in this particular instance, but no one would believe me.

You would have thought it was the lawyer being sentenced instead of me, the way he carried on. He called it a terrible miscarriage of justice and said we might as well be back in the Eighteenth Century when they hanged children.

Well, that was an exaggeration, if ever there was one; nobody was being hung and nobody was a child. That policeman had died and I had had a part in it. Maybe I had pushed him. I couldn't be sure. In my heart I really hadn't meant him any harm. I was just scared. But he was dead all the same. And as far as stealing went, I hadn't stolen the box but I had stolen other things more than once.

And then it happened. It was a miracle. All my life I'd dreamed of a nice room of my own, a comfortable place to stay. And that's exactly what I got.

The room was on the small side, but it had everything I needed in it, even a wash basin with hot and cold running water, and the walls were freshly painted, and they let me choose whether I wanted a wing chair with a chintz slipcover or a modern Danish armchair. I even got to decide what color bedspread I preferred. The window looked out on a beautiful lawn edged with shrubbery, and the matron said I'd be allowed to go to the greenhouse and select some pot plants to keep in my room. The next day I picked out a white gloxinia and some russet chrysanthemums.

I didn't mind the bars at the windows at all. Why, this day and age some of the finest mansions have barred windows to keep burglars out.

The meals—I simply couldn't believe there was such delicious food in the world. The woman who supervised their preparation had embezzled the funds of one of the largest catering companies in the state after working herself up from assistant cook to treasurer.

The other inmates were very friendly and most of them had led the most interesting lives. Some of the ladies occasionally used words that you usually see written only on fences or printed on sidewalks before the cement dries, but when they were scolded they apologized. Every now and then somebody would get angry with someone and there would be a little scratching or hair pulling, but it never got too bad. There was a choir—I can't sing but I love music—and they gave a concert every Tuesday morning at chapel, and Thursday night was movie night. There wasn't any admission charge. All you did was go in and sit down anywhere you pleased.

We all had a special job and I was assigned to the infirmary. The doctor and nurse both complimented me. The doctor said that I should have gone into professional nursing, that I gave confidence to the patients and helped them get well. I don't know about that but I've had years of practice with sick people and I like to help anybody who feels bad.

I was so happy that sometimes I couldn't sleep at night. I'd get up and click on the light and look at the furniture and the walls. It was hard to believe I had such a pleasant place to stay. I'd remember supper that night, how I'd gone back to the steam table for a second helping of asparagus with lemon and herb sauce, and I compared my plenty with those terrible times when I had slunk into supermarkets and nibbled overripe fruit and raw vegetables to ease my hunger.

Then one day here came that lawyer, not even at regular visiting hours, bouncing around congratulating me that my appeal had been upheld, or whatever the term was, and that I was as free as a bird to leave that minute.

He told the matron she could send my belongings later and he dragged me out front where TV cameras and newspaper reporters were waiting.

As soon as the cameras began whirring and the photographers began to aim, the lawyer kissed me on the cheek and pinned a flower on me. He made a speech saying that a terrible miscarriage of justice had been rectified. He had located people who testified that Mrs. Crowe had given me the box—she had told the gardener and the cleaning woman. They hadn't wanted to testify because they didn't want to get mixed up with the police, but the lawyer had persuaded them in the cause of justice and humanity to come forward and make statements.

The lawyer had also looked into the personnel record of the dead policeman and had learned that he had been judged emotionally unfit for his job, and the psychiatrist had warned the Chief of Police that something awful might happen either to the man himself or to a suspect unless he was relieved of his duties.

All the time the lawyer was talking into the microphones he had latched onto me like I was a three-year-old that might run away, and I just stood and stared. Then when he had finished his speech about me the reporters told him that like his grandfather and his uncle he was sure to end up as governor but at a much earlier age.

At that the lawyer gave a big grin in front of the camera and waved goodbye and pushed me into his car.

I was terrified. The nice place I'd found to stay in wasn't mine any longer. My old nightmare was back—wondering how I could manage to eat and how much stealing I'd have to do to live from one day to the next.

The cameras and reporters had followed us.

A photographer asked me to turn down the car window beside me, and I overheard two men way in the back of the crowd talking. My ears are sharp. Papa always said I could hear thunder three states away. Above the congratulations and bubbly talk around me I heard one of those men in back say, "This is a bit too much, don't you think? Our Bat is showing himself the champion of the senior citizen now. He's already copped the teenyboppers and the under thirties using methods that ought to have disbarred him. He should have made the gardener and cleaning woman testify at the beginning, and from the first he should have checked into the policeman's history. There ought never to have been a case at all, much less a conviction. But Bat wouldn't have got any publicity that way. He had to do it in his own devious, spectacular fashion." The other man just kept nodding and saying after every sentence, "You're damned right."

Then we drove off and I didn't dare look behind me because I was so heartbroken over what I was leaving.

The lawyer took me to his office. He said he hoped I wouldn't mind a little excitement for the next few days. He had mapped out some public appearances for me. The next morning I was to be on an early television show. There was nothing to be worried about. He would be right beside me to help me just as he had helped me throughout my trouble. All that I had to say on the TV program was that I owed my freedom to him.

I guess I looked startled or bewildered because he hurried on to say that I hadn't been able to pay him a fee but that now I was able to pay him back—not in money but in letting the public know about how he was the champion of the underdog.

I said I had been told that the court furnished lawyers free of charge to people who couldn't pay, and he said that was right, but his point was that I could repay him now by telling people all that he had done for me. Then he said the main thing was to talk over our next appearance on TV. He wanted to coach me in what I was going to say, but first he would go into his partner's office and tell him to take all the incoming calls and handle the rest of his appointments.

When the door closed after him I thought that he was right. I did owe my freedom to him. He was to blame for it. The smart-alec. The upstart. Who asked him to butt in and snatch me out of my pretty room and the work I loved and all that delicious food?

It was the first time in my life I knew what it meant to despise someone.

I hated him.

Before, when I was convicted of manslaughter, there was a lot of talk about malice aforethought and premeditated crime.

There wouldn't be any argument this time.

I hadn't wanted any harm to come to that policeman. But I did mean harm to come to this lawyer.

I grabbed up a letter opener from his desk and ran my finger along the blade and felt how sharp it was. I waited behind the door and when he walked through I gathered all my strength and stabbed him. Again and again and again.

Now I'm back where I want to be—in a nice place to stay.

Honoré de Balzac

The Mysterious Mansion

About a hundred yards from Vendôme, on the banks of the Loire, there stands an old dark-colored house, surmounted by a very high roof, and so completely isolated that there is not in the neighborhood a single evil-smelling tannery or wretched inn such as we see in the outskirts of almost every small town.

In front of the house is a small garden bordering the river, in which the boxwood borders of the paths, once neatly trimmed, now grow at their pleasure. A few willows, born in the Loire, have grown as rapidly as the hedge which encloses the garden and half conceal the house. The plants which we call weeds adorn the slope of the bank with their luxuriant vegetation. The fruit-trees, neglected for ten years, bear no fruit; their offshoots form a dense undergrowth. The espaliers resemble hornbeam hedges. The paths, formerly gravelled, are overrun with purslane; but, to tell the truth, there are no well-marked paths.

From the top of the mountain upon which hang the ruins of the old château of the Dukes of Vendôme, the only spot from which the eye can look into this enclosure, you would say to yourself that, at a period which it is difficult to determine, that little nook was the delight of some gentleman devoted to roses and tulips—to horticulture, in short, but especially fond of fine fruit. You espy an arbor, or rather the ruins of an arbor, beneath which a table still stands, not yet entirely consumed by time. At sight of that garden, which is no longer a garden, one may divine the negative delights of the peaceful life which provincials lead, as one divines the existence of a worthy tradesman by reading the epitaph on his tombstone.

To round out the melancholy yet soothing thoughts which fill the mind, there is on one of the walls a sundial, embellished with this commonplace Christian inscription: ULTIMAM COGITA. The roof of the house is terribly dilapidated, the blinds are always drawn, the balconies are covered with swallows' nests, the doors are never opened. Tall weeds mark with green lines the cracks in the steps; the ironwork is covered with rust. Moon, sun, winter, summer, snow, have rotted the wood, warped the boards, and corroded the paint.

The deathly silence which reigns there is disturbed only by the birds, the cats, the martens, the rats, and the mice, which are at liberty to run about, to fight, and to eat one another at their will. An invisible hand has written everywhere the word "mystery."

If, impelled by curiosity, you should go to inspect the house on the street side, you would see a high gate, arched at the top, in which the children of the neighborhood have made numberless holes. I learned later that that gate had been condemned ten years before. Through these irregular breaches you would be able to observe the perfect harmony between the garden front and the courtyard front. The same disorder reigns supreme in both. Tufts of weeds surround the pavements. Enormous cracks furrow the walls, whose blackened tops are enlaced by the countless tendrils of climbing plants. The steps are wrenched apart, the bell-rope is rotten, the gutters are broken. "What fire from heaven has passed this way? What tribunal has ordered salt to be strewn upon this dwelling? Has God been insulted here? Has France been betrayed?" Such are the questions which one asks one's self. The reptiles crawl hither and thither without answering. That empty and deserted house is an immense riddle, the solution of which is known to no one.

It was formerly a small feudal estate and bore the name of La Grande Bretèche. During my stay at Vendôme, where Desplein had left me to attend a rich patient, the aspect of that strange building became one of my keenest pleasures. Was it not more than a mere ruin? Some souvenirs of undeniable authenticity are always connected with a ruin, but that abode, still standing, although in process of gradual demolition by an avenging hand, concealed a secret, an unknown thought; at the very least, it betrayed a caprice. More than once, in the evening, I wandered in the direction of the hedge, now wild and uncared for, which surrounded that enclosure. I defied scratches and made my way into that ownerless garden, that estate which was neither public nor private, and I remained whole hours there contemplating its disarray. Not even to learn the story which would doubtless account for that extraordinary spectacle would I have asked a single question of any Vendômese gossip. Straying about there, I composed delightful romances, I abandoned myself to little orgies of melancholy which enchanted me.

If I had learned the cause of that perhaps most commonplace neglect, I should have lost the unspoken poesy with which I intoxicated myself. To me that spot represented the most diverse images of human life darkened by its misfortunes. Now it was the air of the cloister, minus the monks; again, the perfect peace of the cemetery, minus the dead speaking their epitaphic language; today, the house of the leper; tomorrow, that of the Fates; but it was, above all, the image of the province, with its meditation, with its hourglass life. I have often wept there, but never laughed. More than once I have felt an involuntary terror, as I heard above my head the low rustling made by the wings of some hurrying dove.

The ground is damp; you must beware of lizards, snakes, and toads, which wander about there with the fearless liberty of nature. Above all, you must not fear the cold, for after a few seconds you feel an icy cloak resting upon your shoulders like the hand of the Comendador on the neck of Don Juan.

One evening I had shuddered there; the wind had twisted an old rusty weather-vane, whose shrieks resembled a groan uttered by the house at the moment I was finishing a rather dismal melodrama by which I sought to explain to myself that species of monumental grief. I returned to my inn, beset by somber thoughts. When I had supped, my hostess entered my room with a mysterious air and said to me:

"Here is Monsieur Regnault, monsieur."

"Who is Monsieur Regnault?"

"What! Monsieur doesn't know Monsieur Regnault? That's funny," she said as she left the room.

Suddenly I saw a tall slender man dressed in black, with his hat in his hand, who entered the room like a ram ready to rush at his rival, disclosing a retreating forehead, a small pointed head, and a pale face, not unlike a glass of dirty water. You would have said that he was the doorkeeper of some minister. He wore an old coat, threadbare at the seams, but he had a diamond in his shirt-frill and gold rings in his ears.

"To whom have I the honor of speaking, monsieur?" I asked him.

He took a chair, seated himself in front of my fire, placed his hat on my table, and replied, rubbing his hands:

"Ah! It's very cold! I am Monsieur Regnault, monsieur."

I bowed, saying to myself:

Il Bondocani! Look for him!

"I am the notary at Vendôme," he continued.

"I am delighted to hear it, monsieur," I exclaimed, "but I am not ready to make my will, for reasons best known to myself."

"Just a minute," he rejoined, raising his hand as if to impose silence upon me. "I beg pardon, monsieur, I beg pardon! I have heard that you go to walk sometimes in the garden of La Grande Bretèche."

"Yes, monsieur!"

"Just a minute," he said, repeating his gesture. "That practice constitutes a downright trespass. I have come, monsieur, in the name and as executor of the late Madame Countess de Merret, to beg you to discontinue your visits. Just a minute! I'm not a Turk and I don't propose to charge you with a crime. Besides, it may well be that you are not aware of the circumstances which compel me to allow the finest mansion in Vendôme to fall to ruin. However, monsieur, you seem to be a man of education and you must know that the law forbids entrance upon an enclosed estate under severe penalties. A hedge is as good as a wall. But the present condition of the house may serve as an excuse for your curiosity. I would ask nothing better than to allow you to go and come as you please in that house, but, as it is my duty to carry out the will of the testatrix, I have the honor, monsieur, to request you not to go into that garden again. Even I myself, monsieur, since the opening of the will, have never set foot inside that house, which, as I have had the honor to tell you, is a part of the estate of Madame de Merret. We simply reported the number of doors and windows, in order to fix the amount of the impost which I pay annually from the fund set aside for that purpose by the late countess. Ah! Her will made a great deal of talk in Vendôme, monsieur."

At that, he stopped to blow his nose, the excellent man. I respected his loquacity, understanding perfectly that the administration of Madame de Merret's property was the important event of his life—his reputation, his glory, his Restoration. I must needs bid adieu to my pleasant reveries, to my romances; so that I was not inclined to scorn the pleasure of learning the truth from an official source.

"Would it be indiscreet, monsieur," I asked him, "to ask you the reason of this extraordinary state of affairs?"

At that question, an expression which betrayed all the pleasure that a man feels who is accustomed to ride a hobby passed over the notary's face. He pulled up his shirt collar with a self-satisfied air, produced his snuffbox, opened it, offered it to me, and, at my refusal, took a famous pinch himself. He was happy; the man who has no hobby has no idea of the satisfaction that can be derived from life. A hobby is the precise mean between passion and monomania. At that moment I understood the witty expression of Sterne in all its extent, and I had a perfect conception of the joy with which Uncle Toby, with Trim's assistance, bestrode his battle-horse.

"Monsieur," said Monsieur Regnault, "I was chief clerk to Master Roguin of Paris. An excellent office, of which you may have heard? No? Why, it was made famous by a disastrous failure. Not having sufficient money to practice in Paris, at the price to which offices had risen in 1816, I came here and bought the office of my predecessor. I had relatives in Vendôme, among others a very rich aunt who gave me her daughter in marriage.

"Monsieur," he continued after a brief pause, "three months after being licensed by the Keeper of the Seals I was sent for one evening, just as I was going to bed (I was not then married), by Madame Countess de Merret to come to her Château de Merret. Her maid, an excellent girl who works in this inn today, was at my door with madame countess's carriage. But, just a minute! I must tell you, monsieur, that Monsieur Count de Merret had gone to Paris to die two months before I came here. He died miserably there, abandoning himself to excesses of all sorts. You understand? —On the day of his departure, madame countess had left La Grande Bretèche and had dismantled it. Indeed, some people declare that she burned the furniture and hangings, and all chattels whatsoever now contained in the estate leased by the said—

"What on earth am I saying? I beg pardon, I thought I was dictating a lease. —That she burned them," he continued, "in the fields at Merret. Have you been to Merret, monsieur? No?" he said, answering his own question. "Ah! That is a lovely spot! For about three months," he continued after a slight shake of the head, "monsieur count and madame countess led a strange life.

"They received no guests. Madame lived on the ground floor and monsieur on the first floor. When madame countess was left alone, she never appeared except at church. Later, in her own house, at her château, she refused to see the friends who came to see her. She was already much changed when she left La Grande Bretèche to go to Merret. The dear woman—I say 'dear,' because this diamond came from her, but I actually only saw her once—the excellent lady, then, was very ill; she had doubtless despaired of her health, for she died without calling a doctor, so that many of our ladies thought that she was not in full possession of her wits.

"My curiosity was therefore strangely aroused, monsieur, when I learned that Madame de Merret needed my services. I was not the only one who took an interest in that story. That same evening, although it was late, the whole town knew that I had gone to Merret. The maid answered rather vaguely the questions that I asked her on the road; she told me, however, that her mistress had received the sacrament from the curé of Merret during the day and that she did not seem likely to live through the night.

"I reached the château about eleven o'clock. I mounted the main staircase. After passing through diverse large rooms, high and dark and as cold and damp as the devil, I reached the state bedchamber where the countess was. According to the reports that were current concerning that lady—I should never end, monsieur, if I should repeat all the stories that are told about her—I had thought of her as a coquette. But, if you please, I had much difficulty in finding her in the huge bed in which she lay. To be sure, to light that enormous wainscoted chamber of the old régime, where everything was so covered with dust that it made one sneeze simply to look at it, she had only one of those old-fashioned Argand lamps. Ah! But you have never been to Merret. Well, monsieur, the bed is one of those beds of the olden time, with a high canopy of flowered material. A small night-table stood beside the bed and I saw upon it a copy of the *Imitation of Jesus Christ,* which, by the by, I bought for my wife, as well as the lamp. There was also a large couch for the attendant and two chairs. Not a spark of fire. That was all the furniture. It wouldn't have filled ten lines in an inventory.

"Oh, my dear monsieur, if you had seen, as I then saw it, that huge room hung with dark tapestry, you would have imagined yourself transported into a genuine scene from a novel. It was icy cold, and, more than that, absolutely funereal," he added, raising his arm with a theatrical gesture and pausing for a moment.

"By looking hard and walking close to the bed, I succeeded in discovering Madame de Merret, thanks to the lamp, the light of which shone upon the pillow. Her face was as yellow as wax and resembled two clasped hands. She wore a lace cap, which revealed her lovely hair, as white as snow. She was sitting up, and seemed to retain that position with much difficulty. Her great black eyes, dulled by fever no doubt and already almost lifeless, hardly moved beneath the bones which the eyebrows cover—these," he said, pointing to the arch over his eyes. "Her brow was moist. Her fleshless hands resembled bones covered with tightly drawn skin; her veins and muscles could be seen perfectly.

"She must have been very beautiful, but at that moment I was seized with an indefinable feeling at her aspect. Never before, according to those who laid her out, had a living creature attained such thinness without dying. In short, she was horrible to look at;

disease had so wasted that woman that she was nothing more than a phantom. Her pale violet lips seemed not to move when she spoke to me. Although my profession had familiarized me with such spectacles, by taking me sometimes to the pillows of dying persons to take down their last wishes, I confess that the families in tears and despair whom I had seen were as nothing beside that solitary, silent woman in that enormous château.

"I did not hear the slightest sound, I could not detect the movement which the breathing of the sick woman should have imparted to the sheets that covered her; and I stood quite still, gazing at her in a sort of stupor. It seems to me that I am there now. At last her great eyes moved, she tried to raise her right hand, which fell back upon the bed, and these words came from her mouth like a breath, for her voice had already ceased to be a voice: 'I have been awaiting you with much impatience.'

"Her cheeks suddenly flushed. It was a great effort for her to speak, monsieur. 'Madame,' I said. She motioned to me to be silent. At that moment the old nurse rose and whispered in my ear: 'Don't speak; madame countess cannot bear to hear the slightest sound, and what you said might excite her.' I sat down. A few moments later, Madame de Merret collected all her remaining strength to move her right arm and thrust it, not without infinite difficulty, beneath her bolster. She paused for just a moment, then she made a last effort to withdraw her hand, and when she finally produced a sealed paper, drops of sweat fell from her brow. 'I place my will in your hands,' she said. 'Oh, *mon Dieu!* Oh!' That was all. She grasped a crucifix that lay on her bed, hastily put it to her lips, and died. The expression of her staring eyes makes me shudder even now when I think of it. She must have suffered terribly! There was a gleam of joy in her last glance, a sentiment which remained in her dead eyes.

"I carried the will away; and when it was opened, I found that Madame de Merret had appointed me her executor. She left all her property to the hospital at Vendôme with the exception of a few individual legacies. But these were her provisions with respect to La Grande Bretèche: she directed me to leave her house, for fifty years from the day of her death, in the same condition as at the moment that she died, forbidding any person whatsoever to enter the rooms, forbidding the slightest repairs to be made, and even setting aside a sum in order to hire keepers, if it should be found necessary, to assure the literal execution of her purpose. At the expiration of that period, if the desire of the testatrix has been carried out, the house is to belong to my heirs, for monsieur knows that notaries cannot accept legacies. If not, La Grande Bretèche is to revert to whoever is entitled to it, but with the obligation to comply with the conditions set forth in a codicil attached to the will, which is not to be opened until the expiration of the said fifty years. The will was not attacked, and so—"

At that, without finishing his sentence, the elongated notary glanced at me with a triumphant air and I made him altogether happy by addressing a few compliments to him.

"Monsieur," I said, "you have made a profound impression upon me, so that I think I see that dying woman, paler than her sheets; her gleaming eyes terrify me and I shall dream of her tonight. But you must have formed some conjecture concerning the provisions of that extraordinary will."

"Monsieur," he said with a comical reserve, "I never allow myself to judge the conduct of those persons who honor me by giving me a diamond."

I soon loosened the tongue of the scrupulous Vendômese notary, who communicated to me, not without long digressions, observations due to the profound politicians of both sexes whose decrees are law in Vendôme. But those observations were so contradictory and so diffuse that I almost fell asleep despite the interest I took in that authentic narrative. The dull and monotonous tone of the notary, who was accustomed, no doubt, to listen to himself, and to force his clients and his fellow citizens to listen to him, triumphed over my curiosity.

"Aha! Many people, monsieur," he said to me on the landing, "would like to live forty-five years more. But just a minute!" And with a sly expression, he placed his right forefinger on his nose, as if he would have said: Just mark what I say. "But to do that, to do that," he added, "a man must be less than sixty."

I closed my door, having been roused from my apathy by this last shaft, which the notary considered very clever; then I seated myself in my easy-chair, placing my feet on the andirons. I was soon absorbed in an imaginary romance à la Radcliffe, based upon the judicial observations of Monsieur Regnault, when my door, under the skillful manipulation of a woman's hand, turned upon its hinges. My hostess appeared, a stout red-faced woman of excellent dispo-

sition, who had missed her vocation: she was a Fleming, who should
have been born in a picture by Teniers.

"Well, monsieur," she said, "no doubt Monsieur Regnault has
given you his story of La Grande Bretèche?"

"Yes, Mother Lepas."

"What did he tell you?"

I repeated in a few words the chilling and gloomy story of Madame
de Merret. At each sentence, my hostess thrust out her neck, gazing
at me with the true innkeeper's perspicacity—a sort of happy me-
dium between the instinct of the detective, the cunning of the spy,
and the craft of the trader.

"My dear Madame Lepas," I added, as I concluded, "you evidently
know more, eh? If not, why should you have come up here?"

"Oh! On an honest woman's word, as true as my name's Lepas—"

"Don't swear; your eyes are big with a secret. You knew Monsieur
de Merret. What sort of a man was he?"

"Bless my soul! Monsieur de Merret was a fine man, whom you
never could see the whole of, he was so long; an excellent gentleman,
who came here from Picardy, and who had his brains very near his
cap, as we say here. He paid cash for everything in order not to have
trouble with anybody. You see, he was lively. We women all found
him very agreeable."

"Because he was lively?" I asked.

"That may be," she said. "You know, monsieur, that a man must
have had something in front of him, as they say, to marry Madame
de Merret, who, without saying anything against the others, was
the loveliest and richest woman in the whole province. She had
about twenty thousand francs a year. The whole town went to her
wedding. The bride was dainty and attractive, a real jewel of a
woman. Ah! They made a handsome couple at that time!"

"Did they live happily together?"

"Oh, dear! Oh, dear! Yes and no, so far as any one could tell, for
as you can imagine we folks didn't live on intimate terms with them.
Madame de Merret was a kind-hearted woman, very pleasant, who
had to suffer sometimes perhaps from her husband's quick temper;
but although he was a bit proud, we liked him. You see, it was his
business to be like that. When a man is noble, you know—"

"However, some catastrophe must have happened to make Monsieur and Madame de Merret separate so violently?"

"I didn't say there was any catastrophe, monsieur. I don't know
anything about it."

"Good! I am sure now that you know all about it."

"Well, monsieur, I will tell you all I know. When I saw Monsieur Regnault come up to your room, I had an idea that he would talk to you about Madame de Merret in connection with La Grande Bretèche. That gave me the idea of consulting with monsieur, who seems to me a man of good judgment and incapable of playing false with a poor woman like me, who never did anybody any harm and yet who's troubled by her conscience. Up to this time I've never dared to speak out to the people of this neighborhood, for they're all sharp-tongued gossips. And then, monsieur, I've never had a guest stay in my inn so long as you have, and to whom I could tell the story of the fifteen thousand francs."

"My dear Madame Lepas," I said, arresting the flood of her words, "if your confidence is likely to compromise me, I wouldn't be burdened with it for a moment for anything in the world."

"Don't be afraid," she said, interrupting me; "you shall see."

This eagerness on her part made me think that I was not the only one to whom my worthy hostess had communicated the secret of which I dreaded to be the only confidant, and I listened.

"Monsieur," she began, "when the Emperor sent Spanish or other prisoners of war here, I had to board, at the expense of the government, a young Spaniard who was sent to Vendôme on parole. In spite of the parole, he went every day to show himself to the subprefect. He was a Spanish grandee, nothing less! He had a name ending in os and dia, like Bagos de Férédia. I have his name written on my register; you can read it if you wish. He was a fine young man for a Spaniard, who they say are all ugly. He was only five feet two or three inches tall, but he was well built; he had little hands, which he took care of—oh, you should have seen; he had as many brushes for his hands as a woman has for all purposes!

"He had long black hair, a flashing eye, and rather a copper-colored skin, which I liked all the same. He wore such fine linen as I never saw before on anyone, although I have entertained princesses, and among others General Bertrand, the Duke and Duchess d'Abrantès, Monsieur Decazes, and the King of Spain. He didn't eat much, but he had polite and pleasant manners so that I couldn't be angry with him for it. Oh! I was very fond of him, although he didn't say four words a day and it was impossible to have the slightest conversation with him; if anyone spoke to him, he wouldn't answer. It was a fad, a mania that they all have, so they tell me.

"He read his breviary like a priest, he went to Mass and to the services regularly. Where did he sit? We noticed that later: about two steps from Madame de Merret's private chapel. As he took his seat there the first time that he came to the church, nobody imagined that there was any design in it. Besides, he never took his face off his prayer-book, the poor young man! In the evening, monsieur, he used to walk on the mountain, among the ruins of the château. That was the poor man's only amusement. He was reminded of his own country there. They say that there's nothing but mountains in Spain.

"Very soon after he came here he began to stay out late. I was anxious when he didn't come home till midnight. But we all got used to his whim; he would take the key to the door and we wouldn't wait for him. He lived in a house that we have on Rue de Casernes. Then one of our stablemen told us that one night, when he took the horses to drink, he thought he saw the Spanish grandee swimming far out in the river, like a real fish. When he came back, I told him to be careful of the eel-grass. He seemed vexed that he had been seen in the water.

"At last, monsieur, one day, or rather one morning, we didn't find him in his room; he hadn't come home. By hunting carefully everywhere, I found a writing in his table drawer, where there were fifty of the Spanish gold-pieces which they call portugaises, and which were worth about five thousand francs; and then there were ten thousand francs' worth of diamonds in a little sealed box. His writing said that in case he didn't return, he left us this money and his diamonds, on condition that we would fund Masses to thank God for his escape and his salvation. In those days I still had my man, who went out to look for him. And here's the funny part of the story: he brought back the Spaniard's clothes, which he found under a big stone in a sort of shed by the river, on the château side, almost opposite La Grande Bretèche.

"My husband went there so early that no one saw him. He burned the clothes after reading the letter and we declared, according to Count Férédia's wish, that he had escaped. The subprefect set all the gendarmerie on his track, but, bless my soul, they never caught him! Lepas believed that the Spaniard had drowned himself. For my part, monsieur, I don't think it; I think rather that he was mixed up in Madame de Merret's business, seeing that Rosalie told me that the crucifix that her mistress thought so much of that she had it buried with her was made of ebony and silver. Now, in the early part of his stay here, Monsieur Férédia had one of silver and ebony, which I didn't see afterwards. Tell me now, monsieur, isn't it true that I needn't have any remorse about the Spaniard's fifteen thousand francs, and that they are fairly mine?"

"Certainly. But did you never try to question Rosalie?" I asked her.

"Oh! Yes, indeed, monsieur. But would you believe it? That girl is like a wall. She knows something, but it's impossible to make her talk."

After conversing a moment more with me, my hostess left me beset by undefined and dismal thoughts, by a romantic sort of curiosity, a religious terror not unlike the intense emotion that seizes us when we enter a dark church at night and see a dim light in the distance under the lofty arches; a vague figure gliding along, or the rustling of a dress or a surplice; it makes us shudder. La Grande Bretèche and its tall weeds, its condemned windows, its rusty ironwork, its closed doors, its deserted rooms, suddenly appeared before me in fantastic guise. I tried to penetrate that mysterious abode, seeking there the kernel of that somber story, of that drama which had caused the death of three persons.

In my eyes, Rosalie was the most interesting person in Vendôme. As I scrutinized her, I detected traces of some inmost thought, despite the robust health that shone upon her plump cheeks. There was in her some seed of remorse or of hope. Her manner announced a secret, as does that of the devotee who prays with excessive fervor, or that of the infanticide who constantly hears her child's last cry. However, her attitude was artless and natural, her stupid smile had no trace of criminality, and you would have voted her innocent simply by glancing at the large handkerchief with red and blue squares which covered her vigorous bust, confined by a gown with white and violet stripes.

No, I thought, I won't leave Vendôme without learning the whole story of La Grande Bretèche. To obtain my end, I will become Rosalie's friend if it is absolutely necessary.

"Rosalie?" I said one evening.

"What is it, monsieur?"

"You are not married?"

She started slightly.

"Oh! I shan't lack men when I take a fancy to be unhappy!" she said with a laugh.

She speedily overcame her inward emotion, for all women, from the great lady down to the servant at an inn, have a self-possession which is peculiar to them.

"You are fresh and appetizing enough not to lack suitors. But tell me, Rosalie, why did you go to work in an inn when you left Madame de Merret's? Didn't she leave you some money?"

"Oh, yes! But my place is the best in Vendôme, monsieur."

This reply was one of those which judges and lawyers call dilatory. Rosalie seemed to me to occupy in that romantic story the position of the square in the middle of the chessboard; she was at the very center of interest and of truth. She seemed to me to be tied up in the clew. It was no longer an ordinary case of attempting seduction; there was in that girl the last chapter of a romance. And so, from that moment, Rosalie became the object of my attentions. By dint of studying the girl, I observed in her, as in all women to whom we devote all our thoughts, a multitude of good qualities: she was neat and clean, and she was fine-looking—that goes without saying. She had also all the attractions which our desire imparts to women, in whatever station of life they may be. A fortnight after the notary's visit, I said to Rosalie one evening, or rather one morning, for it was very early:

"Tell me all that you know about Madame de Merret."

"Oh, don't ask me that, Monsieur Horace!" she replied in alarm.

Her pretty face darkened, her bright color vanished, and her eyes lost their humid, innocent light. But I insisted.

"Well," she rejoined, "as you insist upon it, I will tell you; but keep my secret."

"Of course, of course, my dear girl; I will keep all your secrets with the probity of a thief, and that is the most loyal probity that exists."

"If it's all the same to you," she said, "I prefer that it should be with your own."

Thereupon she arranged her neckerchief and assumed the attitude of a story-teller; for there certainly is an attitude of trust and security essential to the telling of a story. The best stories are told at a certain hour, and at the table, as we all are now. No one ever told a story well while standing, or fasting. But if it were necessary to reproduce faithfully Rosalie's diffuse eloquence, a whole volume would hardly suffice. Now, as the event of which she gave me a confused account occupied, between the loquacity of the notary and that of Madame Lepas, the exact position of the mean terms of an arithmetical proportion between the two extremes, it is only necessary for me to repeat it to you in a few words. Therefore I abridge. The room which Madame de Merret occupied at La Grande Bretèche was on the ground floor. A small closet, about four feet deep, in the wall served as her wardrobe. Three months before the evening the incidents of which I am about to narrate, Madame de Merret had been so seriously indisposed that her husband left her alone in her room and slept in a room on the floor above. By one of those chances which it is impossible to foresee, he returned home on the evening in question two hours later than usual from the club to which he was accustomed to go to read the newspapers and to talk politics with the people of the neighborhood. His wife supposed that he had come home and had gone to bed and to sleep. But the invasion of France had given rise to a lively discussion; the game of billiards had been very close and he had lost forty francs, an enormous sum at Vendôme, where everybody hoards money and where manners are confined within the limits of a modesty worthy of all praise, which perhaps is the source of a true happiness of which no Parisian has a suspicion.

For some time past, Monsieur de Merret had contented himself with asking Rosalie if his wife were in bed; at the girl's reply, always in the affirmative, he went immediately to his own room with the readiness born of habit and confidence. But on returning home that evening, he took it into his head to go to Madame de Merret's room to tell her of his misadventure and perhaps also to console himself for it. During dinner he had remarked that Madame de Merret was very coquettishly dressed; he said to himself as he walked home from the club that his wife was no longer ill, that her convalescence had improved her, but he perceived it, as husbands notice everything, a little late.

Instead of calling Rosalie, who at that moment was busy in the kitchen watching the cook and the coachman play a difficult hand of *brisque*, Monsieur de Merret went to his wife's room, lighted by his lantern, which he had placed on the top step of the stairs. His footstep, easily recognized, resounded under the arches of the corridor. At the instant that he turned the knob of his wife's door, he fancied that he heard the door of the closet that I have mentioned close, but when he entered Madame de Merret was alone, standing in front of the hearth. The husband naïvely concluded that Rosalie was in the closet; however, a suspicion that rang in his ears like the striking of a clock made him distrustful. He looked at his wife and detected in her eyes something indefinable of confusion and dismay.

"You come home very late," she said.

That voice, usually so pure and so gracious, seemed to him slightly changed. He made no reply, but at that moment Rosalie entered the room. That was a thunderclap to him. He walked about the room, from one window to another, with a uniform step and with folded arms.

"Have you learned anything distressing? Or are you ill?" his wife timidly asked him while Rosalie undressed her.

He made no reply.

"You may go," said Madame de Merret to her maid, "I will put on my curl-papers myself."

She divined some catastrophe simply from the expression of her husband's face, and she preferred to be alone with him. When Rosalie was gone, or was supposed to be gone, for she stayed for some moments in the corridor, Monsieur de Merret took his stand in front of his wife, and said to her coldly:

"Madame, there is someone in your closet?"

She looked at her husband calmly, and replied simply:

"No, monsieur."

That "no" tore Monsieur de Merret's heart, for he did not believe it; and yet his wife had never seemed to him purer and more holy than she seemed at that moment. He rose to open the closet door. Madame de Merret took his hand, stopped him, looked at him with a melancholy expression, and said in a voice strangely moved:

"If you find no one, reflect that all is at an end between us!"

The indescribable dignity of his wife's attitude reawoke the gentleman's profound esteem for her, and inspired in him one of those resolutions which require only a vaster theater in order to become immortal.

"No," he said, "I will not do it, Josephine. In either case, we should be separated forever. Listen. I know all the purity of your soul, and I know that you lead the life of a saint, and that you would not commit a mortal sin to save your life."

At these words, Madame de Merret looked at her husband with a haggard eye.

"See, here is your crucifix. Swear to me before God that there is no one there and I will believe you, I will never open that door."

Madame de Merret took the crucifix and said:

"I swear it."

"Louder," said the husband, "and repeat after me: 'I swear before God that there is no one in that closet.' "

She repeated the words without confusion.

"It is well," said Monsieur de Merret coldly. After a moment's silence: "This is a very beautiful thing that I did not know you possessed," he said as he examined the crucifix of ebony encrusted with silver, and beautifully carved.

"I found it at Duvivier's. When that party of prisoners passed through Vendôme last year, he bought it of a Spanish monk."

"Ah!" said Monsieur de Merret, replacing the crucifix on the nail. And he rang. Rosalie did not keep him waiting. Monsieur de Merret walked hastily to meet her, led her into the embrasure of the window looking over the garden, and said to her in a low voice:

"I know that Gorenflot wants to marry you, that poverty alone prevents you from coming together, and that you have told him that you would not be his wife until he found some way to become a master mason. Well, go to him and tell him to come here with his trowel and his tools. Manage so as not to wake anybody in his house but him. His fortune will exceed your desires. Above all, go out of this house without chattering—"

He frowned. Rosalie started, and he called her back. "Here, take my pass-key," he said.

"Jean!" shouted Monsieur de Merret in the corridor, in a voice of thunder.

Jean, who was both his coachman and his confidential man, left his game of *brisque* and answered the summons.

"Go to bed, all of you," said his master, motioning to him to come near. And he added, but in an undertone: "When they are all asleep, *asleep,* do you understand, you will come down and let me know."

Monsieur de Merret, who had not lost sight of his wife while giving his orders, calmly returned to her side in front of the fire and began to tell her about the game of billiards and the discussion at the club. When Rosalie returned, she found monsieur and madame talking most amicably. The gentleman had recently had plastered all the rooms which composed his reception-apartment on the ground floor. Plaster is very scarce in Vendôme and the cost of transportation increases the price materially, so he had purchased quite a large quantity, knowing that he would readily find customers for any that he might have left. That circumstance suggested the design which he proceeded to carry out.

"Gorenflot is here, monsieur," said Rosalie in an undertone.

"Let him come in," replied the Picard gentleman aloud.

Madame de Merret turned pale when she saw the mason.

"Gorenflot," said her husband, "go out to the carriage house and get some bricks, and bring in enough to wall up the door of this closet; you can use the plaster that I had left over to plaster the wall." Then, beckoning Rosalie and the workman to him, he said in a low tone: "Look you, Gorenflot, you will sleep here tonight. But tomorrow morning you shall have a passport to go abroad, to a city which I will name to you. I will give you six thousand francs for your journey. You will remain ten years in that city; if you are not satisfied there, you can settle in another city provided it is in the same country. You will go by way of Paris, where you will wait for me. There I will give you a guarantee to pay you six thousand francs more on your return, in case you have abided by the conditions of our bargain. At that price, you should be willing to keep silent concerning what you have done here tonight. As for you, Rosalie, I will give you ten thousand francs, which will be paid to you on the day of your wedding, provided that you marry Gorenflot. But in order to be married, you will have to be silent; if not, no dower."

"Rosalie," said Madame de Merret, "come here and arrange my hair."

The husband walked tranquilly back and forth, watching the door, the mason, and his wife, but without any outward sign of injurious suspicion. Gorenflot was obliged to make a noise. Madame de Merret seized an opportunity when the workman was dropping some bricks and when her husband was at the other end of the room to say to Rosalie:

"A thousand francs a year to you, my dear child, if you can tell Gorenflot to leave a crack at the bottom. —Go and help him," she said coolly, aloud.

Monsieur and Madame de Merret said not a word while Gorenflot was walling up the door. That silence was the result of design on the husband's part, for he did not choose to allow his wife a pretext for uttering words of double meaning; and on Madame de Merret's part, it was either prudence or pride. When the wall was half built, the crafty mason seized a moment when the gentleman's back was turned to strike his pickaxe through one of the panes of the glass door. That act gave Madame de Merret to understand that Rosalie had spoken to Gorenflot. At that moment, all three saw a man's face, dark and somber, with black hair and fiery eyes. Before her husband had turned, the poor woman had time to make a motion of her head to the stranger, to whom that signal meant: *"Hope!"*

At four o'clock, about daybreak, for it was September, the work was finished. The mason remained in the house under the eye of Jean, and Monsieur de Merret slept in his wife's chamber. In the morning, on rising, he said carelessly:

"Ah! By the way, I must go to the mayor's office for the passport."

He put his hat on his head, walked towards the door, turned back, and took the crucifix. His wife fairly trembled with joy.

He will go to Duvivier's, she thought.

As soon as the gentleman had left the room, Madame de Merret rang for Rosalie; then, in a terrible voice, she cried:

"The pickaxe, the pickaxe! And to work! I saw how Gorenflot understood last night; we shall have time to make a hole and stop it up."

In a twinkling, Rosalie brought her mistress a sort of small axe and she, with an ardor which no words can describe, began to demolish the wall. She had already loosened several bricks when, as she stepped back to deal a blow even harder than the preceding ones, she saw Monsieur de Merret behind her. She fainted.

Anticipating what was likely to happen during his absence, he had laid a trap for his wife; he had simply written to the mayor and had sent a messenger to Duvivier. The jeweller arrived just as the disorder in the room had been repaired.

"Duvivier," asked Monsieur de Merret, "didn't you buy some crucifixes from the Spaniards who passed through here?"

"No, monsieur."

"Very well. I thank you," he said, exchanging with his wife a tigerlike glance. —"Jean," he added, turning towards his confidential valet, "you will have my meals served in Madame de Merret's room; she is ill, and I shall not leave her until she is well again."

The cruel man remained with his wife twenty days. During the first days, when there was a noise in the walled-up closet and Josephine attempted to implore him in behalf of the dying unknown, he replied, not allowing her to utter a word:

"You have sworn on the cross that there was no one there."

"Q"